COMPLETION

TIM WALKER

COMPLETION

WILLIAM HEINEMANN: LONDON

Published by William Heinemann 2014

2 4 6 8 10 9 7 5 3 1

Copyright © Tim Walker 2014

First published in Great Britain in 2014 by
William Heinemann
Random House, 20 Vauxhall Bridge Road,
London SW1V 2SA
www.randomhouse.co.uk

Addresses for companies within The Random House Group Limited can be found at:
www.randomhouse.co.uk/offices.htm

The Random House Group Limited Reg. No. 954009
A CIP catalogue record for this book
is available from the British Library

ISBN 9780434022564

The Random House Group Limited supports the Forest Stewardship Council® (FSC®),
the leading international forest-certification organisation. Our books carrying
the FSC label are printed on FSC®-certified paper. FSC is the only forest-certification
scheme supported by the leading environmental organisations, including Greenpeace.
Our paper procurement policy can be found at
www.randomhouse.co.uk/environment

Typeset in Fournier MT by Palimpsest Book Production Limited,
Falkirk, Stirlingshire

Printed and bound in Great Britain by Clays Ltd, St Ives plc

For my family

FOUNDATIONS

Years ago, between dessert and coffee, their dinner party guests would demand the guided tour of Jerry and Pen's loft conversion. So while the six-cup espresso-maker gurgled on the eight-ring stove, Jerry and/or Pen would lead them up the several steepish flights of stairs from the dining table to the top floor. Catching their breath, they'd tiptoe past young Conrad's half-open bedroom door and crowd into the upstairs shower-cum-loo, where the visitors would finger the aquamarine mosaic tiles and whisper about grouting for as long as it took to exhaust their collective knowledge of bathroom DIY, which was not at all long.

Jerry and/or Pen would allude to the excellent water pressure, and then lead them all, shuffling in ones and twos, along the hardwood landing to the children's playroom. There, a male guest might absent-mindedly nudge a puck across the air hockey table, while his wife, girlfriend or life-partner made an abortive attempt at small talk with Barunka the Czech au pair, who by that point of the evening could usually be found curled on a beanbag watching American sitcoms with the sound way down.

At length, the members of this ad hoc tour party would step through the sliding plate glass onto the balcony, where each would gasp and then chuckle at the uninterrupted view of London's skyline. How on earth, they tended to ask, did you find this house anyway? At this, Jerry or Pen would raise a large-arsed wine glass to his or her lips, swallow a mouthful of whichever plonk the Sunday supplements had recently been

3

recommending, and reply that really, you might say the house found them.

One high summer at the start of Thatcher's second term, shortly before the Islington boom began in earnest, the Manvilles – just married – heard from an old art-school boyfriend of Pen's: his grandparents wanted to retire, he said, from their big, *c.*1890 semi-detached house on Highbury Hill to less unwieldy accommodation. He thought he ought to organise the viewing, as his family didn't much care for the spiv estate agents who'd been busy conjuring fat fees from the gentrification of nearby Canonbury and Barnsbury. Their neighbourhood, he explained, had preserved its authentic, multicultural feel.

As they crunched across the gravel from the pavement to the door, Jerry was already weighing up which sports car he ought to buy to best fill the yard. The elderly couple ushered them from the hallway into the open-plan ground floor, where the light from the bay window at the front reached through the sitting room and into the dining area beyond, teasing the rays from the French window at the back. We could fit our whole crappy Kentish Town flat into this one room, thought Jerry, and still leave space for a roller-disco. Pen had what she would eventually describe as her Television-Property-Show Moment; she was seized at once with the desire to make the place her own. Of course, it may just have been a dizzy spell brought on by the pregnancy. And, of course, television property shows did not yet exist. But one day Pen would watch them, and she would recall the sensation vividly.

Below the ground floor, in a half-submerged basement, were the kitchen and downstairs loo. A shallow set of steps led up from the back door to the long, lovingly kempt garden. One flight above the ground floor were a spacious bathroom, a study, and the – frankly, vast – master bedroom. On the second floor: another, more compact bathroom and three charming bedrooms, two of them rear-facing, one of which Pen decided simply must become her studio just as soon as she'd torn up the lace curtains and the ghastly patterned carpet. The gentleman of the house directed Jerry up a tremulous wooden ladder and told him to poke his head into the loft space. It was musty, with symptoms of woodworm. But it had potential.

The smitten second-time buyers doubted they could raise sufficient capital to put in a non-insulting offer, even with the assistance of a kindly high street bank. But the owners had taken a liking to Jerry and Pen, and to Pen's five-month bump, and decided to sell them the house at a knock-down price without a bothersome agent's intervention. They all agreed it would make a fine home for a young family. The Victorian fixtures and fittings notwithstanding, at somewhat less than £100,000 it was a steal, even then. There were tears from the women on both sides of the transaction when the day of the exchange came. Be kind to our little house, the gentleman implored Jerry politely. I will, he replied, thinking, It's *not* little, and I'm going to tear it to pieces.

Gifted with a convenient spell of gardening leave, he acquired the necessary plumbing and electrics manuals and set to work opening up the walls, connecting as much new pipe and wiring as his beginner's expertise would allow. It took longer than he'd anticipated, but he persevered, and when the man from the local electricity board finally came to approve his work, he congratulated him on his thoroughness and precision. Jerry, dusting his palms on his jeans to shake the bureaucrat's hand, had never felt so much like a man.

Electricity and running water were nevertheless limited for a few long autumnal months, during which the couple camped in the sitting room with a portable heater and all the blankets they could muster. Jerry was not entirely pleased to yield to Pen the single fold-out camp bed, which he'd transported from his parents' garage in Macclesfield. But there was no denying that her condition gave her the greater need for comfort – and waking to a light-filled room that he could truthfully call his own was some consolation. They raced to install new radiators in time for the winter and the arrival of their first child: a girl, Isobel. (Afterwards, Jerry would regret having succumbed to the fad for cheap electric storage heaters, and replace the ugly units with a gas boiler and central heating.)

Almost every weekend, they invited their friends over for DIY parties. They refitted the first-floor bathroom, then the basement kitchen-diner, then the second-floor bathroom. They re-floored, re-carpeted, replastered, repainted and re-roofed. Tony Glassop, Jerry's nominal best friend, would loiter in the bay window drinking bottles of continental lager and laughing that they were fools for not having called in professional decorators at the earliest available opportunity. But everyone else was happy to muck in, as long as Pen laid on a buffet lunch. They'd smoke and eat sand-wiches on the front steps, and watch the football fans thunder past on their way to the Arsenal ground.

Pen enhanced the paint job in every room with custom-designed stencils and sponge effects, all the while wondering whether the emulsion fumes would harm her sleeping baby. She picked out furniture from catalogues and mingled it tastefully with furniture from the local junk shops. The previous owners' kitchen dresser was stripped and sanded and heaved to the dining room. Through trial and error, Jerry honed his carpentry skills sufficiently to fit shelves for the large photographic volumes that they would now be obliged to buy. He inserted original nineteenth-century skirting boards and architraves, and overmantels for the old cast-iron fireplaces they'd sourced from salvage. There was a brief debate about the colour of the front door, which, at Pen's insistence, was painted in Racing Green. (Jerry had argued for Mustard.)

With the essentials of the interior complete, they commissioned repairs to the crumbling chimneystack, and to the lead roof flashing. Jerry dug a trench in the back garden and sank a soak-away, to drain the excess rainwater from the gutters and the clay soil – unearthing, as he went, a not-insubstantial collection of buried gin bottles. Thus he surmised that at least one of the former occupants had been a covert alcoholic. Well, every home has its secrets. They used some of the bottles as candlestick holders. Pen designed a rock garden with a water feature, and planted her first bed of herbs just beyond the kitchen door. She tilled soil, laid down turf and, to her husband's horror, started listening to *Gardeners' Question Time*.

By the time the house was complete – or, at any rate, complete enough to hold a house-warming – Jerry estimated that the renovations were between 40 and 60 per cent his own work. He knew where the contours of coloured wire and copper piping clustered and diverged behind each plastered and painted wall. He knew that the slates of the roof would protect his family from weather, because he'd battled his vertigo to put most of them up there personally. When a floorboard creaked beneath a snugly fitted carpet, he could recall having sanded and varnished said floorboard himself.

And yes, of course, when they came to re-redecorate each room in its turn over the course of close to fifteen years, their original efforts were improved upon by specialists, their amateur handi-work buried beneath layers of expert craftsmanship. But Jerry's legacy remained, memorialised in torchlit trips to the fuse-box, in trickling taps, and in the occasional rust-tinged circle of damp on the ceiling of Isobel's bedroom.

The loft conversion was the long-planned *pièce de résistance* and, perversely, Jerry's least favourite bit of the whole endeavour: he was obliged to surrender its construction to professionals early in the house's second decade under his ownership, when the children had grown out of their nurseries. By then his work at the agency had robbed him of the spare time to devote to such an undertaking, yet it had also rewarded him with the cash to pay somebody else to project-manage it – and an architect to realise Pen's dream design. Thanks to new governmental red tape, he wouldn't have been legally permitted to do the work himself. Besides, the technical know-how had by then deserted him, and the pages he had learned it from were lost to spring cleans and second-hand bookshops.

As for the house's trifling fame beyond its own four-or-so walls, it wasn't long after Conrad was born that Pen had left the art department at Manville Glassop Cohn to go freelance, and resolved to try writing a children's book in the surplus hours supplied by the presence of the au pair. '*Conrad and Izzy and Mum and Dad too,*' she wrote – almost without thinking – on her first morning at the drafting table in her so-called studio, '*lived in the house with the very best view.*'

Then and there, she conceived a series of illustrated books for two- to seven-year olds, in which a cheeky young boy named Conrad with grand schemes would get himself into scrapes, from which his clever older sister, Izzy, would invariably rescue him. At the end of each adventure the pair would return, tired but happy, to their large and desirable home (the one at the top of the Hill) where they would eat Marmite on toast under their parents' adoring gaze. Pen would extrapolate the stories from her children's wild imaginings, and compose the illustrations herself.

Gathered on the balcony, the guests would coo obligingly at whichever details of the building's backstory Jerry and/or Pen had chosen to recount that particular evening. Some of those present would have heard chunks of the narrative before. Others might even have featured in one of the preceding anecdotes. Satisfied, they would study the horizon for a while, hugging them-selves to fend off the chill as somebody's husband pointed out the BT Tower or Centre Point. Somebody else would make a risqué joke at the expense of the Major government, or tentatively lament the mainstreaming of Britpop. The smokers (there were more of them in those days) would finish their cigarettes and stub them out in the soil of a window box, from which the cleaner would extract them with a tut the following week. And then they would step inside, slide the plate glass back into place, whisper goodnight to Barunka the Czech au pair, and descend the stairs – all four flights – to the basement kitchen-diner, where Pen or Jerry would have poured the coffee.

Finally, as fading conversation was replaced by the sound of night buses grumbling down Highbury Grove, somebody's wife would offer half-heartedly to help with the washing-up. Coats would be retrieved, air-kisses distributed, and the visitors would drift off into the North London night, leaving Jerry and Pen alone in the house on the Hill, among the devastated remains of dinner.

DERELICTION

Jerry Manville's most enduring mid-career triumph was the campaign he'd devised to launch *Ppalleena!*, a then-obscure Korean probiotic yoghurt drink, into the UK marketplace. His work helped to grow the brand by £50 million in a single year, which, in the 1990s, made it a masterpiece. This feat had been achieved by suggesting to the consumer that one small bottle of the stuff per day could, by some ill-defined alchemy, make its drinker feel better physically, and therefore psychically. Almost at once, in their thousands and hundreds of thousands, the dissatisfied masses had flocked to supermarkets in search of digestive bliss. They added the innocuous placebo to their refrigerators and their daily nutritional routines without ever once subjecting it to proper scrutiny.

Granted, Jerry had flown first class to Seoul to attend a mildly convincing presentation by the manufacturer's in-house dietary specialists. But the science in the sell was cursory. Manville Glassop Cohn's creative team magicked up an ad in which a grumpy, sickly-looking woman in pyjamas received an unexpected early-morning visit from a Buddhist monk driving a *Ppalleena!*-branded milk float. The monk handed the woman a bottle of the Korean yoghurt, which she drank on her doorstep (the firm hired animators to depict the gloop reaching her gut and filling it with 'friendly bacteria' in the least creepy way possible), at which point she and her pyjamas were instantaneously suffused with a healthy, enlightened glow. As he trundled away on his float, the monk waved excitedly and yelled, 'Feel better!' in Korean, which they subtitled with some brightly coloured East Asian typography,[1] and then repeated in more measured English: '*Ppalleena!*: Feel Better.' The Buddhist milkman starred in a series of calculatedly and increasingly bizarre commercials, briefly became a cult figure among housewives and teenagers, and earned MGC a coveted spot in the D&AD annual. More importantly, the ad worked: 30 seconds, £50 million.

Of course, they'd never get away with the same material these days. Advertising Standards were far stricter about the stated benefits of friendly bacteria – as they were about over-generalised, faintly patronising depictions of Asians. Yet it seemed, nevertheless, as if every second product on the shelves in Jerry's local Waitrose was now eager to brag that it contained some allegedly active ingredient that reduced cholesterol or the risk of heart disease. He felt partly responsible, and the manufacturers must have felt that he was partly responsible, too, because they'd rewarded him with a lifetime's supply of probiotic Korean yoghurt. Every Monday he received, by registered post, a chilled jiffy bag containing seven 70ml bottles of *Ppalleena!*. When they had first begun to arrive, soon after the campaign launch, he'd been going through some personal difficulties and was committed to a programme of self-improvement. What remained of that programme now, if nothing else, was the yoghurt. He still drank his shot every morning, without fail. Needless to say, it did not make him feel better. Not physically; not psychically.

In retirement, though, the Korean yoghurts were proving as good a way as any to deduce which day of the week he'd woken on. Which is why, that morning, but for his tortoiseshell-framed spectacles, sandbag paunch and a pair of Calvin Klein Y-fronts, Jerry was standing naked before his open fridge-freezer, calculating the implication of the two remaining 70ml shots: Saturday.

---

1 빨리나았으면좋겠어!

14

On the shelf below the yoghurts, and arrayed with equal precision, was a stack of single-serving ready meals. On the shelf above, the last two bottles from a box of mail-order white wine, and a solitary lager, left there by Glassop on a rare home visit some months previously. Jerry plucked a yoghurt shot from its perch, peeled off the foil lid with a veteran's panache, and downed it in one, tonguing the rim to extract the last of its contents. From across the apartment, he could hear his BlackBerry's treble-heavy approximation of 'Don't You Want Me'. He ignored the call, as he had twice already, and foraged noisily in the utensil drawer for his omelette pan.

He'd consumed no more than three medium-sized glasses of claret the previous evening but, at the dawn of his seventh decade, Jerry found that each new day brought with it a hangoverish fug, and each night a drunk's wee-hours dash to the loo. As recompense, he'd decreed that every breakfast would contain at least one fried or buttered item. He draped an apron across his fleshy middle and prepared himself a cheddar omelette, half a pack of grilled bacon, fresh coffee and two slices of toast. Afterwards, the slap of his feet on the floorboards echoing around the studio, he strolled with his dish to the dining table where his BlackBerry lay.

The flat was a spacious third-floor, one-/two-bedroom warehouse conversion in fashionable King's Cross: artfully exposed brickwork, high windows and all mod cons, a stone's throw from the necessary amenities and unbeatable transport links. The mezzanine master bedroom and its en-suite wet-room both boasted an enviable view of sky and the neighbouring rooftops. Once, it had presumably stored vast amounts of something bound for somewhere. He'd done nothing much to personalise the place in the past year or two, besides strewing it with a few of his most treasured belongings: his Eames lounger and ottoman; his triptych of signed Paul Rand prints; his Anglepoise.

The £900,000 asking price posed some financial risk to a recent retiree, but Jerry and his ex-wives had become accustomed to a certain standard of living. And, since so much of his modest fortune was incarcerated in the properties that Pen and Genevieve part-owned, he'd decided he should spend his few remaining fluid assets on himself, and hang the consequences.

The day was bright and baby blue, and from beyond the double glazing came the comforting hum of a London weekend. Jerry took a contrary pleasure in eating alone at the table alongside seven empty chairs, chewing his omelette slowly and relishing the results of his own rudimentary culinary skills. The BlackBerry blinked with the arrival of an email. He finished his mouthful before picking it up.

From: 'Pen' <penelope.bowles@dotmail.com>
Sent: 09 July 2011 10:32
Subject: House
Have tried calling with no luck. Long lie-in? Don't forget you must check on the house this week as the agent is keen to start viewings next Mon. Do call Monielle to give it a proper clean if you think it needs one. She is £12/hr now. Will email her mobile no again if you have mislaid.
P

As he thought about composing a reply, the phone rang again, this time with the riff from 'The Rockafeller Skank'. Jerry had assigned a different ringtone to each of his former wives, on the basis of vague chronology: the Human League for Pen, Fatboy Slim for Genevieve. He answered it reluctantly.

'Hello.'

'Jerome?'

Genevieve called him by his full name. Once a sign of affection, it was now an accusation.

'No, Genevieve, I have not forgotten.'

'Have— Well, I'm just checking, because you know Xander and I want to get out of London by midday.'

It was an irony of retirement that Saturday and Sunday were now the busiest days of Jerry's week; the days when his dependants took their opportunity to make demands on his time. Monday to Friday, he would rise late for breakfast, then go to a nearby café to read the newspaper and drink a cup of coffee. Back in the flat, he might play a round or two of Solitaire on the computer, before opening the Microsoft Word document that contained the patchy first draft of his ad-man's memoir. An hour or so later, he'd close it again, having made little or no progress. Once a week, for old times' sake, he ate a long lunch with Tony Glassop in a restaurant on Charlotte Street. Afternoons were spent skulking at his club in Soho, or browsing in stationery stores for expensively bound notebooks to add to his informal but growing collection. Later on, he might meet some friend or former colleague for a drink, or take in an art-house film at the Curzon.

Recently, if he happened to be at home in the evening, he'd developed a twice-weekly habit of masturbating to YouTube clips of attractive female newsreaders, or Nigella Lawson – whose frequent expressions of sensual pleasure inevitably stirred his dormant loins. (He had once met Nigella at a drinks party, pre-YouTube, and persuaded himself that flirting occurred.) He was scared of straying too far from the Internet mainstream in search of titillation, after an embarrassing episode featuring a virus that flooded his computer with hardcore pornography. He'd been forced to rifle through the Yellow Pages at 11 o'clock in the evening to find an engineer who could rescue the shuddering wreck of his hard drive. The man had completed the repair job without passing judgement on its sordid causes, for which Jerry was grateful and gave him a large tip.

'. . . Jerome?'

'I know, I know. Xander prefers to be punctual.'

'Oh, for God's sake . . .'

'I'll be there at half eleven.'

Jerry hung up and bit a hunk from his toast. His decision to say screw it all and revert to white bread might have been seen as a small personal victory after life with Genevieve: gluten-avoiding, green-tea-drinking, farmers'-market-frequenting Genevieve. But the very fact that he even considered it as such made it, in truth, a defeat. Still, he had to claim an advantage whenever he could. For instance, he already had the morning's schedule mapped perfectly so as to be twenty minutes late to pick up his daughter – late enough to wind up Genevieve, but not so late that he couldn't plausibly blame the traffic on Marylebone Road.

Jerry knew from his friends' experience that third wives were the thing. Andy Brandt, a former ad director who at one point in the late 1990s briefly held the Guinness World Record for the largest volume of gasoline ever detonated for use in a feature film, had informed Jerry with great conviction that a first wife represented naivety and misplaced optimism. Post-divorce, she would merely remind you of your lost innocence, and of the richly deserved guilt of leaving her for your (probably) younger, (probably) better-looking second wife.

A second wife was a symptom of your overbearing pride and unfounded confidence. Once shed, she would inevitably inspire resentment, even rage: at her, for having led you astray, and at yourself, for having been led. Third marriages, however, commonly emerged from a period of self-reflection, and the subsequent acceptance of one's immutable failings. They constituted, finally, contentment. And, bluntly (Brandt had insisted), most men who'd managed to accumulate three wives lacked the remaining time or energy to fit in a fourth. Brandt himself, it's worth noting, was already on his fifth wife – but he was, he told

Jerry in all seriousness, exceptional. Jerry was still awaiting that elusive third.

After finishing breakfast and clearing the debris into the dish-washer, he laid out his linen suit and a soft white cotton shirt. He stood under the shower for a good fifteen minutes, gazing short-sightedly at the blurred peaks of St Pancras as they vanished beneath the condensation on the wet-room's window. He dressed and made the bed, then he sat on it half-listening to the end of *Week in Westminster*. His DAB radio lived on the bedside cabinet next to his glasses case and the copy of Proust that Glassop had given him as a joke – on top of which lay whatever thriller he'd actually been reading that week. He patted his pockets unconsciously, checking for wallet, BlackBerry and keys.

His car was parked in the basement; a rare signal red 1972 Lotus Elan +2 coupé. His first boss always boasted of having purchased one direct from the production line, and Jerry had promised himself that he'd someday drive the same. The restorer had done a fine job exposing the original silver metal-flake roof and trimming the interior with real oatmeal leather.

Jerry had tired of computerised cars, each new microchip or power-assisted steering component removing him from the feel of the road by degrees. But since owning the Lotus, he'd started to appreciate their reliability. He had to avoid driving at night, because the headlamps often flickered or failed for no particular reason, leaving him to fumble aimlessly with fuses in lay-bys. He had to avoid parking on slopes, because the handbrake was not to be trusted. He enjoyed all the knowing smiles he received from passers-by, but he had to avoid being seen getting in and out of the car: the chassis sat unfeasibly low to the ground, and exiting it was a challenge fit only for a younger man.

* * *

There really was traffic on Marylebone Road, so, by the time the Lotus growled to a halt outside his former home in Notting Hill and Jerry managed to clamber from it, he was in fact a whole half-hour late. He stepped around the designer luggage in the doorway and found Genevieve adjusting her hair frantically at the hall mirror, a frizz of tension in the cool white corridor. When they'd bought the house at the turn of the century – a wedding-cake slice of Georgian terrace in a crescent behind Kensington Park Road, for almost half of Jerry's take-home from the sale of MGC – Genevieve had been adamant that they hire a minimalist interior designer to redecorate it to within an inch of its planning permissions. Jerry had acquiesced, and then watched with mounting disgruntlement as whitewash consumed every wall. By the time it was complete, he wasn't even allowed to leave a magazine lying around, for fear of disrupting the passage of clean lines through the space. He had pretended not to despise it, simply so as not to cause any more rows than were strictly necessary.

'Late again, Jerome?'

'Sorry, I got caught in—'

'I'd booked the taxi for 12.15, anyway,' said Genevieve, wrenching her eyes from herself and settling them disdainfully on her ex-husband. 'Seeing as there's always such terrible traffic on Marylebone Road.'

Rumbled, thought Jerry. Damn her.

'Where to this weekend, then?' he asked, hoping to fill their obligatory chat with inconsequential pleasantries.

'A house party, in the Cotswolds. One of Xander's art chums just bought an estate there.'

'Hmph. All right for some.'

'Do you have anything planned for Alice?'

Jerry puffed his cheeks. 'Thought I'd take her to lunch first. See what she fancies.'

'I've told her to take her guitar with her so she can practise.'

'Hmph': a puzzled 'hm', and a peeved breath out through his nostrils. Jerry wasn't sure that he approved of Alice's music lessons – not to mention her Spanish lessons, her acting lessons and her horse-riding lessons. He had genuine concerns about putting his child under excessive pressure to achieve, thus potentially jeopardising her future mental health. Also, it was bloody expensive.

'She's getting quite good, Jerome. Ask her to play you a song.'

'Does she do requests?'

Genevieve put one hand on her hip. Jerry vainly searched the monochrome hallway for something to look at that wasn't his ex-wife. Her boyfriend, Xander, emerged from the sitting room wearing a gratuitously tight sweater. Xander was a contemporary-art auctioneer and had, fittingly, selected the most pretentious possible variation on his prosaic Christian name, Alexander. Beyond these two facts, Jerry had deliberately taken no interest whatsoever in the details of his successor's life, career or ambitions. Xander treated Alice with the wariness of a novice lion-tamer, and he took Genevieve away for luxury holidays and mini-breaks at every possible opportunity, both of which suited Jerry just fine, thanks very much.

'Jerry,' said Xander.

'Xander,' said Jerry.

As if sensing a conversation reaching its nadir, Alice appeared on the stairs with her rucksack and a child-sized guitar case.

'Hi, Dad,' she said, trotting down the steps and offering Jerry a high-five.

When Jerry met Genevieve, she'd been slumming it as a stylist in a fashion photographer's studio. Her work was passable, in Jerry's opinion, but considerably less alluring than her face, legs, tits, arse, etc. She resented him now, he suspected, not merely for the decline of his own talents and influence, but also for having fooled her into trusting an inflated estimation of her own gifts.

She wasn't quite so young that their union had been unseemly, and though she was technically young enough to have been his daughter, she was somewhat older than Isobel, his actual daughter. He had divested her of some of her most precious years, and she had punished him for it. Yet Alice – just eight, and already destined to be beautiful in a more interesting way than her mother – remained as a trophy of their time together: living proof of his sometime demigod-like status among ad-men.

'Hello, sunshine,' he replied, obliging her with his open palm. She was wearing a customised vintage Madonna T-shirt that, as she turned to kiss Genevieve goodbye, displayed the words 'The Virgin Tour' across its back. Jerry had given it to her for her last birthday. It was important to him that Alice should develop not only a taste for high-quality eighties pop music, but also a healthy appreciation of irony. She was going to need it.

He always hoped his daughter would find it a treat to be driven in the Lotus, but he was invariably disappointed. 'Mummy says you drive too fast,' she would say, or 'It's very noisy, isn't it?', or 'Dad, why does your car smell funny?' She was referring to the stink of leather mixed with petrol, which, to Jerry's mind, was one of the great smells of the world. Today, she'd already complained that the vibrations of the 1.6-litre engine made her ears itch.

'How's school?'

''S okay.'

It certainly ought to be okay, at £5,000 a term. She fiddled with the old Philips radio as they sped down the Embankment, the sun shuffling streetlamp-shadows across the dashboard. Jerry displaced his irritation by putting his foot down.

'What do you want for lunch?'

'Don't mind.'

They ended up in a Pizza Express on the South Bank, for lack of any better ideas. Tourists bleated around them in thirty different languages. The pizzas arrived under-seasoned, and with suspicious alacrity. Jerry could tell by the extra-friendly smiles from the waitress that she took Alice to be his granddaughter. As she bent over to grind the black pepper, he deliberately stole a second-long look down the front of her blouse: if he was to be considered an old man, then he would act like one. He hosed his Sloppy Giuseppe with chilli oil.

'How's your pizza?'

'Nice.'

'Your mum says you're getting pretty good at the guitar.'

Alice grimaced with a mouthful of dough and cheese, and said something indistinguishable.

'Can you play any Dylan?'

Now she raised one eyebrow as if to say, *Daa-aaa-ad*. Jerry was impressed by her physical vocabulary. He used to practise for hours in front of the mirror, trying to get his eyebrows to move independently of one another, with little success. He had to think about the manoeuvre for too long to make it worthwhile. But it seemed to come naturally to Alice.

They shared a plate of profiteroles and wandered along the crowded riverside to the Tate. There was a retrospective Jerry had been meaning to see, and Alice provided the necessary excuse. He occasionally forced her to accompany him to age-inappropriate shows (gratis, Alice being under twelve), while insisting to himself and others that it was educational. He needed someone with whom to discuss the art – and he had absolutely no intention of letting Xander hold sway over his daughter's cultural opinions.

The exhibition was by a Chilean artist whose modus operandi was to take everyday objects – cars, furniture, kitchen appliances – and render them useless. He removed motors or wheels or drawers and replaced them with random secondary objects: lamp-shades, pieces of fruit. He sabotaged product design. The idea,

Jerry presumed, was to draw attention to each object as an object, rather than as a device. To celebrate not its function, but its mere existence.

It wasn't bad, given Jerry's firm belief that most conceptual artists were posturing idiots, who once in a while created something exciting or witty by pure chance, and then retroactively justified its existence with pages of impenetrable monograph codswallop. Too self-regarding to be straightforward; too dense to do anything that actually communicated anything to anybody from beyond the art-world circle jerk. And yet, he often found it expedient to borrow their half-baked ideas, so as to realise them more fully himself, in the service of something useful: brand management.

Alice bounced through the vast gallery ahead of him, all but oblivious to her fellow visitors. It must be bliss to be so at ease, thought Jerry. There had to have been a moment in his own childhood when he'd been conscious without being self-conscious, but he could not recall it. Give her another couple of years, he supposed, and she'll probably have an eating disorder. He caught up with her as she stood transfixed by a cylindrical sculpture welded together from re-purposed bicycle parts. *Tornado IV*, read the caption card.

'Do you like it?' he asked quietly, resting his hand on the crown of her head.

'It's cool,' said Alice.

'You know, a lot of contemporary art is about taking something familiar, and encouraging people to look at it in a different, unexpected way.'

'Oh,' she replied.

'That's sort of what I used to do, as well.'

'What, art?' she said, and gave him a sceptical look.

'Yes. Well, no. Advertising.'

She giggled.

'What?'

'That's funny.'

His BlackBerry honked in his pocket. A couple of the other gallery patrons glanced at him disapprovingly. A text.

Did you get my email? P

Jerry exhaled, deleted the message, put the phone back in his pocket and proceeded to complete his leisurely tour of the exhibition. He sought out his daughter again, and found her gaping through the window towards St Paul's. He took her hand and guided her to the lifts. In the gift shop, he bought himself the more costly version of the exhibition catalogue, and helped Alice to pick out a poster of some Monet water lilies for her bedroom wall that he thought Genevieve and Xander would both hate. When they got back to the Lotus, he was obliged to weather the approval of some American students, who were taking pictures of it with their cameraphones. To Alice's bemusement, Jerry waited until they had dispersed before lowering himself gracelessly through the driver's door and inserting his bulk behind the wheel.

'Are we going home now?' she asked.

'Hmph. Not exactly.'

Jerry aimed the Lotus nose-first into a large space on the street opposite the house. The parking spot was sufficiently level to put the handbrake on and walk away without concern for the car in front. He didn't like to use the driveway, just in case a chunk of gravel happened to flick up and scratch the bodywork. The road was quiet save for the tinny pings of the cooling motor, and what sounded like reggae drifting from an open window somewhere nearby.

'Isn't that where you used to live, Dad?'

'That's right,' said Jerry, sizing up the old place.

When Pen had called in January to say she was finally ready to sell, he'd felt the pang of ownership for the first time in a decade. And when she told him she thought the first- and second-floor bathrooms could do with a refit to boost the resale price, he'd surprised her and himself by offering to oversee the work. So, for six blissful weeks in spring, he'd consulted designers, enlisted building contractors and eagerly supervised the renovations.

'With Auntie Pen?'

'Er, yes.'

(*Auntie* Pen? Christ, the ideas Genevieve put in the poor girl's head.)

'And Conrad and Izzy?'

'Er . . . ?'

'From *The House on the Hill*?'

'Oh, right. Yes, and Conrad and Izzy. Now look, stay here; I'm just going to go inside quickly. Listen to the radio if you want.'

He'd been almost sad when the painters completed the last of the touch-ups. He'd enjoyed driving up there now and then to drink coffee in the kitchen with the workmen. Sometimes he'd watched a bit of television. Once, he'd even mowed the lawn. With the work complete and Pen's possessions all but moved out, there was little left in the building besides curtains and carpets. Yet it remained reassuringly familiar. He opened the car door and put one foot on the tarmac, bracing himself for extraction.

'Can't I come with you?'

'No, you just wait here,' he replied. 'I'll only be a minute.'

'Oh, puh-leeeeeeeez, Dad.'

She squirmed in her seat to demonstrate her enthusiasm, and the car rocked gently back and forth. Jerry was always reluctant to permit too much traffic between the compartmentalised subdivisions of his life. Letting Alice see inside the house on the Hill would be a serious breach of those restrictions. But then again, the place was all but empty and, if everything went according to plan, it would belong to somebody else by next month. It couldn't hurt.

'Okay. Come on then, we're not staying long.'

Alice skipped after her father as he crossed the road, searching his fob for the appropriate pair of keys. As he mounted the steps to the door, she crouched in the driveway, picking up a handful of gravel and letting it trickle out through her fingers.

'Don't do that,' Jerry muttered.

He inserted the thickest key on the ring into the lower of the door's two locks. But, as he tried to turn it, he met with some form of invisible resistance. Hmph. He grabbed the knob and pulled the door towards him with a grunt of exertion, hoping to loosen the mechanism. There was no give, but he tried turning the key again anyway. Nothing. Jerry studied the fob, and teased a Yale key free from the pack. Perhaps he hadn't double-locked the door last time he was here? It was possible. Alice was still crouching in the gravel – now, apparently, digging to discover what lay beneath it.

'Alice, don't do that!'

He raised the Yale key to the second lock, but it refused to slide more than half an inch into the keyhole, however much he wiggled it. Feeling a little foolish, he pressed his lips to the door and blew into the hole, as if that might dislodge the hidden obstacle, then he tried the key once more. Still nothing. There was no escaping it: the key did not match the hole. Would Pen have had the locks changed without telling him?

'Dad, what does this say?'

'Hang on a minute, Alice.'

He stared at his handful of useless metal. There were three more Yale-style keys there, but he could identify them all: the King's Cross flat; the Notting Hill house (Emergencies Only!); and the padlock for the 100 square-foot storage space that he rented in Paddington.

'. . . Dad?'

Alice had stopped playing with the gravel now. She was peering at something in the bay window. Jerry could hear the sound of reggae in the air again: was that Peter Tosh?

'What does this mean, Dad?'

There was a sheet of A4 paper fixed to the outside of the glass — or was it the inside? Jerry couldn't quite see from where he was standing.

'Read it out, Alice.'

'"Section Six",' she replied, reciting the words slowly and precisely. '"Criminal Law Act. 1977."'

'Fuck,' said Jerry, and the hand that held the keys dropped to his side. Alice let out a little yelp — in response, he presumed, to his swearing. He was about to apologise, when he heard a gentle slap on the step beside him. He looked down. There, on the ground, were the smashed remains of an eggshell, most of the contents of which had spattered over the lower half of his left suit-leg, darkening the linen like dog piss on a lamp post.

'Fuck,' he said again. There was laughter from above, and Jerry looked up just in time to watch a second large egg travel the final foot or so to his forehead, where it exploded, spraying his face with slime.

'Fuck!' he cried, staggering backwards.

'Daddy!' Alice squealed.

Jerry peeled off his spectacles and squinted up at the window of the master bedroom, where there were two indistinct dark shapes bobbing with glee. One of them sounded female, and he could just about discern her dayglo pink hair.

'What the fuck do you think you're doing?! This is my fucking house!'

'PROPERTY IS THEFT, MOTHERFUCKER!' yelled the girl with the pink hair, sticking her arm out and making what Jerry could only assume was a lewd gesture, before she disappeared back inside the master bedroom. Her companion cackled, and then coughed mightily.

'Sorry, mate,' he said in a Midlands accent, his croak that of a seasoned smoker of something or other. Jerry couldn't make out the man's face without his specs, which were still slick with goo. The reggae suddenly grew much louder: someone had turned the volume up. It was definitely Peter Tosh.

2

Kneeling before the wall at the back of the barn, where the cool yellow brickwork catches the mid-afternoon sun, Penelope Bowles, née Barclay (formerly Manville), plucked a fat tomato from the vine and breathed it in. It was firm and earthy and sweet. She resisted the temptation to take a bite, plopping it into the trug with its companions. Clutching her secateurs, she reached over to harvest a thick sprig of basil, and then rose slowly to her feet, knees creaking with the effort. She brushed her soiled hands on her smock, which was already freckled with years' worth of paint splatter, and tucked a thread of her greying hair behind her ear. The shadows were lengthening in the valley, a breeze rippling the nearest cornfield. Above the chatter of birds came the familiar cough of Bruno DeLambre's Land Rover approaching up the track. Bliss, all things considered.

The vegetable garden at Le Boqueteau was proving a triumph. Already that summer it promised to yield bell peppers, courgettes, cabbages, runner beans, lettuce and purple sprouting broccoli. Were she not so fond of them, Pen could have paid the plants only scant attention, and they would still grow in abundance thanks to the large quantities of sun, the regular – but not too regular – rain showers, and the fertile Dordogne clay. Some of the flowers on their modest handful of hectares really did plant themselves, such as the violet-blue Viper's Bugloss that blew in on the wind and scattered like ink flecks in the long grasses at the fringes of the property. Herbs, too, grew profusely, and in her fruit grove she'd successfully cultivated damsons, greengages, strawberries, raspberries, rhubarb and quince.

She took up the trug and rounded the barn, meandering across the lawn towards the farmhouse. The grass around the swimming pool was mown short, but a few strides from the water's edge she allowed it to grow roughly, like a meadow. Her calculated neglect had been rewarded with a dappling of wild gladioli. From the poolside lounger she retrieved her spectacles, paperback and glass of now-flat mineral water, in which a drowned bug floated next to the curled-up lemon slice. The lawn was dotted with crab apple trees, which had blossomed in spring, but were still bearing fruit in the form of David's spicy crab apple preserve. The path that led from the pool to the front of the house was bordered with lavender, battled over by butterflies and bees.

Bruno's jeep was parked on the drive under a magnolia. His skittish pointer, Remy, tumbled up to her, wagging his tail furiously, and she obliged him with a ruffle of the ears. She could hear David and Bruno's faltering, pidgin conversation from behind the house, so she walked along the terrace to the kitchen entrance, Remy sniffing at her ankles. Passion flowers and Californian lilac crept around the latticed porch awning, and two small bay trees stood sentry either side of the kitchen door. Pen's plans for the garden felt sickeningly close to completion. Her most cherished project, however, was to convert the run-down barn – presently a garage – into a gîte, so she could invite her London friends to France without feeling that she had to play hostess twenty-four hours a day.

The kitchen was clogged with the smell of David's damson jam bubbling on the stove. Pen found her husband's passion for jam-making just the slightest bit effeminate, but she didn't tell him so, for fear of bruising his ego. And, in any case, it had proved an excellent way to bond with the local community. Whenever either of them went to church on Sunday armed with a new consignment of *confitures*, expat congregants would crowd about them far more eagerly than they did the vicar. Often, when he was at work in England, their thrice-weekly phone conversations would conclude with David asking Pen to pick some fresh fruit and freeze it in preparation for his arrival. He had been in France for just a week now, and already his dedicated jam shelf was filling up with various flavours, each labelled in painstaking calligraphy, ready to distribute after the following morning's service.

She deposited the tomatoes on the kitchen table, where there already sat a small wooden crate filled with wild *cèpe* mushrooms. She picked one up and thumbed it softly, smiling to herself and silently rethinking the supper menu. Her mobile phone was on the worktop near the sink, but there was still no message from Jerry. Not that she'd expected one; she knew him too well for that. She had sent emails to her children, too, to tell them it was finally going on the market; that after years of hemming and hawing, of hesitation and procrastination, and months more of logistics and bathroom refits, there would – a week from now – be a card in the estate agent's window, with a price and a picture of the house on the Hill.

As she washed her hands under the cold tap, David loped in, pursued by a limping Bruno.

'Oh, bugger,' said David, hurrying to the stove to check his jam thermometer. He quickly lifted the pan free of the hob and placed it on the chopping board to cool. 'Bugger, bugger, bugger. Think I may have left this batch on the heat for too long.'

'Oh, dear,' replied Pen, privately contemplating the absurdity of this tall, distinguished man fussing over a little pan of jam. She dried her hands on a tea towel. '*Bonsoir*, Bruno.'

'Hello, *madame*.'

Bruno was probably ten years younger and half a foot shorter than her husband, though he balanced these discrepancies with a surplus of hair – on his head, his arms, the backs of his hands.

David was wearing a shirt tucked into his burgundy corduroys, a woollen sweater draped across his shoulders; Bruno, grubby jeans and an old polo shirt torn from its collar to an inch or two below where the buttons ended, exposing yet more of the dark tufts on his chest. He was clutching a bag of tobacco. Remy scuttled across the quarry tiles of the kitchen floor.

'Have you seen what Bruno's brought us?' asked David, still prodding needlessly at the saucepan with a wooden spoon.

'Yes, the *cèpes*. Lovely,' she said.

'Very kind, don't you think? Foraged just this morning, eh, Bruno?'

'*Oui*,' Bruno replied. 'Yes.'

Pen smiled at him, and David, recovering from the trauma of his overcooked jam, went on.

'Now, Bruno says he's happy to rebuild the woodshed. Shouldn't take him more than a few days. He'll use corrugated plastic for the roof, if that's agreeable to you. Is that correct, Bruno?'

'Yes,' said Bruno, making a sloping-roof gesture with his hand. 'Plastic, yes?'

The woodshed protruded from the back of the house, where they piled logs in advance of winter to keep the wood dry. Its pine frame had long been rotted through.

'That's fine,' said Pen. 'It sounds perfect.'

'Good, good,' said David. 'Well, hopefully he can make a start next week.'

'Super.'

Bruno started to roll a cigarette, pursing his lips, watching Pen steadily. Agitated by his gaze, she picked up a tomato and turned back to the sink to rinse it. David reached into a cupboard and brought out a pair of tumblers.

'Can I make you a drink, Bruno?' he asked.

Bruno politely demurred, explaining in halting English that he really ought to leave, and he and David moved out into the hall, Remy panting behind them. A drink. Pen needed a drink. She placed the tomato on the chopping board and opened the freezer cabinet. As she broke two cubes of ice into a glass, she could hear what sounded like David pressing a euro note of unnecessarily high value into the reluctant Frenchman's palm. She poured herself a Pernod.

David returned to the kitchen and hovered over his jam again, skimming the scum from its surface and depositing it in the sink. Then he studied the deep purple concoction as it dripped slowly from a wooden spoon. Satisfied, he lifted the spoon to his lips, blew across it, and poked at it tentatively with his tongue.

'Hm,' he said. 'It might be all right, actually.'

He offered Pen the spoon and she humoured him, licking a dab of the sugary mixture.

'Yes,' she said. 'Lovely.'

The gasps from Bruno's old 4x4 grew quieter, as it clattered down the track towards the road. Pen sipped her drink to dilute the sickly damson taste.

'You shouldn't have given him money yet, David.'

'Why ever not?'

'He was embarrassed.'

David cracked a pair of ice cubes into his own glass. 'Well, I can't imagine why he should be. He's just a handyman, taking on a job. And he brought us those mushrooms. It was the least I could do.'

'The mushrooms were a gesture; he wasn't *selling* them.'

'Well,' he huffed, 'Bruno is made of stern stuff. I'm sure I haven't offended his sensibilities too deeply.'

'You're probably right,' said Pen after a pause. David leaned over and patted her hand where she'd balled it on the worktop.

'Has Jerry got back to you?' he asked.

'Not yet.'

'He really takes the cake, doesn't he? I ought to call him myself.'

'No, David. No, he'll have got the message. He'll just ignore it for a while.' She threw her hands up: 'It's just a control thing.'

'It's damned rude, is what it is.'

David made himself a gin and tonic, and then turned back to the saucepan. He'd lined up six warm, sterilised jars on the kitchen counter, and now he began, ever so carefully, to decant the jam. Pen put some potatoes on the boil and went upstairs to change out of her smock. When she returned, she found her husband delicately handwriting labels for each jar with a felt-tip pen, detailing the flavour and the date of its preparation.

Try as she might, Pen still could not banish a tiny, unwarranted niggle of resentment at having her bucolic idyll interrupted. Of course it was utterly delightful to have David around, and one naturally hoped for companionship as old age approached. But after so many years alone, she had grown accustomed to a generous allowance of personal space. Yes, a good husband could be indispensable. It was just that she preferred not to have to put up with him all day, every day. As time went on, and as he eased into semi-retirement, he had begun to spend more and more time in France – so she would simply have to get used to it. They both would. Given how little they actually saw of one another, it was really no surprise that their relationship remained perpetually over-polite: he telephoning her from England at precisely 8 o'clock every Tuesday, Friday and Sunday; she suppressing her irritation at having to prepare supper while he dithered around her, spooning his fucking jam into jars.

She chopped the parboiled potatoes, pan-fried them in goose fat with a fistful or two of the *cèpes*, and stirred in garlic and chopped parsley from the garden. Eventually, David retired to the terrace with his drink and a copy of the *Spectator*, to shrug off all the excitement of the past half-hour. Pen sliced the tomatoes to make a salad, which she garnished with chopped basil, and then laid out some cold beef and mustard.

The sun was setting under pink clouds as they settled down to eat on the terrace, lights flickering in the far-off farmhouses on the other side of the valley. David poured the wine and placed the bottle on the table next to a tall canister of extra-strength insect spray. Perfect summer evenings in the South of France were plagued by the immigrant population of North African wasps; thumb-sized beasts with bulbous abdominal undercarriages, they were drawn not so much to supper as to the light from the house. A sting, it was said, sometimes required a trip to the doctor to be prescribed an antihistamine. Pen thought they were best ignored, but David was obsessed; he'd hardly troubled the food on his plate before he was up, attacking his first victim. A wasp bounced in vain against the bright kitchen window, and he blasted it until it buzzed feebly to the ground. He squirted the thing once more to be certain, and then stamped on it, finally walking to the grass to wipe the sole of his shoe clean.

'I've been thinking about the barn again,' said Pen.

'Oh, yes?' David replied, flapping his napkin back across his lap.

'Yes, I was wondering what you thought of having a second bedroom – so that, say, Harriet and Gareth could have Jasper to stay in there with them.'

Harriet was David's daughter. Pen liked her, and her husband. Really, she did. But she would not have minded in the least if their boisterous young son Jasper were exiled to the barn when they next came to stay.

'Sounds like a fine idea,' David replied, patting her hand again. 'And it's your project, after all. Do whatever you think is best. These mushrooms are fabulous.'

She blinked.

'Yes. Aren't they just?'

Pen still could not decide whether David was genuinely unin-terested in the barn conversion, or simply trying to please her by giving her free rein. She was planning to pay for most of the work with the proceeds from the sale of the Highbury house. But she wanted to feel as if the design decisions had been made jointly; and, more importantly, she did not wish to be blamed later for any faults in their execution.

Her mobile phone vibrated, rattling the cutlery on the table.

'Is it him?' David asked pointedly, as she picked it up.

'Yes. He's been to the house. All fine, apparently.'

'Finally. The swine.'

Pen knew that David's extravagant exasperation was a sympathetic attempt to mirror her own, but it made her instinctively defensive. Every time he sighed or swore at Jerry's expense, she wanted to stand up for him. It was an odd sensation, after so many years of sighing and swearing at Jerry herself. Perhaps she ought to explain all this to David, but she hadn't the energy to tackle the tension it might create. She tapped out a reply, accompanied only by the clink of cutlery on crockery.

'These tomatoes are magnificent, Pen. Really, really magnificent.'

'They have come on marvellously, haven't they?'

She chewed a forkful of Bruno's *cèpes*, thinking about London. About Jerry and his myriad flaws. Without warning, David leapt from his seat, grabbing the insect spray and firing it into the half-dark.

'Bloody thing!'

He left his plate unattended to go after the wasp. Pen watched him as he stalked off into the garden, canister in hand, ducking among the lavender in search of prey.

3

The soft throb of reggae still stirred the air, but the intruders had retreated into the depths of the house. Alice hugged the gatepost where the gravel yard greeted the pavement, snivelling safely beyond the reach of any further projectiles. After calming her down sufficiently to leave her side, Jerry had returned to the front door, where he crouched and poked open the letter box with his thumb. He'd scraped some of the gloop off his glasses using a leaf from one of Pen's shrubs, though by then the coughing man with the Midlands accent had disappeared inside, closing the window of the master bedroom behind him.

Jerry called through the door, faux-forlornly: 'Hello? . . . *Hello?* Can we just talk, please?'

There was no reply. The hallway, or what he could discern of it from that narrow angle, was bare down to the brushed wooden floorboards. He thought he could see shadows moving in the sitting room, but the curtains had been drawn, leaving only the notice of squatters' rights on display. Lord knows what was going on behind those designer drapes. Drug-taking and vandalism, probably. Group sex, most likely. Just think of all the stains: blood, piss, sweat, semen, spray-paint. Were they drinking his tap water? Were they watching his 32-inch television? Were they leaving skid marks in his toilet? He felt like some old nobleman returning from a long and fruitless war in the Holy Land, only to find his castle overrun by the serfs, his family seat usurped.

'. . . Dad?' Alice whimpered.

'It's okay, Alice. Just give me a minute . . . HELLO?'

Nothing. His back twinged, so he stood up with a little groan of discomfort and banged the door-knocker twice. No one came. He banged it again, just because.

'Bastards.'

He gingerly fingered his hair. It was gelled into clumps by the raw egg, threatening to stiffen like meringue. He wiped his sticky hand on the brickwork, and then dug his BlackBerry from his trouser pocket, blessedly unscathed. His hands trembled with outrage. He didn't think he'd ever dialled 999 before; sixty years and not a single emergency call. Was it so unreasonable to have assumed he'd never need to?

'Hello, emergency service operator, which service do you require?'

'Police, please,' he muttered impatiently, confident that his problem would soon be solved.

'I'll just connect you now.'

Jerry sighed and tapped his soiled shoe on the top step, wondering how far away the nearest patrol car might be, how long it would take to arrive, sirens blaring, blue lights ablaze.

'Hello, police emergency. Where are you calling from?'

'From Highbury Hill. Look, there are people in my house.'

'I'm sorry, sir. Could you repeat that?'

'There. Are. People. In my *house*.'

'You're being burgled?'

'Not exactly . . .'

The woman's voice was kindly, but robust.

'I'm sorry, sir. Could you give me the exact address?'

'They're squatters.'

The operator paused. 'Squatters.'

'Yes, there are squatters in my house.'

'Ah, I'm sorry, sir. That's a civil matter, I'm afraid.'

'Excuse me?'

'I'm sorry, sir. That's not a police matter, and it's not an emergency. You'll have to get off the line.'

'What?'

What?!

'I'm sorry, sir. You should talk to a solicitor. I'm afraid you'll have to get off the line.'

The phone went dead. Jerry stared at it in disbelief.

'Bastards.'

He clomped down the steps and stood in the driveway, glowering at the house, bunching and unbunching his fists. He paced the gravel in a circle as Alice looked on warily. He scanned the ground for a brick, something to hurl through a window. He considered screaming some new obscenities, but that would only scar his daughter's youthful subconscious yet more deeply than the previous five minutes. And it wouldn't exactly endear him to the neighbours.

The neighbours. He grabbed Alice's outstretched hand and led her forcefully along the pavement to the adjoining house. There was a petite G-Wiz electric car parked outside on the God-awful granite paving that Pen had complained about more than once (to him, of course; never to its owners). Jerry tried to recall the name of the couple that lived there as he jogged up the front steps and pressed the doorbell for half a second longer than was really necessary. They'd once tried to organise a street party; Pen had complained about that, too. Stuart and . . . Anna? Angela?

'Andrea!' he remembered breathlessly, as she opened the door.

'Oh, um . . . Jerry, isn't it? What a surprise!'

Andrea was forty-something and starting to show it around her middle. She wore a baggy T-shirt over yoga pants and bare feet, and her mousy hair was clenched in a ponytail to reveal a face bereft of make-up. There was a small sports towel slung over her shoulder, and a large mole on her neck. She was not, Jerry quickly deduced, wearing a bra. When she grinned, she opened her gapped

40

teeth an inch and thrust her tongue forward. He flinched involuntarily.

'I must be a sight!' she said, still grinning. 'I was in the middle of a downward-facing dog!'

Jerry tried to smile in sympathy, but failed. 'Andrea, look. I'm very sorry to bother you, but there are squatters in the house. In *our* house.'

'Oh, yes,' Andrea replied. 'We know. They seem jolly nice, actually. Considering!'

She did the thing with the teeth and the tongue again, and then used the towel to wipe a film of perspiration from her face. When she spotted Alice at the foot of the steps, she wrinkled her nose and waved eagerly, mouthing a babyish 'Hello'. Alice did not respond.

Jerry recovered himself. 'You *know*? Didn't you think to tell Pen?'

'Oh! Well, at first we thought they must be relatives of yours or, y'know, friends of the children. They're very discreet . . .' She raised her arms in the air and stretched one, then the other, behind her head as she went on, her speech interspersed with tiny grunts of exertion. 'And, um, when Stu found out they were squatters I suppose we just thought, y'know, "Pen hasn't been living there; what's the harm?" I mean, they've really been perfectly polite so far. They play a bit of music, but not *too* loud. I'm sorry, um, I suppose we just sort of assumed you already knew, y'know.'

Jerry folded his arms and nibbled his lower lip, trying to tease away a scrap of dead skin with his teeth. The mood he was in, anybody could have made him irritable. Even Nigella, or Fiona Bruce. Andrea was especially unlucky, in that she was an exceptionally irritating person already, and thus, at this particular moment, doubly – triply – irritating to Jerry. He could just imagine her, proudly informing her *Guardian*-reading chums that she had squatters next door, as if it added some kind of credibility to her yoga stretches and her stupid little fucking car.

'Well, I *didn't* know,' he said. 'Nobody bloody *told* me, did they?!'

She stopped grinning, finally, and put her hands on her hips the way Genevieve did when she was about to give him a bollocking. 'Well, I'm sorry, Jerry, but I don't think we even have a phone number for either of you. I don't know if Pen left a forwarding address with somebody else on the street, but the house has been empty for some time. So I'm not sure quite what you expected us to do about it.'

Jerry suddenly felt very, very tired indeed.

'How many of them are there?' he asked.

'I couldn't say. A good handful, I suppose. Some of them are foreign. I think they might be students.'

'How long have they been there?'

'How long . . . ?'

'The squatters. How long have they been in the house?'

'Oh, I don't know. A month, maybe? Two?'

'Two *months*?! Bloody hell.'

Andrea opened her mouth and closed it again. Jerry turned on his heel and stomped down her front steps, taking Alice once more by the hand. His daughter had grown pale and unresponsive; she appeared to be suffering from some variety of post-traumatic stress disorder.

'Have you tried calling the police?' Andrea called after him, as he swept past the G-Wiz.

'Yes!' he replied, not looking back. He crossed the street to his car, Alice dumbly keeping pace.

'Get in,' he said.

Jerry circled the block twice, becoming increasingly irate, before he found a parking spot close to Holloway police station that wasn't on a double yellow line. A bolus of rage had settled in his gut like a badly digested kebab. If he were to get a parking ticket now, he thought, he might just have to start gunning people down in the street. He wasn't entirely keen to leave the car unattended in this part of town, so close to Hornsey Road's low-rise council blocks, but there was nothing else for it. He heaved himself from the Lotus and waited for Alice to follow. She had allowed her hair to fall across her face and remain there, veiling her troubled features; he almost had to drag her limp form up the ramp to the station entrance.

The small reception area was quiet and dim, blinds lowered to keep out the broiling sun. There was a single policeman on duty behind the bulletproof glass at the front desk, a middle-aged constable with ruddy cheeks and a bum-chin. A sticker on the glass in front of him proclaimed that the Met was '*Working together for a safer London*'; an inordinately facile bit of branding, thought Jerry, his ad-man instincts distracting him momentarily. The place had that air of public buildings badly designed by brutalists: condensation, sweat, boiled cabbage. A teenager in sweatpants and an Arsenal shirt sat on the wipe-clean metal chairs by the door, flipping through a copy of the local free sheet too fast to take in anything but the pictures. If Jerry was jumping a queue, then nobody tried to stop him.

'Yes?' said the constable.

'I'd like to report a home invasion,' said Jerry.

'A home invasion,' the policeman repeated, scanning his computer screen for no apparent reason. 'Do you mean a burglary, sir?'

Jerry tried hard to think of a way that he could frame his complaint, so that the police would agree to forcibly remove the squatters without his having to lie to them. The constable clicked his mouse aimlessly.

'Not really, no. A home invasion. There are people in my house.'

'I see. Was it a forced entry?'

'I don't know. I suppose so.'

The policeman studied Jerry properly for the first time, taking in his suit, his fury-red face and his ossifying egg-bouffant.

'You suppose so. And you're saying they're still there?'

'Precisely.'

'I see. And what, they're burglars?'

'Well, no. No, not burglars. Students, I think. They *terrified* my daughter.'

Jerry grasped Alice by the shoulder and shoved her towards the desk, so that the policeman could see what he hoped would be her terror-stricken expression. The constable glanced at her, but he failed to register any interest.

'Sorry, sir. Did you say "students"?'

'Squatters,' said Alice, opening her mouth for the first time in about half an hour. Now the constable took a proper look at her. She smiled up at him, sad-facedly.

'What was that, m'love?'

'They're squatters,' she replied.

Jerry cleared his throat. The policeman looked at him levelly again, unimpressed.

'Squatters is it, sir?'

'Hmph. That's right.'

'I'm afraid that's a civil matter, sir. Nothing the police can do about it. You'll have to take it up with the courts. I can give you a phone number . . .'

'They attacked me.'

'Pardon?'

It was a desperate tactic, but it was all he had left.

'They attacked me. The squatters.'

'Attacked you how, sir?'

'They threw eggs at me.'

The constable smirked and flicked his eyes furtively over Jerry's shoulder. Jerry turned. The teenager in the Arsenal shirt was snickering into his newspaper. Jerry turned back, unable to conceal his apoplexy.

'They've ruined my fucking suit!'

'Now, there's no need to swear, sir.'

'I beg to differ. This is a one-thousand-pound suit. And it's a FUCKING TWO-POINT-ONE-MILLION-POUND HOUSE they're in, for that matter!'

The policeman had regained his composure. He folded his arms and leaned back in his chair.

'Now look, Mr . . . ?'

'Manville.'

'Mr Manville. Squatting is not currently a criminal offence in this country. It's a pain in the behind, and I apologise for the inconvenience. I really do. But I suggest you call your solicitor. I presume you have one of those?'

On reflection, thought Jerry, mentioning the asking price for the house had probably been a mistake. He was tempted to tell the policeman to go and perform some revolting auto-erotic act, but he restrained himself. Getting arrested was not going to aid his cause. He bottled the insult and let it buzz vainly in his gullet.

'Thanks for nothing,' he said, taking Alice's hand again.

'Bye,' she smiled, as her father escorted her to the exit.

'Bye-bye, m'love,' the constable replied.

Jerry sat in the driver's seat of the Lotus, gripping the wheel as if about to snap it in half. What, precisely, was the point of the police, if not to protect law-abiding, homeowning citizens such as himself from just this sort of violation? The perpetrators were *in situ*, and eminently arrestable. Surely the Met ought to welcome any opportunity to improve their mediocre stats? Weren't they 'Working together for a safer London'? The day was coming to a close, and he couldn't face another trip back up to the house in the dark just to yell futile pleas through the letter box, or be sworn at by kids with stupid hair. Alice looked at him expectantly. She had perked up since her brush with the long arm of the law. Damnably resilient, children.

'Dad?'

'Just a minute, Alice. Dad's thinking.'

He was, bluntly, rather testy with his daughter for having told the policeman the truth, but even he knew that berating her for it would set an uncomfortable precedent. And while he was reluctant to take that self-satisfied constable's advice, it struck him that there was presently no other option. He yanked out his BlackBerry again and scrolled through the contacts list until he reached his solicitor, Clive Billings, a stout, florid Scot whose advice alone cost the equivalent of a modest provincial mortgage.

'Jeeeerry,' drawled Clive as he answered, with a warmth that only a man who gets paid for small talk could muster. 'Saturday. Must be an emergency. What can I do for you?'

Jerry explained the situation as quickly and concisely as he could, his own mental clock ticking noisily as he did so. He could almost hear the rustle of pinstripe on the other end of the line as Clive made himself comfortable.

'So Pen hasn't lived in the house for . . . ?'

'Oh, a year. At least. Eighteen months.'

'But you both have keys.'

'Yes. It's taken us a while to get round to selling it. We were doing up the bathrooms.'

'Sure, sure. So which of you was the last to visit? Before today, I mean.'

Jerry was convinced that Clive practised his leisurely Celtic inflections so as to draw out every conversation to its maximum achievable length.

'Me, I think.'

'And is it possible that you left a door unlocked, or a window open, the last time you were there?'

He racked his brains. Could he have been that stupid?

'Hmph. It's possible.'

'Because, you see, Jerry, if they broke in, then that's a criminal act. But if they got in without causing any damage, then they can stay for as long as it takes us to get a court order to regain possession. Until then, the place is theirs.'

'Well, they've changed the locks.'

'Then nothing's provable. Truth is, they could say they found the front door kicked in by somebody else, and that they just walked through it. If there are no witnesses . . .'

'Okay. So the court order.'

'We need to apply for something called an interim possession order. The judge will decide whether to issue it, and when he does – which he will – we serve the squatters with the documents. The judge sets a date for a hearing, at which he will find in your favour. And then – but only then – you'll be able to retake possession, or have the squatters evicted.'

'Perfect. Great. How long will that take?'

'Oh, a few weeks, a month. I could pull some strings, maybe hurry things through in a fortnight or so. Depends how much of a fight the little pricks put up.'

'A fortnight?! No. No, that won't work. The agent is starting viewings Monday week.'

'Jerry, my son. I'm afraid all that's going to have to wait.'

Jerry's brow prickled with sweat.

'Now,' said Clive, 'I want you to promise me something, Jerry.'

'What's that?'

'I don't want you going back to the house and confronting them, making threats – anything that could work against us in court.'

'How much has this call cost me already, Clive?'

'Promise me, Jerry.'

'Fine. I promise. So how much? Three figures?'

'Oh,' Clive chuckled. 'Aye, I should think so. How long have we been talking?'

'Long enough.'

'Do you want me to set things in motion?'

'Fine.'

'All right, then.'

'Clive, I'm hanging up now. Give me a call when you have some news.'

'Good to talk to you, Jer—'

Jerry hung up. And before he could talk himself out of it, he typed a text:

Been to house. Everything fine. No need for cleaner. J

He held his breath, watching the message intently as it flew south.

'Dad?' said Alice.

'Just a minute, Alice.'

The phone shuddered in his hand.

Good. Will be back in London next Sunday to finalise everything with the agent. Perhaps see you then. P

He read it twice, to make sure it betrayed no suspicions. Pen would be mightily displeased to discover what was going on – and something told him it would play out as having been his fault. It probably *was* his fault. She might even parlay from it a larger slice of the proceeds from the sale. Next Sunday. That gave him a week to get rid of the bastards, somehow. He put the phone back in his pocket and let his head loll backwards, then jolted upright again, concerned that he'd stain the oatmeal leather headrest with the crusted egg white in his hair.

'Are you okay, Dad?'

'Not really,' he sighed. 'Let's go home.'

4

Jerry bathed and washed his hair, twice, and then he and Alice shared a pair of Waitrose ready meals for dinner: a moussaka and a Jamaican shrimp curry. They spoke little, except to comment on the quality of the food, which was passable but hardly transcendent. In any case, Jerry was preoccupied. He looked around the cavernous flat on which he'd splurged so much cash without a second thought, and then thought of the house on the Hill, of how he'd strained and striven for so long to mould a home in his own image. Now that image was being defaced, with anarchist slogans and marijuana cigarette ash.

He allowed Alice to watch some gaudy television talent contest while he sat glumly in his Eames chair, sinking the rest of a bottle of wine and trying to concentrate on an article about Syria from the previous week's *Sunday Times*. Despite reading with a spare pair of clean spectacles, after a few paragraphs he gave up and surfed the Internet instead, where he soon found himself perusing a forum for people who'd fallen victim to squatters. None of their stories filled him with much hope. Quite the opposite, in fact: here were countless tales of middle-class woe; genteel households and healthily aspirational property developments infested by students, gypsies and the homeless, all of whom had proven unable to perform such basic domestic tasks as taking the rubbish out or bleaching the toilet pan. Invariably, the process of eviction took far longer than even the most pessimistic owner had feared. So he gave up on that as well, wrenching himself from the computer to gaze, eyes glazed, at the television alongside his daughter.

When the programme ended, Alice dutifully went to brush her teeth and change into her pyjamas. Her bed was in the box room beneath the mezzanine. Jerry roused himself from his funk to switch off the television and shuffled across the studio to go and tuck her in. She had removed her guitar from its case and sat propped on a pillow, carefully plucking arpeggios. It was a small Spanish-style acoustic, with a fretboard narrow enough to accommodate her eight-year-old fingers. Jerry had allowed himself to be up-sold by the sales assistant at the music shop when he'd gone there, on Genevieve's orders, to buy it in the weeks before Christmas. The man had played him a tune on a cheap guitar, and then played it again using the model that cost twice as much and sounded three times as good. If Alice was to plague the adults in her life with her inexpert finger-picking, Jerry had concluded, then she might as well do so on an instrument that made an attractive noise. He'd admired the sales assistant's technique, and opened his wallet to reward him.

Now he perched at the foot of the bed and watched Alice across the wide expanse of her *Monsters, Inc.* duvet cover. Her face was adorably creased with concentration.

'Go on,' he said. 'Play me something.'

Self-consciously at first, and then with growing confidence, she began to pick out the looping introductory riff to what Jerry eventually identified as 'Everybody Hurts' by REM.

'Bloody hell! Not that!' he cried, clamping a hand to his forehead. 'Can't you play something a bit more jolly?'

Alice sighed and rolled her eyes.

'Come on,' said Jerry. 'Dad's in a bad mood.'

She pondered the question for a moment or two.

'Okay,' she said. 'Ummm. What about this one?'

She meticulously repositioned her fingers, and then started to strum a tune that Jerry didn't think he recognised. Somewhere beneath the bum notes and the flubbed chord changes, though, was a pleasant refrain. Alice had plainly forgotten or failed to learn some of the lyrics, but she hid the gaps in her remembrance by humming, or by singing something nonsensical that resembled them. Jerry lay back on the bed and let her play it all the way to the end, pretending he was enjoying it by occasionally waggling a finger in time to the music.

'That was nice,' he said when she finished. 'What is it?'

'Taylor Swift,' Alice replied, zipping her guitar back into its case.

'Hmph,' said Jerry, unsure whether this 'Taylor Swift' was a male or a female. 'Well, your mum's right; you are getting pretty good.'

Alice shrugged, uncomfortable with the compliment.

'Do you want to go to sleep?'

'Ummm. I might read for a bit.'

'Okay,' he said. 'Don't be too late.'

He watched her organise her duvet and pillows by the light of the Conran bedside lamp. She opened her book. It was large-format, and it looked colourful.

'What is that?' he asked. 'Aren't you a bit old for picture books?'

'*Daa-aaa-ad*. It's *The House on the Hill*!'

He reached across and snatched it from her. *The House on the Hill 3*, it said on the cover, *The Birdseed and the Bumblebees*. Beneath the title was one of Pen's vivid illustrations, of two chil-dren standing at the foot of a giant sunflower, and a cluster of fat bees buzzing around it. He turned to the page that Alice had been reading.

Izzy watched Conrad planting the seeds,
at the foot of the garden where Mum wouldn't see.
'Sunflowers grow fast,' she warned with a frown.
'I know!' grinned her brother, and patted the ground.

'Wow,' said Jerry. There was a dull ache in the pit of his stomach. Indigestion. 'Shouldn't you be reading *Harry Potter* or something by now?'

'I read *Harry Potter* as well, Dad.'

'Okay, okay,' he replied, a lump in his throat.

He handed her back the book and, exhausted as he was, felt an up-swell of affection. He leaned over, and she submitted to a kiss on the crown of her head. 'G'night,' she said.

Jerry stood and stepped back into the studio, closing the bedroom door behind him. He turned the television on again quietly, if only for the illusion of company, and went to the fridge. Generally he preferred to drink wine, but having polished off a bottle already, he was now curiously drawn to Glassop's abandoned lager. He wrenched the cap off and gulped down a large, foamy mouthful.

The enjoyment of booze, he had long ago learned from various focus groups and semi-scientific studies, was directly related to its cost. Almost anyone would believe that a wine was of quality if the price tag told them so, if a vintner or an advertiser or a marketing exec had somehow invested it with an intangible value that outweighed its intrinsic worth.

He'd hoped it might drown out his angst, but twenty minutes later, the lager long drained, his mind continued to race with the consequences of the afternoon. He was dog-tired, but restless. He tried to enjoy whichever action B-movie he'd alighted upon in the lower reaches of the satellite TV spectrum, but found himself prowling the apartment instead, his head filled with violent revenge fantasies. Perhaps he needed something stronger. He checked his wristwatch. The pubs would be open for a while.

He shrugged into a dark canvas blazer and slipped on a pair of preposterously adolescent trainers, which he'd convinced himself he could just about carry off, so long as they were paired with the correct accompanying outfit. A seam of light still glowed beneath Alice's bedroom door, but when he pressed it open she was fast asleep. Jerry felt a familiar twinge of guilt at abandoning his daughter; like back pain, it was a sensation he'd long since trained himself to suppress. He tiptoed across her floor with the absurd caution of the slightly inebriated, and switched off the bedside lamp.

Out on the pavement, he shambled towards the bright lights of King's Cross like a brainless insect. On the station forecourt, feral teens fought over boxes of fried chicken; awkward first dates pecked each other goodnight; backpacking tourists tried to hail taxis, or studied their city maps bewilderedly. He turned east up the hill and walked until he found a pub on Pentonville Road. The place was packed, but he managed to clamber to the bar and order himself a double Bushmills with water. The staff wore generic, brewery-branded polo shirts and jaded expressions. He huddled over his glass, trying to savour the single malt as he was jostled by the crush of punters. Identikit indie rock music had turned to sludge in the overpowered speaker amps. This would never do. He downed the drink and fought his way back to the street.

At the Angel crossroads, he paused for a moment and considered going into one of the busy cluster of bars, but insufferable young Estuary men with short-sleeved shirts spilled onto the pavements, sloshing their pints and shouting what passed for conversation on a Saturday night, over the impatient hoots of the number 73 bus. He thought of turning onto Upper Street, but that would take him inexorably towards Highbury. There were a lot of pubs between here and the house and, were he to patronise enough of them along the way, he might well find himself beating angrily on his own front door at four in the morning, against the express advice of his solicitor.

Instead, he headed straight down the City Road, still brooding on his predicament. He resolved to continue walking until he was too tired or drunk to brood any longer, at which point he would hail a cab home to bed. He passed darkened houses and flats, the pavement black but for the occasional puddle of light from a street lamp. To his regret, no pubs presented themselves for almost half a mile, but the whiskey had begun to take effect, so he stopped in at a 24-hour petrol station to soak up the alcohol with a Ginster's chicken and bacon pasty. He slipped a Toffee Crisp into his inside pocket, too – for the road. At an off-licence next to the Old Street roundabout, he bought himself a quarter-litre of Jameson and a ten-pack of Marlboros, and then let himself glide on, direction-less, through the late-night crowds, puffing a cigarette and sipping surreptitiously from the bottle.

On the oft-repeated recommendation of his GP, Jerry had all but ceased to smoke, but he could still drink – in moderation, of course. When he'd first started out in the advertising game, booze and fags were the industry's biggest clients – and he and his colleagues their most loyal consumers. Later it was cocaine; and later still, when the money drained from the trade and the account-ants took over, it was lattes and the subsidised company bar. But Jerry's generation was still steeped in alcohol.

He'd always liked to think of himself as an accomplished drunk, the sort of creative who'd have a cocktail or two with lunch and return to the office to do his best work, who'd sip Scotch late into the night when alone, and keep abreast of Glassop or Brandt when boozing competitively in company. And yet, and yet. If Jerry were to think about it seriously, he'd recall that Glassop could always out-drink him with ease, that beer in excess made him gassy, and that certain spirits caused him to become bilious and regretful.

The chip shops were a-squeeze with famished revellers, and on Old Street the bars heaved. Jerry flicked his cigarette butt away and slid the Jameson into his belt, to hide it from the bouncer at the door of one mildly inviting establishment. The man looked him up and down, seemingly amused by the solitary old fart who'd chosen to infiltrate this youthful territory. But he didn't perform a body search, so Jerry pushed through the swing door into the club, the bottle nuzzling his bum-crack, chuckling to himself and feeling twenty-one again.

The decor was that of an unreconstructed East End boozer, yet judging by the age of the clientele, Jerry guessed this was some kind of retro-ironic design choice. The walls wore flocked wallpaper and a series of sepia-toned photographs, of supposed former owners and regulars. Flushed with what-the-hell confidence, he offered to buy a drink for the pretty young blonde at the bar. She declined; he insisted and ordered her a vodka and cranberry, but failed to catch her name before some giggly friends drew her away again, each of them blessed with glistening teeth, perfectly sloped breasts and boyish behinds. He smiled at the group to feign a cool complicity in their joke – the punchline, he supposed, being himself – and then hastily downed his double.

The music in this place was better, he thought, strutting to the Gents for a lengthy and pleasurable piss. An Afro-Caribbean fellow stood by the basins proffering a paper towel as he washed his hands. Since he felt obliged to leave 50p in the man's silver tray, he thought he might as well have a spritz of one of the expensive colognes on display. Chanel, Prada, Hermès, Davidoff Cool Water. He chuckled again, recalling Andy Brandt – Brandt of the five wives – who wore Cool Water. Not because he liked the scent, and not because young women really 'liked' the scent, but because it tended to remind them of their first boyfriends, and was therefore (Brandt alleged) sexual catnip. There was a killer ad campaign in there somewhere but, to Jerry's regret, MGC had never handled an aftershave account. He patted it liberally onto his cheeks and throat.

Upstairs, the blonde girl and her friends had been hijacked by a huddle of lusty young blokes, so he stumbled back out into the night, venturing ever deeper into the East End. He lit up again and drank some more whiskey from the bottle, the burn of the undiluted spirit on the back of his throat a penance for past and present foolishness.

He lost his bearings somewhere in Shoreditch, but carried on walking regardless, his footsteps becoming increasingly erratic. In the dimly lit doorways of the neighbourhood's numerous dingy clubs, rebel consumer youths with curious hair and curious facial hair, non-prescription specs and non-essential sunglasses, band T-shirts, brand T-shirts, plaid, flannel, gingham, flat caps, baseball caps, trilbies, skinny jeans, hotpants, floral prints, flowy dresses, vintage jewellery, vintage hosiery, winklepickers, brogues, Nike Hi-Tops, Converse Chuck Taylors, Dr Martens 1460s, handbags, manbags, denim, double-denim and triple-denim, smoked roll-ups and simpered over each other's shoes or piercings or bicycles or body art.

Who were all these juvenile creatures of the night, Jerry asked himself; who were these under-worked youngsters, parading the pavement as if they invented haircuts? They couldn't all be artists' technicians or trendy sales assistants. Could they? Some of them, he argued hazily to himself, must surely spend their weekdays wearing more sensible outfits. With a sudden lurch, physical and intellectual, he wondered whether his tormentors might be among them.

He lumbered to a halt outside a friendly-looking pub in a quiet road, many of its young patrons scattered on the pavement in the still-warm summer night air. The bottle in his hand was empty, and a fleeting destructive urge caused him to lob it across the street, where it smashed noisily into tiny shards on the tarmac. Some of the kids stared at him. He stared back, searching for pink hair, listening for a Midlands accent, sozzled enough to hope that fate might have brought him face to face with his enemies.

Not seeing anyone who resembled the squatters – whose faces

he could not, in any case, have identified – Jerry made his way inside, just in time to hear the peal of the bell for last orders. The lino floor was sticky with spilled beer, the music was from the 1970s, and at the bar sat a motley selection of grizzled locals – all of which made Jerry think, with the few active brain cells at his disposal, that this pub was still only halfway to gentrification. He could drink to that. He strung together enough words to order one last double Bushmills, not bothering with the water this time, since his taste buds were already too far gone. He ordered one more lager as well, to chase the spirits down. When the drinks came, he lunged a hand into his pocket to fetch out a tenner and sprayed change all over the lino.

'Bollocks,' he said, but left the coins where they were.

He necked the whiskey at the bar, some of it dribbling warmly from the side of his mouth, down his neck and into the collar of his T-shirt. He felt a burp rising in his throat and suppressed it, for fear it might be vomit in disguise. The nicotine in his bloodstream was having a minor disagreement with the alcohol, and the Waitrose Jamaican shrimp curry seemed eager to step in, too. Conscious that the butch landlady was eyeing him, anticipating trouble of some variety, Jerry retreated with his pint to the pool table, where two young toughs in vests were contesting a tight game. Bowie was on the sound system: 'Young Americans'. He shuffled about between shots, trying not to get in the way of the players, but getting in the way nonetheless. When one of them sank a ball from a difficult angle, he cheered heartily and clapped him on the shoulder. Down the fellow's tricep swam a large tattoo of a koi carp. His arm, Jerry noted, was particularly muscular – as was his glare. Jerry staggered away before he was pushed.

He spotted a spare chair at the end of a nearby table of youngsters and slid onto it clumsily before they could object. The pair closest to him registered his arrival, and then went on talking to their friends. Jerry counted six of them, though there may have only been four. Or possibly seven. Mostly male but, broadly speaking, effeminate. One of them, he noticed as he placed a steadying hand on the tabletop to keep from tumbling sideways, was dressed as a giant yellow cat, with whiskers and pointy yellow cat ears. Jerry was pretty convinced this was not a hallucination, though by now he could not be entirely sure. He cradled his forehead and examined a beer mat on the table in front of him, studying the word '*Foster's*', and spelling it out to himself letter by letter. Sitting down had been a colossal error. His half-finished pint now tasted like spit and piss, so he slid it away from him towards the nearest nattily dressed boy, moaning inwardly (or was it outwardly?) and wishing he hadn't wandered so far from home.

He rose to his feet, thinking this might improve matters, but it only made things worse. His head drained of all blood and sense, so he sat back down again with a thud. Now the kids at the table were watching him, their features stricken with a mixture of apprehension and disgust.

'Do any of you know,' he said loudly, through the fuzz of intoxication, 'a girl with pink hair?'

He'd hoped the question might make his presence seem planned, deliberate. But their faces were blank, and he wondered whether the words in his head were, in fact, the same ones that were coming out of his mouth; or whether, like Alice conjuring her nonsense lyrics to that Swift Taylor song, he was merely mumbling gobbledygook.

'Hmph.' He tried again. 'Do any of you, by any chance, know a girl with pink hair? Or a bloke with a Midlands accent, who smokes a lot?'

The young man dressed as a yellow cat spoke first. 'Miaow,' he said.

'What?!' said Jerry.

'Man, are you all right?' the cat-boy repeated.

'Ah!' said Jerry, and cackled at the misunderstanding. 'Are you supposed to be a cat?'

Now somebody else spoke: 'Jerry?'

Jerry was puzzled. Had he introduced himself? He scanned the faces at the table, but they were a blur.

'Jerry!'

Okay, he'd figured out who was addressing him now. A new kid was standing at the far end of the table, carrying a round of drinks. Jerry removed his spectacles, thumbed his eyes and squinted to see if the face would come into focus: a nice-looking young chap in Elvis Costello glasses and Breton stripes; short back and sides, whipped-cream quiff, and an unfortunate scrap of brown bum-fluff on his upper lip . . . Oh. The boy moved around the table towards him.

'Dad, what are you doing here?' he said, sufficiently confused and angry to resort to the more accurate appellation.

'Conrad,' said Jerry. I should leave immediately, he thought. Before this gets embarrassing. So he stood up again, clutching his specs. But it was too much to bear. The walls rolled away, and he stumbled sidelong into the pool player with the koi carp tattoo, who'd been lining up a shot on black. The cue ball thudded ineffectually against the cloth rim of the table.

'Motherfucker,' the man growled.

'Sorrymatesorrysorry,' said Jerry. But it was too late. The man poked him angrily in the eye with the fat rubber end of his cue.

'Ow!' Jerry put a hand to his face, dizzied. He spun around. The rest of the pub had turned to look at him, hushed, heads like cancer cells dividing and dividing and dividing in his splayed vision. The floor seemed to rock beneath him, and the corner of Conrad's table hurtled his way. Then blackness, and blissful sleep.

5

Three time zones and approximately 3,400 miles away, Isobel crept downstairs in the pink-grey glow of pre-dawn. She padded across the cool kitchen tiles in her slipper-socks and filled the kettle from the tap. The house was silent save for the quiet rush of water on water. She couldn't hear anything from beyond the door to Carmen's suite, so she supposed she must be the only person awake. Carmen's accommodation was offensively small. But Emirate villas all came with pre-built digs for Filipina maids, and Carmen's tiny bedsit conformed to their generic dimensions. They couldn't exactly give her the guest bedroom, could they? Isobel swallowed a yawn.

As the kettle came to the boil, she started to empty the dishwasher, slowly and carefully so as not to strike any plates together and rouse Carmen or the twins. She often found herself performing the tasks that were intended for the maid, because she felt guilty and over-rich – rich! ha! – and under-worked. And yet, she worried that work was what gave Carmen pride and satisfaction, and that to do it for her was to patronise her, to rob her of her hard-won place in the world. She sometimes wanted to sit the maid down and ask her how she'd made it here from the back streets and barrios of Manila, or whichever was the city of her birth. But they could barely converse in the same language.

Isobel worried about the subcontracting of labour to the Third World – be it entire nations, or just Carmen and their Indian gardener (who may, in fact, have been Pakistani) – especially since she had so much time on her hands to read online news sites and spot the global trends, the macro-master-servant relationships that characterised geopolitics. She worried, too, that her browser history was being studied by the Sheikh's security services, and that they'd see treachery in her search terms: 'uae+corruption'; 'dubai+development+environment'; '"jake gyllenhaal"+girlfriend'. She had no evidence to back up this suspicion, but she worried nonetheless. All this worry. It was a steady hum in her gut.

She poured a cup of strong tea and tiptoed through to her office. The desk lamp was still on as she'd left it late last night. There were two designated offices in their rented house, though Isobel struggled to make hers appear businesslike. Yes, she had a desk, a chair, a lamp, a laptop. But also a beanbag, and an Ikea KLUBBO side table with a television and a selection of knock-off DVDs from the souk. A scatter of old CDs. A photograph of Torsten and the twins; a couple of the twins' crayon scrawls; a publicity shot of her and Conrad reading cheerfully from *The House on the Hill*, aged fifteen and eleven or thereabouts, just before the divorce. In one of the Ikea JONAS desk drawers: her passport, driving licence and assorted official documents. In another: stationery. And in the bottom drawer, secreted beneath an old issue of *Elle*, all the credit card receipts that she didn't want Tor to see.

She switched on her laptop and rubbed her arms. Ridiculous to be cold, she thought, with the desert looming just behind the back garden. But she and Tor, with their shared Northern European heritage, both liked to have the a/c on full blast overnight. It was one of the first things they'd agreed upon three years ago, lying awake after a round of distinctly un-Islamic coitus in a suite at the Jumeirah Beach Hotel. Their nostalgic affection for cold air had become one of those running in-jokes that couples share in the early days of a relationship; the glue that binds two people who barely know one another but want to know more,

and which, recalled or recounted later, seems never to have been
funny at all.

Through the window the pool lay still and blue in the windless
air, framed by implausibly green grass. A Swingball set. A pair
of plastic loungers. A few shrubs she couldn't identify, but which
were tended by the gardener, mainly so she had something to pay
him for. Beyond the fence, power lines twisted away into the
dunes. Their housing development encircled a primly landscaped
golf course, but for sound financial reasons Isobel and Tor had
chosen to rent a villa on the sand side of Blue Sky Grove.

Her loganberries needed fertilising. She opened the browser and
clicked on the bookmark labelled 'Acres'. Like every house in the
gated community, theirs was graced with superfast broadband, so
she was greeted at once by the Web game's jolly rustic jingle. She
clicked the volume down a notch. The laptop screen sprouted
great yellow ears of wheat and demanded her Facebook log-in
details. She tapped in her password with unconscious swiftness.

Maintaining a virtual online farming business, especially one
as ambitious as Isobel's, could be a full-time occupation. Her Acres
farm was the first place she visited each morning, and the last
place she went at night. There was much to do: ploughing,
planting, harvesting, feeding, slaughtering. Each crop and farmyard animal had its own schedule to be administered. Sometimes
she'd rise in the small hours just to water a field – otherwise,
certain sensitive crops could wither and die overnight, wasting
valuable Acres coins. As soon as she'd worked out how to do this
from her iPad using the Acres app, rather than getting out of bed
and going to the laptop, her sleep patterns had markedly improved.

Isobel had accumulated 800 acres – no longer a smallholding,
but an online industrial farm, staffed by five dozen dungaree-
wearing virtual workers, moving hither and thither with ploughs
and watering cans. Her personal avatar and the farm's manager,

'122y', wore a red plaid shirt and her hair in pigtails. The farm was about 70 per cent arable, 30 per cent livestock. Arable was more straightforwardly profitable, but livestock were more valuable in the long term. They also made farmyard animal noises, which gave her twins the giggles.

Her early successes had been built on basic crops such as wheat and corn, barley and soya beans. She'd then progressed to fruit and veg: strawberries were labour-intensive, but could be turned around quickly and lucratively. Aubergines were low maintenance, but yielded fewer coins per acre. She was now cultivating a handful of loganberry fields, which seemed to offer the best of both worlds: a decent profit, but without the 2 a.m. watering times.

The larger your farm grew, the more outbuildings you needed to store ploughs and spades and fence-building gear. Isobel was particularly proud of her tractor, a top-of-the-range AcreMaker500, which absolutely earned its keep in increased crop yields. On the other hand, she felt a little uncomfortable about the vast barn of battery chickens in the south-east corner of the farm. She kept the rest of her livestock in large, free-range pens at the north end, so as not to subject them to the melancholy cheeping of the ill-treated birds, which had been expertly rendered by whoever sound-designed the game. There were lengthy Acres Web forum threads dedicated to digital animal rights, and she was aware that many of her fellow players would disapprove. Battery eggs were an unsavoury profit booster, but a necessary one.

There was even a safari animal option, the product of an Acres synergy with a virtual zoo game; Isobel occasionally considered purchasing a lion or two. She could create a visitors' centre and invite (simulated) paying customers. She wondered what would happen if she put a lion cage next to a sheep pen – whether the game was smart enough to account for inter-species animosity, or whether its utopian sensibilities would dull the instincts of even the most powerful predators. For now, she'd decided to maintain the integrity of her virtual farm, and to keep it within the confines of real-world plausibility.

Of course, there were no real-world profits to be accrued from Acres, and mostly she bought fields, crops, livestock and equipment only with the virtual credit derived from her digital agricultural successes, or smart Acres trades made with her Facebook acquaintances. But there was an option to spend real money, in order to give oneself an edge over the competition. Isobel was generally wise enough to refrain, but not long ago she had, for example, spent US$50 on the AcreMaker500, $40 on an AcreSprayer crop sprayer, and $25 each on two shire horses (which could pull a plough for five times longer without rest than a normal horse), as well as $10 here and there buying new plots and seeds to plant in them when her friends and virtual neighbours had failed to furnish her with coins, or fertiliser, or hog feed. She coveted the AcreHayMaker1000 combine harvester, but at $100 it had always seemed too extravagant for a single purchase. (Its virtual cost was a bank-breaking 1,000 Acres coins, meaning few thrifty players could ever hope to acquire it.)

Thanks to the game, Isobel had upwards of 100 Facebook friends whom she'd never met, except via Acres. She came across them on fansite forums, where dedicated players such as herself often went to find new Acres neighbours. Each one brought with them, according to the game's rules, fresh acreage and a modest coin boost. She'd altered her Facebook privacy settings to allow most of them only limited access to her profile, so they couldn't find out much about her besides her kick-ass farming skills. But she'd conversed with some of her more loyal neighbours via Skype. They came from five continents and at least twelve countries.

She had more rosettes than almost any of her Acres neighbours, the result of virtual county fairs where her produce had been deemed the most impressive. (There were six plots set aside by the south fence, where she would slow-grow giant marrows purely in order to win prizes.) She was ranked in her friends list only below Cindy Welch of Boca Raton, Florida. Isobel attributed this to Cindy's AcreHayMaker1000, which her husband Bob had bought her as a birthday present. She didn't think Torsten would understand, were she to make a similar request.

Isobel had built her virtual agricultural empire in a remarkably short space of time. She assumed that some of her Facebook friends had proper jobs, whereas she could programme her life around the farm. Even the twins could be offloaded onto Carmen for an hour or two if there was harvesting or fertilising to be done. She used to jog every day. Now she did so twice a week if she was lucky. But her weight seemed to stay down. She was rarely hungry. Tor seemed baffled by her hobby, but he could see that it made her happy – or, at any rate, that it kept her from going bonkers. So he tolerated it as long as she didn't discuss it over dinner.

Having initiated the fertilisation of the loganberry fields, she sat watching as I22y piloted the AcreMaker500 back and forth across the plot, dragging the AcreSprayer behind her. She'd purchased the tractor in blue, with a yellow stripe on the side. She wasn't sure she'd ever actually eaten a loganberry. What did real loganberries even look like? Isobel had never been a great fan of the countryside as a girl, too grossed out by insects and animal excrement. But Acres somehow reminded her of home. There was greenery in London, oxygenating plants, discreet pockets of nature that she'd only appreciated after years away in the desert.

She checked her Facebook. There were some game queries from fellow Acres players, and a pair of unfamiliar friend requests, which she decided to deal with later. Conrad had been tagged in a photo album called 'Shoreditch Shenanigans'. He was leaning against his bicycle in a park somewhere (Shoreditch, she supposed).

He had the beginnings of a moustache. She worried that he looked glum, but maybe that was just his way of trying to look cool. She'd never persuaded him to join Acres, much to her irritation.

In her Gmail, she found a courtesy message from the bank, which she ignored. And a credit card statement, which she also ignored. There was an email from her mother, which she postponed opening, already well aware of what it would say. Isobel rubbed her arms again. It troubled her to think of the house on the Hill belonging to someone else. Home was the anchor that kept her from slipping off the edge of the world.

The clock in the top right-hand corner of the computer screen turned to six. Within minutes, Tor would be awake and showering, Carmen brewing his first coffee of the day, the twins tottering down the stairs to watch *SpongeBob*. Isobel savoured the last of the silence, as her overalled avatar trundled from row to row. From beyond the office window came the whir and hiss of the electronically timed lawn sprinklers scudding into life.

6

Conrad stood back as his father heaved onto the cobbles, hoping
to save his Puma Blue Stars from the splash. Jerry was doubled
over, propped against the alley wall with an outstretched palm.
The vomit stank of whiskey, with a hint of . . . what was it?
Prawns? He seemed to have finished, so he turned to look up at
Conrad despondently. Conrad battled to suppress his own gag
reflex. There were phlegmy strings of sick at the corners of Jerry's
mouth, and the collar of his T-shirt was damp with dribbled booze.
His forehead was bleeding, and a hefty bruise had started to form
just below the hairline. One arm of his spectacles had snapped
off in the fall, and they now balanced lopsidedly on the tip of his
nose. Conrad proffered the fistful of napkins that the hot barmaid
in the Cow-Shed had given him; Jerry took them with what looked
like gratitude, but then his eyes turned fearful, and he lowered
his head to puke again.

Polly, Jamie and Beagle were watching from under the street
lamp a few feet away; at the dread sound of cough followed by
splatter, Polly squeaked and pressed her face into Jamie's chest.
Jamie muttered something disparaging.

'Dude,' said Beagle. 'Why do you call him Jerry?'

'Because that's his name,' Conrad replied.

'Huh. Sort of weird, though.'

Conrad ignored this. Given that Beagle had recently taken to
wearing his bright yellow *Pokémon* onesie round the clock, he
could surely be considered a poor judge of what was weird and

what was not. Jerry moaned softly, like a baby deciding whether to cry. He'd evidently reached another lull in the retch cycle. Conrad felt a hand on his shoulder.

'Don't you think you should take him to hospital?' asked Polly.

Conrad adjusted his own large-framed specs. He didn't really need glasses; he'd found these ones in a vintage store and their effect on his vision was negligible. But he liked the feel of them, the look. Polly was smiling at him from beneath her dirty blonde fringe: her pity smile. She had a smile for every occasion. She squeezed his arm sympathetically. Behind her, Jamie was fidgeting with his keffiyeh, eager to get away. Beagle was eating pork scratchings.

'I guess,' said Conrad.

'Okay. I'll get you a cab.'

Jamie offered to walk Conrad's bike home for him, but he preferred to take it along for the ride. The cabbie was cool with that, but he wasn't so keen on his other prospective passenger.

'Not going to be any trouble, is he?' he said when he saw Jerry.

'No, he's all right.'

'Well, if he sicks up on my seats, it's fifty quid.'

In the taxi, while Conrad tried to keep the bike propped against the partition, Jerry put his head between his knees and moaned some more, holding a wad of bloodied napkins to his wound. He managed not to puke again, though, and when they got to Whitechapel and Conrad realised he hadn't enough cash, his father wordlessly handed the cabbie a £20 note for the fare.

Unfortunately, A&E at the Royal London was where the worst of Saturday night ended up. Overdoses, stomach-pumpings, street fights, domestics. So an old soak with a knock on the head settled like dregs at the bottom of the priority list. After locking up his bike outside and whispering a little prayer to the bicycle gods that it not be nicked, Conrad found them the quietest spot in the noisy waiting room, and then waited for Jerry to lower himself into a chair with a great big sigh. To alert the duty nurse to their presence, he was first required to negotiate a pair of tramps clinging to one another like punch-drunk boxers beside the reception desk. The woman at the counter said Jerry would be called soon for a check-up. Conrad went to buy a coffee and a bottle of water from the vending machines near the entrance, where some threateningly large men in scuffle-torn Arsenal shirts were arguing about the transfer market. He kept his head down lest he be noticed.

He returned to find Jerry snoring, his mouth wide and his broken glasses drooping across his face. Conrad regarded his father's somnolent form in the blank artificial light. The worst of the bleeding had stopped, and Jerry had stuck a folded napkin to his forehead with congealed blood, as if the wound were a giant shaving cut. His gut poked out from under his T-shirt, each deep inhalation revealing a thick stripe of pasty flesh. How are the mighty fallen. Here was one more item for which Conrad could blame Jerry — a list including, but not limited to:

- The genetic inevitability that he, too, would one day be a fat, blind, selfish old cunt.
- The divorce.
- 'Conrad'. He'd always resented his father for naming him that, in defiance of his mother's objections. Pen claimed to have given Jerry a handful of sensible names to choose from: Ben, Dan, Tom, Tim. But his father persevered, and Conrad stuck. These days, he had to admit grudgingly, he was almost grateful for the distinction. He knew no other Conrads, and nobody who knew him knew any other Conrads. He was like Cher, or Tiger, or Boris: he had first-name recognition. Jerry had once told him this gave him a brand identity. As far as he was aware, he was still the UK's only Googlable Conrad Manville.

He sat down next to his father. His denim shorts were cut just above the knee, and his legs were getting chilly. He drank a mouthful of coffee, hoping it might heat him up. It burned his tongue. There was an old black lady a few seats along, staring so intently into the middle distance that Conrad started to think she might be dead. Eventually, she blinked. Jerry grunted back into consciousness. He thanked Conrad for the water.

'I'm really sorry about all this,' he said.

'You were looking for somebody,' said Conrad.

Jerry gulped from the bottle and gave him a blank look. He rebalanced his glasses on the end of his nose. They came to rest at a jaunty angle.

'At the pub, before you passed out? The others said you were looking for someone.'

Jerry frowned fleetingly.

'Ah. No,' he said. 'That was nothing. Just drunk. I thought I . . . It's nothing. Sorry. Hmph.'

He took another swig of water.

'You weren't looking for me, then.'

'For *you*? No! I mean, no . . . No. Nice surprise, though.'

Conrad sipped his coffee. He couldn't taste it now, thanks to his burned tongue. Which was probably a good thing. He had a favourite blend of superior Kenyan beans that he got from the organic supermarket where he worked. He doubted hospital machine coffee could compete.

'How do you feel?'

'Middling,' said Jerry, tentatively prodding his bruise.

'Sounds like Mum's finally selling the house.'

Jerry flicked his eyes around the waiting room, apparently uninterested.

'Yeah,' he replied. 'The house.'

'Cool,' said Conrad, who had no great love for the house on

the Hill and, quite honestly, was in dire need of the windfall it promised to bring his way.

'Yup,' said Jerry, still failing to meet his son's eye.

The nearby argument about football grew louder for an instant, and then subsided again. The nurse at reception called out a name; it wasn't Jerry's.

'So,' Conrad asked, 'how's the single life treating you?'

'Oh,' Jerry replied. 'Fine.'

'Clearly.'

Jerry blinked at him, puzzled.

'Oh, this?' he said at last, referring to his present state of dereliction. 'Nah, this is just . . . No, I'm fine. Fine. What about you?'

'Er,' said Conrad. 'Fine.'

'I like your, erm . . .' Jerry dangled a hand above his head and wiggled his digits. 'Hairdo?'

'Really?' said Conrad, retouching his quiff unconsciously. 'Thanks. I think.'

Jerry patted his pockets, pulled out his phone and made as if to check his texts. Conrad sipped his coffee again. Now the old black lady was staring at him. He smiled nervously, but her expression remained fixed: eyes wide, mouth slack. Jerry appeared to have discovered an uneaten Toffee Crisp somewhere in the folds of his blazer. He emitted a little 'Oh' of pleasure, peeled open the wrapper and took a bite. He offered the chocolate bar to Conrad but, seeing as he'd been vomiting less than an hour previously, Conrad thought it best to decline. He studied a family planning poster that was pinned to the opposite wall: '*Your options if you are pregnant, including keeping the baby, adoption and having an abortion.*'

'Do you get to see much of Alice?' he asked.

Jerry stopped chewing his Toffee Crisp.

'Oh, fuck,' he said.

'What?'

Jerry looked at his watch.

'Fuckety fuck.'

'What is it?'

Jerry stood up abruptly, blinked twice to beat the inevitable head rush, and started to stagger away. Then he turned back.

'Good to see you, Conrad,' he said. 'I have to go.'

'What? But you haven't even seen a doctor yet!'

'I'm fine, I'm fine.'

Jerry put a steadying hand on Conrad's shoulder, and for an awful moment Conrad thought he was about to hug him, there in the waiting room of the Royal London, with dried sick on his shirt and the old black lady staring at them and drooling. But he seemed to decide against it at the last minute.

'It's been too long,' he said instead, blinked once more, and then belched quietly.

'Jerry. Dad. What if you're concussed or something?'

'I'm fine,' Jerry said again. 'I feel much better. Do you need money for another cab?'

'No.'

'Okay. I have to go.'

'Dad . . .'

But he was already stumbling away, and this time Conrad let him go, concerned though he was. As he reached the exit, Jerry tripped over himself and inadvertently shoulder-barged one of the large men in Arsenal shirts. They fell silent, and Conrad winced in anticipation of violence. But the man just took Jerry by the arm, balanced him upright and gave him a little encouraging push through the door.

The streets were almost empty as Conrad rode home. Buses, taxis, a few bedraggled hipsters hanging outside the late openers. On

Commercial Street he dived between a number 67 and the minicab coming the other way, feeling a gust of air on his face as he tunnelled through the tiny gap. The minicab's beeping horn drifted off in his wake. His customised fixie was an old Peugeot frame from the eighties, fixed up by a Brick Lane bike sage called Bananaman (real name Eric), who had ground the braze-ons off the old frame and stripped it back to bare steel, then welded on horizontal drop-outs and an arched rear brake bridge. At Conrad's request, the frame was powder-coated in Racing Green, his favourite shade. Afterwards, just to teach himself how, he'd taken it home to build up on the floor of the sitting room: old Campag cranks with MKS pedals; a Nitto quill stem and track bars, wrapped in white bar tape; DT Swiss Deep rims in white, laced to Shimano track hubs; a Thomson seatpost; and a Selle San Marco Concor saddle, also in white.

It had only a single, front brake – no flapping leads, and no lights to disrupt the frame's purity of form. Yes, it was a signifier of coolness: fixie bikes were still cool, despite their ubiquity in the lower E postcodes. But what endeared it to Conrad most of all was that it worked. He had created a functioning piece of machinery. His Pumas applied pressure to the pedals, which yanked the chain, which turned the wheels, which engendered forward motion. Its single gear, moreover, gave it the greatest possible measure of authenticity, cool or not: it put Conrad closer to the mechanism, to the bike and therefore to the road, until he became velocity embodied. Man and bike, one.

He jumped a red light at the junction of Shoreditch High Street and Bethnal Green Road, narrowly avoiding a clip from a white van. He had an ongoing inner duologue about the wearing of a helmet. He didn't want to die or get brain-damaged, obviously. But he did want to appear nonchalant and unafraid of death or brain damage. The first time he'd come off was in a downpour: he'd taken a corner too fast and the bike slid out from under him.

He and the machine had planed in parallel across the rain-slick tarmac, and he still recalled fondly the illicit thrill of seeing his bike spin away as he came to rest on his side, cars honking around him. In the saddle was the one place he felt truly fearless, free of the neuroses that otherwise afflicted him. Tonight, he was four drinks down and helmetless, the wind ruffling his hair.

The flat comprised two floors above a late-night pho noodle place on Kingsland Road. The cooks were chucking out the rubbish and their final customers as Conrad unlocked his front door. They nodded hello and, like always, offered him a complimentary box of noodles. Free Vietnamese food had been one of the big draws when he, Polly and Beagle first moved in. Now, he wouldn't mind if he never saw another spring roll in his life. The stink of sweet-and-sour seeped up into the flat day and night, secreting MSG fumes in his clothes and his hair. He respectfully demurred, lifted the bike onto his shoulder and carried it up the cramped stairs to the landing, letting the door slam behind him.

With the landlord's permission, he'd rigged a pair of bicycle racks high on the wall in the narrow first-floor passageway, to keep the fixie and his road racer – a 1993 Giant Peloton Superlite – out of the way. But Polly often left her Pashley there, too, so navigating a path to the kitchen could be tough. He hefted the fixie onto its rack and went into the sitting room.

It was past 3 a.m. and the lights were low, but everyone was still up. Beagle was on the beat-up old sofa smoking a joint and playing *Gears of War*, a half-eaten carton of noodles on his lap. Jamie sat next to him, arranging drugs on the back of one of Polly's cutting-edge fashion photobooks. Polly was curled up asleep on the antique armchair they'd reclaimed from a skip in Hoxton the previous summer. There was an open bottle of red wine and three glasses on the coffee table, along with the candles and the ashtray and the stacks of style magazines. Jamie was really into late-nineties ambient trance – ironically, or so he claimed – so

74

there was some awful synthy crap coming from the Freecycled home cinema speakers.

'You fancy a bump, Conrad mate?' asked Jamie, offering him the photobook. A bag of ket and three house keys lay perfectly spaced across the face of the model on the cover. Conrad suspected Jamie had assembled this tableau carefully; Jamie was pretty OCD about cool shit.

'No, thanks.'

Jamie offered the K to Beagle instead, who waved it away. He paused the Xbox, rested his joint expertly on the arm of the sofa, peeled back the pointy-eared hood of his *Pokémon* onesie and forked another mouthful of noodles.

'How's your dad?' Polly asked drowsily.

'Okay,' Conrad replied. 'Think I might go to bed.'

'Dude,' said Beagle, restarting the game.

'Me too,' said Polly, and closed her eyes again.

Conrad creaked up the stairs to the top floor. In the bathroom, the extractor fan rattled while he pissed. Below the waterline, the toilet bowl was coated in a layer of brown limescale that must have been there long before their tenancy; no legally available cleaning product was capable of shifting it. The cold tap dribbled as he brushed his teeth; the water pressure in the flat plummeted whenever the Vietnamese cooks downstairs were washing up, which was most of the time. He studied his would-be moustache in the mirror. Should he even grow a moustache? Would carefully tended facial hair constitute an extension of his essential self: the verifiable Conrad? Or merely add to the mask that divided him from the world? Would it make him unique, or predictable? Perhaps the answer rested on the size and variety of moustache he chose, and how much evidence of careful tending it betrayed.

He sought to emulate the lustrous 'taches of cycling's Heroic Era, specifically that of Eugene Christophe, the Old Gaul, who'd repaired his own forks at a roadside forge on the 1913 Tour de

France. But maybe he should just grow a full beard instead, without intervention. An untrimmed beard, he supposed, was an authentic beard. But he wasn't sure he could grow a beard. He'd never tried. In fact, he'd never grown a moustache either – and his present effort was taking somewhat longer than anticipated.

Conrad's was the bedroom at the front of the flat, with access via window and stepladder to the patch of roof above the noodle place that they optimistically called 'the roof garden', and had decorated with rusty old garden furniture and a plant-pot full of cigarette butts. The bedroom itself was bare-walled but for a few scraps of Blu-tack, left over from the posters he'd removed when he resolved to practise a kind of neo-minimalism. Beagle was a hoarder: he collected trainers and vintage T-shirts and Japanese designer toys. But Conrad had shed stuff until his room contained only a wooden table for his MacBook Air and networked external hard drive; a reclaimed leather swivel chair; a clothes rack for his handful of jackets; a mattress and bedside lamp; and three stackable Muji storage boxes: one for clothes, one for shoes, and the last for gadgetry and bicycle equipment. His books had all gone to charity shops, with essential texts downloaded to an e-reader as necessary. His music was all on the hard drive. His correspondence was entirely paperless.

Did minimalism say something about him, or nothing? Was it a badge or a blank space? Was his meticulous *mise en scène* a reflection of his real character, or a flawed construction of the ideal Conrad to which he aspired? A handful of cherished brands remained in his life, but only those that were of genuine quality or utility; those that made him feel legitimately individual, or part of a tangible community. He set a high bar for such loyalty.

He pulled down the window blind, kicked off his Pumas and booted up the computer to check the interwebs. He'd been tagged in a Hipstamatic album; he considered de-tagging the picture, which depicted him leaning against the fixie in London Fields, but eventually decided that he looked moody, which was cool. His Facebook News Feed informed him that Isobel had watered her loganberries, whatever those were. He'd thought about unsubscribing to his sister's status updates, so that he wouldn't have to keep reading all her stupid Acres crap, but she'd probably never forgive him.

He stripped to his boxers and retreated to bed with the laptop, where he browsed some FB profiles of girls he fancied. The weekends always yielded new pictures or revealing status updates. He'd friended Tasha the hot barmaid from the Cow-Shed, on whom he had a huge and unhealthy crush, and who'd posted an intriguing photo album of her recent tattoos. A few of his East End acquaintances had spent the previous evening at an electro night up the road in Dalston. Some photographer with a Tumblr and a flashbulb had captured them looking cool drinking fluoro mixers from jam jars, and then artfully overexposed the print in Photoshop.

Finally, he typed the name 'Florence' in the search box. There she was: Flo Dalrymple, graduate student in something or other, and presently the most hardcore of Conrad's many minor romantic obsessions. She'd STILL not accepted his friend request. What did she think, that he was some sort of Facebook stalker? No matter; he could still check out her profile picture. Her hair was a bright red shock: not Lindsay Lohan red, Coca-Cola red. Not a lot of people could pull that look off without being mistaken for a provincial emo, but Flo made it work, with her elfin features and expert eye make-up. He gazed at her face for a few too many seconds. She had a tiny stud in her nose.

Through the paper-thin wall between his and Polly's bedrooms, he heard Polly and Jamie preparing for bed and who-knows-what-else. Conrad and Polly were close enough that their friends all assumed they'd had a thing – but not close enough to have, in fact, had a thing. Conrad was forced to listen to her and her douchebag boyfriend arguing and then fucking almost every night: her douchebag boyfriend who didn't, by the way, pay any rent. It threw into sharp relief Conrad's own sorely lacking sex life. He thought about having a wank to take the edge off, but it was late and he couldn't be bothered. Instead, he pulled on his headphones and fired up the Beat Takeshi movie he'd violated copyright law by downloading that afternoon.

By the time it was over, dawn had broken, and Conrad had fallen asleep.

7

Shortly after the collapse of the Soviet Union, a newly enriched young Russian named Guznishchev had landed at London Heathrow, in pursuit of an advertising campaign to garland his latest venture. Guznishchev, the origins of whose fortune Jerry was disinclined to investigate, had come into possession of a car manufacturing plant in the town of Sergiyev Posad, near Moscow. The factory and the cars it produced were known by their unfortunate acronym: SPAZ, or Sergiyev Posad Avtomobilny Zavod.[1] Guznishchev firmly believed that SPAZ's speciality model, the small and not entirely unattractive SPAZ-1102, could be sold to his nation's new friends in the West as a budget city runaround. With some expert rebranding, he felt certain the SPAZ would be a huge success, heralding the Russian motor industry's grand arrival on the world stage.

Guznishchev had already conducted some basic market research of his own – which, as far as Jerry could make out, consisted of watching a lot of second-rate Hollywood movies – and had decided to rename his modest vehicle the 'Pizzazz'. He turned up at the Mortimer Street offices of MGC armed with his fearsome optimism, a large bodyguard in a too-small suit, and a briefcase filled with cash. (Or so Jerry imagined. Guznishchev never actually opened the briefcase.) MGC's profits tended to fluctuate, and every ad firm wanted a new car brand on its books, so Tony Glassop was keen that they make a good first impression. Jerry

---

1 Сéргиев Посáд автомобúльный завóд

needed the money to fund his planned loft conversion. Theirs was one of only a handful of London agencies in front of whom the Russian dangled his considerable business; like strippers down on their luck, they hungrily grabbed hold.

The TV campaign that Jerry created for the Pizzazz was an Eastern Bloc take on the classic American road trip. Its hero was a dashing Siberian in an animal-skin poncho who, at the beginning of the full, one-minute version, leaves his hut in the forested mountains of the frozen North and points his Pizzazz towards civilisation. Along the way, he passes vast freshwater lakes and snow-capped faraway peaks, packs of wolves and a bellowing Russian bear. Grim Soviet industrial towns and ranks of clapped-out Red Army hardware are reflected in the car's gleaming curves, accompanied by the waltz from *Swan Lake*. The driver is drawn into vodka toasts with coal-smeared miners, and persuaded to swim in a cold canyon river with a group of deer hunters.

Finally, he arrives in the glittering city of Moscow, by which time he has miraculously changed into a dinner jacket. He parks the Pizzazz in a tight spot between two Kremlinesque limousines, then canters up a red-carpeted staircase. Cut to him emerging from a glitzy party, some time later, a towering Russian supermodel on his arm. He leads her to the Pizzazz and opens the passenger-side door. As she climbs into the car, she thumps her head on the door frame. The hero winces. The waltz from *Swan Lake* grinds to a halt. The supermodel looks up at him, rubbing her head, and then smiles coyly. They drive off together, and in the empty space between the two limos are left the words: '*Big Country. Small Car.*'

Jerry found the shoot a harrowing experience, involving far too many drunken domestic flights on decrepit Aeroflot planes, and a wrap party in a Moscow nightclub with Guznishchev from which he feared he might never emerge. Andy Brandt, who directed the ad, was in his element. Brandt personally filmed the close-up of the angry bear – which, though officially tame, was nonetheless terrifying. He was eager to find an excuse to include an explosion, since Guznishchev seemed happy to throw cash at the production, but he eventually contented himself with a shot of the distant gas flares from a Siberian oil refinery. During the wrap party, Brandt inevitably shagged the Russian supermodel in the loos ('Epic tits, Jerry! *Doctor Zhivago* tits!'), while Mrs Brandt the Second waited for him back at the hotel.

The ad was called 'Odysski', and it won MGC a Yellow Pencil at the following year's D&AD Awards. Glassop was over the moon. The Pizzazz, of course, turned out to be total crap. Despite the flurry of hype, very few Westerners were persuaded to buy one, and the difficulty of acquiring replacement parts from Russia became the subject of some amused media commentary. Guznishchev eventually sold the factory to a more competent car firm in the Far East and, much to Jerry's relief, they never heard from him again. Glassop still owned a Pizzazz – a gift from Guznishchev – and would occasionally email Jerry links to a website for its tiny handful of fierce brand loyalists, who met up with each other once a year at a services somewhere on the M1. Recently, a Pizzazz had appeared on *Top Gear*, for a challenge in which the presenters raced three notoriously unreliable old Eastern European cars across the Australian outback for no discernible reason. The Pizzazz was the first to break down.

What came back to Jerry of it all now, however, as he stood before his open fridge staring at the last of his 70ml shots of probiotic Korean yoghurt, was the image of the supermodel banging her head as she got into the car. Brandt had insisted she perform about thirty takes of that scene, which Jerry had always assumed was part of his aggressive pulling technique. In any case, Jerry's head now felt as if it had been banged repeatedly against the roof of a Pizzazz. As he peeled the foil lid from the week's final *Ppalleena!*, he knew that it still wouldn't make him Feel Better. In spite of his erratic bowel movements, bad back and deteriorating eyesight, he was mostly able to dispel any dark thoughts of his own mortality. But not today.

'Come here, Dad,' said Alice. She was standing beside the Eames lounger in her pyjamas, a wad of cotton wool in one hand and a bottle of TCP in the other – both sourced from somewhere in his bathroom cabinet, he supposed. He had returned home to find the flat quiet and his daughter safe, and retreated to his bedroom for a few hours of fitful, fully clothed sleep. When he rose to brave her presence following a long, dark and dissatisfying shit, she'd been watching cartoons. Having temporarily surrendered his best tortoiseshell specs to the dried-on egg whites, and after snapping his spare pair in the fall, Jerry was reduced to the discomfort of contact lenses. His face was shapeless and fleshy without frames. Alice had shrieked at the sight of him, asked whether she might study his cut and bruised forehead, and finally demanded to know where he kept the antiseptic.

Jerry drained his *Ppalleena!* shot and shuffled to the chair as he was told, so that Alice might tend to his wound. He blamed it on his bedside table, saying he'd tripped in the night on his way to the bathroom, which was true in parts. He flinched as she cleaned the cut carefully with TCP and warm water, and then allowed her to apply a plaster.

'Better?' she said.

'Much better,' he replied, which was not true at all, not really.

She left him sitting there as she went to prepare breakfast, which turned out to be a slice of toast, smeared with Marmite from her special corner of the kitchen cupboard, a glass of orange juice and a rather pale-looking, bland-tasting bit of reconstituted egg.

'It's an egg-white omelette,' she said, when she saw the look on his face. 'Xander taught me.'

Jerry smothered his in sea salt. Alice tutted. When he rose to brew coffee, she told him he ought to cut down on his caffeine intake. Xander had taught her that too, then.

'Have my toast,' he said. 'I don't like Marmite.'

'But you always eat Marmite,' she said, hurt.

'Do I?' He didn't.

'In *The House on the Hill* you do.'

Right. In *The House on the Hill*. He rubbed his eyes, the lenses stinging.

'Okay, okay.' And he ate the toast.

Jerry didn't feel much like exerting himself, so they sat together and watched a *Shrek* film on demand. He considered calling Clive Billings again, to see if there had been any legal developments overnight – such as, say, an Act of Parliament restoring the house on the Hill to the Manville family, they being its rightful owners. But Parliament wasn't in session, and Clive probably charged even more than usual for his time on a Sunday. He considered texting Conrad to assure him that he was in good health, but thought it better to let the night's events lie. The morning successfully whiled away, Alice packed her rucksack and guitar in preparation for the journey back west.

Jerry was fairly certain that he wasn't concussed. But then again, he didn't relish the prospect of blacking out on the Euston Road and causing a pile-up with Alice in the Lotus beside him. So they took the Underground from King's Cross, changing to the Central Line at Oxford Circus. To Jerry's outrage, the line was closed beyond Marble Arch due to maintenance work, so they had to transfer to a replacement bus. He had not blacked out by the time they arrived at Notting Hill Gate, and he walked the last leg of the journey to Genevieve's place furious at himself for not having driven after all. Alice unlocked the front door and trotted upstairs with her stuff. Jerry went looking for his ex-wife.

'Christ,' she said, as he entered her chrome-and-white kitchen. 'You look like shit, Jerome. What happened to your face?'

'Walked into a floor,' said Jerry.

Genevieve had a blanket wrapped around her shoulders, bags

beneath her unmade eyes and a large cup of green tea in front of her on the kitchen table. Her hair stuck to itself, like spaghetti to the bottom of a saucepan.

'Good party?'

'Mmm,' she grumbled.

'Where's Xander?'

'Gone for a run.'

'Naturally.'

She failed to offer him a cup of tea.

'You were right about Alice,' he said.

'Was I?'

'She is getting pretty good at the guitar.'

Alice was in her room when he left, sticking her new Monet poster to the wall above her bed with fat balls of Blu-tack. Jerry knew just what it was like to be an only child in a house overseen by tedious adults: that had once been his story, too. He leaned against the door jamb.

'Do you think Xander will like it?' he asked.

'No,' she grinned, still standing on her bed. He walked over to give her a little hug, and she kissed him gently goodbye on his forehead, where the bruise still ached.

Jerry soon found himself underground again. This was where he'd end up one day, he reflected. Underground and alone. And what would he have to show for his shortish life? It meant little now that he'd once been a leading figure in the field of Fast-Moving Consumer Goods (FMCG) advertising. These days only media studies students would be interested in his show reel. None of his campaigns would outlive him, unless you counted the existence of the Pizzazz UK Owners' Club, or the sad young men he sometimes saw wearing ironic Buddhist Milkman T-shirts.

His flat was little more than a place to hang his Paul Rand prints and lay his bruised, bloodied head. Mathematically speaking, he owned at least three storeys of Genevieve's place, but it contained no trace of him. He and Glassop and Bill Cohn had built MGC from scratch, but the agency no longer survived under their names. No; what he had to show for himself was the house on the Hill. That was his legacy. Pen may have given it a new paint job in the years since his departure, but he was intimate with its workings. He'd installed the central heating, for pity's sake; with his own two hands he'd plastered and shelved and roofed and floored. He knew the fuse-box by heart; could tell you, by feel alone, which switch corresponded to which room, to which corridor. The house on the Hill, he could see now, was a reflection of his very best self: optimistic, energised, ambitious. And a bunch of pseudo-Bolsheviks had the temerity to take it from him? No, he told himself. This would not stand.

The train ground to a halt in the tunnel, its motor idling. The lights flickered.

'Very sorry, Ladies and Gentlemen,' said a voice over the tannoy, in muffled cockney. 'Seems the train in front is having trouble with its doors. I'm afraid we'll be stuck for just a few minutes while they sort it out. On behalf of Transport for London, I'd like to apologise for the delay. Hopefully we'll have you on the move very shortly.'

Inappropriately cheerful, that message, Jerry thought. Without the natural passage of air through the carriage, the temperature began to rise steadily. He felt his sweat glands going to work. His forehead throbbed.

As a child of the Cheshire suburbs, Jerry had been obsessed with the very idea of London. Its music, its lights, its clothes – and, most of all, its women – were once a distant, cherished dream. His dad was a bank manager in Macclesfield, his mum a naval man's daughter. They'd lashed themselves to Empire values. But his was a generation with ambitions, with disposable income, and the only place to squander them both to his satisfaction was here, in this city. Now, though, it had roughed him up and left him bleeding, just another out-of-towner muggee. The police, arms crossed smugly behind a desk somewhere, manifestly not 'Working together for a safer London'. The hospitals, which couldn't even find time to attend to a sensible person's bump on the head, so swamped were they with junkies and drunks, nutters and louts. (Is it any wonder he paid through the nose for a Harley Street GP?) And now this Tube carriage, halted on behalf of Transport for London.

In the vacuum left by the train's lack of movement, he could hear the dum-thwack of a rap song from the earphones of the young man next to him. Further down the carriage, a group of Spanish schoolchildren were yammering noisily. Someone nearby was, or had recently been, eating a tuna melt sandwich. Round them all up, Jerry thought to himself, and slap ASBOs on the lot of them – along with the traffic wardens and the yoga practitioners, the art dealers and the overpriced lawyers and the whingeing trade unionists, the investment bankers and the Islamic fundamentalists and the greedy MPs, the pootlers in the fast lane and all the people who can't just stand on the fucking right on a fucking escalator like they're fucking supposed to.

This is about right, he thought. This is about the bloody size of it. Trapped, as usual, in a tiny world full of bastards. Underground; alone.

RENOVATIONS

8

Pen had loitered at the scene of her old life for far too long. In the basement of the house on the Hill, the kitchen-diner still echoed with Isobel and Conrad's adolescent spats. At the dining table one flight up squatted the ghosts of soirées past, while in the bedroom lurked the spectre of her and Jerry's sex life. Her studio was cluttered with reminders of her neglected career. And the loft conversion laughed at the folly of her foundational project: to make their home an example to their peers, a series of children's books – and even a lifestyle feature in a newspaper property section. (The *London Evening Standard*, 10 July 1996, to be precise.)

She occupied the empty afternoons with cinema excursions and exhibitions; magazines and popular novels; half-realised paintings and creative writing endeavours; phone calls to girl-friends and, very occasionally, to family members. She fought the urge to overeat: making sure not to fill the fridge; always walking, never driving, to the butcher and the bakery on Upper Street; ordering biweekly boxes of organic, locally sourced fruit and vegetables online. She actively maintained a handful of human relationships, dotting her diary with dinners, brunches, coffees. She went to Pilates classes. She looked after the garden. Thanks to Jerry's divorce settlement and her late father's will, money was almost no object. There was a difference between being alone and being lonely, and Pen rarely experienced loneliness. No, this was independence. This was freedom, in a roundabout sort of way.

Still, there was no avoiding it: with Jerry gone, and now both children too, it was clear the house was far too large for one. She had provided herself with years of distraction from this fact, by embracing any and every interior design fad she came across: exposed brickwork, distressed woodwork, pendant lamp assortments, frame clusters; taupe, avocado, plum; William Morris, Terence Conran, Kevin McCloud.

But with the catalogues exhausted, and since she didn't care for cats or lodgers, Pen had resolved to sell. A parade of estate agents soon drew up in their branded Minis, saucer-eyed at the prospect of a commission. They quoted her outlandish asking prices, so she sounded out her parvenu neighbours, Stuart and Andrea, who assured her that yes, that really was the going rate for a house like hers in such a desirable locale. She prepared to negotiate with her ex-husband, who technically still owned half the property and, having recently signed a second set of divorce papers, would doubtless be amenable to the idea of a significant cash injection.

After splitting the proceeds from the sale between herself, Jerry and the children, she could find a cottage in the Shires reminiscent of her childhood haunts: somewhere to wind down quietly into old age. Then again, she might prefer something small in central London – close to shops, friends, a park, a good hospital. While she considered her options, she'd rent something temporary nearby. It was imperative to sell the house swiftly, before her nerve failed her.

But just as she prepared to erect the For Sale sign, the news bulletins became a glossary of unfamiliar financial jargon: 'subprime' and 'mortgage-backed securities' and 'credit default swaps'.

All of a sudden, selling up sounded foolish. Or, at least, every person whom Pen consulted counselled against it. So she flinched, and was once again burdened with the house for as long as it took the market to recover, and the property to creep back up to its optimum worth. In the interim, she needed something else to fill the unforgiving hours.

When her friends first suggested Internet dating, the very idea struck her as breathtakingly undignified. But after some concerted and coordinated encouragement, she was reassured that it was, in fact, the most reliable way to meet a fitting companion. Pen was far from convinced that she needed a companion at all, but her darling pal Francesca insisted plenty of fifty-somethings swore by it. Everyone knew of a friend, or of a friend of a friend, who'd met their partner online. Facebook had all but dispelled the taboos. But I'm not *on* Facebook, Pen said. Well, you *should* be, Fran replied. And *really*, who wanted to be put next to some awful bore at a dinner party and then have to ignore his unwanted advances for weeks or months thereafter, when one could instead condemn unsuitable wooers with the click of a computer mouse?

Fran was the former television producer who in the nineties had created a short-lived animated version of *The House on the Hill* for Children's BBC. They'd been fast friends ever since. But given that Fran had been happily remarried for going on ten years, Pen wasn't entirely sure how she knew so much about Internet dating. It must have been from women's magazines. In any case, she could muster no watertight counter-arguments. Together, spurred on by a bottle of rosé, she and Fran sat at the dining table with Pen's laptop and composed a dating profile.

Pen-Pal[1]

54[2], London

Height: 5'6"

Hair: Blonde[3]

Body type: Average[4]

Relationship Status: Single (divorced)

Relationship Sought: Friendship; Let's See What Happens; A
  Soul Mate[5]

Children: Two, grown-up

Looking for: A Man

From: London; The South-east

Aged between: 50 and 63[6]

Words to Describe Me: Creative; A Free-Thinker; Sexy; Smart;
  Witty; GSOH; Sociable; Honest; Active; A Home-Maker[7];
  Reliable; Independent[8]; Happy-Go-Lucky[9]; Caring[10].

As a profile photograph, Pen selected her eight-year-old, black-
and-white professional author's head shot. Neither she nor Fran
was absolutely sure this was a good idea, since it might appear
pretentious, or raise unrealistic expectations. It was, though, the
only picture of herself that Pen could bear to publish.

---

1 The username was Fran's idea; she claimed it sounded approachable and witty.

2 There was some discussion of shading Pen's age by a year or two, but they agreed that,
while a lie was often the best way to end a relationship, it was rarely the best way to begin
one.

3 (Grey-blonde.)

4 She almost chose 'Slim', which she most certainly was, for her age, but she didn't wish
to begin any dates with a disappointment. Better, she guessed, to be a pleasant surprise.

5 The choice of categories was fatuous; wasn't everyone here for sex or a spouse? *'Let's
See What Happens'*?! For God's sake.

6 She deliberated at length over what seemed like arbitrary numbers, but elected in the
end to aim for somebody beneath retirement age.

7 Fran insisted on this, declaring that it was not only true, but also necessary to attract
the right sort of chap at Pen's age.

8 Well, obviously.

9 Occasionally.

10 Mostly.

Finally, underneath all this superficial nonsense, she was required to write a personal introduction. She and Fran thought it best to be brief:

I'm an art school graduate, although I now have a post-graduate degree from the University of Life (!). I've lived in north London for over 30 years, and I adore the city – but I love the country too. I enjoy meeting friends and hosting or attending dinner parties, though I'm just as happy at home with a good book/DVD, a bottle of wine and some intelligent conversation. I'd be happy to provide the wine, if you can bring the conversation!

Once she'd created the profile, Pen had to be coached in its maintenance. Internet dating was like an eBay auction, Fran explained. Most still-single men over a certain age were ugly, weird or irreparably psychologically damaged by some long-repressed childhood trauma. So when a fresh, ostensibly sane divorcé or widower popped up in your profile's Suggested Dates sidebar, you had to place your bid immediately. There must be no doubt about your interest in the product, no haggling. = Buy It Now.

For about a fortnight, Pen surprised herself with her impatience to return to the keyboard, to surf the site in search of eligible suitors. Several awful men – ugly, weird or both – selected her as one of their Favourites. She ignored their advances and snickered uncharitably about them on the phone to Fran. After a few days of this, though, she decided she ought to engage, not merely observe. However, her first promising email exchange, with an anaesthetist from Twickenham, took an unexpected turn towards the sexually graphic. When she recoiled from her correspondent's vivid prose imagery, he bombarded her with apologies, and she felt obliged to block his messages. She had not, thank God, offered him her telephone number yet.

She next agreed to a lunch date with a divorced public relations executive, at a tapas bar in Soho. The man talked at length about himself and, after slack-jawedly munching a spoonful of *patatas bravas*, neglected to wipe the tomato juices from the corners of his mouth, causing Pen to dab her own lips compulsively with a napkin, in the hope that he might do the same. When he learned she'd been married to Jerry, he spent some ten minutes singing the praises of MGC. He insisted on paying the bill, but then studied the receipt carefully before slipping it into his wallet, as if he planned to charge it to his company expense account. When she kissed him goodbye – an air-kiss, to evade those tomato-crusted lips – she was kissing him goodbye.

It would be a funny story, she supposed, nothing more. And yet, when the divorced public relations executive failed to call and offer her the chance to reject him, she grew morose and moped about the house for forty-eight hours in her dressing gown, cursing herself and eating and wondering why she even bothered. She told Fran that she wished to retire her dating profile. Fran rushed over with another bottle of rosé. One last try, she said. Third time lucky.

David Bowles was handsome; that was the first thing. Even if he'd added an extra inch or two to his true height to boost his profile stats, he would still be six foot tall, with gunmetal grey hair and a stiff but somewhat dashing smile. At sixty-two, he grazed the upper limit of her age preference, with a dead wife, a grown-up daughter and a house on the West Berkshire borders – plus a pied-à-terre in Hammersmith. He soberly listed travel, reading and walking among his interests in an otherwise unrevealing introductory paragraph; Pen imagined him reluctantly dictating it to the daughter. They exchanged polite emails, in which he betrayed no hint of depravity. When, at last, he asked her to dinner at a bistro in Covent Garden, he thoughtfully sent her a weblink to the menu.

She wore a black dress, a red shawl and kitten heels, and arrived early to steel her nerves with a vodka tonic. She was trying to make herself comfortable on the banquette when she spotted her date striding purposefully towards her across the dining room, like a colonel in mufti. Her stomach fluttered with social anxiety, and she was glad of the preparatory alcohol. He wore a navy-blue blazer and a smart gingham shirt open at the neck, golden-brown corduroys and suede loafers. He was gently tanned. He apologised for being late (he was a minute or two early), shook her hand, and then apologised again.

'I'm terribly sorry, but this is all rather new to me. Should one shake, or kiss?'

'Oh, I'm sure a shake is fine for now,' she replied, and cringed as she realised the implication: that a kiss would be acceptable later. They tittered self-consciously at each other's non-jokes. A solicitous French waiter was hovering nearby, eager to take David's brolly to the cloakroom. After much faffing with jackets and flapping of menus, they faced each other across the table, discussing public transport as she sipped at her aperitif. David toyed with his cufflinks. He strongly recommended the bouilla-baisse, though not so strongly as to seem severe.

'Oh, so have you eaten here before?'

'No, no,' he said hastily, blushing. 'But I hear it's the most authentic Marseillaise in town.'

To her shame, Pen was not sure she'd be able to rank bowls of bouillabaisse Marseillaise by their authenticity. In the end, her nerves subsiding, she ordered the veal. David had a cultured palate; the wine he chose, with her assent, was a perfect match.

He positively stank of propriety. He was a partner in a small but, he claimed, well-respected management consultancy firm. It sounded terribly dull to begin with, until he revealed that one of his clients was a global chain of hotels, and that he was often obliged to travel by business class to interesting countries with appealing climates. He was thus a practised conversationalist who read and digested the newspapers – albeit the stuffy, right-wing ones. His demeanour reminded Pen of her dear departed father, and of the life she'd left behind in the home counties when she fled for art school all those years ago. By her count, he made two mildly racist comments during dinner, a habit to which white well-to-do men of a certain age were prone, alas. But he spoke with great affection of Kenya (which he called 'Keen-yah').

Pen explained that she'd harboured dreams of being a painter, but quickly discovered that her talents were more commercial. She'd worked in advertising, as a graphic designer and illustrator, where she met her first and only husband, Jerry. After childbirth, she toiled part-time in the art department of his fledgling firm, but, reluctant to return to full-time work, she had eventually started to write children's books instead. David took all of this in with tiny nods, as if ticking each item on her CV against a mental checklist.

He teased from her the name of her book series, *The House on the Hill*, and instantly recalled it from his young grandson's reading list. He seemed a little flushed with the excitement of recognition. Pen knew of the effect from Conrad's schooldays, when teachers and fellow parents had seemed keen to make her acquaintance on the basis of her handful of middlingly successful stories. She'd often wondered whether this experience constituted fame, and how Meryl Streep might have dealt with it. It was undoubtedly a pleasurable sensation, if a touch pathetic on the part of her admirers. She was glad when David changed the subject.

Pen had the sense she was being subjected to a sort of cost-benefit analysis; that he was assessing her as a potential investment, and that over the course of the evening she had indeed proven herself an attractive prospect. She enjoyed his approval, yet she already felt sure that he was not at all her type, nor she his. She had in mind someone more creative, less conservative. He probably voted Tory. Could she be a Thatcherite's consort? She thought not.

They ordered a dessert to share, followed by espressos. David chose this intimate, wine-blurred instant to mention his wife, who'd died two years previously, following a long and drawn-out battle with a horrific wasting disease. He spoke of it in a few clipped sentences, as if he'd been meaning to get it out of the way all evening, and had only just plucked up the courage. Pen made sympathetic noises and stared at a tiny stain on the tablecloth where he'd spilled a dot of bouillabaisse.

After finishing his coffee and his morbid endnote, David paid discreetly and, as they emerged into the evening drizzle, he opened his brolly to shield her from the damp. He flagged down a taxi, resolving the need for any after-dinner small talk. She thanked him for a lovely evening, and allowed him a kiss on each cheek in the continental manner. By the time the cab dropped her at her door half an hour later, she'd concluded that he was wooden, and overall uninteresting, and that she was turned off by his incessant, nervous tweaking of his cufflinks. She mixed her second vodka tonic of the night and sat sipping it at the kitchen table. Who needed a man, anyway?

On the other hand, David was neither ugly nor weird, nor did he seem irreparably psychologically damaged, and so when he emailed her the following day to propose a second date, she agreed – after first letting him stew for twenty-four hours, at Fran's suggestion. Her instincts were rewarded: he bought tickets to an RSC production of *The Seagull*. Pricey ones, in the stalls. This was, he informed her over interval drinks, only his second-favourite Chekhov. Pen began to wonder whether he might be worth cultivating, after all: a man familiar with more than one fin-de-siècle Russian play must surely have some hidden depths.

Of course, what really piqued her interest was the house in France. David had first mentioned it fleetingly at the theatre – not in his online profile: a significant omission – but she picked her moment to pursue the subject after he offered to drive her to Cambridge one Saturday. He picked her up from Highbury in his BMW estate, stopping in the kitchen-diner for a coffee. She gave him a tour of her lower floors, at which he nodded appreciatively, complimenting her on the garden. She told him she was keen to sell. With a professional seriousness, he advised her to await a sustained upswing in the market. Then he jangled his car keys and muttered darkly about the roadworks on the M11.

David was a Queens' alumnus, so they strolled about the college's courtyards, went punting on the Cam, and motored out to Grantchester village in the late afternoon. At the tea garden, they sat outside beneath an apple tree, the long grass tickling their ankles. Pen nursed a coronation teacup of Earl Grey and a scone. Already, David had begun to speak obliquely of their imagined future life together. She indulged his hypothetical talk of cohabitation and merged financial interests, and his optimistic assumptions about the rapport she would strike up with his daughter, Harriet. She smiled non-committally, but she was not entirely ill-disposed to it all. They could doubtless lead a comfortable existence. Fran would claim it as a triumph.

Nevertheless, Pen had to weigh the prospect of life with David against the advantages of independence; her own cost-benefit analysis was pending, and its outcome would decide whether he could offer her anything besides polite conversation and pleasant day trips.

'I haven't even seen your home yet,' she said eventually.

David had a pained look that she later came to recognise as the grief-mask of the recently widowed, and it passed across his face then. The house in West Berkshire, he explained, needed some work before he'd be comfortable having her to stay – by which, she surmised, he meant he ought to cleanse it of some of the remaining evidence of the dead wife. He was, he went on, reluctant to have her visit his Hammersmith flat. It had been bought as

Harriet's starter home, and she'd married and moved out in the same year that her mother passed away. Lonely, David had decamped to bustling West London for much of every week. But the flat was not really his. He looked pensive.

'Come to France with me,' he said at last. 'For a long weekend. I'd love you to see the place.'

Pen sipped her tea, adjusted her shawl and gazed away into the orchard, pretending to ponder the invitation.

'That sounds delightful,' she replied.

It was love at first sight. The farmhouse at Le Boqueteau perched adorably close to the top of a long, low valley: an empty hammock of patchworked arable fields, cushioned with coppices. It was more than two miles from the nearest village, silent but for birdcalls and distant tractors. The lawns needed serious attention, and the pool had fallen out of use, but the building itself was an immaculate mix of mod cons and original farmhouse features: a vast kitchen, a genuine fireplace, authentic wooden shutters. The barn, meanwhile, had oodles of potential. Pen had never been drawn to the suburbs, but the countryside was a different matter – not to mention the French countryside. This was a genuine rural idyll. She could paint here; she could garden; she could write.

David had flown out ahead of her, so as to pick her up from the airport at Bergerac in the old Volkswagen Passat that he kept in the barn. He and his wife had bought the house together with the intention of retiring there, he explained as they sped down through the Dordogne – but then she had been diagnosed with the horrific wasting disease, and they'd never been able to take full advantage. Pen again made sympathetic noises. The area was popular with expats, David went on, but one could avoid them if one preferred. Unlike many of the English residents, and despite his poor French, he continued to employ a local – a Mr Bruno DeLambre – to do all the work around the house and garden.

David offered her the use of her own bathroom, and there was an excruciating moment when it seemed he might suggest she sleep in the spare bedroom. But having seen the house and decided that it was to her liking, Pen decisively deposited her weekend bag in the master bedroom. She showered and changed into her favourite cashmere dress for dinner, knowing that it flattered her shape and was easily removable. David cooked a casserole with some gnarled local potatoes; Pen hoped this would not send them both to sleep too quickly, and ensured that they fortified themselves with half a bottle each of burgundy from the makeshift wine cellar at the back of the barn.

The sex was awkward at first, but pleasant enough. Both parties spent some time preparing themselves in the bathroom beforehand, with unguents and toothpaste and Viagra pills. David folded his clothes prior to the commencement of foreplay, and the couple had to remind themselves of the etiquette of the bedroom after years out of service. (David's wife's horrific wasting disease, he explained, had prevented her from enjoying intercourse for some time before her death.) It was, technically speaking at least, a success. They clung to one another's loose-skinned limbs for a minute or two afterwards, out of politeness, but the mattress was more than large enough for them both to enjoy a decent night's sleep without troubling one another. David snored briefly, and then was silent. When Pen awoke, some hours after dawn, it was to an empty room and the smell of toast under the grill.

In another life, she might have hoped to spend all weekend in bed, pausing only for meals and bathroom breaks. But in this one, they filled the next two days instead with long walks and paperbacks. On Saturday morning David drove her to the market in Agen, which was certainly cheaper than any North London farmers' market, if less exotically stocked. On Sunday, at his suggestion, they went to church for the fortnightly Anglican service, where he introduced her to his expat acquaintances, whose names she quickly forgot, so discombobulated was she by her first

Eucharist in decades: a full hour's unnerving talk of eating flesh and drinking blood.

Pen wondered whether the wife's death had made David more or less devout. He was not a noticeably religious man, except on Sunday mornings. Yet in spite of their growing closeness, she didn't think it appropriate to tell him that she believed life was a series of arbitrary events, explained away by the gullible as luck, fate or the design of a higher being; that destiny was claptrap, and that we had only ourselves to blame for bad choices; that they could both easily continue as they were, alone and counting down the hours until death (after which, by the way, there came nothing at all); or that they could choose to count those hours together – but that neither choice had any intrinsic value, since God was merely a comforting figment, and nothing really meant anything.

That evening, they drove to a nearby hill-town for dinner. As they strolled back to the car at dusk, David stopped abruptly and asked her to sit. The bench boasted the best view in the vicinity, overlooking the winding road to the valley floor. With some difficulty, given his height and age, he sank to one knee and produced the ring that he must have bought before even leaving England. Pen watched a pale Citroën slalom down the slope below them in the gloaming, rounding each hairpin bend with leisurely ease. They had known each other for approximately four months. It was almost a blessing, Pen reflected, that David had a dead wife whom he so clearly still adored; it would remove the obligation to love him as perhaps she should. As he squeezed the ring onto her finger, her eyes welled, though she couldn't really say why.

Together, they quickly concluded that Pen should relocate to France while David commuted back and forth from London. It was a mutually beneficial arrangement, allowing Pen to lay claim to the farmhouse, and David to split his time between her and the spirit of his dead first wife. But there was one, unexpected condition. The dead wife had a dog, a fact that David had slyly kept to himself until now. Bennett, a black Labrador, had the bad luck to live at David's Berkshire house and, when David was in London, a neighbour's. David was keen that the bereaved pet should live out his own final years in comfortable surroundings, and he wanted Pen to take him with her to Le Boqueteau. Bennett, he explained, had been jolly lonely since the death of his mistress and of his fellow Labrador, Gordon. Pen and the dog could keep one another company when he wasn't there. Pen could not summon a sincere excuse without sounding heartless (she was not a dog person [true]; she abhorred the idea of cleaning up another animal's shit [true]; she was allergic to dog hair – it gave her asthma attacks [false]). So she reluctantly agreed. In a property that large, she felt sure that she and Bennett could stay out of each other's way.

David knew better than to demand a church wedding, and so their union was certified in the spring of 2010, with a small affair at a register office. The guest list was short. David's daughter and her husband and their toddler. Isobel and the babies – Torsten couldn't make it; he was tied up with work. Conrad. Fran was her maid of honour. One of David's long-standing colleagues acted as best man, and then rushed off to another engagement.

Afterwards everybody retired to the house on the Hill for tea, where Isobel and Harriet swapped child-rearing notes, while David and Conrad chitchatted awkwardly. Fran wept a little at the thought of her friend moving abroad, but Pen insisted she come and stay. There was a barn at Le Boqueteau that she was already planning to convert into a gîte. The sunsets were unbeatable. The pool was simply heaven.

9

Bennett drooled. The drool dangled from his chops as Pen prepared his lunch or his dinner, spooning biscuity meal and chunks of Chum into the bowl labelled '*Dog*'. He drooled as she ate, too – sitting patiently, just within reach, watching and waiting with pathetic eyes for a food scrap or a pat on the head, until she grudgingly relented and tossed him a morsel, which he'd tease around the terrace or the tiled floor of the kitchen before swallowing. He drooled on Pen's lap when he placed his chin there, hopeful for affection. It had the opposite effect; she would shoo him away in disgust and rub at the stain with a square of kitchen roll. Labrador drool did not resemble human saliva: it was thicker, stickier, like raw egg white. Every evening, as he lay in front of the television, Bennett would leave an unwelcome little damp patch on the Persian rug where his jaw rested. He was a blemish on the meticulous pattern of Pen's new life.

His eyes sagged wearily, and his jowls hung slack. He panted with each effortful step. His coat was wiry and stiff, where once it must have been glossy, nutrient-rich. He stank: that deep dog smell of dirt and sweat and infrequently scrubbed scalp. He never ate fish, yet his breath reeked of it, and he released brutal, rotten-egg farts that made Pen gag as she tried to concentrate on the US Open semi-finals, or the series finale of *Spooks*, or whichever British programme was presently saved on her Sky+ box.

He pursued her relentlessly, moping in her wake wherever she went. If she closed a door behind her to keep him out, he would never whine or complain – but, when she emerged again, there he was, waiting to trail along behind her once more. During the days, he watched her as she painted, never quite letting her out of his sight as he wandered around the garden, snapping half-heartedly at insects, or inspecting the plants as if copying Pen, like a child does its parent. When she took her morning and afternoon swims, he would stand at the poolside, tongue lolling, forever threatening to leap in after her. At night, thank heavens, David had recommended she confine the dog to the utility room with the walking boots and the washing machine, and so she did.

Pen had laid plans to paint a collection of conspicuously French scenes, to flog to credulous punters back in London or West Berkshire. For this she had bought oils and brushes, dusted off her sketchbook and easel, and had canvases stretched by a man in Holloway Road, which she'd shipped over with the rest of her things from England. She painted the house. She painted the barn. She painted the neighbouring fields as the seasons turned, and the garden as it grew closer to her specifications. Bennett, lying on his belly in the middle of the lawn, became a smudge of ochre among the vibrant greens. She drove to nearby valleys and hill-towns to paint new landscapes. She sat on the bench where David had proposed, and sketched a watercolour of the winding road below. She found a square close to the church where the local men played boules, and she drew and photographed them for a future composition, certain that such material would sell. She found a disused water tower, standing alone in a field of yellow rape, and painted it once every six weeks or so, under a variety of skies. At first, she left Bennett behind at Le Boqueteau. Once it became clear that he was unlikely to run away and get lost, she allowed him to accompany her on painting excursions. He rarely strayed far from the easel.

Pen's restaurant-level French steadily improved. Courtesy of Robert, the proprietor of Chez Robert's cellar and wine merchant on Av. Barbusse, she began her education in the undervalued wines of Bergerac, so as to impress future visitors with her local knowledge: crisply acidic Saussignacs; rich, spicy Pécharmants; elegant, complex Montravels. Robert gave her oral tasting notes whenever she bought a new case, and she scribbled them down from memory in her sketchbook as soon as she returned to the Passat. She learned the biographical details of each producer, and the adjectives best suited to their product. Then she matched each wine to a regional cheese: hard, Cheddar-like Cantal; sharp blue Fourme d'Ambert; mild, creamy Saint-Paulin. She soon shed any of the ethical objections she might have previously felt obliged to hold towards pâté de foie gras, and limited her weekly intake for health reasons alone. She learned the layout of the *hypermarché* at the edge of Agen by heart, and in early summer found a pick-your-own cherry orchard on the drive into town, where she took to stopping for a punnet once a week. Sometimes Bennett came with her to sniff the ground in search of loose fruit. French children would pet him fondly, regardless of the pong.

She slept late. She raced through the classics, finally vanquishing the complete works of Austen, Eliot (George) and Trollope (Joanna), and forging onward into Forster and Lawrence. She succumbed to temptation and spent entire evenings watching DVD box sets. Thanks to digital radio, she could still listen to *Gardeners' Question Time*. Now and then, she had Fran send her consignments of her favourite magazines. Far from the judgemental eyes of friends or family, she felt liberated to indulge in selfish pastimes.

David visited weekly, or fortnightly, and each time insisted that Bennett seemed happier, more energised. Pen wondered exactly what the poor beast must have been like before the move. Her husband was pleased with the progress she was making in the garden. Her first task had been to plant a herb bed, and her ambitions had expanded from there, to fruit and vegetables and flowering creepers. That first summer, with the help of Mr DeLambre

– Bruno – she started to experiment with free-standing bamboo thickets, planted to mark the invisible lines where the Bowles land ended and the neighbouring farms began. When, during the night, she heard wild boar grunting and squeaking, chewing up some nearby turf, Bruno offered to install an electric fence. Should the boars venture into her garden, he said, they could cause untold damage. But she declined – she didn't move to the country to build fences. Well then, he said, perhaps he would shoot them and give her the fillets for her freezer. She laughed nervously at that.

Bennett and Remy, Bruno's pointer puppy, had taken to one another immediately. Remy would hop up and down in front of the old dog with inconsiderate vigour, and Bennett would nose at him affectionately. Bruno was decent enough to clear any canine excrement from the garden as part of his duties. He would collect the dogs' doings in a shovel, and then toss them into the next-door field. On hot days, stripped to the waist to reveal his hairy and perfectly rounded Gallic gut, he would break off from watering the plants to hose the dogs down. Even Pen had to admit that Bennett was grinning when he shook himself dry in the sun. In his dreams, the dog was young again. This she knew because, as she watched him slumber, drooling into the carpet or the grass or his beanbag bed, he twitched and jerked as if bounding after rabbits – his tongue and ears a-flap, the wind at his back, his lungs full and his heart strong.

Meanwhile, the house on the Hill sat empty, and on each of Pen's few visits home she removed more of its remaining contents to France, to friends or to the dump. Though the London property market had stabilised, she now felt strangely reluctant to sell. She wanted the money to fund the barn conversion, for which she often found herself drafting designs on napkins, or conjuring mental colour schemes. But what if the farmhouse was inhospitable in winter? What if David failed to improve with time? Selling now would signify an absolute commitment to her new life, her new marriage. It was an unsettling thought.

And besides, she saw nothing of her children for months on end; in what sense, exactly, would they be a family, if the family home were sold? Isobel schooled her in Skype, and they spoke irregularly via Pen's unreliable broadband connection, so she could claim to be watching her grandchildren grow. Conrad was monosyllabic on the phone, so meeting him in person was the only way to engage him properly; given that he'd failed to take up her offer of a French vacation, such opportunities were scarce.

In fact, her only guest had been Fran, whose visit in May was merely satisfactory. Fran loved France, she loved the garden and the pool, she loved the wine and the cheese and the foie gras. She even professed to love Bennett. Fran and David, however, did not complement one another quite so well as the Haut-Montravel and the Fourme d'Ambert. He was not like North London husbands; she was not like West Berkshire wives. Dinner conversation was stilted. Pen made a mental note to ensure her husband was abroad the next time her friend came to stay.

In the absence of other company, Pen tentatively befriended some of David's churchgoing acquaintances. This required home visits, since she remained uneasy at the thought of attending a service. She took tea with the Stewarts and the Garrick-Smiths, whose invitations to play bridge she persistently declined. Her favourites were the Cutlers, a couple from across the valley. Patrick, the English husband, worked a four-day week in Bristol. Pen brought Bowles jam to their cottage for his French-Algerian wife, Maz, and old, unsold copies of *The House on the Hill* series for the children. Maz would make her coffee or a simple lunch, as Pen chatted to the wonderfully complexioned Cutler youngsters, who always begged bilingually to play with *le chien*. The whiffy old black Lab was unexpected social glue. She sometimes had the sense that it was she, not the dog, who was the subject of the Cutlers' pity.

Towards the end of summer, after months of panting in the

heat, Bennett's bowels began to fail him. Soon, the days when incontinence had affected only his saliva glands seemed halcyon. Pen would find him standing bashfully beside a pool of unplanned urine or sick. Unless such accidents occurred in the garden, dealing with them was well beyond Bruno's remit. David was rarely present, so Pen had to return to the well of resolve she'd once discovered for changing her children's nappies. She became accustomed to the process: mopping, disinfecting, and then spraying the area with lavender bathroom fragrance.

Soon he started eating less, too, and she imagined he did so in order to reduce the frequency of the revolting task; he did so hate to impose. After one such incident, the dog was so doleful that she decided to give him a proper wash, and stood him in a large metal tub meant for nasturtiums to lather him with shampoo. Once his coat had dried in the sun, she groomed it with a clothes brush. He looked better, the way a Chelsea pensioner looks better for a fresh uniform. 'Don't you look smart?' she said as she finished, before she realised that she was conversing with a dog, and checked herself.

David, when he learned of Bennett's condition, warned her that the end was probably near. It was, he explained, precisely how Gordon, Bennett's fellow Labrador, had passed. His prediction proved correct – once it had begun, Bennett's decline was swift. Pen's parents had both gone the same way: sprightliness and oft-commented-upon good health, followed by a fall, or a short illness. Then a sickbed, complications, and haste unto death.

One humid autumn morning, Bennett couldn't seem to persuade his back legs to propel him into the garden after his mistress. Pen found Bruno's phone number pinned to the kitchen board at the top of David's emergency list. She'd never called the handyman before; he simply appeared on his allotted days. A woman answered – his wife, she supposed – and Pen asked frantically for Mr DeLambre, in what she hoped was adequate colloquial French.

Bruno drove Pen and the dog to the veterinary surgery in Agen. The vet gave Bennett a cursory examination before recommending the needle. She and Bruno left Pen alone with her pet to say goodbye. Bennett lay exhausted on the padded table, his chest rising and falling with each laboured breath. Pen sat in a chair, stroking his flank. Tears streamed down her cheeks, as stinging a shock as too-hot bathwater. Bennett, however, appeared oblivious to his fate. He smiled broadly, content to be next to her, finally to have her full attention. His blind loyalty had been rewarded at the last.

Afterwards, Bruno drove her home in silence, the dog wrapped in a blanket in the back of the Land Rover. Stupid woman, she thought, blowing her nose. To grow so attached to an animal – and without even realising she'd done so. Stupid, stupid. At her request, Bruno dug a hole under a chestnut tree at the top of the back lawn, from where one could see down over the house and into the valley. Bennett had often trudged up this slope behind her, to lie nearby as she sipped Sauvignon and sketched the undulating cornfields. Remy sniffed sadly at the blanket in which his dead friend was rolled. Though she knew that there was no more an afterlife for dogs than there was for humans, and that Bennett was now just dust and ashes in the ground, Pen nonetheless felt inclined to say something to mark his passing. So she thanked him, guiltily, for his friendship. Then she left Bruno to fill in the grave.

Ah, thought Pen, as the rattle of Bruno's Land Rover receded –
so this is loneliness. She lowered herself into the chair at the head
of the kitchen table, palms sticky with sweat and soil. Bennett's
half-full water bowl sat shimmering beneath the window. Through
her weary eyes, the afternoon sun seemed soft-focus, bathing the
kitchen like the cover of some seventies folk LP, or an early-Delia
recipe book. How long ago that was. Recalling her youth made
Pen feel her age. The decade came back to her often: as a series
of scents, which, smelled elsewhere, returned her to the leather
upholstery of her father's Daimler; to the turpentine and tobacco
smoke of artists' studios; the marijuana and mildew of unloved
squats; sweet curry-house spices blended with Jerry's bitter, first-
date cologne.

She wished, for a second, that she could still be as insensitive
as her twenty-something self. It was always easier to worry about
oneself than to invest emotionally in others. Start caring about a
family pet and you soon find yourself caring about the family.
Then friends, neighbours, the community, society: a world of
prospective emotional vulnerabilities. No one felt guilty about
anything in the seventies; self-centredness had been so easily intel-
lectualised, explained away by whichever pseudo-radical young
man was hoping you'd cheat on your boyfriend.

She dragged herself to the dresser. There was an open bottle
of Château Monteil 2005 (intense, grapy, rich), but she wanted
something stronger. She slid the ice tray from the top shelf of

the freezer and broke two cubes into a tumbler. They squeaked and split deliciously as she poured on the Pernod. A pinch of earth from the grave plot had plonked into the drink, but she hadn't the energy to fish it out, so she sipped from the other side of the glass.

For the first time, and with some force, she felt her geographical isolation: the hundreds of miles that separated her from anyone who'd give a damn. David was in England, and she was uncomfortable talking to him of strong emotions; she thought it best to wait a day for his regular 8 o'clock phone call before informing him of Bennett's demise. She almost rang Isobel or Fran, but told herself that Isobel had the twins to contend with, and would be too flustered to feign interest in the death of an unfamiliar animal. Fran would be baffled by her bereavement; she liked dogs the way she liked handbags. She couldn't call the Cutlers; the dog was the only reason they were friends with her! She yearned to call her mother, her father. She wanted to call Jerry. But the first two were as dead as Bennett, and the third . . . well, the third was Jerry.

She finished her first glass of Pernod before the ice had even begun to melt, swallowing the gritty soil dregs as if she deserved it, and poured another. The straps of her swimsuit creased her shoulders. She'd been on the way to her morning swim when Bennett collapsed, and she hadn't changed or showered since. Maybe a dip would raise her spirits now. Her towel was on the hall table. She picked it up, and then knelt beside Bennett's beanbag, putting her hand to the crater left there by his curled form. His wiry hairs cross-hatched the fabric. Pen felt herself welling up again, so she walked outside before she could be borne away by grief.

The heat of the afternoon was beginning to subside. Overripe crab apples littered the grass, rotting sweetly. She fished some desiccated leaves and a handful of drowned wasps from the pool with the net. Death was everywhere! The water, when she plunged in, was cool and clarifying. She breasted ten lengths, concentrating solely on her breathing and her stroke, and pushed the sadness aside for a few minutes. As soon as she paused to catch her breath, however, melancholy skulked back to claim her again. She shuddered as she dried herself in the sun, padding down her flaccid old flesh with the sandpapery towel. She tensed, pinched the skin where her tricep ought to have been, and found a fist of loose-hanging flab. Already she was thinking more of herself than of the dog, which might have been promising, but for the thoughts being so doom-laden.

Indoors, third Pernod in hand, her swimsuit seeping damp into David's favourite armchair, Pen scrolled through the channels on her Sky+ box in search of a comforting period drama. Nothing. Was the whole universe arrayed against her? She started to watch a repeat of *Grand Designs*, but it was one that she'd seen before, twice, and it yielded few ideas for the barn conversion. There remained a dark saliva stain on the rug where Bennett liked to rest his chops. When the chill of the drink and her wet hair began to bite, she went up to prepare a bath. She ran it hot and deep, with bubbles and a perfumed candle and Radio 4 long wave, and then lowered herself in gently, letting it warm her pores with lavender scent. Five minutes went by. Even self-indulgence had lost its pleasurable itch. She soaked for a miserable twenty more, while the water grew tepid and the sun sank ever further.

Pen was dressed and drying her hair glumly in front of the bedroom mirror when she heard the hollow slam of a car door. She scanned the driveway from her window, and saw Bruno's Land Rover. The handyman had returned. Had he forgotten his spade, she wondered, or come to invoice her for the digging? She checked her eyes for signs of weeping – not so evident now – and descended the stairs. Bruno stood in the kitchen in fraying jeans and one of his grubby polo shirts, breathing noisily. Under his hairy arm was a small cardboard packing box, lined with kitchen paper, and filled with *cèpes*. Remy shimmied against his ankles.

'*Madame*,' he said, and tipped his head towards the box of mushrooms. 'Dinner.'

She could have kissed him. Her eyes prickled with tears again. In times of sorrow, Pen found, the sympathy of others served to refine the upset, turning it bitter-sweet. A kind thought, a gift, company: how unexpectedly considerate he was – for a handyman.

'Oh, thank you, Bruno,' she said; a familiar phrase, rarely spoken with such conviction.

She stepped towards him, arms open to receive the box, but he kept a firm hold on it.

'*Non*,' he said. 'You sit.'

Bruno shambled to the range and put the box on the worktop. Spotting the open bottle of Château Monteil, he plucked two glasses from the drying rack beside the sink and poured a large glug of wine into each of them. He put one on the kitchen table in front of Pen.

'*Bon?*' he said, raising a furry eyebrow.

She stared at the glass dumbly.

'Er, yes. Thank you.'

'Sit, sit,' he said again, satisfied.

Taken aback by Bruno's firmness, Pen felt she had little choice but to comply. She sank into the chair, where Remy ministered to her immediately, nosing at her thigh and offering her his ears to ruffle. Bruno sipped at the second glass of wine.

'You have a shock, *non?*' he said. 'The dog. Very sad. I have many dogs before Remy. Is always very sad. Very sad.'

'Yes,' said Pen. 'Very sad.'

'But wine is good.'

'But wine is good,' she agreed. '*Bon santé.*'

They drank, the silence broken only by the swish of Remy's tail wagging back and forth across the tiled floor. Then Bruno put down his drink, clapped his rough hands together and plucked a mushroom from the box.

'So,' he said, turning its stem between thumb and forefinger. '*Le bolet orange*'. He pointed to the mushroom's plump, orange-brown cap. '*Ouais?*'

'Ah,' Pen replied, smiling. 'Orange.'

He turned, rummaged in the box again, and picked out a darker, more squat specimen. '*Tête de nègre*,' he said.

'Did you pick them yourself?' she asked.

'*Bien sûr*,' he replied emphatically, holding up one last variety: '*Voilà! Le cèpe d'été.*'

He handed it to Pen, and she examined the fat stem in her palm.

'Summer mushroom,' she translated, to herself.

By some instinct, perhaps innate in all Frenchmen, Bruno found the kitchen's best frying pan in the first cupboard he opened. He pulled the finest knife from the magnetic strip that was screwed to the wall above the worktop. Pen kept the garlic in a clay jar, which he reached for almost without looking, breaking off a pair of cloves, peeling and chopping them like a television chef. He put out his palm to take back the *cèpe* Pen was holding and, as she passed it to him, she saw that his hand was still earthy and unwashed. She nearly ordered him to run it under the tap, but restrained herself. He cut the stem from the cap, and began doing the same with the rest, slicing the stems thinly as he went.

'You have told Monsieur Bowles?' he asked, his eyes on the chopping board.

'Yes,' she lied quickly. 'David was . . . He was very sorry.'

'Mmph,' Bruno grunted. 'He is nice dog, Bennett. Good, ah . . .' He searched for the correct term. '. . . character?'

'Yes,' Pen agreed again, stroking Remy's soft coat unconsciously. 'A very good character.'

114

Bruno lit the gas without asking how, located the butter dish, cut a ragged chunk and slapped it into the skillet. He casually sloshed some olive oil, turning the pan over the heat to shift the warming fat around its surface. David followed recipes to the letter for every culinary endeavour, including jam. Bruno seemed sufficiently confident to press on without instruction.

'Are you married, Bruno?' she asked, and was instantly struck by her own impertinence.

He was facing the range, and seemed not to have heard her.

'*Madame*,' he said, 'you must please have some, ah . . . *le persil.*'

'Oh, do call me Pen, please,' she replied.

'Parsley,' he said in English.

It took her a moment to grasp his meaning. 'Parsley?'

'Yes,' he said, lending the request a hint of urgency. He deposited the mushroom caps in the pan, where they started to sizzle gently.

'Ah,' she cried finally. 'I see! Parsley.'

Pen swigged the last of her glass of wine, pushed back her chair and rushed from the kitchen so eagerly that she forgot to fetch her secateurs. She was halfway down the gravel path to the herb garden, Remy trailing concernedly behind her, before she noticed their absence. Ho-hum; she would have to harvest the necessary leaves by hand. The task had given her purpose, and for a few minutes her worries were forgotten. Evening was falling rapidly as she rounded the barn and knelt in the warm grass close to the parsley plants. Birds chirruped the dusk chorus. She wrenched a fistful of stems from the bed, brushing away clumps of soil from the roots with her other hand. As she stood up again, she became aware that she might be somewhat tipsy. Most of the valley's fields had already been stripped by combines of their yellow corn; she watched the stubble turn to umber beneath the darkening sky, waiting for the blood to return to her head. The sensation made her oddly euphoric.

She strolled back to the house again, stopping by the porch trellis to sniff at an especially aromatic passion flower. When she re-entered the kitchen, now rich with the smell of sautéing mushrooms, Bruno opened and closed his palm, silently demanding the parsley. She pressed the stems into his hand and poured herself another glass of wine, then she stood and watched him as he chopped the herbs. He slid the mushroom caps from the pan onto a plate and replaced them with the sliced *cèpe* stems, the parsley, the garlic, tossing the mixture deftly to coat it in butter and oil. His face, blotchy with burst capillaries, bore a healthy glisten of perspiration. A pale crescent of underbelly sagged from beneath his polo shirt, and hair tufted from his collar. She was mesmerised by his sheer competence at the stove. The French! He'd almost finished his wine, so Pen poured him another glass, too. She wished she'd had time to put some make-up on.

'Should I make a salad?' she asked.

Bruno thrust his lower lip out and half-nodded as if to say, '*Bof*, why not?' Then he tipped the mushroom caps back into the pan, and tossed it once more.

They were two-thirds of the way into a bottle of Domaine des Herbiers 2007 (berries, liquorice, tannin) by the time Pen forked her last mushroom. She had taken her time over the dish, and not simply because it was delicious: seasoned so impeccably as to shake her confidence in her own salad dressing. Despite her initial surprise that he should have turned up at all, she was reluctant to let Bruno leave. She craved his company, anybody's company. The talking cure. She had watched him eat brutishly – at odds with his plainly sophisticated palate – and mop the juices from the plate afterwards with a breezeblock of farmhouse French bread.

'It is like I am *un amérindien*,' he was spitting, between mouthfuls of wine. The British middle class, he'd haltingly explained, were slowly but surely colonising the restaurants, the supermarket aisles, *l'église*. When potential clients called and found his spoken English lacking, they just hung up the phone. How was he to go on making a living, when his native tongue was now the region's second language?

'I'm sorry,' Pen replied. '*Un amérind . . . ?*'

'*Un amérindien,*' he said again, tersely. 'A. Red. Indian.'

She pondered this idea as seriously as she could, given how much she had drunk: that she might be the unwitting ambassador for some foreign occupying power; a lady of the Raj; a frontier settler, laying waste to south-west France with her linguistic smallpox.

'But who,' she asked, slurring a little, 'will do all that work for them, if not you, Bruno?'

'More English!' he replied. 'English plumber, English builder, English carpenter, English gardener . . .'

'Gosh,' she said, and sipped some more wine. 'Well, you can rest assured that David and I won't be hiring anybody else.'

Bruno grumbled and lobbed another chunk of bread into his mouth, chewing it audibly. Remy mewled at Pen's feet, so she reached down to pet him again. By showing affection to Bennett's young protégé, by feeding him scraps and rubbing his coat, she felt she was doing some kind of service to his memory – demonstrating, to the dead dog's lingering spirit, that he had succeeded in altering her for the better.

'Monsieur Bowles . . . You have been married not long?'

'Not long at all,' Pen replied. 'We only met last year.'

'Ah,' he sighed, as if disappointed, and studied the grain of the oak tabletop. 'A romance.'

'Oh, I wouldn't say that,' she said (thinking, *Why* wouldn't I say that?). 'Did you know Mrs Bowles? The first Mrs Bowles, I mean.'

'Yes.' Bruno looked up at her and smiled – sadly, she thought. 'She was very nice lady, like you. But not *like* you. You see?'

'Mm,' she said, not entirely sure that she did see. 'I was also married before, but a long time ago. My husband, my first husband . . . We have two children, but they're grown up.'

He nodded, and lunged his lower lip forwards again.

'Do you have children, Bruno?'

He breathed in deeply, then he shook his head and let the air out through his nose, his eyes fixed on hers. Unabashed, but unforthcoming.

What, precisely, did she know of the mysterious Monsieur DeLambre, this man to whom she gave the run of her garden three times a week? Did he have any family at all? A woman answered his telephone: his wife? Some local floozy? Or just a friend who happened to be in the house the one time Pen had called? He was good with his hands: a natural in the kitchen, an accomplished planter and feller of trees and other flora, a practised erector of trelliswork. He'd restored the back door and a number of dining chairs, and had laid the stones for the terrace single-handed. (David had told her all this proudly, as if he ought to be admired for having paid another man to do his hard work.) She sometimes noticed him tinkering beneath the bonnet of his Land Rover, apparently au fait with complex mechanics, too. Where does one acquire so many manual talents? she asked herself.

Bruno was not a wealthy man, to judge by his car and his clothes – the jeans, the polo shirts – though, of course, that might merely be his work attire. His wages were modest. Remy, and the other dogs he professed to have owned, proved he was an animal lover. Pen had recently come to believe that this was a sign of good character, not of emotional incontinence or of poor personal hygiene, though Bruno was certainly guilty of the latter. He was significantly younger than Pen, she presumed, but his age remained indeterminate, shaded by the unmistakable effects of labour and vice. He smoked at any opportunity. To judge by his skin and this evening, he drank furiously. His weight and his skill in the kitchen suggested he ate well, too. And yet he seemed entirely unashamed of any of it, which made it all somehow forgivable. He was simple, hard-working and honest: the very best variety of Red Indian.

He emptied his pockets of smoking apparatus and began to make himself a cigarette, dextrously pinching and rolling the tobacco into a perfect little paper cylinder. He put it to his lips and picked up his lighter, looking to her at the last moment for her permission.

'Of course, of course,' she said, and stood to fetch an ashtray. The nearest suitable thing was a saucer from the drying rack, which she placed in front of him, and breathed in a noseful of his smoke. She hadn't had a cigarette in years, but the thick scent – as bitter and complex as the Domaine des Herbiers 2007 – was invigorating.

'May I?' she asked as she sat across from him again.

'*Bien sûr*,' he replied, sliding the paraphernalia towards her. She grimaced; she'd rarely smoked roll-ups, and never rolled them personally – even at art school, she'd had family money to fund her negligible Silk Cut habit.

'*Bon*,' he said, understanding, and started to roll a second cigar-ette, keeping his own balanced on that prominent lip. Then he propped it on the rim of the saucer so as to run his tongue along the fresh Rizla paper. Silently, he handed her the finished cigarette, lighting it for her as she leaned across the table towards him.

Pen inhaled, and immediately felt light-headed. She recalled her drug use in the far-off years before responsibility, remem-bering how changeable her reactions could be from one joint to the next: sometimes relaxed and garrulous, others silently para-noid. Now, brain hazy with plain tobacco, she felt as though she'd been lifted free of grief and despondence. She laughed a little to herself, breathing the smoke out slowly and watching it twist in the light.

'Thank you, Bruno,' she said.

Bruno finished his cigarette and stubbed it out mercilessly on the fine porcelain. Pen reached over to pull the saucer closer to her but, without warning, he quickly clasped her hand in both of his. She flinched, feeling the softness of her own skin contextualised by his coarse palms.

'We must try to be happy,' he said, the heavy clouds of his accent clearing for an instant, as he held her gaze assuredly.

Desire lanced through her, making her giddy. Or was that the cigarette? He left her hand resting limp on the table again, beside the smouldering saucer. Whatever did he mean? Did 'we' refer to all humanity, or just the two of them? What was 'happy', in any case? And how did he suggest 'we' ought to go about it?

Just as she felt they might come to some understanding on that final point, Bruno stood abruptly and took up his now-empty box from the worktop. Remy, alert to his master's every whim, jumped to attention. Pen was breathless. The handyman seemed agitated, and stared for a second or more at the dirty pan, still cooling on the stove, as if he were deciding whether or not he should offer to do the washing-up. It was almost midnight.

'*Bonsoir, madame*,' he said. And then he walked briskly out, to the terrace and to his jeep – leaving Pen alone in the house, her cigarette half-smoked.

11

David, when he called, was reliably ineffectual.

'Oh, dear,' he kept saying. 'Oh, dear. You poor thing.'

It would be more than a week until his next visit, and a change of plans was quite out of the question: one of his clients was expanding into North America, and his feet had hardly touched the ground. But he sounded pleased with Pen's choice of burial plot, and passed on his thanks to Mr DeLambre for having done the necessary spadework. She didn't tell him about Bruno's dinner, nor that she had lain awake for hours, imagining the handyman's manly hands roving across her haunches and flanks. In her fantasy, the previous evening would have ended where it began: in the kitchen, on the broad farmhouse table. A reclaimed refectory antique, made from sturdy Provençal oak. She felt sure it would have taken their weight, hers and the Frenchman's.

Bruno was not due to tend her lawns again until Thursday, so she'd spent the daylight hours alone, in a state of frustrated distraction, yearning for the uninvited Land Rover to appear on the driveway once more. If anything, this high anxiety was harder to endure than the self-pity of the previous day. She was certain something had passed between them at the kitchen table, helped along by the heady melange of wine and smoke and just-foraged fungi. She turned the evening's events over in her mind, analysing their exchange – what she could recall of it, when sober – from every conceivable perspective. He'd visited on the pretext of sympathy for her loss, but Pen knew men better than that. If

Bruno had a wife to whom he intended to be faithful, then he would surely have mentioned her, even brought her with him for dinner. Then again, if he were unmarried, why the sudden departure? So sudden, in fact, that he'd left behind his leather jacket, which still hung on the back of a kitchen chair. Pen furtively checked its pockets, finding nothing but crumpled cigarette papers.

Fearful of sentimentality, she collected Bennett's things and put them in a black refuse bag, which she tied and deposited in a dark corner of the barn. His food and water bowls, his half-finished bags of meal, his handful of mangy toys. A bone. A blanket. A beanbag. Her dog had been happy to lead a spartan life. Admirable, really. If only she could be so free of frippery. She passed an hour staring at herself in the mirror, toying with her hair, reassuring herself that yes, she was still an attractive woman, and that Bruno's attentions would be well deserved. She gazed obsessively at his telephone number on David's emergency list: a sheet of lined A4 notepaper, fixed to the kitchen cork-board with a drawing pin at each corner, the names and numbers spelled out in her husband's prim, jam-label handwriting. What if the woman answered Bruno's phone again? She couldn't quite bring herself to dial it and find out.

In the afternoon she took herself over to the Cutlers' in the Passat, to deliver a copy of *The House on the Hill 4: The Wheelbarrow and the Watermelons*. The children said thank you in their adorably accented English, and Maz, their mother – seeing Pen was somehow preoccupied – asked her whether everything was all right. She'd been fantasising about Bruno again, but she used the moment to break the news of Bennett's death. Maz offered Pen a hug, and said she would decide how to tell the children herself, in her own time. Pen said she thought that was a good idea, and then finished her coffee.

Her appetite had deserted her, and she ate little. Some bread, cheese and a dollop of David's tomato-and-chilli jam were all she could manage for lunch. She'd never felt so self-conscious with David, so unsure of herself, so disconcerted by desire. And for whom? The fat gardener! Hardly your typical dashing Frog. Perhaps this was all just some pathetic Lady Chatterley fantasy, though he made an entirely unconvincing Mellors. Or was it all in her head, like Adela at the Marabar caves in *A Passage to India*, imagining sexual motives in the behaviour of an upstanding local? Recalling Bruno's talk of Red Indians, she thought of *Dances With Wolves*: the suicidal frontiersman, who falls for a squaw and goes native. She recalled, wretchedly, having been unmoved when they killed Kevin Costner's animals at the end.

Would she feel this attraction in another context? If Bruno were some itinerant continental labourer, say, laying down decking in the garden at Highbury? Certainly not. She couldn't imagine raising the subject with her London friends and being taken remotely seriously. But perhaps that was the point: Fran wasn't here to judge her. Who was? Not even the dog. She was alone with her cravings. And in a world without consequences, sex was suddenly ever-present. If a woman sleeps with her gardener and there's nobody around to hear her, does she make a sound? Yes, she guessed: Yes, yes, yes.

Pen had never been fucked by a Frenchman. God, she'd only ever been *made love to* by Brits. As a student, she'd prided herself on being pretty racy, but that was mostly an act. She'd slept with an Irishman with whom she briefly shared a room in a squat near Notting Hill Gate – what was his name again? Conor? Kieran? – in a decade when consorting with the Irish was thought of as rather dangerous. In fact, she'd suspected him of being English all along, and putting on Irishness so as to stir the loins of impressionable young women. Then there was Alec the Jamaican, whom she'd petted heavily to see if the rumours were true. (They were, but, being nineteen and a touch naive, she'd stopped short of fourth base.)

Jerry had been a clumsy but adorable lover: never quite the screw he aspired to be, rarely the womaniser that his worst friends would have encouraged. In the decade between husbands, she'd barely been made love to at all, unless you counted that abortive fumble with Fran's ex-husband, which Fran must *never, ever* find out about. Oh, and Tony Glassop had snogged her in the back of a taxi after offering her his shoulder to cry on. She'd seen it coming – invited it, really – but then instantly regretted it, and refused to allow him into the house. What if this was it? What if these were her final pangs of sexual yearning, the very last of lust?

So when David had phoned – as ever, at the stroke of eight – Pen delivered the news, and he responded with stiff solicitousness. She assured him that she was in good spirits, and – as soon as he'd changed the subject, asking her to pick some greengages for his next batch of jam – she lied and said her supper was burning.

It was approaching dusk when she first heard the rumble from the far end of the driveway; she was sitting on the terrace, watching cirrus clouds and picking at a tomato salad. A forbiddingly large wasp hovered close by, probing the lilac. With Pavlovian certainty, she identified the sound as that of Bruno's Land Rover. She hurried inside, clenched by terror and desire, planning to pour herself another glass of Clos du Saint-Sebastian 2009 (citrus, herbs) and drink it before he could discover her there, trembling at the table. She heard his dragging footsteps come to a halt at the kitchen door.

'*Bonsoir, madame.*'

She'd managed to pour a half-glass, spilling a few drops on the tabletop with shaky hands, and she took a large mouthful before turning to face him.

'Good evening, Bruno,' she croaked, a parody of seductiveness.

The handyman's features were flushed. He had nothing with him to explain his presence: no box of mushrooms, no gravedigging invoice. His green polo shirt was as grubby as ever, the crest embroidered over his heart – of some country club or amateur sports team or cheap clothing designer – obscured by grime. Remy stood loyally beside him, tail bobbing against the door jamb. Bruno seemed out of breath, and his deep inhalations duetted with the dog's crazed panting. Pen took another mouthful of wine, so big that it required two gulps to swallow.

'Was there something—?'

'I am sorry, is late,' he interrupted her, taking a step into the room so that they were just a foot or so from one another. 'I was all day in the garden of Madame Garnett, at Puygaillard.'

Pen felt again their remoteness from the rest of her world, the plains and hills and cities and seas that separated her from consequence or repercussion. She put her glass on the table. Bruno looked at her with hangdog eyes – Bennett eyes – and at once she saw through the blotchy, middle-aged face to the young man and the little boy beyond. The wine had done its work on her again. She rushed across the few inches of terracotta quarry tile that separated them, and hurled her mouth into his.

Her eyes were determinedly closed, but she felt Bruno flinch and pull away. Perhaps, though, she'd simply bruised his lips with the force of her kiss, because after a long, yawning instant of uncertainty, his unwieldy arms closed around her, and his jaw softened into the caress. Good God, it was happening. It was really happening. Her continental smelled not of garlic or fine wine or fresh bread, but of dog hairs, soil, stale tobacco. They snogged and groped and slurped, affronting the very fundamentals of French kissing. When finally they separated for a second, to look at one another for confirmation of what was to come, his eyes were blank with lust.

Like a pair of arthritic waltzers, Pen taking the lead, they shuffled together to the table, where she clambered backwards to balance her buttocks on its edge. Bruno reached hairily into her skirts and found her knickers, dragging them south to her knees. She'd put on Rigby and Peller underwear, in preposterous anticipation of just such an eventuality; the choice now seemed entirely immaterial. And then, Christ, he was lapping at her, his thumb circling her arsehole. Her right arm went out from under her in shock, spanking the pepper grinder straight off the table and to the floor, where it cracked in two and sent scores of black peppercorns scurrying away over the quarry tiles. Remy yelped and pounced at them excitedly. Pen bunched Bruno's thick, curly hair in her fist and spasmed again, against her will. He roared and reared up, clutching his scalp.

'My God, I'm sorry,' she said, but he silenced her with another graceless kiss. She could smell herself on his snout. He pulled her knickers the rest of the way down, till they dangled off one ankle; while he was distracted with that indelicate operation, Pen moved the wine glass to another corner of the table so as not to shatter it accidentally in the throes of passion. Thank heaven for Pilates, she thought, as she splayed her legs to greet his advance.

Her sleeveless linen blouse had fiddly buttons, and it took Bruno too many seconds to open the top two, so he resorted to wrenching the remainder of the garment downwards until it came to rest around her middle. In his increasing haste, he failed to properly unclasp her bra, and liberated just one of her breasts. With her second nipple stubbornly refusing to reveal itself, they moved on to Bruno's trousers instead. Pen tried clumsily to unbuckle his belt, but he batted her hands away and did it himself, letting the shabby jeans collapse to his ankles. She thought of the dark-capped *tête de nègre* as she pulled his erection from his briefs, thick and shortish and veiny like its owner. Bruno's hands rubbed and poked in search of the appropriate orifice, and then, with a mutual shudder, he thrust his way in.

126

Pen, ecstatic, lay back on the kitchen table as the handyman lunged at her again and again. She felt his belly moving against her own through the scrunched blouse, a rough palm on her sole free breast. He grunted like the wild boar she often heard in the woods behind the farmhouse at night, tilling the earth in search of truffles. A tiny moth fluttered into the light bulb above her, which seemed to brighten and dim rhythmically. The kitchen table. It had to be the kitchen table. The wood squeaked against itself in sympathy, quivering and scraping incrementally across the floor. Pen fought against the question of whether it would take their weight after all, and whether it would leave scratches on the terracotta. She gripped Bruno's short, grizzly neck with one hand, and with the other clung moaning to the edge of the tabletop. His leather jacket, she saw, still hung over the back of one of the kitchen chairs. Could it be that he'd come merely to collect it?

In her abstracted state, she only now became aware that she'd left her Le Creuset stoneware butter dish out in the afternoon heat. She could see it on the worktop, beyond reach, as Bruno's eager convulsions rocked her back and forth across the Provençal oak. It would have softened to slurry by now, in the heat. The butter. The butter in the butter dish. The butter. The butter dish. The butter dish. The butter dish. The BUTTER dish. THE BUTTER DISH. THE. BUTTER. DISH. THE! BUTTER! DISH!THEBUTTERDISHTHEBUTTERDISHTHEBUT-TERDISHTHEBUTTERDISHTHEBUTTERDISHTHEBUT-TERDISHTHEBUTTtterdish.

12

Isobel turned the warm sand with her flip-flop and thought about crop yields. A single dune separated her from the rest of the New Year revellers, but that was enough to put her at the far tip of civilisation, beyond the point where the world met the wilderness. The landscape shifted and stirred relentlessly, imperceptibly, pointlessly: sand, and then more sand. Here was the earth without water or trees, without grasses, animals, birds, humanity. Even the light was fading, the desert horizon dissolving into dusk. Creation in reverse.

She imagined the grey-brown wastes as blank pixels, primed to welcome squares of digital corn, virtual soya beans, make-believe maize. In her head she conjured ploughs, feed troughs, hydroponic fertilisation apparatus. Row upon row of fences, pen after pen of poultry and pigs. Her farm was still in its infancy but I22y, her avatar, had recently hired five new hands to build a second barn. If she harvested enough barley next week, she'd raise sufficient Acres coins for a horse. And with one horse to drag a plough, she'd turn fields faster, earning more coins in less time. Her second horse would come easily. Then she could begin to think about fruit and veg.

She emptied the rest of her gin cocktail onto the sand, where it made a sickly blue smear. She'd never been much of a drinker: she'd watched her mum and dad embarrass themselves that way one too many times. The lemon wedge slid out of the glass with the ice and hit the ground, soundless. It looked odd there, wilted on the desert floor – a singular item of once-living, biodegradable matter – and she instinctively thought to pick it up. Litterbug. Would it even rot out here, in this climate, or mummify? Or would it be consumed by a colony of resourceful insects? She kicked over the spot until the fruit and the blue gunge were obscured.

It always required unexpected effort to climb a dune, each step sinking back halfway to the last. Her flip-flops and her flowery maxi-dress compounded the difficulty. When she reached the top of the rise, she stopped to catch her breath. The breeze carried tiny, stinging sand grains. In the far distance, the chrome spires of downtown glinted in the Gulf sunset. Closer, the highway tarmacadam shimmered with the preserved heat of the afternoon. And below her, in the well of the great wave of sediment, there slumbered a pride of SUVs.

She could hear the shouts of the Bedouin as they set about raising the last of the marquees. (They were always 'Bedouin', these desert caterers, but Isobel was never entirely sure what that meant. Half of them were clearly subcontinental. Some of them had turned up in a Mercedes G-Class.) She could smell meat cooking on makeshift barbecues. Two of the men were lighting a circle of torches, two more trying to force a low table level on the shapeless ground. Vast, intricate carpets had been unrolled to fashion a floor, plump cushions arranged in place of chairs. And on the dining tables: candelabra, flowers, fruit platters. Under one of the canopies was a DJ booth, with coloured disco lights and a not-insubstantial sound system. Presently it was playing gentle Arabian muzak, but there would be dancing later, and Isobel would be expected to take part.

Bankers and their wives clustered around the cool-boxes at the drinks bar, always any such encampment's first completed construction. She could pick out Tor from a distance in the half-dark without even trying: he was the tallest, and the most blond.

He chose that moment to turn and look up at her, silhouetted against the orange sky. He waved, and she waved back – but tentatively, from her waist, not wishing to attract undue attention. Then she shuffled crabwise down the slope towards him.

There was a burst of laughter as she approached. The white males of Dubai were always laughing. Laughing or drinking, or eating or swearing or leering or pissing or shitting. Isobel blushed, as if it were at her expense, but she needn't have. A balding Australian with a goatee was talking about the Burj. (When they weren't laughing or drinking, they were talking about the Burj.) Tom Cruise had just been filming a movie there; up near the summit, with wires and a helicopter. The Australian's audience chugged their lagers and listened for a punchline.

'. . . So this mate of mine works for the developers. And he's got the job of taking visitors to the top. Sounds bloody great, I know. This is like two years ago we're talking. Tower's passing a hundred and forty storeys, something like that. And there's no glass, no shell. Just the concrete guts and that eight-hundred-metre drop. And before he agrees to take me up there, he asks me am I afraid of heights? Okay, I think: he's considering my mental welfare. But no, I told him, I'm not: I've done two skydives and a bungee jump, but thanks for your fackn concern!'

Goatee put a hand in the air, to forestall the incipient laughter. He wasn't done yet. As Isobel lingered at the back of the group, an over-conscientious Bedouin ('Bedouin') waiter thrust another gin cocktail into her hand. She tried to object, but the man looked so eager to please, desperate even, that she felt obliged to accept it.

'. . . And he says, "It's not you I'm worried about. It's me."
See, people with vertigo get up that high and something happens to them. They get this uncontrollable urge to jump. It's insane, I know. And the month before, this fella tells me, he'd taken some lady up there. Big, y'know? Real *fat* chick. And she's chilling,

she's fine – till they step out at floor one-four-zero, or whatever. Suddenly, she's making for the edge!'

The laughter began to build, as goatee mimed grappling with his imaginary fat chick. His shirt hung open to reveal his stomach, of which he really ought to have been less proud.

'. . . So she's jogging towards the void, right? And my friend has to fackn rugby-tackle this lady and wrestle her to the ground! Said it was like harpooning a whale, like Moby fackn Dick! He had to get two more guys to help carry her back to the lift. Three guys, it took. Three big guys. Sheila just lost her shit, y'know?'

They were all laughing now, the bankers' puce, mottled features distorting with hilarity, their wives' fake tits jiggling. Isobel forced a smile so as not to appear uncharitable.

'. . . And now, he says, if anybody admits they're just the tiniest bit afraid of heights, he has to chain them to him, in case they try to take the plunge! I know! *Chain* 'em. And he's a big guy, like six foot something. But he says there's no way he's taking me up there if I'm a risk. He says, "Brian. You are a large fella. You try to jump, you're gonna pull me down with you!"'

A final, cresting roll of laughter. Brian-with-the-goatee slapped a nearby male colleague on the back, clearly overjoyed with his story's reception. Some of the bankers were gasping for breath, so utterly fucking side-splitting had they found it. Except Tor. Tor stood just two men apart from Brian: six foot three and unselfconsciously unmoved, his blank German features conspicuous above the heads of those around him. Tor rarely laughed. She loved that. If something wasn't funny, he refused to patronise it with false amusement. His eyes met hers, and he moved towards her through the group. His shirt was open just enough to show his tanned, hairless chest. He had on shorts and plimsolls, divided by long, bronzed legs. Beautiful man, she thought, for maybe the millionth time.

'Where'd you go?'

'Just a little walk.'

'Find anything interesting?'

Tor didn't smile, but he was joking. Probably. A hand appeared, gripping his shoulder, followed by the ruddy face of the storyteller.

'Well, this must be the famous Mrs Meier,' the man said, still grinning with pride. He removed his hand from Tor's shirt and held it out for Isobel to shake: 'How are ya, darln?'

His palm was clammy; fair enough – hers was, too. Isobel smiled and muttered hello. The man, Brian, pumped her hand firmly, holding her gaze as if to demonstrate fascination. He was probably forty-five-ish, but booze and excessive tanning had conspired to confuse the ageing process. His hair loss was unfortunate; the beard, unforgivable.

'Isobel,' said Tor, 'this is Brian. He is a Senior Fund Manager—'

'I'm his *boss*, is what I am! Right, Torsten?' he laughed. 'Isobel, a pleasure.'

Tor widened his eyes a fraction, as if to say, Yes, he is my boss – and, as you can tell, he's an idiot. Brian glanced at Isobel's tits, and then tried to disguise it by taking a long gulp of his lager. She had no feel for regional Australian accents – did Australia *have* regional accents? – but Brian somehow struck her as provincial, retrograde: as though maybe he'd grown up on a farm.

'Now,' he said, 'how is it we never see you two at our beach barbecues? You must've heard about our barbecues, Isobel. Torsten lock you in the house at weekends or something?'

He chuckled and clapped his free hand to Tor's chest. Isobel bristled proprietorially. She looked to her husband for some kind of plausible negative response to the invitation.

'Ah, well,' Brian continued, oblivious. 'I guess you guys have young kids, right? But seriously, bring 'em along, too. We have a pool, video games. Y'know? They'll *love* it.'

They were rescued, then, by the arrival of two more SUVs, which had swung off the road a few hundred yards away and were fast approaching the camp. Brian evidently knew their owners, because he yelled an ear-splitting 'Hey!', waved enthusiastically and walked in their direction without taking his leave of Tor and Isobel.

'So this is *his* party?' she asked.

'I'm afraid so,' said Tor.

Isobel hadn't much of an appetite, but she paced herself so as not to be seen to under-indulge. The forty or so guests, sagging ever further into fat cushions, poked down barbecued lamb, chicken boti, mutton kebabs, grilled prawns, halloumi, tabbouleh, raita, hummus, flatbreads, fruits, ice creams, baklava. They drank and drank: beer and wine and whisky and cocktails. Isobel had been placed between Tor and a young, rugby-shouldered accountant from Ireland, and she smiled and nodded as the man rambled on, his mouth full, about the idiosyncracies of expat living, the frustrations of business-class air travel.

All the while, she was thinking of her Acres farm. She'd neglected her smallholding for a few days over Christmas, stuck at the house in London *sans* twenty-four-hour Wi-Fi access, and returned to the Emirates to find she'd lost crops and coins as a result. The consequences of inattention were severe; she wouldn't make the same mistake again in a hurry. She calculated her plot's profit margins and growth forecasts, while her dinner companion weighed Etihad service against Emirates.

The waiters replaced the ravished dinner settings with shisha and oil-thick local coffee, the music increased in volume and vigour, couples rose to boogie arrhythmically – and before long, in the absence of any actual belly dancers, more than one man had laughingly displayed his own stomach and wobbled it back and forth. Tor, conscious of their reputation for antisociability, persuaded Isobel to gather up the hem of her dress and shimmy in time to some weary classics.

It was nearing midnight when she wandered out of the ring of torchlight towards the cars. Tor was trapped in a conversation about the commodities markets with one of his colleagues, and she'd begun to feel a chill in the desert air. She paused beside the Pathfinder to admire the clear night sky: the perfect moon, the pinprick stars, the wash of galaxies. Then she opened the passenger-side door and grabbed her Abercrombie hoodie from the front seat.

'Hey there,' said a voice near by. 'You must be Isobel.'

She slammed the car door shut as she turned to see who'd spoken, thus extinguishing the only light source in the vicinity. There was a woman leaning against the bonnet of a Land Cruiser. Her dark outline part-eclipsed the view back towards the camp.

'Erm, yes.'

'Sorry to startle you.' Another Australian accent. 'Came out here for a bit of quiet time.'

'Oh,' said Isobel, slipping on the hoodie and zipping it halfway up. 'Yeah, me too.'

The woman moved towards her to shake her hand, ice clinking in her glass. On the breeze came the awful sound of bankers singing along to Bruce Springsteen.

'I'm Shauna, by the way.'

'Isobel. But you knew that.'

'Darln, only because you're the one person here I've never seen before. That husband of yours is keeping you under wraps . . .' The woman gripped her arm conspiratorially, and Isobel could smell fish tikka on her breath as she stage-whispered, 'And I don't blame him; you're the most beautiful wife here!'

'Ha!' Isobel laughed, flattered in spite of herself. 'No, just the youngest, I think.'

That was true. There were bankers here who were younger than her, but they were all single men. Shauna laughed in reply, and then fell into step as Isobel sauntered back towards the light.

'You have kids, right? Twins? They must be gorgeous.'

'They are,' said Isobel, those proud-parent reflexes kicking in like always. 'Nothing to do with me, though. Blondies, like their dad.'

'Boys?'

'Yeah, two boys.'

Closer to the torchlight, she turned to look at Shauna again, and made out a turquoise blouse, white linen pants, and the features of a woman at the panicked beginnings of middle age. The excessive, corporate-wife make-up that Isobel could never bring herself to emulate; breasts of dubious provenance; complexion pink despite a deep, disconcerting tan. They paused at the edge of the party, between two flaming torches. A waiter materialised with a tray of champagne, and Shauna picked up a glass, putting her empty cocktail tumbler back on the tray. The man waited for Isobel to take one, too – which she did at last, reluctantly.

'We're lucky,' Shauna said, nodding towards the big Persian rug in front of the DJ booth, where an overweight man with no shirt on was attempting the caterpillar. 'Sheikh cancelled almost all the other desert parties. Somebody at the bank knows somebody.'

'Huh,' said Isobel, who'd heard as much from the news, and hoped in vain that she and Tor might earn a last-minute reprieve. She looked forward to his office's extracurricular get-togethers even less than he did, and managed to avoid almost all of them.

'Solidarity with Gaza, something like that,' Shauna went on. 'Honestly, I can't see why it should affect us. We're way out here in the desert! Nobody can even hear us. And anyway, *they're* the ones always making a racket – all that bloody praying!'

She tittered at her own joke, and Isobel smiled weakly. She knew she ought to object to Shauna's argument on the basis of cultural sensitivity, but she supposed it had a kind of brutal logic. Certainly, it concerned her that the Sheikh could cancel all fun on a whim. Brian, she now noticed, had been standing nearby listening, and he staggered over, whisky in hand.

'Fackn Emiratis. It's not like this is a bloody *mosque*, am I right?' He laughed, like a naughty schoolboy who'd flipped the bird at his headmaster's back. His accent had broadened under the influence. 'Oi mean, cahm on, these fackn Arabs just wonner squeeze another cash bribe out of us. 'S all about the money, baby!'

'You'll have to excuse my husband,' said Shauna. 'He cannot hold his drink.'

'Hey!' said Brian, objecting, and then put his arm around her and kissed her clumsily. She pushed him off and tutted, rolling her eyes for Isobel's benefit. Brian grinned and stumbled away to the tables.

'Y'know, we should hang out sometime,' said Shauna.

'Yeah,' said Isobel, nodding, meaning 'No.'

'I'm *serious*. Brian always speaks so highly of Torsten. It can get pretty lonely here without friends. Do you work?'

'Not exactly,' Isobel replied, meaning 'Not at all.'

Shauna smiled at her, almost pityingly. But they were interrupted by the noise of Brian, and a swelling chorus, counting down loudly from ten, nine, eight, seven . . . Then Tor was walking towards her with long, even strides, making sure to be beside his wife for a kiss when the New Year finally came.

They were supposed to stay the night – the first of 2011 – out there in the desert on that temporary 'Bedouin' encampment, but neither of them wanted to. The first time they'd met was at a brunch; the only two people in the whole hotel dining room who weren't drunk. Isobel didn't like to drink, and Tor's constitution staunchly resisted intoxication, no matter how much alcohol he consumed. Now, once again, they were the only sober guests at a party – apart from the catering staff, who observed their clients' grotesque antics bemusedly. Some time before 1.30, Isobel and

Tor agreed they'd done their duty and strolled back across the sand to the Pathfinder.

Isobel had drunk the least, and insisted on driving. She wanted to get home and water her barley fields. The a/c came on hard as soon as she turned the key in the ignition. She kicked off her flip-flops in the footwell, put the jeep in gear and guided it over the uneven ground to the empty highway. She liked to drive late at night, headlights playing across the clear black tarmac. Normally, the roads were a nightmare: terror, or gridlock. People here thought safety was Allah's concern, but Isobel didn't believe in Allah, and she thought safety ought to be the concern of the Emirati boy racers in the fast lane, or the speed-freak bus drivers in the slow lane. When you weren't steering clear of collisions, there was the chaotic road planning to contend with. The streets kept changing as the city sprawled. You couldn't get a handle on the place. Taxi drivers, twenty years' resident, got lost all the time: tied up in traffic cones, diverted by unexplained road barriers, foiled by incomplete avenues that just gave up and gave in to the rubble of the desert edge.

13

The rectangular plot that held their rented home had first belonged to the desert, and to the shuffling groups of genuine Bedouin who criss-crossed its unforgiving expanse. The sand had no care for days or years, but at some arbitrary moment a seaside village was crafted from the mud at the mouth of a creek that whispered away into nowhere. The people were resourceful: when the *daba* locust descended, they cooked and ate it; the insects were a feast, not a plague – and they gave the village its name. Fishers and traders and smugglers came, pearl divers and Islam. The calendared Portuguese laid violent claim to the land; then the French, the Dutch and the English, who saw intangible value in this stretch of barren, blistering coastal real estate partway to the Raj. A sheikh was negotiated with, treaties signed, and the desert took on a kind of worth that any visitor could comprehend: dollars and dirhams and pounds.

The Sheikh established holding companies, hired property contractors, constructed towers and a taxless economy. The creek was bridged, fresh water was drilled, streets were paved and electricity generated to power televisions, fridge-freezers, financial exchanges. The old town was scuffed away like litter in the scrub, bazaars and *barastis* kicked over by golf courses and shopping malls and water parks. The world's cranes converged on the Emirate, which grew up and then out into unchecked suburbs of so-called ranches and faux-Moorish McMansions. And two years ago, as the twins tussled in Isobel's belly, Tor had consulted a rental agency and picked theirs from a thick brochure of near-uniform residential tracts.

The plaster facade of the villa in Blue Sky Grove, its jutting beams and artful curves, were a kind of homage to the mud forts of the pre-modern era, an Arabian mock Tudor. When they'd moved in, Tor left the decorating to Isobel, who decided not to do any, on the unspoken understanding that the Emirate was a temporary home, and that they'd return to Munich or London in due course. She retained the white walls and the off-white carpets, said 'whatever' to the sterile, generic furniture that was already there, and took a day trip to Ikea to purchase the necessary extras. Their appliances were unlovely but ultra-functional. The water ran clean. The fuses never blew. Into the garage went the Pathfinder, the Audi A4 and Tor's rowing machine. They hired the gardener from an agency (though it would've been simpler and cheaper to have had no plants at all). And they hired Carmen from another, trusting her unquestioningly with their keys, their kitchen and their toddlers.

If someone had asked Isobel for her five-year plan – beginning, for the sake of argument, some time after university graduation, and ending here, at twenty-eight – then okay, she wouldn't have picked this destination: a home on the rim of the tropics, a husband, children. Not because she didn't want that, exactly, but because it would've been so far beyond her frame of reference. And because, when she was shortlisted for Feature Writer of the Year at the 2004 *Guardian* Student Media Awards, she'd assumed the universe had set her a different assignment.

She didn't win the prize, but her report for the campus tabloid on the alcoholic misadventures of the Student Union executive committee had been quoted extensively in a follow-up piece by the *Daily Mail* about the '*Booze Shame of Britain's Students*', and described (by her undergrad editor, in the awards submission) as a tour de force. Soon enough, she imagined, one or more national newspapers would offer her a platform from which to condemn the evils of Tesco, or rail against the dastardly foreign policy of the New Labour government. Though such things rarely stoked any sincere passion or anger in her heart, she knew in her head that they were important, and that to write about them would be admirable and worthwhile. Honestly, she probably cared more about the latest plot twist in *24* than she did about climate change. But she wanted to be a serious person, she really did.

What actually happened, though, was that she was offered a year-long graduate traineeship at a B2B journal for the interior design trade, covering the designer furniture beat. She blinked and she'd been there eighteen months, bullshitting about hand-made Danish dining sets when all she could afford for herself were Swedish flat-packs. So she quit in a spasm of self-pity, and went on to endure another year of underpaid, under-appreciated freelancing, supplemented with shifts at a pub on Essex Road. Occasionally, she spent a fruitless fortnight on work experience at a broadsheet or a glossy women's mag, where she'd transcribe another journalist's tedious celebrity interview, or laboriously type out TV listings – only to be told, with a consolatory shrug, that there was little likelihood of a permanent (or semi-permanent) position opening up, and that no, they did not pay their interns' expenses.

Without the structure of school or college terms, the seasons flew by seamlessly, adulthood overtaking her before she'd the time or the means to prepare for it. Conrad was away at university by then, and living alone with her mum was becoming an embarrassment. She'd never repainted her bedroom's lilac walls, never taken down her Britpop posters or clip-framed gap year photo-collages. Pen was both pushy and needy: wanting her to leave, not wanting to be left. Isobel worried they'd develop some sort of symbiotic, spinsterish mother-daughter support system. So for pride's sake, she moved out of her old room in the house on the Hill, and into one half its size in a shared flat in Hackney. By the time her double bed and BILLY bookcase were in, there wasn't space for much else.

Over time – as she waited glumly for delayed Tube trains, got jostled in teeming pubs, swore at the faulty self-checkout machines in Tesco – she grew to resent London's crowds, its rents, its emotionally charged weather. Her student debts weren't exactly going away. So when a friend of a friend offered her a job on a start-up culture weekly in the Gulf, she scrounged the airfare from her dad and packed a bag.

She could barely raise her arm to hail a taxi from the airport terminal in the thirty-something-degree heat. Jonathan, the friend of the friend, had warned her the traffic was pure terror – but, if she were to be horribly maimed in a pile-up, the hospitals were swank. Sure enough, as his speedometer nudged 70, her cab driver delivered an unbroken, near-unintelligible ten-minute monologue about his decision to move here from (she thought) Yemen, without once studying the road ahead. She resolved to ask him no further questions, and to ignore his driving and that of the other swerving vehicles on the seven-lane highway. She raised her gaze instead to the pitiless blue sky. Who waters all the palm trees, she wondered, and where does the water come from?

She jacked the a/c right up in her hotel room as soon as she arrived in one piece. And she did the same when she moved into a rented studio flat of her own the following week. It was on the fourth floor of a nearly-new tower block, with satellite TV, a communal pool and a small balcony perfect for sunbathing. She returned from her first trip to the Emirates Mall with a bagful of bikinis. Frankly, Hackney could go fuck itself.

Dubai was a chance to go wild while her twenties peaked. She'd always been sort of a square at heart, but she struggled against type to embrace the whirl of pool parties and karaoke nights. She gamely joined Jonathan and friends for Friday brunches in the big hotels while the locals were at prayer, to watch her fellow Westerners gorge themselves on seafood and champagne. By day she dressed modestly so as not to offend any religious sensibilities; by night, she went clubbing in short skirts at the Ayer's Rock and the London Underground. She shagged a couple of yuppies and afterwards blamed the booze, though in fact she was sober for most of it, and suspected herself of wanting a story to tell the other mag staffers. There wasn't much else to talk about.

Even on her modest salary, she had sufficient disposable income to hire a daily. Isn't it amazing, asked the other expatriates at the brunches and the barbecues: isn't the Lifestyle amazing? By the Lifestyle, she guessed they meant the maids, the gardeners, the drivers waiting in Bugattis and Bentleys and Lexae while their masters shopped for designer sunglasses or reproduction art. The sprawling themed malls, where the service was so good it was scary, where bored sales assistants spent their days folding Armani and forming dead smiles for foreigners. The bargain knock-offs at Karama market, where she acquired most of her pirated DVDs. The blissfully cheap curries at Ravi's in Satwa. The strange, compromised taste of a halal Big Mac. The heat. The wind. The water. The beach. The harmonious citizenry sourced from every nation on earth. The leader fabled for personally distributing wealth to his people. That was the Lifestyle. And yeah, it was kind of amazing.

Sometimes the rock was lifted to reveal the lice beneath, like when human faeces washed up on the beach because the sewage treatment facilities were too clogged with waste; or when gleaming new residential/retail developments sat empty and powerless because the electricity grid spread too slowly to match the housing boom. The English-language papers reported these PR shitshows sparingly, but Isobel became acutely aware of her reliance on technology to exist: the shipping network that brought fresh produce from far away; the a/c that kept her cool in defiance of the climate. If the desalination plants that made the seawater drinkable were to fail, the taps would run dry in a week, and she'd have to drink the swimming pool.

Her inner Pulitzer-winner might've been troubled by the toxic sludge that came as a by-product of hydrating the city. To build the Palm Jebel Ali, they'd destroyed a coral reef. Her beloved a/c accounted for most of the Emirate's summer energy use. She was contributing to the world's biggest per capita ecological footprint. No one walked anywhere, everyone drove. And then there was the politics, or lack of it: no voting, no opposition. She'd never once heard anyone, even a Westerner, criticise the man whose benevolent face watched them steadily from his countless official portraits.

But Isobel tried not to stop and think about these things too profoundly. Make hay while the sun shines, etc. It was easy enough, when life itself was so easy. She'd been hired to write about culture, not politics. And face it, she told herself, you're not a serious person. The allure of the trivial was too strong, too persuasive.

Nobody was here for democracy, anyway; they were here for the money. That went for the blue-overalled South Asians who built the skyscrapers, as much as for the pinstriped business class who occupied them; it was true of the Filipina maids and the Iranian developers and the Kyrgyzstani hookers; of the rare, unsmiling Emiratis and their fat, rude kids.

Still, it soon became clear to everyone at Jonathan's culture weekly that there wasn't much culture in the city besides the crap nightclubs. Like everything else, culture was imported: Hollywood movies, Premier League football. The weather might be an improvement, but there was no theatre, no museums, scant music to suit Western tastes, and precious few galleries that exhibited anything worth writing about. The magazine folded in a little under a year.

As she cleared her desk, Isobel thought she might try to sell some pieces about the scandalous treatment of workers, or of the environment, to British publications. All the best journos in town were just passing through on the way to a war zone; the rest were too wary of the Sheikh to write anything boat-rocking. Maybe, she mused, she'd be the one to break that implicit embargo. But she never got beyond sending a couple of speculative emails to foreign desks in London, both of which went unanswered. And besides, by then she was knocked up.

Torsten was here for the money, too. He worked in the private equity department of a multinational bank. Bankers chatted Isobel up all the time in the nearby hotel bars, each of them as subtle as a caps-locked status update: I AM DESPERATE. But her future husband was the first one she'd hit on herself, over Friday brunch at the Desert Well. She'd never seen the tall, beautiful blond man before, standing alone by the buffet with his modest plate of food. Jonathan fairly launched her in his direction.

'Not a fan of the terrine?' she said, indicating, with a tilt of her flute of Buck's Fizz, the untouched heap of salmon on his plate. He looked at her, then at the terrine.

'Actually, the food is very nice,' said the *Übermensch*. 'But the people are quite boring.'

She giggled and tossed her hair. God, I'm *outrageous*, she thought. And then flushed as his face remained resolutely straight. Wait. Was he not joking?

'I'm Torsten,' he said, wiping his fingers on a napkin to shake her hand. 'And you are . . . ?'

He took her parasailing the next weekend. He seemed to feel no fear, but Isobel's terror was an aphrodisiac, and she let him fuck her senseless afterwards. Their first date. He gave so little away that she wasn't sure whether to expect a second. But they bonded over their mutual craving for the cool of air-con. She wouldn't have called him charming, exactly: he declined to laugh at almost anything, which made it hard to tell if he was teasing or not. (It'd never occurred to her just how much the wheels of conversation were greased by inane laughter.) But she found his blankness a kind of comfort, a symptom of strength. And as she burrowed down into his personality, she thought she glimpsed deep, hidden seams of humour and warmth. She ached for him, even after the first time, and the second; months later, she was still awed by his lean, tanned body atop her, beneath her, inside her. Beautiful man. Beautiful fucking man.

Of course, they could've been more careful. Work visas were wedded to employment. So when she broke the news to Tor – I've lost my job; we're having twins – he knew precisely what it meant. He didn't get angry or upset. The opposite, in fact. He was the son of schoolteachers: unselfish, a rock. And maybe a little bit in love with her, too. Everything happened so fast. Jonathan delayed his flight home to give her away. Isobel was either blissfully happy, or in shock. Or both. Either way, the day was a blur. That whole year was a blur.

Jonathan wasn't the only one leaving. The crash had come to the Gulf. It hushed the city, halting the construction cranes, silencing the Sheikh's boasts, devastating the oil price. The rest of the magazine's staff, just about anyone Isobel called friends; within a couple of months, they were gone. She was left alone with the lifers. The gold rush was over, and all that remained were a handful of delusional prospectors, sieving through the mud of the creek-bed.

Tor insisted there was still money around. His department survived the worst. He didn't make as much as Isobel had assumed bankers made; he was still some kind of junior, waiting for the right pay grade. But this cheered her up, made her think his motives must somehow be noble: a non-wanker banker. He wasn't being selfish. He stayed simply to earn what he needed to take care of his wife, his sons. He found them the villa to rent in Blue Sky Grove. And the hospitals, Isobel soon discovered, truly were swank. Suddenly, her life was small again. She kept to the house with the newborn twins, willing them to be big enough for the beach, the water park at the Atlantis Palm, or the ice rink at the Mall, the places she used to go at weekends with Jonathan and the culture club.

But, for now, they just stared: at the television – they adored Japanese-style game shows, strangely calmed by the bodily harm to which contestants were subjected; or at her – quietly, mouths smeared with organic baby food, like tiny, Teutonic secret police officers awaiting a misstep. Funny. They were Meiers, not Manvilles. They didn't look like hers, with their perfect blond hair and blue eyes. They didn't even sound like hers; when they began to burble words, they did so with the indistinct accent of the international crèche. Before they'd even finished their frequent and arduous bouts of breastfeeding, they seemed to have ceased to need her in any meaningful psychological way. After all, they had each other. They were a self-sufficient unit: fascinating and duplicating one another to the exclusion of their parents. Isobel loved them, though. She was their mother, wasn't she? Jesus: she was their *mother*.

Pregnancy had given her a glow, but she was left with extra flesh. And when she studied herself some time after the birth, she could see the crow's feet starting to form at the corners of her eyes. Her breasts were losing their former firmness. She daren't study the backs of her thighs in the bathroom mirror, for fear of encroaching cellulite. She saw Jerry and Pen in her own features. Whoa, she thought, reeling: that is when you *know* you're getting old. Jogging in 40-degree heat helped with the weight loss. But now, as she drove past the cosmetic surgery clinics on Jumeirah Road, she began to understand their allure.

Isobel had been sick of the house on the Hill, but just occasionally she got nauseous with not being there, in her old room, with the lilac walls and the Britpop posters and the clip-framed gap year photo-collages. She even missed London's rain: months went by here without a drop. And okay, sure, it was the Lifestyle, but it didn't always feel like a life. Oh, for fuck's sake, she thought, whenever she caught herself complaining. Am I turning into my mum?

She managed to place some bland and uncritical articles about Emirates property with foreign publications. She blagged a handful of hotel reviews for in-flight magazines: a chance to leave the kids with Carmen and spend a complimentary night at the Desert Palm or the Royal Mirage, where she and Tor snatched glimpses of the romance that had so quickly receded. At the Jumeirah Beach Hotel, scene of some of their first furious couplings – and, just maybe, of the twins' conception – you could hear morning prayers from a nearby muezzin. It sounded like a reprimand, reminding the post-coital couple of their responsibilities. They collected their scattered underwear and the Pathfinder, and drove home.

LOAD-BEARING WALL

14

Jerry lurked in the driver's seat of the Lotus, watching the house. It was tricky to remain inconspicuous at the wheel of a rare vintage sports car, but he was doing his best. After downing his daily *Ppalleena!*, the second of the week (Tuesday), he'd thrown on some dark clothes and clip-on sunglasses, and driven over to Highbury. On the way, observing the traditions of the stake-out, he'd bought himself a large Americano, three sugar-glazed Krispy Kreme doughnuts, and a copy of *The Times* to hide behind, in case he was spotted by his quarry. It had been two hours now, and he was beginning to feel like a rotisserie chicken, twisting beneath the windscreen in the midday sun. There was nothing left of the doughnuts but crumbs in the footwell and, thanks to the coffee, nature called. Urinating, however, would require him to desert his post.

So far, the house had seen zero activity. He wondered whether he'd turned up early enough; it was possible some of the squatters had disappeared to day jobs, though he found it hard to imagine them actually working for a living. Regardless, he knew from his Internet research that there had to be at least one of them in the property at all times to retain possession. Soon after he'd parked, a couple of young blokes had walked up the street beside the car in casual clothes, chatting about Arsenal, and Jerry almost jumped out to confront them – but his nerve failed him, and they kept on walking past the house, innocent and oblivious.

He was hoping to catch one or two of the unsavoury occupants coming out, not going in. That way, he could follow them to a neutral location, where they'd be unable to retreat into the house to escape him. He also wanted to confront them somewhere relatively public, rather than be drawn into a fracas with a potentially dangerous young offender on this quiet street, bereft of witnesses. An adult, scared of kids: the world was upside down.

Frankly, it made Jerry sick to think that London had once more become a city one couldn't walk across at will, without fear of being stabbed in broad daylight by some child wearing a hooded sweatshirt. Liverpool, maybe. Glasgow, obviously. But *London*? He didn't know who to blame first for society's moral collapse: an ineffectual police force, or the laissez-faire liberalism of North London's bourgeoisie, who seemed to think the squatters gave their street a bit of colour and cosmopolitan charm. Given his recent dealings with the Met and his next-door neighbours, he was inclined to blame both equally.

He had spent the previous day mulling over these disappointments, or distracting himself from them with menial tasks, such as a trip to the opticians to have his spectacles cleaned and repaired. He'd gone to his usual café for a post-breakfast coffee and tried but failed to focus on the newspaper. Still afflicted by a needling headache, he'd avoided his club in the afternoon, staying home to play Solitaire and squander a while on YouTube with some attractive female newsreaders. One more brief, frustrating phone conversation with Clive Billings had ended with his solicitor again insisting that Jerry not go up to the house.

It was in Clive's interests that they resolve the issue slowly, and by legal means. But Jerry had done some further reading of his own. The Web forums had yielded more than one example of homeowners who'd managed to talk their squatters into leaving, by laying out the facts of their predicament and – assuming said squatters were, deep down, reasonable people – making them feel guilty enough to give up the door keys. If Clive was paid extortionate amounts to wield a stick, then Jerry had once been paid equally well to wave a carrot. Persuasion was his game. And if he could corner one of his young adversaries, perhaps he could cajole them politely into relinquishing the property.

The twenty-first-century consumer considered him- or herself immune to certain traditional advertising techniques. But youthful rebellion was really just another brand identity. You couldn't sell these people products, so you sold them sponsored alternative lifestyles, grass-roots movements, Facebook campaigns. It was time for some of the old Manville magic.

Just as he was debating whether to find a quiet tree somewhere around the corner in Highbury Fields, or to knock on Stu and Andrea's front door and demand the use of their loo, Jerry heard footsteps and a familiar cough. A smoker's cough. A Midlands cough. He flipped down his clip-on sunglasses and sank as low as possible on the oatmeal leather seat to study the approaching figure in his wing mirror. The jeans were loose and paint-spattered, the workers' boots scuffed, the military surplus jacket flapping open to reveal a tatty vest. He risked only a fleeting look at the fellow's face as he passed: stubble, sallow cheeks. He was wheeling a bicycle – stolen, probably – tick-tick-ticking towards the house. The man could have been anything between twenty-five and forty, but Jerry was certain this was the same suspected egg-thrower who'd been at the window of the master bedroom, cackling at his plight.

Sure enough, the man strolled into Jerry's driveway and carried the bike up to the front door, banged the knocker three times and waited. Jerry lifted *The Times* level with his face and peered over the top of the page. He knew the importance of patience, of sticking to the plan, but what if this was the only chance he'd get to speak to one of the bastards all day? While he wrestled with this dilemma, the door opened and Midlands man stepped inside, taking the bike with him. Dammit, thought Jerry, presuming he'd missed his opportunity. But then another figure emerged, closing the door behind her and trotting down the steps. She stalked across the gravel and up the road away from the Lotus, petite and pert-arsed and with spiky blonde hair. Jerry hurriedly folded his news-paper, rolled up the driver's side window and, with a succession of grunts, hauled himself up and out of the car.

The faster he walked to keep up with her, the more his bladder protested, so it was a great relief when the girl finally slowed her pace and turned into a café. She'd taken a circuitous route through a series of deserted residential back streets, which on the one hand forced Jerry to hang back so as not to be detected, and on the other meant he had to jog as quickly as he could to keep her in sight whenever she turned a corner. He would not have made a particularly competent spy. Getting his bearings, Jerry deduced that they were now at the corner of Newington Green. He flipped his clip-on shades back up. The café looked Moroccan-themed, or possibly Lebanese. It was quiet but for a couple of yummy mummies at a pavement table outside, their children enthroned on ruinously expensive pushchairs.

The bell on the door pealed as Jerry walked in, and the barista and her sole customer turned to look at him. A boxed salad and a glass of smoothie lay between them on the counter. Beneath the perspex were deli trays of falafel, tabbouleh, baklava. The barista was punching numbers into the till. An amused smile wormed its way across the girl's face. She was twenty-something, and she had on tight, black jeans and a loose grey T-shirt, with a keffiyeh around her neck. Freedom for Palestine, Jerry supposed.

'I'll get this,' he said, flourishing a tenner. The barista looked to the girl for confirmation. The girl shrugged and picked up her lunch.

'Anything for you, sir?'

'No, thanks,' said Jerry, still feeling the uncomfortable effects of his previous coffee. The woman gave him his change, and he plonked an extra pound into the tip dish to appear magnanimous.

'So you're a blonde now,' he said to the girl, who'd failed to make a run for it. 'Didn't your hair used to be pink?'

He couldn't decide whether her smile was promising, or disconcerting.

'I like to change my identity now and then,' she replied.

'What, to throw people like me off the scent?'

'Could be.'

She turned and walked out the door but, rather than walk away, she took a seat at a table near the yummy mummies and opened her salad box. There was an empty chair opposite her, which seemed to invite his presence. This was good. This was going well. He was establishing a rapport. The café had a loo, he noticed, with artisanal wooden cut-outs of a man and a woman nailed to the door. It could wait. He followed her outside.

'I'm Jerry,' he said, positioning the chair with a scrape of metal on concrete, and then settling on it. He put his folded copy of *The Times* on the table in front of him. She glanced at it and smirked.

'Hello, Jerry. That's a nasty bruise. What happened to your head?'

She stuck her fork in a cherry tomato and lifted it to her mouth, watching him as she ate. She had big eyes, brown and kohl-rimmed. Impeccable cheekbones. Porcelain complexion. A tiny stud in her nose.

'What's your name?'

She exhaled. 'Why don't you call me . . . Rosa Luxemburg.'

'I'd rather not.'

'Fine. Call me Ulrike.'

'Ulrike?'

'Ulrike Meinhof.'

'Oh, for fuck's sake,' he said, without thinking. Her eyebrows

155

shot up. He was losing her. Keep your cool, Jerry. Be reasonable. He took a deep breath: 'Okay, then. Hmph. Ulrike.'

'Jerry. What's that short for? Gerald? Gerard?'

'Jerome,' he confessed, reluctantly.

'Of course. Jerome.'

Only Genevieve called him Jerome. And when this girl said it, she sounded just like Genevieve: well bred, contemptuous. She chewed a chunk of sweet potato.

'Look,' he said. 'Whatever your real name is. The house you're squatting in. It's not just some empty property. I – we, my family – have been there for thirty years. Three decades. My kids grew up there. When I moved in it was nothing, it was . . . Well, I redid the whole house myself. It's very dear to me.'

'I like what you've done with the place.'

'Well, I don't like what *you've* done with it.'

'You don't *know* what we've done with it.'

'Okay, look.' Jerry was running out of patience already, and he couldn't seem to find a sitting position that de-pressurised his bladder. 'I'm not here to play silly buggers. You're going to get evicted eventually. You are aware of that?'

'Not necessarily. We have some law students.'

'Ha. Well, I have a lawyer. An actual, real-life, grown-up solicitor. An expensive one. So why bother postponing the inevitable? I need you to get out of there before this weekend. By tomorrow, preferably.'

She took a sip of her smoothie.

'Where do you live, exactly?' she said. 'Do you rent?'

'Do I *rent*? No. What's that got to do w—'

'So, you don't rent. You own another place. At least one other place. Those are expensive clothes, I bet. You're obviously not starving. So why do you give a shit?'

'"Obviously not starving"?! What's that supposed to . . . Are you joking?'

This was not going to plan, thought Jerry, becoming increasingly indignant.

'How long since you lived there? Actually lived in the house, I mean.'

'Er, well. About twelve years or so . . .'

'*Twelve years?*!'

'But my ex-wife—'

'You're divorced?'

'What?'

'You're divorced. You said you have an ex-wife.'

'I have two. What's it to you?'

She sipped her smoothie again, unmoved.

'Just doesn't surprise me, that's all. Two, though. Wow.'

'Oh, please. What is this? Some sort of sisterly intervention? "All Men Are Bastards"?'

She chuckled slightly at that. Jesus Christ, he thought, some women can't walk past a fucking Wonderbra billboard without bleating about the patriarchy.

'We are selling the house,' he said. 'We want other people to live there. But I don't think it's too much to ask that they pay for the privilege!'

'Who?'

'"Who"?'

'Who do you want to live there? Some other rich white family? Some hedge fund manager and his kids? Or will you split it into overpriced flats for desperate first-time buyers?'

A wise ad creative once said the most valuable piece of real estate in the world was a corner of someone's mind – and Jerry had been a gifted speculator, buying up the green-belt brain cells of the consumer masses and building ideas, desires, brands. But he could tell he was losing his touch. He really needed that piss now. It was time to wrap this thing up.

'Okay,' he said, 'how much do you want?'

'I'm sorry?'

She didn't look sorry. She looked as though he'd just slapped her. He would have liked that: slapping her.

'How much do you and your friends want, to get out of my house?'

'You're amazing. How many houses do you need, Jerome? Y'know, there's almost a million empty properties in this country. Hundreds of thousands in London alone, including at least one of yours. And there's a *housing crisis*! Can you believe that? What were you planning to offer us? A hundred quid each? Five hundred . . . ?'

He'd been hoping fifty would do it, actually.

'How much did that place cost you, when you bought it thirty years ago? Not more than a hundred grand, I bet.'

'How did you . . . ?'

'Educated guess. And it must be worth well over a million now, right? More like two, even. So basically, accounting for inflation, you'll quadruple your money, I reckon.'

'If you'd let me.'

'And when you bought it, I bet it cost about twice your annual income. Three times, maybe. Something like that?'

Jerry didn't respond, but he had to admit her maths were sound.

'But if I wanted to buy it,' she went on, poking her fork in his direction about once every other sentence, for emphasis. 'Or if one of my – how shall I put it? – "housemates" wanted to buy it, well then maybe it would cost about twenty or thirty times our annual income. Because your houses have been getting more expensive, while our wages have stagnated. But then, plenty of us don't have an income to speak of, so it's irrelevant anyway. And if we did, well, we couldn't get mortgages because the banks have jacked up the deposits, because your lot rigged them to fail and fucked the economy. And meanwhile, you forgot to keep building houses for the rest of us. You just sat on your own piles and got fat from the proceeds . . .'

It just gets worse, thought Jerry. How had this ended up as a conversation about current affairs? He rarely cared enough about anything any more to have strong opinions. And he certainly hadn't the patience to debate with some student revolutionary. Would it make her feel any better to know he'd always voted Labour – even in the eighties? Probably not. He'd supported CND, the miners, Rock Against Racism. Or, at any rate, he'd worn the relevant pin-badges. And yes, he'd sometimes wondered whether his life's trajectory was predetermined by the dumb luck of his mid-century, middle-class birth.

But he could see where this was going, this Red-Army-Faction/Free-Palestine/Property-is-Theft posturing. He'd never been impressed by that futile teenage urge to reject consumerism and therefore the values of Western Capitalist Democracy. People liked property. They liked *things*. They liked to accumulate *things*. Things – houses, vintage sports cars, keffiyehs – helped them to define themselves. Things were a comfort, a repository for memories. He had spent the better part – yes, the *better* part – of his life engaging with people's desire for things that would say something about them: that they were independent, or intelligent, or happy-go-lucky. Why suppress humanity's instinct to acquire? Why apologise for that instinct, as long as it's legal? He was fed up with liberal guilt, with feeling bad for being white and male and wealthy-ish. Of being expected to feel ashamed for having *things* and enjoying it. Of that constant implication that anything pleasurable must have come at the expense of some poor child worker crushing coffee beans between his thumb and index finger in a sweatshop in El Salvador for Caffè fucking Nero. The girl was still talking. He still needed to piss.

'. . . So now we can't buy houses. Only forty-year-olds can buy houses. And there *you* go, old man, buying three of them. Why? As investments? To build equity? To buy-to-let? So you can make us pay your exorbitant London rents and stop us saving enough for a deposit, while we fund your crippling energy bills because you couldn't be bothered to insulate properly, while we sit around with beige walls because you won't let us paint them and make it feel even slightly like a home, while we wait to see whether you'll chuck us out for no particular reason at the end of our six-month lease? Well, in your case it sounds like it's mainly because you couldn't keep your prick in your pants. But either way, you see my point.'

Her speech complete, 'Ulrike' forked and ate another tomato. Jerry wondered whether it was possible to laser a hole in somebody's head, just by looking at them.

'Did you practise that?' he asked.

'Fuck you,' she said calmly.

'Fuck me? Fuck *me*? FUCK YOU. Get out of my house. Get out of my house. GET. THE. FUCK. OUT OF MY. HOUSE.'

By now people were, of course, staring. The yummy mummies with the expensive pushchairs were whispering shockedly to one another. Some wag in a passing white van yelled, with mock disapproval, 'Language!' Jerry had been banging the table quite violently, and the girl's smoothie had fallen over to form a puddle of orange gloop that was now advancing towards him across the Formica. In spite of this, she was smiling again, serenely. Every curse he hurled imbued her with greater power. She was like fucking Obi-Wan Kenobi.

'You think it's my fault,' he said, 'that I worked hard and earned money and you haven't?'

'Not *just* your fault, dickhead. But you boomers let it happen, all of you.'

'Oh, so whose fault is it, then? Thatcher, I bet. Thatcher or Blair.'

'Them too.'

'Jesus Christ, you people are tedious. And what is this "you" and "us" bullshit, anyway? You're telling me you don't have money? You sound like you went to bloody Pony Club, for fuck's sake. You're posher than I am!'

This last part was certainly true. Jerry was convinced of it. Whatever her politics, only generation upon generation of wealthy men and their trophy wives could have cultivated such effortlessly magnificent offspring. What joy it would have been, to shag such a specimen when in his prime!

'What did you earn all that money doing, Jerome?'

'What?'

'What was it that you worked so hard at, to earn all this money? What do you *do*?'

The yummy mummies had tutted enough, and were rolling their pushchairs away. The heat and his exertion had made Jerry clammy. His urethra was clenched tight. His headache was burgeoning again.

'None of your business.'

'Go on,' she said. 'Tell me. You want to, I can feel it.'

She was right. He did want to.

'I was in advertising.'

When she opened her mouth to laugh, really laugh, she opened it wide enough for him to see every one of her perfect, sparkling teeth, from her lower molars to her near-vampiric canines. Flawless dentistry. Still laughing, she stood and picked up her salad box, tossing it adroitly into a nearby litter bin. Jerry felt his crotch dampen: not piss – not yet – but smoothie, which had dribbled under his newspaper, over the lip of the table and into his lap. He leapt up. She was walking away, and he wanted to follow, but by now he was bursting – and so, defeated, he ran with pigeon-toes to the loo in the café instead.

As the urine flowed noisily into the toilet bowl, fast and strong and clear, he thought of what he ought to have said: 'Didn't you shout "property is theft" at me? And now, young lady, you tell me that what you really want to do is . . . buy a house?' That would have been clever, clever and disarming. *L'esprit de l'escalier.*

When he got back outside, there was no sign of the girl. The barista was mopping up the orange smoothie from the table with *The Times.* Jerry hoped the damp patch on his chinos would dry quickly in the afternoon sun. No longer preoccupied by the need to piss, he now became fully aware of his headache's resumption.

By the time Jerry had moped back to his car, the house seemed quiet again. Had the girl returned, or gone elsewhere? Did it matter? He remembered Clive Billings's advice and wished he'd heeded it. He squeezed into the Lotus and drove home. Later that evening, while he was watching TV and poking inexpertly at a Chinese takeaway with a pair of chopsticks, he heard his BlackBerry buzz on the dining table. He rose effortfully from his Eames chair and went to pick it up. One new email. The sender's address, he guessed, had been faked up purely for the purpose of delivering this single, two-line message:

From: 'Ulrike' <71117@dotmail.com>
Sent: 12 July 2011 20:19
Subject: House
Nice meeting you, Jerome.
If it makes you feel any better, I'm sorry about the eggs.
x

VALUATION

15

Conrad recalled Flo Dalrymple vividly. Like a Post-It scribbled with a dying biro, she was etched hard on his remembrance. In actual fact, he considered his and Flo's first and only serious encounter to have been archetypal: of his continuing failure to meet attractive girls and have sex with them. It happened in the spring. At Jamie's gallery opening. Well, not a 'gallery' as such – Cumulonimbus, the big old Dickensian warehouse-type venue, behind Kingsland Road's E8 stretch, where people did exhibitions and parties and stuff like that.

Dijon yellow masonry climbed to the high factory windows; iron struts spanned the vaulted roof. Grand cinematographer's lamps lit the scuzzed concrete floor. The buzz of chat and the shush of shuffling feet was subsiding as the crowd thinned, but up on the mezzanine level, by the mojito bar, some posh DJ was still playing coffee-table dubstep.

Conrad was standing with Polly, cradling a bottle of Corona and staring at Jamie's spotlit 3x5 selfie. In the picture, Jamie was posing among a cluster of dudes who had big beards and machine guns, on a ridge somewhere near the AfPak border. The reddish tint on the image gave it a nostalgic feel, like they were still fighting the Soviets, as opposed to whoever it was they were fighting now: the Americans; each other. It was dusk or dawn, and they were all squinting manfully into the sunlight. Jamie had on his keffiyeh and combat fatigues and maybe six days' stubble. One of the fighters had taken the shot. It was all explained on the handwritten title card next to the photo.

Most of Conrad's acquaintances weren't actual artists, by the way. They worked in Hackney's bars and coffee shops, for graphic design firms or guerrilla marketing teams. And they talked about art and music and films a lot, but they didn't actually make anything. They just consumed it. Doubtless there were some visionaries in their midst, serving them Red Stripes or flat whites because they were *genuinely* struggling to pay the bills. On the whole, though, the people he knew did not create, they traded: small-batch baked goods, or limited edition trainers, or fonts.

Take Polly. She had a market stall, where she sold knick-knacks and vintage oddities that she'd found in junkshops, or on eBay and Etsy. And clothes, like the custom-cut collectible New Order T-shirt and Navajo print leggings she had on that evening. She had her own website, where you could mail-order her selected *objets*. She made a monster profit from all that retro tat, merely via skilful curation. She was an entrepreneur. They did a whole page on her in *Dazed & Confused*.

But Jamie Doohan was different. Polly's boyfriend was an actual artist, probably. His exhibition, 'Take the Boy Out of Shoreditch', consisted of photo-portraits he'd shot in Iraq, Pakistan and Afghanistan. He'd applied a Hipstamatic lens to the conflict-torn, turning Taliban tribespeople and Iraqi insurgents – or whatever they were – into iterations of East End cool, all facial hair and sunglasses. His cameras were Holgas and Lomos and Polaroids; the pictures were faded, colour-saturated, under- or overexposed, tinted, grained, scratched. They smacked of some kind of authenticity. Were they more or less real than those of a normal war photographer? Conrad didn't think Jamie was intellectually equipped to tackle that question. The guy just thought they looked awesome. Alas, he was correct.

Jamie could legitimately wear a keffiyeh: he'd bought it in a souk in Basra. He could carry a Leica slung around his neck to Columbia Road flower market on Sundays, like every other hipster douchebag, and blame it on his profession. He was unimpeachable, a bona fide creator. And brave with it. Ultra-alpha. Iraq, FFS!

Afghanistan! He was the sort of guy who pissed unthinkingly at the middle urinal. He was, in Conrad's considered opinion, a total wanker. But Conrad dared not say so. Who would believe him? He thumbed the thick slice of lime down through the bottleneck and let his beer bubble furiously.

'So. What d'you think?' said Polly.

'Well, he didn't take this one, did he? So it doesn't really count.'

'No, *dumbass*. Of the whole thing. The exhibition. What do you think?'

'Oh. Yeah. Yeah. I think it's cool.'

Of course it was cool. That was the whole point. Was it any *good*? Someone obviously thought so, because some of Jamie's bigger prints were already selling for well over a grand. But really: who knew? Conrad hadn't come for the pictures, anyway. He'd seen them all before, many times, because Jamie was always showing off his Tumblr to anyone who happened to drop by the flat. (If Conrad had to listen to that story about the opium-dealing rickshaw driver in Quetta one more fucking time . . .) No, he'd come because he knew that Jamie was friends with loads of fit girls, and he'd wanted to stand by a wall and drink and stare at them.

He'd not been disappointed; the soirée was winding down, but earlier it had been rammed with pretty partygoers, and Conrad had stared at lots of them. Not *stared* stared. He wasn't a pervert or anything. He just stole repeated glances at them over Polly's or Beagle's shoulder, and looked away quickly if they clocked him. There were bohos like Polly in pretty dresses, knit tights, brogues: the kind of girls that read really long Russian novels. There were clubbers in fluoro and denim. There were West London bottle-blondes in classy office-casual. Jamie had a lot of friends from a lot of places; they just all happened to be extremely good-looking. And whaddya know: here he came, approaching Conrad and Polly from across the warehouse with one such young lady. Solar-eclipse eyes, vampire-pale skin, black bob, grey/black outfit, cheekbones. #GucciGoth.

'Who's that?' asked Conrad, who knew already.

Polly sighed, the breath fluttering her fringe. 'Flo Dalrymple,' she said. '*Kiiind* of a dick.'

He'd actually been introduced to Flo Dalrymple once before at some rubbish house party in De Beauvoir Town. At the time he'd been preoccupied inhaling nitrous oxide balloons and vainly chirpsing Polly's friend, Xanthe: a serious but since-dissolved crush. He didn't expect Flo to remember him. But the thing was, when Conrad was reintroduced to friends of friends – especially the attractive ones – he was often forced to pretend to have forgotten certain details about their lives that he'd already gleaned from Facebook.

People edit their FB pages to present their best selves, the ideal interpretation of their actual, unremarkable lives. Conrad knew that all too well. But when he saw some hot chick's tastefully compiled profile pictures album, and studied her carefully constructed lies about her badass life, he had a tendency to believe the hype. Flo's account presented few facts to non-friends, but he'd been able to deduce, for example, that she used to be a redhead. That she'd seen Gorillaz play Glasto last summer, and that her favourite film was *One Flew Over the Cuckoo's Nest* – or, at least, that's what she wanted everyone to *think* was her favourite film. People really needed to be more careful about their privacy settings.

Conrad steeled himself as Jamie and the girl came towards them.

'Quick,' he muttered. 'Laugh, like I've just said something hilarious.'

Polly laughed, exasperated but obedient, and punched him softly on the arm.

'Hi, babes,' said Jamie to Polly. 'Conrad, mate. This is Flo.'

Jamie had gone to a boarding school, so he called everyone 'mate' in a posh accent.

'Hello,' said Conrad, and they shook hands. Wow, he thought. We're touching.

'Hey,' Flo said. 'We met before.'

'Oh. Did we?' YES, he thought. WE DID.

'Nice speech,' Conrad said to Jamie, who'd delivered a characteristically self-regarding address at the beginning of the evening, in which he'd neglected to thank Polly, who'd done most of the framing and hanging and lighting. She didn't seem to mind, which made it worse.

'Thanks, mate,' said Jamie, then he slung an arm round Polly's neck and whispered something to her. She giggled and they turned away, strolling along to the next wall of 3x5s. Dead subtle. Thanks, mate. Conrad cleared his throat to fill the awkward silence, fighting the urge to ask Flo something inane. What did you say in these situations? He never quite knew.

Flo was holding a Corona, too. She gestured at the room with it: 'What do you think?'

'Of the show? Yeah. Cool.'

'Huh. Seriously?'

'Oh. Er. You don't . . . ?'

'But it's awful, right? I mean, he's basically taken all these amazing people from all these amazing countries and just put a sort of a "Western" filter on them. Cool, sure. But, I mean. *Terrible*, really. Right?'

Conrad adjusted his non-prescription spectacles. He wondered whether Jamie was still close enough to have heard all that. This girl was already incredible. She smiled, seemingly content to be controversial. To agree or disagree? This was one of small talk's great, timeless dilemmas.

'Wow,' he said. 'Er. Yeah. I guess so.'

'Actually,' said Flo, giving him a friendly nudge with her elbow, 'I sort of knew who you were already.'

'Really?' REALLY.

'Yeah, Jamie said your mum wrote *The House on the Hill*? So you must be *the* Conrad. From the books?'

'Oh. Okay. Yeah, true. That's weird.'

She chuckled. Conrad imagined her chuckling, naked. Pearly skin, peach-soft breasts. Don't look at them. Don't look at them. DON'T LOOK AT THEM.

'I used to love that one about the bees,' she said.

'Oh, right. Yeah. *The Birdseed and the Bumblebees*.'

'Yes! Exactly. Gave me nightmares, though.'

Conrad didn't exactly adore being known as 'Conrad', but he was accustomed to it. So the two of them talked about *The House on the Hill*, and about the house on the Hill. He told her it was empty now. The Manville Museum, he called it. She sympathised, and then she changed the subject: to kids' cartoons they used to watch, and teen movies from the nineties. And from there, somehow, they got on to music, and some band named after a woodland animal that they'd both read about on Pitchfork. Conrad found bantering about cool shit like music and films and art intellectually exhausting: a persistent interplay of the earnest and the ironic, one or other attitude struck according to the subject at hand. What to endorse, what to condemn. (Sometimes, he really just felt like listening to some fucking Coldplay. But he could never admit that to ANYBODY, could he? He couldn't even add Coldplay's new album to his Spotify playlists, for fear of accidentally sharing the fact with his friends.)

Good God, he thought too much. He was over-thinking right now, this second, as Flo was talking about whatever she was talking about. Argh. Politics, maybe? Was she talking about *politics*? Wasn't there some rule about NOT talking about politics? How did they get on to politics in the first place? Was it something *he* said?

Whenever he was feeling unlucky in love, Conrad had always comforted himself with the idea that Nice Guys Finish Last. Until he realised that he probably wasn't particularly nice – or, at least, no nicer than anyone else – and that people just thought him nice, because he was shy and cute (said Polly) and sufficiently considerate to others. But he buried his bad thoughts and animosities – disguised them, even. Did that, in fact, make him of worse than average character? Could everyone see RIGHT THROUGH him?

He had a habit of becoming obsessed with girls: *any* girl, but usually one girl at a time, and almost always a girl with zero sexual interest in him. Xanthe, Polly's fashion blogger friend; Natasha, the cute barmaid from the Cow-Shed; Sadie, the strawberry-blonde Philosophy undergrad from his student halls – for whom he'd wasted the whole of Freshers' Week making MP3 mixtapes. The list went back way further than it should. When he was objective about it, he knew he was decent-looking. He had excellent hair. Yet his so-called sex life was a litany of near misses, fumbled catches and spectacular, explosive crash landings. This time, he supposed, would be no different.

So the bar at Cumulonimbus closed up, and Jamie invited the stragglers back to his place – which was not his place at all, but Polly's place, and therefore Conrad's and Beagle's place, too. Flo said the overground was down for the weekend, and she had to catch the Tube across town; weird, thought Conrad, because she seemed like she'd be from Es 1–5 or 8/9. Rolling up his superslim-fit jeans legs for cycling, he offered nervously to walk her to the station at Highbury & Islington. 'Yes,' she said. YES.

They both knew full well that Flo didn't need to be walked to the station by a boy. She could've caught a bus. She was probably a lot tougher than Conrad. Besides, these were streets being gentrified in real time. The south end of the Dalston strip still had a sheen of shiftiness, but it was more bourgeois by the month, as bookies and badman pubs were pushed up and out into deepest Hackney, replaced by latte shacks and pop-up bars. Nowadays, if you saw what you thought was some unshaven tramp stumbling towards you in the shadows, chances were he'd hit a pool of street light and turn out to be a drummer in a folk band, or a male model, just some middle-class white guy with facial hair. And the closer they got to Highbury, the more wisterias there were, clinging to the neighbourhood: social climbers.

Later, Conrad remembered that she talked about her postgrad as they were walking up St Paul's Road. MSc in Social Policy at LSE, something like that. He remembered that he complimented her high-tops, but that the comment came out sounding insincere. He remembered that she liked his bike, the customised Racing Green Peugeot, which he was wheeling alongside him; and that he explained its provenance, and the physical and psychological benefits of riding a fixie. He remembered that she was sceptical, but in a sort of flirty, teasing way that he suspected suggested admiration. (Foolishly, he'd discover in about twenty minutes' time.)

But his memory of the conversation gets a bit blurry after that, because he was pretty much freaking out about the possibility that he might get to snog her, and about the possibility that if he didn't try, it'd somehow be impolite – but that if he did try, and failed, it'd be world-ending: an Extinction-Level Event. He ran the numbers in his head and calculated that there were at least five ways this could go really badly, and only about two in which it could go well.

'So you live with Jamie and Polly?' she asked.

'With Polly and our friend Beagle,' he replied. 'Jamie doesn't pay rent. He just stays over all the time.'

She laughed. Conrad got the sense that Flo didn't much like Jamie, which made him like her all the more. Mutual animosities were as attractive as shared passions. It was raining a bit by the time they got to the busy roundabout at Highbury Corner, but she suggested he show her the house on the Hill.

'Really?'

'How far away is it? Like, five minutes?'

'Yeah. Maybe ten.'

'Come on. It'll be interesting.'

'For *you*, maybe.'

She wrinkled her nose. There was a little stud in it, gleaming. Of course, Conrad's reluctance was feigned. More time with Flo, on quiet lamplit streets, featuring some charming details from his childhood: his odds of success were surely shortening. They strolled up Highbury Fields towards the house, between the park and the darkened tennis courts. She asked about his parents, he remembered. He told her Jerry was a semi-famous adman; she said she'd Google him. He told her about the divorce, and Jerry leaving, and how his mum had just sort of stopped writing the books.

'That's really sad.'

'I guess.'

'Wasn't there one where you made, like, a tree house and then got stuck in it?'

'Er. *The Fir Tree and the Fire Truck*?'

'Right! Haha, I loved that one as well.'

What he didn't tell her was that *The Fir Tree and the Fire Truck* was based on a true story, only there'd been no fire truck involved. Just a tree house at an adventure playground, and a four-year-old Conrad suddenly developing severe vertigo and having to be coaxed down by his sister – and then his mum turning his trauma into a hilarious children's book, for money.

By the time they got up to the Hill, the drizzle had coated the pavements. Conrad's plaid shirt was damp through. The house loomed, large and dark and empty: a silent monument to his fuck-up family. Evidence of their ante-diasporic greatness. Now a family in name only, he might've said, but Isobel and his mum no longer shared the name, either. They were linked by this house, like impoverished aristos to their ancestors' stately home. (Conrad Manville: Last of His Line!) Yet no one had lived in the place properly for months, years. He wasn't sure his mum would ever end up selling it. She'd told them all she was ready at least twice, but there was still no For Sale sign in the yard. Logistics, she said. Technicalities. Bathroom refits.

Conrad didn't have his house keys. He stood at the gate, one foot in the gravel of the yard, while Flo walked up to the front door, studying the house from close quarters, standing on tiptoes to peer in through the big bay window.

'There's nothing in there now, anyway,' he said. 'Just furniture.'

'Won't it be weird?' asked Flo, gazing up at his parents' bedroom. She turned and walked back towards him. 'Such a big part of your life.'

'Nah,' he replied. 'I don't care. Somebody ought to at least live in it. My sister and I are going to take a share when it gets sold. Then I can set up a business or something.'

'What business?'

'Pfft. Dunno yet.'

She studied Conrad, bit her lip. 'You ever think it's kind of disgusting?'

'What?'

'Our parents. The boomers. All that money. They rape the planet, fuck up the economy and then they leave us with the mess. You can't do anything with your life until they decide to give you a share. And they're taking early retirement?'

He snorted, amused. But she was serious.

'Er,' he said, and wiped the rain droplets from his specs with his sleeve.

'You know, if *they* wanted to start a business, or they wanted to be artists or something, back then they could just go on the dole. We'll never have that. We'll probably never have pensions even, or decent salaries.'

'Hm. Bummer. But you're not exactly . . . Well. Poor? Sorry.'

'I don't mean *me*. I mean everyone. Our *generation*,' she said firmly. 'And anyway, revolutions happen when the middle class gets angry enough. When the intellectuals get ideas.'

Conrad remembered that she muttered something then about fucking bankers and fucking Tories and fucking rich arseholes. But maybe he was just making that up so the story would sound a bit more dramatic. He remembered that he envied her righteous anger. He supposed he ought to be angry, too, but he wasn't; he was just disappointed. He and his friends thought they were rebelling against the mainstream because they borrowed the poses of past rebellions, but they were just being cool. They didn't *stand* for anything, not like the Punks or the Hippies or the Beats. But Flo stood for something. (He wasn't sure *what* yet, but *something*.)

She was less than a foot from him now, her hand resting on the bike saddle. She was looking at him intently, as if deciding how to frame a question. Conrad shivered – with cold or apprehension, he couldn't tell – and then he leaned towards her. She saw him coming, and timed her escape perfectly, turning her face an inch or two at precisely the right second so that his lips landed there, on the unforgiving ridge of her beautiful cheekbone. Like a battle-field medic, she'd done her best to rescue some of his dignity against overwhelming odds. Conrad felt the palm of her hand pressing softly against his chest. FUUUUUuuuuuuuck. He took half a step back and looked at the pavement. The reflected glow of a nearby street lamp was diffused by the fallen rainwater. It looked like an explosion. Crash. Burn. Pfft.

He walked her back to the Tube, convinced he was in love. The next day, he friended her on Facebook.

16

In the first volume of *The House on the Hill* – published in 1989 and called, simply, *The House on the Hill* – 'Conrad' decided to surprise his parents by redecorating while they were out at the shops. A tyke in short trousers, tiny fists gripping his crayons, he doodled brightly coloured flowers, animals and rainbows all over the white walls and the expensive furniture.

> He drew in his bedroom, red, yellow and blue
> He drew on the bath and he drew in the loo
> He drew on the tables, he drew on the chairs
> He drew in the cupboard under the stairs

On page thirteen, 'Izzy' came back from school and told him he'd be in deep shit if Mum saw what he'd done. Duly chastised, Conrad helped as his sister tried frantically to scrub off all the pictures before their parents got home, but to no avail. Until, that is, she hit on a plan to chuck pots of paint over the crayon scrawls instead: white paint on the white walls and the bathroom facilities, brown on the wooden dining set. They finished the job just as Mum and Dad arrived with the shopping. Mum was delighted to find the place so clean. Dad sat down immediately to eat Marmite on toast. When he got up from his chair, the children saw that his bum had turned brown in the damp emulsion. They chuckled to one another mischievously, Conrad still holding the empty paint-pot behind his back. The end.

It was based very loosely on a real-life incident that Conrad couldn't even remember, when, aged eighteen months, he'd scribbled something illegible on the skirting board in his bedroom. But it cemented the pattern for the rest of the twelve-book series. 'Conrad' would cook up some dumb idea, like walking a dog on roller skates, or building a tree house without a ladder, or planting giant sunflowers in the garden. Then Izzy would save the day by calling the fire brigade, or hiding a pot of honey in next-door's garden to draw away the monster bees.

'Conrad' was Conrad's blessing and his curse. Yes, if you were born at some point in the late eighties, or early nineties, then there was a good chance you'd have read *The House on the Hill* and heard of him, even seen the cartoons on Children's BBC. He was the famous kid in his Montessori class. He had brand recognition, like his dad always said; he was the UK's only Googlable Conrad Manville. But it was a problematic distinction: he was forever that cheeky brat with the ridiculous schemes. His mum had created 'Conrad', and people just presupposed that Conrad shared his characteristics. Teachers, parents, friends – all of them assumed he was charming but hapless, and that his grand plans continually came to naught. In the end, Conrad couldn't help but grow into 'Conrad'. Neurotic, semi-rational and susceptible to outrageous flights of fancy. The difference between the actual and imagined boys was negligible: after all, what are you if not what everyone else thinks you are?

It was to *The House on the Hill*, in fact, that Conrad directly attributed his unfortunate employment history. Every one of his ambitious schemes had faltered in the execution. His first job after graduation was as a runner for a commercials and music video production house, which demanded he degrade himself daily in the service of talentless douchebags who, like him, thought they might be the next Martin Scorsese.

He spent six months shifting at Disastrous TV, which made

177

documentaries about apocalyptic news events for channels at the deep end of the digital listings. Conrad's job was to trawl the most disturbing raw footage on the Web in search of broadcastable material. It was the worst possible work for an anxious person. In six months, he saw more 9/11 clips than most people had in a decade – not to mention the plane crashes, the beheadings, the tsunamis, the kittens. Fucking hell, the kittens.

He undertook a selection of poorly funded internships at Silicon Roundabout start-ups, with a view to creating and marketing his own app. He made the coffees for a music streaming service; he photocopied for an e-learning website. He got an interview with a geo-social networking firm, which was threatened with a trade-mark infringement action before it had time to offer him the job. Meanwhile, all around him, overnight millionaires were selling their iPhone games to California.

After fitting out his 1993 Giant Peloton Superlite with a Shimano Exage Groupset and Vittorio Rubino grey/black tyres, he even spent six weeks trying to be a cycle courier. But he had to surrender almost half his earnings to the courier firm, and in his first month he barely made enough drops per day to cover the cost of his new messenger bag and cycling shoes. When the company cut half its riders due to the recession, he was too inefficient to keep his place. He wasn't sure he could hack it anyway; he'd already crashed twice running red lights, once crushing a set of architectural blueprints that, along with the necessary repairs to the Giant, saw him forfeit his entire weekly pay packet.

His parents had brought him up to be an aspiring creative professional, but they'd never really prepared him to be disappointed. Without the media career he'd taken for granted, it proved difficult to contrive a public face, a brand identity, and so he found himself falling back on the default character traits of 'Conrad': amiable failure. In the books, his big sister was always there to dig him out. But what use was Isobel if she was thousands of miles away, married to some Eurotrash banker? Not much.

So now he stacked shelves at the Kingsland Organic Supermarket. It was part-time – a few days a week. It beat being unemployed, just. He got whatever he wanted gratis from the deli counter at the end of his shifts, and Hannah, the deputy manager, gave him super-flexible hours. Conrad had a feeling Hannah fancied him – and he might've fancied her, too, if she ate a few more of the fresh salads, and not so many of the home-baked cinnamon spirals. Much as he preferred not to admit it, he had an aptitude for retail – a rapport with customers and a gourmand's grasp of the store's produce selection: the artisanal cheeses, the craft beers, the organic condiments.

His redbrick university arts degree ought to have rendered him more employable. At what, though? He was a white-collar grunt: psychically unprepared for manual labour, intellectually ill-equipped for specialist office work. Overeducated, underskilled. He was adamant that he be permitted to strike out on his own, and the only parental support he accepted was a £1,000 monthly standing order from his dad, which he was pretty sure Jerry had completely forgotten existed. It was enough to cover his rent (£630pcm) and a bit more. Conrad resented it, but then he owed rather a lot of money to the bank, and even more to the student loans company, so he couldn't afford to be 100 per cent principled. Some day, he hoped, he'd stand on his own two feet, and be beholden to his parents for precisely nothing. He wished he was as sensible with money as his sister. Isobel always had a handle on her finances.

Of course, the house sale – which was finally, allegedly, about to occur – would clear all his debts at a stroke. It would rid him of his overdraft, of *The House on the Hill* and of the stigma of 'Conrad'. And he was unconflicted about that: it seemed only fitting that he should get a share, since he and Isobel had added so much sentimental value to the property. He didn't want to owe anything to anybody. This was now the extent of his ambition.

When she came in, Conrad was restocking the fruit and veg section, replacing yesterday's perfectly passable Rubinette red apples with today's flawless, freshly delivered ones. The only uniform to set him apart from the customers on the shop floor was a name-badge pinned to his breast pocket and a brown waist apron with the Kingsland logo embroidered on it. He hated the badge and the apron; however uncomfortable he might have been about his name, it was still disheartening to see it wasted on a scrap of store-branded plastic. But at least he didn't have to wear a trademarked fleece like the poor bastards down the road at Tesco.

Out of the corner of his eye, Conrad noticed a bob of vivid pink hair gliding down the ethnic foods aisle towards the deli counter. The girl seemed familiar from behind. Strutting alongside her was a bloke with enviable stubble growth in a khaki vintage army jacket, pushing a trolley full of food: a selection of breads, several boxes of quinoa spaghetti, stacked plastic tubs of hummus and guac. When the girl turned her head to confer with her companion, the stud in her nose caught the light from the deli counter's refrigeration unit: Flo Dalrymple.

Conrad felt his palms go clammy. Should he say hello, or find an excuse to flee to the stockroom before Flo spotted him? Would she even remember him? Of *course* she would. Wouldn't she? Hannah was behind the deli counter, slicing meats. Did he want Flo to know that he worked in a shop? He didn't think he'd mentioned it when they'd last spoken, months ago, on that mizzly April evening after Jamie's exhibition. He'd probably avoided the subject, or told some white lie about his TV career.

Conrad had plenty of prior experience bumping into girls with whom he'd previously crashed and burned – but his years of practice made it no less mortifying. Before he could make himself scarce, however, Flo was heading his way, consulting what looked like a shopping list. He knew for near certain that apples would be on it; everybody always needed apples. It was too late to duck out of the way now without drawing attention to himself, and the bloke with the stubble was already eyeing him suspiciously as he parked the trolley alongside Conrad's crate of Rubinettes.

'Hello,' said Conrad. 'Flo, right?'

He'd never seen anything quite like it. She looked up at him from her list and, for a moment, she seemed puzzled, as though she was trying to place him. But then her dark eyes widened, her pupils ballooned, and a blush crept quickly all the way to her cheeks from the cleft in her low-cut V-neck T-shirt that he was trying not to look at. In fact, to say he'd never seen anything quite like it was not strictly true. He'd seen this precise thing happen whenever girls talked to Jamie Doohan. But he'd never had that effect on a female himself.

'Conrad,' she said. 'Shit. Hey. Sorry, you gave me a shock. What's going on?'

She glanced around quickly, as if checking that no one was following her. Conrad could feel his own face reddening. Had he interrupted something? It felt as though he'd interrupted some-thing. Was this MASSIVELY awkward? Probably. But she seemed flustered, and not in a totally bad way. And she'd remembered his name. Or, wait: had she just read his name-badge?

'Er. Well . . .'

No, she hadn't seen the badge. Because she spotted it then, and she reached out and touched it, and then laughed and sighed at the same time, as though she was relieved to find that it was real.

'Oh, right! You *work* here.'

Conrad looked down glumly at his brown Kingsland waist apron, concealing his loins, denoting emasculation. 'Yeah,' he said. 'Part-time.'

The bloke with the stubble was still sizing Conrad up. He looked

181

unwashed: like one of those people who'd ask you for 20p outside a Tube station, and then pursue you down the street shouting insults if you said no. Conrad shrank a little more beneath his gaze.

'This is Austin,' said Flo. 'Austin, this is Conrad. Maybe I told you about him.'

Austin nodded, said nothing. Conrad wiped his clammy hand on his apron, in case Austin offered his to shake, but he needn't have. Maybe Austin was Flo's boyfriend. Or maybe, 'Maybe I told you about him' was code for: 'This is the guy I told you about, Austin. *Remember?* The super-hot one whose bones I intend to jump?' There was an uncomfortable silence, and Conrad had the sense that one of them should probably leave. But he couldn't leave, because he was supposed to be restocking the fruit and veg section. He pointed at one of the deli purchases in Austin's trolley.

'That maple-glazed ham is really good,' he said.

Austin looked down at the packet of just-sliced meat.

'Oh, yeah?' he replied, gruff and Brum.

'Yup. Really good. Er. In a sandwich or whatever.'

'Austin,' said Flo, handing Austin the shopping list. 'Why don't you go and find the rest of this?'

Austin turned to look at her, expressionless. He took the list and disappeared towards the drinks aisle. Flo smiled at Conrad. She tucked some of her pink hair behind her ear.

'So,' said Conrad. 'Is. Er. Is Austin your boyfriend?'

She chuckled softly. 'No, just a mate.'

Argh. Conrad clutched at a change of subject. 'You having a party or something?'

Her eyes widened again. Conrad gestured towards the brimming trolley.

'What? Oh, no,' she said quickly. 'Just doing a big shop. Austin and I, we live together. We have a lot of housemates.'

'I thought you lived the other side of town.'

'Huh? Oh, yeah. I do. I did, I mean. I moved.'

'Oh, cool. Where to? Round here?'

'Yeah, not far.'

Not far. Conrad chose his words carefully: 'Cool. Er. We should hang out. Or something.'

She blushed again. 'Yeah, definitely!'

Definitely. DEFINITELY. She sounded almost breathless. He liked to think of her breathless. Breathless and naked and drenched in sweat.

'So wait,' he said. 'Where *exactly* are you living? Shoreditch? Dalston?'

She grinned. 'I love your hair,' she said, and reached out her hand to touch his quiff. 'Can I? Do you use product? What is it?'

She touched his hair. SHE TOUCHED HIS HAIR. He didn't much care for people touching his hair, but this was different. Trying very hard not to stammer, he told her the name of the styling clay he used. He told her that he thought her hair was cool, too. What was it, hot pink? Exactly, she said, and giggled coyly, and looked up at him with her head angled down, the way he saw girls do when they were flirting with Jamie. Conrad's stomach played a few bars of free jazz. He could feel Hannah watching him from behind the deli counter. At any moment, she could humiliate him utterly, just by ordering him back to work. But he was gambling with the knowledge that his deputy manager was too insecure to pull rank.

'You want some apples?' he asked Flo. 'These Rubinettes are tasty.'

'Sure,' she said, and watched as he bagged up a handful of fruit from the fresh crate. 'How long have you worked here?'

'Not long. It's sort of a stopgap. I'm planning to get into social media. I had an interview at a geo-networking app-type place.'

'Cool! That is so interesting. Well, remember me when you're a CEO.'

'Ha. I will.'

He would. Maybe she could be his assistant. Then his wife. Maybe they could start a charitable foundation together, travel the world, eliminate child poverty. At that moment – the moment just after she TOUCHED his HAIR – *anything* seemed possible.

'So, which one's your boss? Is it that chubby girl over there who's been giving me funny looks for the last five minutes?'

She said that loud enough that Hannah might have heard. It was mean; it was *incredible*.

'Er. Kind of. She's the deputy manager.'

Flo leaned towards him and whispered, 'Are you unionised?'

He could feel her breath tickling his ear. She was joking, he presumed. So he laughed, nervously, and a little more high-pitched than he'd have liked.

Austin appeared again, carrying a crate of craft beer with several bottles of wine balanced on top. He didn't look at Conrad as he eased them into the trolley.

'You know,' said Conrad, feeling a little more confident around Austin now, 'this place is a real rip-off.'

'No shit,' Austin muttered.

'Yeah,' said Flo. 'But it's the only supermarket round here that adheres to even remotely sustainable practices.'

Sustainable? True, the fruit and veg came in bulk each day from a supplier somewhere in Surrey: its food miles were fifty or less. What Flo didn't know, though, was that – as organic and wholesome as it was – half that precious produce went to waste. Every day they chucked out crates and crates of perfectly good food, simply because it had gone unsold for twenty-four hours. And some sort of governmental or in-house health-and-safety directive stipulated that they couldn't even donate it to the local homeless.

When he worked a late shift, Conrad always went back to the flat with a rucksack full of the day's leftovers. Polly and Beagle would never go hungry.

Though he didn't say so, Austin was plainly agitating to leave. 'We should get going,' said Flo.

'Sure,' said Conrad, and then, hastily, 'Hey, so let me take your number.'

'Oh,' she said, paused, and then, 'I lost my phone. Tell me yours.'

'Er. Why don't I just Facebook you?'

'Oh. Okay. Yeah. Cool. See you soon, then.'

'Absolutely.'

Absolutely. Well, that went well, thought Conrad, as he watched Flo follow Austin and his trolley towards the checkout at the front of the shop. Improbably well. *Unbelievably* well. Energised by the success of the encounter, he quickly finished decanting his crate of apples and made for the storeroom to collect another. On his way, he passed the deli counter. Hannah looked up.

'Who was that?' she said.

'Oh, just a mate,' Conrad replied breezily. 'Why?'

He looked back towards the checkout, where Austin was hefting all four of their bulging paper shopping bags. Flo appeared to be paying, with a gold card.

'No reason,' said Hannah, and went back to potting olives.

17

As far as Conrad was concerned, the Manvilles were in the wind. So if he needed advice or encouragement or emotional support – the sorts of things he imagined a family ought to provide – then he turned to his friends. They weren't always encouraging, and he often ignored their advice. But they were sympathetic, most of the time.

'She told me to Facebook her, but she *still* hasn't accepted my friend request.'

'But she did definitely say she wanted to hang out,' said Beagle. 'Right?'

They were in London Fields, eating banh mi sandwiches from the fusion food truck: Conrad and Beagle and Beagle's boyfriend, Dennis. They slouched on the sunlit grass in Cunts' Corner, that section of the park famed for being the most heavily populated by hipsters. Bikes of every species lazed close by, their back wheels ticking idly. A cluster of cunts was playing frisbee. A solitary cunt in Ray-Bans and a deep-V tee was keepy-uppying with a Hacky Sack. Somewhere, some other cunt was barbecuing. Conrad could smell grilled halloumi and firelighters.

'Yeah, sort of.'

Beagle chewed for a second or two, considering Conrad's situation. 'So, maybe she just doesn't use Facebook that often,' he said. 'Some people don't, dude. I know that seems weird to you. Maybe she's more of a Tumblr person.'

'So wait,' said Dennis, sounding puzzled. 'Who was the other guy again?'

Dennis was an up-and-coming model-slash-actor who'd just shot his first major print and billboard campaign for a new streetwear line and was still half-pretending to be straight for the sake of his tween-girl Twitter followers.

'Never found out. Just a friend, I guess.'

'Maybe he really is her boyfriend,' said Dennis, 'and she doesn't want you to see their FB pictures of, like, their sex holiday in Jamaica.'

'*Jamaica?*' said Beagle.

'Seriously,' Dennis replied.

'Okay,' said Conrad. 'Let's assume for a second that this "Austin" – that's the guy – let's assume that Austin *is* Flo's boyfriend, and that she doesn't want me to find that out on Facebook. Is that a *good* thing, or a *bad* thing? I mean, does that mean she maybe *likes* me?'

'Or,' said Beagle, 'is she so completely indifferent that she just hasn't bothered to accept you yet? Indifference: that is the WORST.'

'Not possible,' said Conrad. 'She was *massively* chirpsing me. Definitely. I'm sure of it.'

'Hmmm,' Beagle murmured, his mouth full of daikon and slow-cooked pork. He was wearing a Buddhist Milkman T-shirt that said 빨리나았으면좋겠어![1] on it. Beagle had suffered vicariously through Conrad's varied sexual travails for years on end, been consulted incessantly on the implications of numberless glances, texts and stray, semi-flirtatious comments. Conrad knew he ought to stop unburdening his imagined romantic problems onto his friends, but he just couldn't help it. He guessed they owed it to him, Polly and Beagle, since they were both happily coupled up. That was the sole privilege of singledom. God, he was boring.

Beagle swallowed. 'And you're sure that you were chirpsing,'

---

1 'Feel Better!'

he said, 'and not doing that thing where you think you're chirpsing but you're actually just being all nervous and creepy?'

'Fuck off,' said Conrad.

He'd recounted both the Flo stories in detail, with what he believed to be minimal embellishment: the gallery, and then the supermarket. There had been serious chemistry, both times. He was convinced of it. Should he message her again? Should he search for her on some other social network and Poke her there?

'Forget about it,' said Beagle. 'If you ask me, she sounds like trouble. All that laughing and touching, then she throws you the cheek? She just loves the attention.'

'Maybe I exaggerated the laughing and the touching,' said Conrad. 'It's just that those are the bits I remember.'

'Whatevs,' said Beagle. 'Trouble.'

But trouble sounds *good*, Conrad wanted to say. Trouble sounds like something you'd like to have sex with, doesn't it? Dangerous, wild, ANIMAL sex. Conrad had never had sex like that. Conrad had not had much sex at all, but that wasn't the point.

'Plenty more fish in the sea,' said Dennis, who was turning out to be no use whatsoever, Gay-Best-Friend-wise. 'What about that Hannah chick? From the shop? She sounds up for it.'

'Nah, not into her.'

Beagle raised an eyebrow: 'Too fat?'

'I didn't say that.'

'Too fat,' said Dennis, nodding.

I should've prefaced this conversation, thought Conrad, with a plea for clemency. He wanted Beagle and Dennis to offer him a sliver of hope, an analysis of his initial crash and burn that allowed for the prospect of future snogging. He'd concocted multiple fantasy scenarios, in which Flo had forced herself to resist his advances that night outside the house on the Hill, despite a burning attraction, due to some item of tragic personal history, or an arsehole boyfriend situation, or take-it-slow propriety. For any of these narratives to feel plausible, though, Conrad had to ignore Flo's patent self-assurance: she was plainly not the type to take it slow if she didn't feel like it. He could conceive of no credible plotline that began with her rebuffing him, and ended with them sleeping together.

The sun passed behind a cloud, and the air cooled. All three of them were wearing pretty much the exact same pair of twill shorts, only in different colours, which Conrad found faintly embarrassing. They looked way too much like a boy band for comfort. Beagle picked at the last crumbs of pork and baguette in the bottom of his brown paper bag, and then crumpled it and lay back on his boyfriend's lap. They sat in silence, accustomed to the leisure time that a lack of work provided. Someone nearby was listening to a grime track on their mobile. Conrad heard the wap-wap of a bass line and the chk-chk of a synth cymbal. He could identify the genre, but not the tune. The summer made him sad.

A stray ball bounced up and dinked into the side of Dennis's head, and then dropped onto the grass beside him. Dennis recoiled as if he'd been slapped, but it was only a beach football. He seemed most concerned about his delicate hairdo and his Wayfarers, both of which he readjusted carefully. Some floppy-haired cunt in a wife-beater bounded over barefoot and kicked the football back towards his friends.

'Sorry, buddy,' he said in a Fulham accent, and bounded away again. Pfft. When did all these rich people start getting interested in the East End, wondered Conrad. They weren't even hipsters. They were pseudo-hipsters, post-hipsters. They swarmed into the E postcodes like locusts, ravaging each neighbourhood's personality, leaving behind a desert of chain bars and corporate streetwear emporia. Spitalfields was lost to blue chipster bankers and bridge-and-tunnellers. Shoreditch and Hoxton, too. Mile End and Victoria Park were well on the turn. Stokey was for dads. Bits of Dalston,

London Fields and Bethnal Green were okay. Shacklewell, Mildmay, Cambridge Heath. Clapton was solid. But someday soon, he supposed, he'd have to consider moving south of the river, where there were still some genuinely trendy shitholes.

What hope was there of tangible cultural authenticity when Conrad was surrounded by this cornerful of late-capitalist cunts, belatedly aping their early Shoreditch forebears, who had in turn mimicked the tropes of some half-imagined New York borough, years ago and thousands of miles away? Dead culture. Hipsters: fucking hipsters. The sun came out again.

'I like your moustache,' said Dennis, and he reached out to Conrad's top lip, stroking what little there was of it. Conrad couldn't help but finger it incessantly himself; he wasn't sure it counted as a moustache just yet, but he was glad of the validation.

'Er,' he said. 'Thanks. I think.'

'Dudes,' said Beagle, sitting up. 'Lunchbreak is over.'

Their banh mis digested, the three of them strolled back out of the park and down Broadway Market, the sun in their faces, Conrad guiding his bike one-handed. Past the gastropub and the cluster of new estate agents, past the posh homewares shop and the pastry waft of the old-school bakery, past the Argentinian steak joint and the organic café and the art house DVD rental place. Council estates towered behind the street on both sides, but nobody ever spoke of them unless their bikes got nicked nearby.

Beagle worked at a coffee shop that was also a clothes shop, but which looked like a charity shop. It didn't have a name, because it did not wish to attract the wrong sort of ill-informed *Time Out* reader on a day trip to the area. Thus its clientele were impeccably cool, and everybody else felt sufficiently intimidated to stay away. It was a strange business model. Beagle's Vespa was parked outside permanently, like a sculpture commission. Conrad left the two of them there at the door, drinking herbals, Beagle feeling up Dennis.

* * *

It would be nice, thought Conrad, to have somebody who'd feel me up in public now and again. He considered himself essentially a lonely person. Was that his parents' fault, too? He wondered how much he could legitimately blame them for. Did divorce create deep but unseen scars of distrust and alienation in a child, or were those wounds there to begin with? Was he congenitally crap with girls? He supposed the children of a happy marriage could be just as fucked up as anyone else. *More* so, maybe: a happy marriage was a high bar to clear. He wanted to think that he just hadn't met the Right Person. But had he maybe met the Right Person – assuming there was such a thing (probably not) – and blown it somehow, without even noticing? Maybe he'd done the thing Beagle needled him for, where he tried to chirpse the Right Person but was all nervous and creepy instead. Maybe that WAS what he'd done with Flo. Maybe, he thought, I just wasn't built for love. Maybe I was built to pine from afar for unattainable women. Specifically, the ones who were trouble. Maybe, eventually, all that pining would turn into perversion, after all. Maybe this was how stalkers started out. Or serial killers. Conrad couldn't be a serial killer, though. He didn't have it in him.

Back home at Kingsland Road, the pho noodle place was steaming, sweet-and-sour stench bubbling between the floorboards as Conrad hefted his bike up the stairs. Nobody ever seemed to eat there until after the pubs closed, but they started cooking at lunch-time nonetheless. The door to the flat wasn't double-locked, which meant someone was home. He hoped it was Polly. Maybe she'd packed up her market stall early. She did that sometimes.

But his heart sank when he reached the top of the stairs to find that her Pashley wasn't there. Instead, in the cramped kitchen at the end of the corridor, Conrad came upon his landlord, Ali, laying Beagle's cheese slices onto bits of Polly's spelt bread. He'd carved the loaf without a chopping board. Conrad could see the new scratches on the Formica worktop.

Ali was a squat, smiling Bangladeshi dude who always wore a flat cap, beneath which there whirred a passable business brain. Thanks to historical luck, or ancestral nous, the guy had a bunch of prime-location properties between Brick Lane and Dalston, which he ran from a little office at the bottom of Hackney Road. He filled them all to the brim with students and skint twenty-somethings, and the tenants were so grateful for the modest lease payments that he never had to perform any refurbishments. The crocked water pressure? The cooker's broken extractor fan? The washing machine's recurring leak? Conrad and his flatmates were reluctant to demand he do anything about them, just in case he decided to bump up the rent at the end of the year. Ali was raking it in without lifting a finger. Conrad admired his tenacity, and he envied his idleness, but he didn't much care for his habit of turning up unannounced. An Englishman's home was his castle – unless he was renting it from a Bangladeshi.

'Oh. Er. Hi, Ali.'

'All right, Conrad,' he said. 'Mind me making a sandwich?'

His name was either Kamal Ali or Ali Kamal; Conrad and his flatmates had never quite figured out which one was his surname, and which his given name. But they called him Ali, and he didn't seem to mind. Conrad always wanted to ask him about the culture of arranged marriages. He often thought it'd be preferable to pining vainly after girls that he met at art parties. None of the pain and pressure of courtship. Maybe his landlord could tell him how it all worked. Ali took a bite of the sandwich.

'I guess not,' Conrad replied.

'Nice one. How's Polly?'

'Er. Fine.'

'Truth is,' said Ali as he chewed, 'I came in to take a dump. Shitter in the office is bust, and yours is the closest flat. You don't mind, do you, mate?'

18

The first time she arrived at Isobel's door, Shauna wore a cerise blouse, baggy beige shorts and a Titleist golf visor.

'Hey, Iz! You ready?' she said, cotton pop socks edging from the tops of her golf shoes. Her legs had a just-waxed sheen.

'Sure,' replied Isobel, who was never keen on 'Iz', but had conditioned herself to endure it from a life's worth of patronising grown-ups and overfamiliar acquaintances.

'You're gonna need a hat,' said Shauna, eyeing up her polo shirt and tennis skirt, with a frown so minimal it might've been calculated to prevent further wrinkle formation. Behind her on the driveway was her Escalade, its bodywork sparkling white in the February sunshine.

'Sure,' said Isobel again.

She turned back into the chilled gloom of the house. She thought she'd maybe left her cap in the laundry room next to Carmen's quarters after her last run: four times around the flat, half-mile horseshoe of Blue Sky Grove. But as she passed her office on the way to find it, she was diverted by the mooing of a digital cow. She went to the laptop, to enact the necessary mouse clicks and Ctrl+ commands that would set in motion the milking and the soya bean harvest.

'Strewth!' said Shauna, who'd appeared in the office doorway behind her. 'It sure is cool in here. You always have the air con on so high?'

'Tor likes it,' Isobel replied, closing the laptop surreptitiously.

'Awww.' Shauna lifted a framed photograph from the Ikea EXPEDIT shelving unit. She poked at it with a long, polished nail. 'Is that *you*? So cute.'

'Oh. Yeah, me and my brother.'

'Aww,' said Shauna again. 'What's his name?'

'Conrad.'

'Conrad,' she repeated. 'Aww.'

Isobel smiled, not sure whether she should be embarrassed or indignant. She left Shauna fussing over the twins' finger-paintings and went to the laundry room. It was stuffy with the smell of tumble-dried bed linen. This was Carmen's domain, and Isobel felt a little like Kate Winslet, dashing through the *Titanic*'s engine room in her posh underskirts. But she found the cap, perched on a basket of unwashed pants and pyjamas.

'So where are the kids?' Shauna's question followed her through the house.

'At the crèche,' she called back, sniffing the sweat-stained rim of the hat, deciding it would just about do. 'Carmen's going to pick them up after her shop.'

She found Shauna in the sitting room, studying the two huge prints of flamingoes that hung above the sofa; they'd been there when they moved in, and Isobel had never summoned the motivation to replace them. She had one of her mum's French paintings, a Christmas present, wrapped in a brown paper parcel in the garage. She really ought to put it up. Instinctively, to create a diversion, she pressed the button that drew up the electric blinds from the plate-glass back windows. Sunlight assaulted the cream carpets and the twins' strewn toys as the yard revealed itself: the patio and the pool; the loungers and swing-set; the gardener in his spotless green uniform, pruning shrubs. The desert.

'You have *such* a lovely home,' said Shauna, with admirable sincerity.

Isobel felt the flush of self-consciousness, seeing it afresh with an outsider's eye. The house had almost no defining characteristics. Those flamingo pictures, the three-piece suite, the magazines on the coffee table: it was about as personalised as a dentist's waiting room. Even after two years, she and Tor were just passing through.

She'd rebuffed every one of Shauna's invitations since the New Year – to lunch, shopping, the races at Meydan, the movies – and by now she'd almost exhausted her stock of believable excuses. But perhaps Tor had been putting Shauna up to it from the start. Because one evening, as Isobel brushed her teeth in the en suite, laughing about the Australian's latest offer – 'golf with the girls' – he'd suggested that maybe, just maybe, it would be good for her to get out of the house, after all. Meet some new people. 'Even if,' he said, perching on the bed in his briefs, 'they aren't . . . Ach, how did you say it? "People Like Us"?'

Isobel knew full well that her husband worried about her: worried that she spent too much time alone at home in Blue Sky Grove. He was cool about it, the way he was about everything, but he worried. So, to alleviate his concerns, Isobel called Shauna back and told her that no, she did not play golf, but she'd be thrilled to give it a bash. Shauna was over the fackn moon.

They drove to the club in the Escalade. Its windows were tinted black. Isobel fiddled with the electronic recliner controls for the passenger seat, while Shauna wittered on about the wondrousness of Tor. How handsome he was, how thoughtful. How she wished he and Brian could be better friends beyond the office. Apparently Brian needed a pal, now their youngest kid was at boarding school in Oz.

'Iz,' she said, 'you are *so* lucky to still have little ones.'

Isobel agreed absent-mindedly, envisioning Shauna's boy as some obnoxious jock like his dad. Is that what Shauna wanted with her, too – a pal? Tor was probably right; she could do with a few more friends out here. Her husband and the maid didn't count, after all. But was Shauna seriously the best she could do? When they arrived at the course, there were two more women waiting at the entrance to the clubhouse, both wearing designer dark glasses.

'This is Isobel, ladies. Isobel, this is Mercedes and Diane.'

They were Jumeirah Janes, just like Shauna, their dental work gleaming between Botox-broad stripes of red lipstick. Isobel sensed a slackness in the skin on their hands as they shook hers, a more accurate clue to their carbon dating. They acted giddy as schoolgirls to meet her. But like schoolgirls, she suspected, they'd bitch like mad behind her back later. Isobel accepted each compliment and crumpled it for tossing in her mental wastepaper basket.

'Who is it you remind me of?' said Diane. 'You look *just like* that actress. Oh, you know the one, Mercedes! Shauna, what is her *name*? She's in that Will Smith movie. You know!'

But nobody knew, and they argued over the name of the Will Smith movie, and the name of the actress whom Isobel allegedly resembled, all the way to their golf carts.

Mercedes and Diane had already rented a set of clubs for Isobel. She offered to pay her course fee, but they wouldn't hear of it. They said she ought to consider membership. They'd pull some strings to get her and Tor to the top of the waiting list. She was non-committal to the point of rudeness. It felt as though she was being interviewed for a job she didn't want, and she knew where that could lead. She sensed she should've worn a proper blouse and trousers, bought golf brogues even – but fitting in would almost be worse than the alternative.

Shauna steered them over the smooth tarmac to the first tee. Like the ladies beneath their lipstick, Isobel noticed, the perfect grass of the golf course was in fact a simulacrum, betrayed by the sections of irrigation pipe visible amid the bushes. Desert sand had settled in the gaps between each green blade. The afternoon was stifling, and she was glad whenever they passed near the lawn sprinklers, because they briefly cooled her bare legs with the spray. She supposed it was good to get outside for once, beyond the bounds of her gated community.

She and Shauna waited while Mercedes and Diane teed off ahead of them. Isobel had never played golf, not even on the course beside Blue Sky Grove. Jogging was her preferred mode of exercise: solitary, contemplative, non-competitive. Frankly, she'd always considered golf a game for lesser life forms – men like Brian, so intellectually bereft that they could think of nothing more rewarding to fill their leisure time than hitting a ball into a hole with a stick.

So she was relieved to learn that her companions were all of no more than intermediate skill: they cackled at their crappier shots, cheated if ever the ball rolled into a bunker or the rough, and allowed her spare putts to bring her score closer to par. The more conservative club members glared and tsked at their uncouth antics as they crossed paths, but the ladies couldn't have cared less. 'Never you mind them, Iz,' said Shauna with a wink. Isobel' had enough beginner's luck to get by. She almost enjoyed herself.

After nine holes, they made for the clubhouse bar and a pitcher of Pimm's. When Isobel protested and asked for juice, she was summarily ignored. They sat on the terrace overlooking the eighteenth green, their chatter mingling with that of the nearby fauna. Colourful birds bobbed in and out of the foliage. Were they really imported by the Sheikh, these unlikely flocks? That's what she'd heard. That they were meant to atone for the migratory birds wiped out by the city's development. One more worthy cause on which she'd never managed to report. She sighed and sipped her drink. Not a serious person.

'I'm going to take you under my wing,' said Shauna, who'd spotted her watching a wagtail, as it pottered along the wrought-iron railings near their table.

Isobel gave up, finally, and smiled her assent. She had to admit it was pleasant to be in company. And anyway, none of her real friends were around to judge her. No Jonathan, sniggering behind his hand at Shauna's deficient breeding. No Conrad, conspicuously checking his texts. Hanging out with these ladies would be like reading one of her glossy magazines: trashy, but kind of fun. Plus the twins were so boring. What with Acres and endless telly, Isobel could feel herself getting stupider and stupider. Adult conversation might at least dam the oceanward surge of her intelligence.

'God, Diane,' said Mercedes, 'I do *love* your tits.'

They all hooted at that. Diane cupped her outrageously pert breasts.

'I know!' she said. 'I can*not* stop staring at them in the mirror!'

Shauna leaned in to Isobel. 'Could you tell? Diane got hers done with this great surgeon on Jumeirah Road, between the Botox clinic and the nose-job shop! But darln,' and she patted Isobel's thigh, 'you won't need to know that for another ten years.'

Isobel laughed. Maybe it was just the Pimm's, but she was loosening up. She'd always preferred the company of men, and men enjoyed her company more than women. But with their cheating at sports and their talk of breasts, these girls might as well be guys. So, it was decided: if Shauna wanted to be her friend, to take her under her wing, then okay, she'd submit. Isobel had resisted her advances until now on the grounds of good taste, but she hereby absolved herself of the obligation.

'So, ladies,' she piped up, when conversation next lulled, 'who's for another round . . . ?'

The three of them looked at her hesitantly. 'Of drinks, I mean.'

'Oh!' said Shauna. She chuckled, patting Isobel's thigh again. 'Of course, darln. Of course!'

They went back to Shauna's in Jumeirah Park, Shauna driving despite her second Pimm's. It would've been an imposing place, were its neighbouring villas not nearly identical: detached four-beds with crusader castle battlements and sandstone, mock-Moroccan turrets. The practical purpose served by a turret in this day and age was unclear, but the Gulf's residential developers couldn't get enough of them. The house wasn't exactly on the beach, as Brian had all but claimed; instead, it backed onto the waterfront of one of the city's inland canals, the real beach a tantalising ten minutes' drive away.

A pseudo-palatial staircase swept up from the reception area. On the grand, imitation-antique table in the hall (which, as a former design reporter, Isobel rated unfavourably) were potpourri and pictures of the kids. Shauna tipsily gave Isobel the tour of her home's key features, letting the others take an audit in case they'd forgotten. Mercedes and Diane soon headed through to the kitchen at the back, but Isobel lingered with her hostess over the home cinema, the gold-plated taps in the downstairs loo, the well-appointed games room. Brian had a foosball table, little used now that their youngest was gone. It was an old, solid thing, maybe the oldest item of furniture in the house. The wood lacquer was pristine, the pitch impeccably kempt, the twisting action of each rod as smooth as if freshly oiled. Engraved amateurishly in the wood beside its built-in scoreboard was Brian's name, the name of his son, and two more that Isobel didn't recognise.

'Brian's had that thing since he was a boy,' said Shauna. 'Him and his brothers.'

'My brother used to have one, when we were kids,' Isobel replied, spinning a goalkeeper.

'Conrad?' Shauna wrinkled her nose. 'Aww.'

The house on the Hill had had a playroom, with air hockey and one of the best views in London. Did Brian have air hockey? He did not. Isobel kept that detail to herself.

The open-plan kitchen was all stainless steel and glass and granite. The maid had laid out hors d'oeuvres. Isobel wasn't hungry. Shauna offered her a G&T; she took an apple juice. Mercedes and Diane were out on the patio, nattering. The pool was bigger than Isobel and Tor's, with more sophisticated side lighting. And there was a big, built-in barbecue on the terrace; it must've been Brian's pride and joy.

'Wow. Is that a pizza oven?!'

'What? Oh, yeah. But we never use it. Come on . . .'

Shauna led her through the yard and down to the strip of sand beyond. It could maybe have passed for a real beach, if Isobel didn't already know better. A couple of kids puttered past them on the canal, piloting a tiny launch. The women strolled right to the water's edge as the boat's wake lapped against it. Shauna was saying how they had a great mall nearby, restaurants. Isobel could see skyscrapers peeping over the top of the house behind her and, far off and heat-faded, the Burj. She understood why people might want to live like this. Shauna's compliments about the house in Blue Sky Grove sounded all the more hollow in hindsight.

'Y'know, Iz, darln, we bought this place before it was even built,' said Shauna, chomping a celery stick. 'Went to the developers' in downtown when the Sheikh passed the freehold law. They showed us a couple of designs, I picked one, Brian pointed to a plot on a map – might as well have been playing Pin the Tail on the Donkey! – and they said they'd hold it for us for five minutes. Five minutes! That was all. But I just closed my eyes and prayed we'd love it. Brian wrote a cheque for the deposit right there and then. Now, I won't tell you how much it cost, but I will tell you that when we walked outside, the people in line tried to buy it off us – and some of 'em offered near-double! Brian says that's when he reckoned we'd made the right decision.'

Mercedes and Diane were walking down the sand to them now, gins in hand.

'Did you get hurt in the crash?' said Isobel.

'Oh, y'know,' Shauna replied. 'Real estate is stabilising.'

'What about that condo of yours?' Mercedes interrupted, and sipped her drink.

Shauna glanced sharply at Mercedes; Isobel noticed it, then forgot it, all in an instant.

'We have this apartment,' Shauna said, explaining. 'In a high-rise downtown. It's an investment. The building isn't finished yet. Construction stalled. But we'll sell it once it's done.'

'Typical,' said Diane, in solidarity with Shauna and her plight.

'They're so short-sighted,' Shauna explained. 'They don't have the history to know how these things work. Any of it – business, economics. No history.'

She meant the Arabs. Mercedes and Diane nodded solemnly in agreement, as if this were a conversation long rehearsed at barbecues.

They ate a late lunch, and, by the time Shauna drove her home, she was way over the limit. She belched once at the wheel, apparently forgetting she had a passenger. Back at Blue Sky Grove, she climbed out of the Escalade just to give Isobel a firm, perfumed hug.

'I will see you soon, darln,' she said, before gliding away in her gilded SUV.

When Isobel got inside, she could hear the twins upstairs, being bathed by Carmen. She'd go and look in on them in a sec. But first she went to the laptop. She'd never yet spent real money on Acres, but she'd been thinking about it all day. The milking was done, the soya beans harvested. She was due some coins – but not enough. She dug her Mastercard from her bag, clicked through to the payments page and added the card number to her Acres account. Now she could convert real money into coins, purchase crops or equipment at will. She bought five acres at $2 (20 coins) per acre. She had an idea to set aside a plot of land to slow-grow some prize-winning giant veg for the Acres county fair. But then, five acres probably wasn't enough. So she bought five more. And a shire horse ($25/250 coins), because her normal horses hadn't been pulling their weight. She sent him to the stable for a feed while she decided what to plough with him first. He was vast, a glossy nut-brown with clean white feathering around his hooves. A fine animal. Something to be proud of.

19

Cindy Welch

hey hon bun. can you believe it?! bob bought me an acrehaymaker1000!!! best. birthday gift. ever!!! i cant stop looking at it! so how was yr weekend?

Isobel Meier

Wow, that's great. Happy bday. Weekend was nice, thanks. Tor and I took the twins to the beach. What's the weather like in Florida this time of year?

Cindy Welch

its good! we just had bobs folks in town frm minnesota. and my kids got a puppy!!! so cute!!! ill put up some pics.

Isobel Meier

Haha, do. Not sure mine are ready for pets yet. Maybe a goldfish . . .

Cindy Welch

so anyways, how about 3 hogs 4 yr cherry blosom cow. cd throw in a few coins 2 . . . ?!x

Isobel was never into games. Throughout their teens, Conrad's array of consoles had cluttered the playroom floor, as he stayed up late practising kung-fu kicks or strafing machine-gun fire. But

Tekken 4 and *Medal of Honor* did not educate or improve; they just turned her little brother into a moron. And it wasn't just video games: she could never get interested in netball or lax, either. Competitive school sport left her cold.

It was Jonathan who first sent her an invitation to play Acres, some months after he'd left the Emirates. Isobel ignored it for a week or two and let it sit there, loitering beside her Facebook News Feed as she scrolled through her London friends' photo albums. But one afternoon, at home in her office while Carmen collected the twins from the crèche, she stopped staring out of the window long enough to click 'Accept'. Tickled by the preposterously jolly theme music, she signed up and decided to spend a minute or two nosing around. She chose the username 'I22y', the same as the prefix for her first ever Yahoo! address, and picked out features for her avatar: dungarees, a red plaid shirt, brunette pigtails just like Izzy from *The House on the Hill*. A minute or two became three hours. By the time she finally shut down her laptop, eyes stinging from staring at the screen, Carmen had brought the kids home, made their dinner and put them in the bath.

At first, she was sucked in simply by the richness of Acres's lush parallel world: the tools, the barns and outbuildings, the marketplace. The crisp detail of the creatures, the comforting farmyard sounds, the colours: green, yellow, blue, more green. She enjoyed the certainties of the game: spend this many coins, get that many crops; sell this many crops, get that many coins. Rise at a certain hour to fertilise, and your wheat will grow high and healthy. Real-life farms, she supposed, suffered floods, droughts or plagues of locusts. In Acres it was always cloudless spring.

She found genuine satisfaction in setting herself goals and achieving them. In seeing her small collection of Acres squares become a collage of arable varieties. In collecting cows and sheep and pigs and arranging their fields in neat lines, just so, divided where appropriate by white picket fences. She'd grown bored and directionless, her days defined by the children's mealtimes, but Acres gave her fresh purpose. Whenever she surpassed one of her weekly online ambitions, she experienced a soothing rush of dopamine.

She formed lasting connections with other players. Every time you welcomed a neighbour, you were rewarded with a coin boost and five extra acres. The more Acres acquaintances you made, the greater the agricultural rewards. Once it became clear that she'd saturated her existing Facebook friends with invitations, she started surfing the Acres blogs and forums in search of fellow players. Cindy Welch was one of the first; a Florida housewife with two girls in middle school. They exchanged hints and tips, and in due course they exchanged pleasantries and personal details, too. The same thing soon happened with Freya Demetriou in Adelaide, Karen Pinsky in Tel Aviv, Cathy Ashman in Vancouver.

To those neighbours who seemed most friendly and trustworthy, Isobel awarded full access to her Facebook profile, including pictures of the twins. Hers was a photogenic family, and she accepted strangers' compliments graciously. She thought her buff husband might even encourage other women to become friendly with her, and thus to make Acres marketplace exchanges in her favour. (Of course, it could easily have the opposite effect.) With Tor at work and the twins at the crèche, her most intense, daily human contact was with her gamer neighbours. They were a village. They were a community.

As I22y's farm grew in influence, power and prestige, Isobel found herself developing more and more fruitful online relationships. Acres, she began to realise, demanded a delicate interplay of accomplishment, a fine balance between virtual-financial capital and social capital. Succeed too conspicuously, and her friends could become rivals; get too generous with her friends, and profits would suffer. These were valuable life lessons. She was learning the skills of a true businesswoman: forward planning, decision-making, leadership. She demanded stolid workmanship from her employees, competence and industry. She was a benevolent autocrat.

At first, Tor caught her playing more and more often. Amused, he mocked her for it. Later, though, he gently chided: wouldn't she prefer to get out of the house, do something with the twins – *anything* besides this silly game? So she learned to disguise her addiction, to indulge when he was out of the room or at work, and he caught her playing less and less. It must have looked to him like ritual tedium: the shepherding of resources; the cultivation of crops; the repetition of menial, apparently meaningless tasks. A mouse click here, a flurry of data entry there. But was it really so unlike her husband's own work? The machinations of the private equity department sounded to her like just that: ritual tedium. Both of them were playing the markets and building their client base. For both of them, the game proceeded – crops and profits grew, diversified, withered – whether they were at their desks monitoring them or not.

Sure, Tor was dealing in real money. But what was money, anyway? A fiction, as unstable as sand. At least Acres had a value system that was static, comprehensible, honourable: an acre of soya bean seed cost 10 coins, an acre's worth of soya beans sold for 12 coins. Strawberry seeds, 20 coins. Strawberries, 25. Isobel never returned from brewing a cup of tea to find the price of her best crop had plummeted. She'd never truly understand why property bubbles ballooned or burst, or why financial markets crashed. The game's good governance, its unquestioned regulation, seemed to her a role model for the world at large.

And it made her think of home, the greenery and the birdsong. When she'd endured a difficult day with the children, or a hazardous drive to the shops, a trip to Acres was like a holiday. She gave the kids her iPad, or left them quietly hypnotised by

TiVoed episodes of *Total Wipeout*, and then crept away to play. Her exasperation at childcare competed with her craving for the game, and before long she was abandoning them to Carmen earlier and earlier each day.

Her cultural life shrank to a dot. When had she last read a book? Months ago. A year, even. She kept track of some serious blogs, because they were brief. She flicked through unserious magazines. Sometimes she watched TV with the twins, or a DVD box set with Tor. She went with Shauna to the IMAX. But she was always thinking of her laptop, and the game. She supposed it was an embarrassing phase that would one day fade, like Ugg boots.

Time passed differently in Acres: winter never came, crops grew at a terrific speed, yet the pace of life was gentle. No hellish traffic. No malls, no nightclubs. None of the city's frantic rush, nor the aimless quiet of Blue Sky Grove. If I22y's farmworkers ever had barbecues together, which Isobel sometimes liked to imagine, they'd be sedate affairs. And the meat would be organic, locally sourced from her own land – not shipped in from a continent away. Prime Acres beef in every burger; I22y's finest pork in each sausage; home-grown lettuce and tomatoes; mayonnaise mixed with Acres chicken eggs.

A cherry blossom cow, incidentally, was a genuine asset. You could choose your farm animals by species at the Acres marketplace, but the breeds were randomised. With cows, for instance, you mostly got Friesians or Jerseys, occasionally a big-horned Highland bull. But there were also deliberate glitches, which now and then threw up a novelty. Isobel's cherry blossom cow was freckled pink, and she'd advertised it to her Acres neighbours on Facebook as a marketplace commodity. Cindy, she knew all too well, collected such rarities avidly. She had a five-acre field full of mutant, multicoloured farm creatures.

Isobel Meier

Hmm. Well, now that you've got the AcreHayMaker1000, do you still need all of your old tractors? I could do with another one myself . . . What if I swapped the cherry blossom for your AcreMaker100 – the red and yellow one? Those strawbs won't harvest themselves!

Cindy Welch

boy, Izzy – you drive a hard bargain, dontcha?! ok i guess i can let the old tractor go. i do love my rare breeds!!! lets do it.

Isobel Meier

It's a deal. Talk soon. Send me a puppy picture when you have a minute.

Cindy Welch

sure thing! say hi to torsten from me! xx

20

Pen's painting suffered an interruption in those first weeks of autumn. But as the season progressed, and as she and Bruno and David fell into a new routine, her creativity flourished and her palette was filled with the *rouges* and russets of late September. Bruno helped her to manage the garden's annual decline. Meanwhile, she found new forms of life in the fields and villages. She sketched scenes at an outdoor market in the hill-town where David had proposed, untroubled now by the summer rush of holidaying Brits; and she finally put her largest canvas to use by painting the abandoned house, on the road to Agen, with the frontage smothered in reddening Virginia creeper. She even started work on a nude self-portrait, but became self-conscious partway through and painted over it with abstract blues and yellows, the first of a series of Hodgkin-like colour studies unlike anything she'd previously attempted.

Leaves dropped each day on the surface of the swimming pool, grass began to grow on Bennett's grave, and after a few weeks the Cutlers came to Le Boqueteau to lay flowers and pay their respects. Maz had decided it would be a good lesson in grief, and promised the children a puppy of their own, which Pen vowed to visit. She gave them some jars of David's greengage jelly to take home. David, when he first returned following the dog's death, spent a few silent minutes alone at the graveside, and Pen suspected the loss meant one more missing connection to the dead first wife. They went for a long walk, talking little, and for the rest of that

209

weekend he quietly immersed himself in jam-making and One
Day International cricket coverage.

Bruno never stayed overnight, and nobly refused to make love
in the marital bed. The mattress in the spare room was equal to
the task but, with the grounds to themselves, he and Pen often
made other arrangements. He would bring her *cèpes* he'd foraged,
wildfowl he'd shot, rustic wines, or cut flowers from the roadside
or the garden of another of his clients. He never asked for
anything, and nor did she. She was curious about his life beyond
the driveway, but – whether due to the frustrations of language,
or to something else – he disclosed little.

She did at least discover that he wasn't married. He lived alone,
he said, and she never learned the identity of the woman on the
phone. She had no cause to call him again, let alone visit him at
home, because he always turned up on his three allotted work
days each week, which they would invariably interrupt or conclude
with sexual intercourse of increasing familiarity. The raking of
leaves from the lawn was sometimes, it had to be said, neglected.

Was it possible to maintain this blissful lifestyle indefinitely?
David had mentioned the prospect of moving to a three-day week
at work, which would allow him to spend far more time in France.
Pen tried to sound enthusiastic, privately hoping the other partners
at the firm would veto the plan a while longer. She was beginning
to entertain the concept of a classic French arrangement: from
her husband, the Englishman, she could have comfort, security,
property. From her lover, the Gaul, passion of a sort, gratification
– and, yes, something she recognised as genuine affection. The
fondness that she'd only acknowledged for Bennett when it was
already too late, she now reassigned to Bruno. She felt more at
ease with him than with her husband; she longed for him more
hungrily. More than once, she allowed herself to wonder what it
would be like to run away with the gardener.

Wine flowed freely through their relationship, and the

household's alcohol consumption more than doubled; Pen made sure Bruno took a portion of each week's empty bottles away with him in the Land Rover, so as not to arouse David's curiosity. She didn't want her husband to think she was turning into some sort of lonely alcoholic, which would have been the natural assumption. The idea of an affair, let alone with Bruno, would be so utterly inconceivable to David that no quantity of clues could have led him to the truth. He once complained that Mr DeLambre had left his chopping equipment lying around out by the wood-shed; Pen remembered that he'd done so in order to ravish her atop the chest freezer in the utility room. She changed the subject, pointing out that the woodshed's frame was rotted through – and suggesting they ask Bruno to rebuild it.

While the weather was still clement, they had sex in the garden: on the lawn and in the long grass where the wild gladioli grew, once upright and uncomfortably squeezed against the trunk of a crab apple tree. Sometimes in the barn, where Pen put down a blanket to protect them both from splinters. Once in the Land Rover, which gave her pins and needles and a grazed shin where she clobbered it on the handbrake. Once beside the herb bed, where Bruno pounced on Pen from behind while she was weeding; her fists gripped the warm soil beneath the basil plants as they came concurrently. When the air grew chillier, they moved inside; the kitchen table had a kind of sentimental value, though the rug in the sitting room was considerably more comfortable. In the end, they seemed to arrive separately but simultaneously at the view that the spare room was the most practical, straightforward location for their lovemaking, and thereafter contented themselves with its more conventional enticements: a bed, fresh linen.

Bruno was an eager lover. Primal, unreconstructed, like an outsider artist painting in oils, without ever having studied the technique of the Great Masters, let alone the nuance of Impressionism. Afterwards, he would roll two cigarettes and they would smoke them together quietly. Pen had to be sure to clean and dry the tobacco-scented bedclothes ahead of David's visits. He did once sniff the air and ask her whether she'd allowed Mr DeLambre to smoke in the house; she claimed to have left the kitchen door open while the handyman was pruning the bay trees just outside, puffing away as he hacked at them with his shears. She said she would give him a stern warning not to do so in future, and David appeared satisfied. From then on, whenever they smoked in the spare room, they made sure to close the door and open the window. She and David were having sex no more or less often than they had previously, which was not especially often, but she had to admit that she was enjoying it more, if only because it introduced some variety.

Conversationally, her relationship with Bruno was somewhat lacking. His English failed to improve, and he often limited himself to portentous post-coital remarks.

'So. You are happy, *madame?*' he would ask, scratching his unclothed gut. 'With Monsieur Bowles?'

'Well, "happy" might be pushing it,' she joked, and Bruno grunted pensively.

'But he is a good man, *ouais?*'

'Yes. He's a good man.'

Also, another time: 'You think ever you will live together? Madame and Monsieur Bowles, *à deux? Ici?*'

And, yet another time: 'If you were not married, you think this happen? *Entre nous?*'

She could hear other, more thorny questions within the ones to which he gave voice, but she chose to ignore them.

In mid-December, she drove back to London, taking with her a selection of paintings. Through some old design contacts, she managed to flog a small handful of them at one of the city's higher-class Christmas craft markets. The money – £3,200 in all

– was not to be sniffed at, but it was sufficient that somebody saw value in her work. Fran had made a few enquiries on her behalf, and a pub gallery in Islington agreed to sell a pair of pictures from her *Boules* series, with a view to repeating the arrangement should it prove successful. She kept aside two of her *Field With Water Tower* landscapes as gifts for Isobel and her new step-daughter, Harriet; and one of the abstract compositions for Conrad.

The Manvilles' Christmas plans were always complex and unsatisfactory. Pen and David squeezed into his Hammersmith flat for a fortnight, and spent Christmas Day with Harriet. On Boxing Day, Pen booked a table at a gastropub for lunch with Isobel and Conrad, which saved her having to prepare a proper meal in the now-sparse surroundings of the house on the Hill. The twins had turned into fully fledged toddlers since she last saw them: blond, moon-faced little boys, who tended to lapse into German when they quarrelled over their Christmas cracker prizes. Pen tried to foster some sort of emotional connection with her grandsons, but they were interested mostly in themselves. She gave them copies of *The House on the Hill 6: Bedtime and the Babysitter*, and *7: Rover and the Roller Skates*. Isobel read to them over the hubbub of the pub dining room, trying to explain that she was the 'Izzy' in the stories, and that Conrad was the 'Conrad':

> Conrad would not go to bed.
> 'I'm too grown-up for bed,' he said.

But they were engrossed in their toys. Conrad was incredulous: 'You're *still* giving those to people for Christmas?' He and David could not seem to find much common ground, so David just talked to Isobel about his own grandchild, while Conrad thumbed his mobile phone.

Isobel and the twins were staying at the house, so Pen came

back with them to help make some beds. She turned up the heating and wandered the rooms, wondering again whether to let the place go. The view from the balcony of the loft conversion was still enviably panoramic. The walls were neutrally coloured and nearly bare, the bathroom fittings good as new; it was as saleable as it would ever be. Yet, much as her life in France was flourishing, a total commitment to David seemed less sensible with every passing day. What if she and Bruno were discovered? Where would she go then?

In lieu of an evening meal, she had bought gingerbread men for the twins to eat while they watched a Pixar DVD; they took what appeared to be sadistic pleasure in breaking off the legs and arms and heads. She and Isobel dined on tinned soup at the kitchen table. There was still snow on the ground in the back garden.

'I suppose the cold must come as quite a shock to you now.'

'Nah. To the twins, maybe. I like it. We sometimes get forty-five degrees out there in summer. *That* is a shock.'

Isobel looked tanned, but tired.

'So, are you really going to sell the house this time?' she asked.

'Well, you could always come back to England and buy it, darling. Torsten must have made a lot of money out there by now!'

This had struck Pen as being a not-inconceivable solution.

'Not nearly enough for that, I'm afraid,' Isobel replied, suddenly glum. She blew cool air across her spoonful of soup. 'Do you have Wi-Fi here any more?'

'I'm afraid not,' said Pen. 'Did you want to Skype him?'

'Mm,' said Isobel, swallowing.

Some part of Pen hankered secretly to return to Bruno. (Was he alone with Remy for Christmas? She'd forgotten to ask. When she announced that she was leaving for a fortnight, they'd been picking the shot pellets from some variety of game bird that he'd hunted and plucked and roasted himself. He'd nodded and started rolling a cigarette.) But back in the urbane world of friends and family, her romance seemed preposterous, unreal, as she'd always expected it would. Red Indians, indeed.

Pen wanted to tell her daughter about the Frenchman, wanted to confide in somebody. But Isobel had gone on and on about how nice David was, how healthy and happy Pen looked. Besides, she'd always had a bit of a puritanical streak – not inherited from her mother, that's for sure. Pen didn't know how well she'd react to the revelation, even if she explained that Bruno was part of the reason for that health, that happiness. In the end, Pen drove to Hammersmith, Isobel and the twins went to bed, and a day later they were gone again, on a return flight to the Emirates. The house on the Hill was empty once more.

David drove back with her to the Dordogne to see in 2011. The farmhouse was just as beautiful in winter, thought Pen, when the frost bleached out the pastel shades of the surrounding landscape. They lit a fire and ate a casserole and David opened some champagne in time for the BBC's Big Ben coverage, which he insisted on watching, despite the French *minuit* having passed an hour previously. He had decided to stay for a whole week. Before Christmas, the other partners had agreed to let him phase his working patterns on a project-to-project basis, which meant that he could return to France for longer tranches of the calendar. The news had made him high-spirited. Pen hid her concern convincingly, or so she thought.

When Bruno's Land Rover returned on the Monday after New Year's Day, she hid in the kitchen with a mug of herbal tea as David strode out to the drive to meet him. She heard the mumble of their conversation, the crackle of their shifting weight on the cold grass, and David's unexpected laughter. He had announced at breakfast that he thought Bruno deserved a Christmas bonus and a basket of jams for all his good work, and that he would give him the week off, too, with the ground being so hard. Pen tried to predict Bruno's reaction: another week without fleshly satisfaction, the knowledge that such weeks would only become more frequent, not to mention David's patronising pay-off. Anybody would feel hard done by after all that. She held her breath until she heard the Land Rover's door close again, and the engine turn over. David looked remarkably chipper when he came back in. He was at his most handsome when he was happy.

'Well,' he said, grinning. 'Isn't that kind?'

'What?' Pen's herbal tea was fast becoming lukewarm.

'Bruno has invited us to go hunting with him tomorrow. Shoot something for our supper. Won't that be fun?'

'Hunting?' she repeated, trying to conceal her alarm. 'With guns?'

'Yes, of course. Don't look so worried, Pen. It sounds like he knows just what he's doing. And I've done plenty of shooting in my time.'

She blushed with panic. 'Well, I haven't!'

'Of course not!' he chuckled. 'That's because you're so damned metropolitan. I'll show you how it's done.'

'I'm not sure, David,' she said, draining the rest of her tea into the sink. 'I'm really not sure.'

'Oh, come on. You're always saying you want to immerse yourself in the local customs and all that. Isn't this just the sort of thing?'

If only he knew. What does the Red Indian do to the Paleface when his way of life is threatened? He takes his woman. And then he claims his scalp.

21

Bruno had arrived at Le Boqueteau at seven, by which time Pen had been awake and fretting for more than two hours. The Frenchman honked the Land Rover's feeble horn and waited there, out on the drive. Pen filled a Thermos with hot coffee, then she decanted some brandy into a hip flask. David spooned quince jam onto croissants and wrapped them in aluminium foil. They'd both piled on layers of warm clothing beneath their Barbour jackets, but Pen was chilly nonetheless.

She'd had twenty-four hours to deter her husband, but all her strategic subtleties had failed. As the one with hunting experience, David would not be persuaded that it was dangerous. He suggested she stay at home while he and Bruno went shooting, but she knew that if she did, she would be powerless to prevent whatever the handyman had planned. The only way to convince David of the peril he faced would be to tell him everything – the kitchen table, the spare bedroom, the chest freezer – and she was not prepared for that. Nor had she been given an opportunity to confront Bruno about whatever the hell he was up to. David had been in the kitchen all day yesterday potting chutneys, and Pen couldn't get to the telephone, let alone to Bruno's number, without fear of making her husband suspicious.

Bruno nodded and muttered a greeting as they approached the Land Rover in the half-dark. Despite David's chivalrous objections, Pen climbed into the back. The seat was a metal bench, padded with under-stuffed cushions that Bruno or some other

217

owner had long ago fixed down using lengths of gaffer tape. Pen glared at the handbrake and remembered the deep bruise it had given her during an assignation. Remy sat up straight beside her in a luminous yellow collar, staring purposefully ahead, while the men filled the leather front seats. They had to leave in time for dawn, Bruno had insisted, because that was when *les bécasses* emerged to feed. David had gathered from the handyman's description that these were small wildfowl with large bills, and sought them in the *Michelin Guide to Birds of Britain and Europe* that he kept on the windowsill in the downstairs loo. Their English name was woodcock, he informed his wife: quail-sized, suitable for roasting, and excellent on toast with Cumberland sauce.

They drove north-east, or so she surmised, towards Bruno's preferred hunting ground. The jeep's suspension was negligible, its heating system non-existent. The corner of the canvas roof flailed in the freezing wind. Pen's teeth chattered, and the dog's steamy breath hung before her. Soon, they were passing through uncharming, utilitarian villages that she didn't recognise and wouldn't have cared to paint if she did. From hamlet to forlorn hamlet, the grey fields slowly shrugged off the mist. David appeared oblivious to the cold and the ungodly hour; he was recounting his past experience of blood sports with boyish gusto: Boxing Day hunts on horseback, pheasant shooting, deer stalking, fly-fishing. He seemed to have partaken of all of them at one time or another. Pen hadn't been aware of any of this, but it came as little surprise.

As her husband rambled on, Bruno silently studied the road ahead, his jaw thrust forward in concentration or irritation: she couldn't make out which. She thought back to the things he'd asked her as they lay in the spare bed, flushed with the question-able shame that followed intercourse. Was she happy? Would she and Bruno be together, if not for David? It was simple enough now to invest them with sinister intent. Of course, even in their first year as man and wife, she had occasionally considered what her life might look like without David. She might thus have given Bruno a somewhat unkind account of their marriage, but she'd never so much as hinted that he should consider doing anything about it – had she? Bruno was a simple man. Did his masculine passions point towards violence? The thought horrified her, thrillingly.

After what might have been half an hour of driving, they turned down a dirt road into woodland. As the car slowed, so did the breeze; the patch of forest lay in a flat dip between two bosomy *collines*, sheltered from the harshest of the elements. The sun was beginning to flicker between the trees. By the time Bruno brought the Land Rover to a halt at the side of the track, Pen could not recall having passed anything but deserted farm outbuildings for at least a mile.

'*Bon*,' said the Frenchman, and stepped out of the jeep. Remy scrambled across Pen's lap and through the gap where the canvas roof was unsecured. David, she saw, had yanked his seat forward to let her out. He stamped his wellies twice to get the blood circulating to his feet.

'Come on, darling,' he said impatiently. Pen was gassy with anxiety, and felt that to remain motionless in the Land Rover might somehow forestall events. Reluctantly, though, she swung her boots out of the vehicle, lowered them to the hard mud, and then tugged her cashmere scarf tight around her neck. Bruno had been rummaging for equipment in the back of the jeep and he emerged with a pair of shotguns, one in either hand. Pen shrank at the sight of them; her nerves bristled as if from vertigo. The Frenchman handed one of the guns to David, who shifted it to the crook of his arm.

'*Quelle direction?*' he asked, in his brutally accented French.

Bruno nodded towards the woods, lifting his stomach to buckle an ammunition belt around his middle. He and David both carried small, leather-strapped pouches at their waists – filled, Pen presumed, with hunting accessories. The handyman plucked a box of ammo from his bag and David copied him, competently cracking open his gun to insert the cartridges. She was briefly reassured: her husband knew how to handle the weapon, should he be forced to use it in self-defence. But then, without any warning, would he even get the chance?

Finally, Bruno produced three high-visibility orange baseball caps, and presented two of them to his new hunting companions. Pen had already put on a woollen hat, and was loath to relinquish its warmth – but safety, she supposed, was paramount. She bunched her hair and squeezed it under the cap. Remy nosed the air impatiently. Bruno closed the rear door of the jeep and shouldered his gun. He gave his guests a grim look, and a jerk of the head that said 'Follow me', then he turned and moved off into the skeletal birches.

The silence was as chilling as the air. They loped through the trees, accompanied solely by the sound of twigs snapping. The handyman had told Pen and David to keep behind him: he would lead the hunt for the first bird of the morning. Pen hung back instinctively, heart thumping. Remy's yellow collar was just visible, ducking and weaving through the frosted woodland ahead, but his mottled brown coat made for effective camouflage. She suffered again that sense of isolation: here, in the woods, in the countryside, in a foreign land, they were so far from the threat of wider consequence that anything seemed possible. Only now it wasn't her own impulses that concerned her, but those of her impassioned lover. He had a gun, for Christ's sake! She could hardly breathe. If Bruno had planned a murder, nobody but Pen would ever know for certain that it wasn't simply a tragic accident, caused by the victim's inexperience of firearms etiquette. And would she ever tell anyone, knowing that she'd have to tell them *why*?

She looked up from the forest floor and saw David's hi-vis cap just a few steps ahead of her; their pace had slowed, and Bruno was muttering commands to his dog in French.

'Has Remy found something—?' she began to whisper, but her husband shushed her with a flap of his hand. The dog was 20 yards ahead, statue-still, snout pointed at a scrap of dead shrub. She squinted, but couldn't make out what it was that interested them.

Bruno, louder now, gave a clear command. Remy pounced at the undergrowth. A frantic rustle, and two brown blurs burst from the foliage, fluttering off fast and low in a zigzag between the trees. Bruno levelled his shotgun and fired twice. One of the dark shapes dropped out of the light. Remy raced off towards it, and the men followed. In spite of herself, Pen couldn't help but be impressed anew by Bruno's native skills. Her Red Indian, tracking and flushing his prey.

Remy returned with what looked like a bundle of leaves in his mouth, which he gave proudly to his master. As Pen drew closer to where the men were standing, David beckoned her over. Bruno held out the woodcock, slumped in his fat palm. She couldn't see the wounds, but it was surely dead. Its long bill pointed limply at the ground.

'*Pour*, ah . . . *des lombrics*,' said Bruno, running his forefinger along the beak. 'Worms.'

David gripped her shoulder excitedly. 'What do you say to that, Pen? Pot-roasted for dinner, with some of those lovely mushrooms?'

Pen looked at her husband, looking at the bird; then at Bruno, looking at her. The gardener smiled. She shuddered.

David was adamant that they should come back with at least a brace of kills: one for the Bowleses, and one for Mr DeLambre. Bruno agreed, but this time suggested David take the lead. Good

God, thought Pen, as they set off through the woods again – Bruno could shoot him in the back at any moment. Yet panic did not persuade her to intervene: what if she was wrong? Or worse, what if she was right, and risked her own skin? After a few hundred yards, they came to a sizeable clearing. Pen slowed to a halt at its edge, but the men pressed on across the grassy scrub, Remy just ahead of them, jittery with anticipation. David turned and saw her standing there, paralysed.

'What time is it, Pen?' he called back.

She looked at her wristwatch. 'Almost half past eight.'

David and Bruno shared a glance and a murmur, and then her husband reached into his pouch and brought out three crumpled foil lumps.

'Time for a spot of breakfast, I'd say!'

She exhaled, realising she'd been holding her breath, and started to walk out into the glade. The hills rose away in the distance on both sides, and light from the early morning sun glinted on the window of a farmhouse on a far-off slope to the west. Warmer now, she unzipped her jacket. The men rested their guns as David unwrapped the croissants. She was halfway between them and the treeline when he looked up and said, 'Where's the coffee, darling?'

Pen was so flustered that, for a second, she didn't grasp what he was talking about. Then it dawned on her: she'd left the Thermos in the Land Rover. She could see it in her mind's eye, lying on the poorly cushioned back seat where, in the fog of apprehension, she'd failed to pick it up. She looked at David, hoping he might spot the plea in her eyes.

'I think I left it in the jeep, actually.'

'Oh, bugger. Well, would you mind going back for it?'

'David, I . . .'

'We'll wait here, Pen. It's only a little way back through the wood if you walk straight.'

She looked again from one man to the other. Her husband,

exasperated by her distractedness; the inscrutable Bruno, now engrossed in the rolling of a cigarette. Remy seemed to have picked up another scent, and was darting to and fro on the grass, as if unable to discern its source. Pen's stomach performed a similar dance as she turned and trudged back towards the shadowy trees, dread reaching out to envelop her.

Beneath the birches, the past night's cold clasped her to it once more. Low branches tormented her, poking at her eyes, kicking at her shins. In the canopy above, she could hear the call of an unfamiliar bird – the dead woodcock's mate, howling in anguish? There it was again: loneliness. Her every step was heavy with regret.

After a minute, she stopped to get her bearings, which was when she heard the shouts behind her. One man's voice, then two. They grew louder, more irate, and she turned in their direction. She couldn't make out the words – they were obscured by the pounding of blood in her ears – but they undoubtedly came from the clearing. As her terror peaked, there followed the clap of a shotgun: one shot, and then a long, ghastly moan.

Pen stifled a cry and stumbled quickly back through the trees, abruptly immune to the scratches they inflicted. She almost lost her footing on the frozen earth, and grazed her palm on a tree trunk as she grabbed at it to maintain her balance. Her flapping Barbour snagged a waist-high branch, tugging her backwards, then tearing free. The unseen horizon spun and she wondered, hysterically, if she'd somehow sprinted in the wrong direction. But then she broke from the cover of the wood and back into the clearing.

The first thing she saw, with a jolt, was David kneeling on the grass. The second, with another, was Bruno lying stricken beneath him.

'Oh God oh God oh God,' she stammered under her breath as she approached. She could hear Bruno moaning and cursing, which meant that he was still alive. Remy licked his face, and neither man shooed the dog away. She could see no blood. The shotguns, Bruno's hi-vis baseball cap and a pair of discarded croissants lay on the dewy ground nearby. David turned to her, mild perturbation in his features.

'I think he's broken his ankle, Pen.'

'What?'

David prodded Bruno's lower leg gingerly, and the Frenchman breathed in sharply through his teeth, swearing again.

'The dog took off after a rabbit and disappeared down a hole; Bruno went after him, stuck his foot straight in it, went over sideways. Think I heard a bone crack before the gun went off.'

'My God,' she replied, beginning to grasp the blessed banality of what had occurred.

'It's jolly lucky neither of us was standing too close, or he might've taken our heads off. The damned dog just popped up out of another hole – three bloody feet away.'

Bruno's face was distorted with agony, the veins in his forehead bulging. Pen met his gaze, but couldn't make out the emotions it expressed: anger, resentment or just straightforward physical pain. She looked down at his left foot, which had indeed come to rest at a very unnatural angle, and felt only relief.

David took charge at once, first unloading both weapons and giving them to Pen to carry. He hauled Bruno to his feet and, though he had to stoop, put one of the injured handyman's arms across his shoulder and helped him to hop back across the clearing. Remy whimpered and bothered alongside them. Pen walked ahead through the woods to the Land Rover, becalmed by her husband's near-military composure. They laid Bruno, still groaning, across the back seat. Remy leapt into the footwell beside him and guiltily nuzzled his belly.

With directions from Bruno, delivered in English even more broken than usual, David quickly found the road to town and, forty-five minutes or so later, the modest hospital on its outskirts. Bruno was soon seen by a doctor; as they waited for word of his condition, Pen marvelled at the efficiency of French healthcare. This wouldn't be such a terrible place to grow elderly, she thought. David said he would stay at the hospital, so she drove the Land Rover into Agen to buy provisions with Remy. When she returned, Bruno was waiting beside her husband, woozy with painkillers and his leg in plaster. He sullenly declined the sandwich she offered, but David wolfed his down at once. The handyman hobbled on his crutches across the hospital car park.

Pen was surprised to learn that David already knew the route to Bruno's house. Passing close to Le Boqueteau and aiming north-east again, he eventually turned the jeep into a driveway just shy of one of the cheerless villages they'd driven through before dawn. In the low afternoon sunlight, the landscape was only a little more promising. Bruno watched it go by silently from the back seat. As they approached the squat cottage at the end of the rutted drive, a dog began to bark, and Remy answered it. The house was blotchy with grey-brown patches of concrete where the white paint had crumbled away, and surrounded by a swirl of churned mud. At the top of the drive was a large, chicken-wire enclosure; within, skinny poultry pecked at the grain-speckled ground. An Alsatian was collared to a metal pole by a 10-foot chain, straining at it so as to bark more violently at the Land Rover's approach. There was an ageing Renault 5 parked beside the back door, its wheel arches rusted. So this was the Red Indian's camp.

Shock upon shock, as they helped Bruno from the jeep, the back door opened to reveal an elderly lady in skirts and an apron. She was familiarly red-faced, and sausage-fingered.

'*Bruno, mon Dieu!*' she cried, and waddled forward to hug him, firing French exclamations too fast for Pen to comprehend. But she recognised the voice from a long-ago phone call. Bruno surrendered to the woman's embrace, and when she stepped back to take his face in her hands, he mumbled an explanation. She looked past him at Pen and David.

'*Monsieur Bowles*,' she said, her plump eyes softening. '*Madame. Merci.*'

'Madame DeLambre,' David replied.

Pen had nothing to say, and so said nothing.

The cottage was small and poky and smelled unpleasantly of animals. At the kitchen table, David conversed in pidgin French and improvised sign language with Bruno and his mother. A wiry cat crept along the top of the dresser, eyeing Pen. At the back door, Remy was munching from a messy selection of food bowls, each one presumably assigned to a different pet.

Pen went to the loo. The tiny lavatory was unheated, and its ceiling clotted with damp from what she assumed to be a bathroom above. She quickly spent a penny, and then listened to the water pipes creaking with resistance as she washed her hands. On the way back to the kitchen, past the narrow staircase, she peered into the sitting room. Its low ceiling and the condensation-fogged windows made the space dark and oppressive. The carpet was threadbare, the original fireplace filled by an unsightly gas heater. Stuffing poked from the seams of the sofa cushions. There were shelves set into an alcove at the back of the room, and displayed on them was a selection of grotesquely kitsch ceramic figurines: a simpering milkmaid; a beatific shepherd boy; a wide-eyed roe deer; geese, sheep, pigs.

Pen was herself again. She had sloughed off her middle-class carapace to indulge her aboriginal fantasy, but, as she disdained those rustic trinkets, she felt it enclosing her once more. She could never live like this. She thought of those sad, middle-aged Dutch women one read about in the papers, who'd fallen for some African gigolo on a beach holiday and run off to Kenya to marry him, squandering the inheritance until they realised they'd been duped, by the gigolo or by their own late erotic urges.

No, she had resolved to be practical, and she would remain so. She had married David because they could comfortably share a lifestyle – and, in the end, that was what truly mattered. She had married for love once, and it had almost finished her off. It struck her now that David and Bruno were like two halves of Jerry: the man of wealth and status, and the man of action, driven by his passions. But there was no middle way. She could not have Bruno and David. She could not have Bruno and Le Boqueteau.

Madame DeLambre called the village taxi driver to take them home. Before they left, David helped to install Bruno on a bruised old armchair in the sitting room. As he lifted the Frenchman's leg to slide a footstool beneath it, Madame DeLambre fussed at the gas fire. Pen stood in the doorway, and Bruno looked at her across the room with the same sad, Bennett eyes that had inspired their first coupling: somehow already aware of his fate; resignedly awaiting the vet's needle, and oblivion.

As they departed, David donated the dead woodcock to Bruno's mother. The old lady kissed him on both cheeks and thanked him again. In her husband, Pen reflected, she had found a man of kindness, integrity and generosity. A man who had shown strength and resolve in difficult circumstances. A man who had loved his wife and worked hard to build them a wonderful old age together – and then, cruelly robbed of her, had been generous enough to give Pen that life instead. Who loved his daughter and his dreadful grandson. Who spent hours, days, making jam for near-strangers. A Christian man, in every sense. And if he was tedious, and if he voted the same way her father had, then so be it. He was good, and that was good enough. She would stay with him. She would make it work. She would convert the barn into a gîte.

'Caroline used to visit Madame DeLambre before she got ill,' David explained, as they sputtered towards home in the back of the taxi driver's Citroën. This was how he'd known the way to Bruno's house.

'She'd buy eggs and things from them,' he went on. 'Just to be friendly. They don't have a lot of money. I believe Bruno's father was a bankrupt. Sold the family farm, that sort of thing. And Bruno never married.'

Pen stared out at the countryside rather than meet her husband's eyes. If he were to see into her soul now, it might all have been for nothing. The landscape became more and more picturesque as they approached Le Boqueteau.

'Happens a lot in the country nowadays,' said David, still filling the silence. 'Farmers without wives. Sad, really. I suppose there just aren't enough suitable women about.'

The following morning, Pen called Jerry in London, to tell him she was ready to sell.

OFFER

22

The first account to appear on the books of Manville Glassop Cohn, in June 1986, was CANoodle, a brand of canned noodles manufactured in Coventry by Harvey's soups. In fact, CANoodle was a rebrand of Harvey's existing range of chicken, beef and mushroom noodles: an attempt to recalibrate the company's product towards a younger demographic than the post-war house-wives who'd long been its core market. Thanks in part to Jerry's 'Lady & the Tramp' print and billboard campaign, CANoodle had briefly threatened Pot Noodle's dominance in the financial year to April, and the new Harvey's CEO let it be known to Tony Glassop that his business would gladly go with him and Jerry, should they decide to strike out on their own.

The two of them had moved agencies together once already, at Glassop's instigation. And for three years or so, over a succession of lunches and dinners and drinks, they'd danced around the idea of establishing their own boutique firm. No more humouring their clients' crap ideas. No more taking orders from dinosaurs. By '86, they had a prospective third partner: Bill Cohn, a diffident but effectual Canadian Jew from the strategic department. (Bill died of stomach cancer in 2007. He was fifty-nine.)

They met to finalise the details at the corner table in a kebab house on Edgware Road, where they knew nobody else in adver-tising would be seen dead during a weekday lunchbreak. Jerry would be Creative Director; Glassop, Accounts Management; Cohn, Planning. They resigned their posts the following day, informed *Campaign* magazine of their plans, and began to build MGC's client base from a small office that Glassop had rented in a loft off Tottenham Court Road. Soon they won breakfast cereals, soft drinks, processed foods. Then a lager and a washing-up liquid. Then a car, a spot cream, a furniture retailer.

When Jerry was a boy, most advertising was conceived with the intention of convincing the consumer that something simply worked. But nowadays *everything* worked, and his job was to appeal to 'Values and Lifestyles', to discern what people saw of themselves in a product, to add intangible value to a brand's intrinsic worth. He thrived for a while, marshalling multiple wild ideas and the nutters in the creative department. He was the beating heart of the company. When MGC took a floor in a building on Mortimer Street in 1989, he demanded brightly coloured brainstorming spaces, beanbags, bonuses. He got them all.

And yet, when the definitive history of advertising was written, his firm would warrant no more than a paragraph. MGC would be buried, and rightly so, somewhere beneath BMP and BBDO; CDP and AMV and FGA; BBH and WPP. Flicking through his portfolio in his darker moments, Jerry feared it had all been a vain folly. They'd never successfully defined what they stood for, so wrapped up were they in the everyday excitements of running their own agency: stealing accounts from competitors, designing logos and letterheads. They caved in too quickly to their clients' demands, agreed to too many tissue meetings and tweaks. They were ordinary, and they too often put their name to derivative campaigns. Despite a decent run of financial successes, in the end, MGC was creatively average – or worse, irrelevant.

At some indefinable moment in the agency's lifespan, moreover, advertising had ceased to be the world's hippest profession, and become a social pariah. Everyone's favourite flash uncle, caught touching up the kids in the spare room. People thought Jerry vulgar, where previously he'd been considered sophisticated. Had he changed? He didn't think so.

In 1999, the firm was sold to Sir Mark Sage and assimilated into his global plc. Glassop negotiated the details, so all three partners were handsomely rewarded. In theory, Jerry was opposed to the sale. In practice, he had a divorce to pay for, and a new fiancée with extravagant tastes. Besides, MGC had recently taken on an ambitious online clothing company, and when the thing went tits up in the dot-com debacle, they lost most of their fee. If not for Sir Mark's infinitely deep pockets, it might have bankrupted them.

Wasn't that the point of advertising? *Loadsamoney?* How else was a lower-middle-class Northern lad supposed to achieve fabulous wealth and a metropolitan lifestyle? Jerry had sanded down his provincial accent, and amassed sufficient funds and professional recognition to keep him comfortable until approximately eighty-five years of age, by his estimate. He didn't expect to live nearly that long. In advertising, though, you were only as good as your next idea. Ideas were the currency of the industry. And as soon as he got comfortable, he ran out of ideas.

Glassop blossomed anew in the corporate environment. Jerry did not. He wanted to do good work, but he was increasingly baffled by the barmy campaigns for which the next generation were being applauded. The product of advertising is intangible value. And Jerry's own intangible value, as a purveyor of profitable thinking, waned with age. Experience had a perceived worth, but not in the native currency of fashion labels or cosmetics brands. They wanted youth. They wanted trendy. Idiots were taking over the world. He blamed the Internet.

By the time the economic crisis bit, Jerry was slouching into the office three days a week, signing off work in which he'd played no active role, still eating lunch on the company dollar. Sir Mark let him go with a generous severance package as part of the restructuring process, and gracefully made it look more or less like Jerry's idea. So he left, supposedly to spend more time with his family – although, in fact, he soon found himself doing dreary consultancy work, just to get out of Genevieve's way. He started a memoir, which briefly became a novel, and then an ad creative's career guide, and then went back to being a memoir. He couldn't be sure exactly when his wife had started bonking the auctioneer, but he was only a year into his retirement when she chucked him out. He was beginning to leave a trail of houses, ex-wives and semi-estranged children.

There was, however, one healthy, intimate adult relationship still left in his life.

'Jesus, Manville! What the hell happened to your face?'

Tony Glassop prodded the bruise on Jerry's forehead.

'Ouch! Don't touch it, Tony.'

'It's fucking *blue*!'

'It's a long story.'

'Well, give me the short version.'

'I fell over.'

Glassop guffawed. Every Thursday almost without fail, since long before Sir Mark Sage started sniffing around MGC, Jerry had been meeting his friend and former partner for a long lunch in Fitzrovia. When their favourite Greek place closed some time in the nineties, they'd become gastro-nomads: eating their way along Charlotte Street, from Italian to Spanish, via a lengthy French sojourn, and then back by way of Lebanese to Thai, Chinese and finally Indian, where they'd settled into a regular spot at their preferred curry house.

Glassop karate-chopped the stack of poppadoms and dipped a big piece in the lime chutney. This was practically the last unfashionable establishment in the neighbourhood that wasn't a fast-food joint. Lunchtimes were quiet but not too quiet. The dog-eared menus were printed on cheap, laminated card; on the walls were amateurish paintings of Hindu gods with multiple breasts. In the corridor to the Gents, for no discernible reason, there was a framed photograph of Princess Di. The waiter brought them two pints of Kingfisher.

'Well,' said Glassop, munching. 'You look a fucking state.'

Jerry had got his specs back from the optician, but his linen suit and his favourite blue blazer were still both at the dry cleaners, and, as he sat opposite Glassop's three-piece and tie, he did feel a touch dishevelled. He hadn't shaved in five days. The bruise on his forehead was large and variable in colour, and it occasionally made his right eye weepy. His stomach strained at his untucked shirt, like a supermarket mango at its cling-film packaging. Glassop continued to schmooze for Sir Mark, hence his classy get-up. The other people in the restaurant might conceivably assume that Jerry was some poor relation, begging for cash.

'What do you expect? There are homeless people living in my house! It's a bloody nightmare!'

Glassop nodded in sympathy and sipped his pint. Jerry had already outlined his predicament on the phone.

'So who are these cunts, anyway? Any idea?'

'I don't know. Students, I think, mostly. One of them's started sending me emails. Listen to this . . .' He took out his BlackBerry and scrolled through his inbox, which was steadily filling up with concise dispatches from 'Ulrike' <71117@dotmail.com>: 'Listen: *"You had free education, free healthcare, free love. You claim you brought the world enlightment, made genders and races and sexualities equal."* . . . blah, blah . . . *"Your parents lived on rations and gave you the NHS and the welfare state. But you mortgaged our futures. You bankrupted us."*'

Glassop chuckled, his shoulders bobbing up and down delightedly.

'Wait, wait, and this one: *"You think, It's okay, they'll get our fortunes eventually. But your life expectancy is so long you'll probably never die. And once we've paid the health service you privatised for your palliative care, the inheritance will be gone. So we're taking it now instead. Think of it as a down payment.*" "Think of it as a down payment"? She's mad! How did she even get my email address?!'

Glassop's hooting had increased in volume until the other diners began to glance anxiously in their direction. 'What do they think?' he almost shouted in his mirth. 'That they're the first fucking generation to be angry at their parents? For Christ's sake.'

Jerry was glad to have a sympathetic ear, finally.

'I know, Tony. I know! Who does she think I am? I'm not even rich! Well off, maybe. But not *rich*. Not Arab rich, or Russian rich. Not banker rich. Not now.'

The waiter returned bearing a large silver tray and began to put their food on the table. For Glassop: one Malabar fish biryani. For Jerry: one lamb dhansak, one pilau rice, one Peshwari naan and a bowl of saag aloo.

'Fuck me, Manville. Does your doctor know you eat this much for lunch?'

'Hmph.' Jerry heaped a spoonful of rice and dhansak onto a corner of naan bread, and scooped it all into his mouth.

'Well, anyway,' said Glassop. 'I spoke to that friend of mine I told you about. Property developer. Has the same problem a lot himself. Big empty houses in Mayfair, Belgravia. These bastards climb in through an open window, change the locks, claim legal rights. He said they leave piles of rotting food lying about. Turds in the corner, that sort of thing. And they're the ones that get legal aid, while he has to pay thousands in lawyers' fees. Disgusting . . .'

Glassop broke off to eat a forkful of biryani. Jerry tucked into the saag aloo.

'At any rate, he's given up on the law. Now he has his own team of chaps. Take-no-prisoners types. He sends them in

– balaclavas, sledgehammers, cricket bats, "bish-bash-bosh" – and they flush the buggers out.'

He gulped his beer, then he reached into his jacket and pulled out a business card, which he handed to Jerry. '*Neil Sweet*', it said. '*Sweet & Sweet Property Consultants*'.

'On the back,' said Glassop.

Jerry turned the card over. He'd managed to smear it with dhansak sauce by mistake, but he could still read the phone number scribbled in biro, and the name: '*John*'.

'Who's this?'

'Team leader. Delta Force. Riot squad. Whatever. My pal Neil says he'll sort it out, soon as you want. Owes me a favour anyway. And his lads are a damn sight cheaper than the lawyers. Less paperwork, too.'

Jerry chewed another hunk of naan.

'But. This isn't legal, is it?'

'Fuck legal, Jerry. Once they're out of your house, the police couldn't give a monkey's arse either way. What are the squatters going to do? Press charges? They'll shit their pants when this lot turn up. It's the last you'll see of them, you mark my words.'

Jerry sighed. This was going to go down very badly with his solicitor. But how else would he get the bastards out before Pen got back? Time was short.

'So, Pen doesn't know about all this?' said Glassop, reading his mind.

'No,' Jerry replied nervously, putting the card in his pocket. 'No, not yet. And I'd rather she didn't find out.'

'Ha! Good luck! She doesn't miss much, that woman. Sharp mind. And *so* fuckable.'

'All right, all right. Not the time, Tony.'

Glassop grinned and ate another mouthful of his biryani. For years, he'd maintained a running joke about wishing to sleep with Pen. At least, it was probably a joke. You never quite knew with

Glassop. He'd always been that bit better-looking than Jerry, that bit better-spoken, that bit more Southern and posh. He had a grown-up son he never saw and didn't much like, but no wives. Jerry estimated that his friend had introduced him to three women, all of whom had appeared to be girlfriends, in the past year alone. One or more might have been professionals, of course. And there was doubtless significant overlap. Jerry had always envied his irresponsibility.

They'd entered the industry at its height, he and Glassop: the era of rented helicopters, six-hour lunches and Savile Row expense accounts. Jerry had worked his way up from the post room to the creative department, waiting for the moment when he became important, and thus sexually irresistible. Then, just as he was approaching his peak, he met Pen, carrying a sheaf of her drawings up to the creative director's office. Their first date had been in a curry house not unlike this one. A fortnight later he'd been sent on his first major shoot, in the Mojave Desert with a bunch of Amazonian underwear models, whom he was unable to chat up because he'd just bloody fallen in love. Of all the luck.

His then agency, Wilson Watson Jarvis Dunn, had a yacht moored at Cannes every summer. The parties were near mythical, but you weren't allowed to bring your wife. And if you had a wife, she wouldn't let you go alone. Jerry had to hear the stories from Glassop instead. He was convinced that he ought to have had more sex sooner. Then maybe he'd have reached his quota before getting married. He'd always resented Pen for taking him off the field, just as he hit his stride.

'Christ,' said Glassop, and downed the last of his beer. 'I remember the way you two did up that house all by yourselves. All that painting and sanding and bloody electrics. Complete fucking waste of time and energy. You should've hired decorators and gone on holiday.'

'Fat lot of good you were. If I recall, you just stood around making snide remarks.'

Glassop chuckled again. 'And eating, remember. *Fabulous* cook, your foxy ex.'

Jerry still had half his rice and some dhansak left to eat, but his bowels were protesting. Curry again; why the hell did he keep doing it to himself?

'You really had it all, Manville. Perfect fucking house. Perfect wife, perfect little fucking kids. I would've killed for your life. Killed *you*, maybe. Ha. You really ballsed it up, you know.'

'I know,' said Jerry. He knew.

'Haha. Sorry, old chum. But I feel like I can say that now. Clarity of distance, all that bollocks. Anyway, don't beat yourself up about it, eh? Ancient history. *Garçon*! Another!'

SURVEY

23

The husk of hulking cargo plane sat empty at the side of the coast road. Its vast wheels had sagged into the sandy airstrip; its insides were stripped of any parts of worth; its original Russian white-and-blue colour scheme was faded and streaked with rust. And down one side, in huge green type, was a phone number, and the name of a nearby hotel. To the UAE's resident expats, the Ilyushin was not a monument to the Soviet super-state, nor even to the establishment whose name it now bore. Instead, after an hour's breakneck drive north-east, through Sharjah and on into the tiny Emirate of Umm-al-Quwain, it marked their arrival at the Barracuda bottle shop.

Isobel swung the Pathfinder into the sprawling car park, already swarming with SUVs. 'There!' cried Shauna, jabbing her crimson fingernail towards a pair of sun-blushed gents in slacks and T-shirts, who were closing the boot of their booze-filled Porsche Cayenne. Isobel waited for their outsize vehicle to perform a clumsy reverse manoeuvre, and then guided the Pathfinder into the empty space. The Barracuda beach resort wasn't even in the middle of nowhere; it was on the far side. She wasn't sure anyone ever actually stayed in its grotsome cluster of low-rises. Alongside the hotel, however, was the vast, virtually unmarked warehouse that contained the Emirates' most celebrated stock of low-cost alcohol.

You didn't need a licence for liquor in Umm-al-Quwain, and Barracuda was famously, fabulously cheap compared to Dubai's few alcohol vendors. Isobel was an infrequent visitor; she and Tor rarely had much to drink at Blue Sky Grove, and whatever they did have lasted so long that they barely ever needed to buy more. But she'd come a couple of times with Jonathan back in the day, and Barracuda was always the same. Next door was a downmarket water park, which relied for attendance on booze-runners and their families. Beyond that was a sewage treatment plant. Beyond that was the Gulf, and beyond that, Iran.

It was a shock to step from the car's prophylactic cool into the vivid heat of noon. The car park reeked of warm petrol. Sand whorled across the tarmac. Isobel made for the shop and its air-conditioning. 'Loving the shoes, Iz!' She turned back to Shauna, who winked naughtily and pointed at Isobel's feet, where they poked from her billowy silk trousers. Somehow Shauna had persuaded her to buy a pair of 1,500-dirham Stella McCartney sandals at Harvey Nicks, and now she couldn't stop wearing them. She grinned sheepishly in reply, yanked a trolley from the chain and pushed it through the doors into the shade of the shop.

The bottle shop was cavernous, windowless, brimming with discount alcohol. Mountains of booze rose up on either side of her as she wove between her fellow shoppers from aisle to aisle, trying to avoid a trolley snarl-up. Countless knock-down cartons of cocktail mixers, endless semi-chilled cabinets of beer, racks and racks of suspect wine, row upon row of whisky, gin and rum. She let Shauna lead the way, seeing as the shopping trip was for her benefit. Isobel watched as her friend heaved boxes of beer and cases of wine into their clanking trolleys with practised competence.

'Now,' said Shauna. 'I want to get double of everything: half the real thing, half the cheap rubbish. We drink the quality grog for the first half of the night, then the rubbish at the end, when everybody's too far gone to tell the difference!'

She cackled, and made Isobel snap an iPhone picture of her

wiggling two vodka bottles like jazz hands. People were staring.

There was little cause to linger. Within twenty minutes, they'd heaped both their trolleys: beer and cheap wine stacked neatly in the bottoms, the better wine and the bottles of hard stuff all clinking against each other on top. In all, it came to 2,000 dirhams, give or take. Isobel had promised to pay half, but as she'd done the driving, Shauna insisted on splitting it 60/40. Eight hundred dirhams was still more than she'd expected to spend, though. Keeping up with Shauna was costly. She told herself that before they'd met, she'd been stuck in the house all day, friendless and frugal. If overspending was what their friendship demanded, then so be it.

Two hyper-attentive staff members pushed the trolleys back across the crowded car park to the Pathfinder and helped them to load up, blinking and perspiring in the brilliant sunshine. '*Shukran, Shukran*,' said Isobel, who tended to get by on that and *As-salamu alaykum*. She put the key in the ignition to get the a/c going again. Shauna had brought a large blue tarp, which they unfolded over their haul of boxes and bottles to disguise them from the prying authorities, as if it would do any real good.

The problem wasn't Dubai; Shauna had a well-worn liquor licence for the parties she hosted. The problem was driving back through barren, backward Sharjah, which hewed to Sharia law far more fervently than its neighbours. Countless ex-pats made the run each week without incident, but there were still stories of people being pulled over and searched by the local police. No one actually knew anybody to whom it had happened, but there were stories all the same. Officially, Shauna and Isobel's purchases could put them both in jail.

Isobel couldn't help but worry, just a little bit. Westerners were less welcome since the crash, as if it were all their fault. And it sort of *was*, wasn't it? There was that British couple locked up for shagging on Jumeirah beach. The judge gave them three months and deportation. 'Iz, darln,' Shauna had reassured her, 'what *those* people were doing in public? They would've been arrested in bloody *Queensland*!'

But then came the expats arrested for kissing in a restaurant, another for wearing a bikini in a shopping centre. Isobel wore bikinis all the time at home. What if the gardener caught her in the pool? (Was he a Muslim? She'd never asked. Would that have been rude?) And what if she forgot herself and kissed Tor in public? It could happen. There were supposed to be hidden cameras everywhere, rooting out immoral behaviour. The city was crawling with secret agents, so people said: locals, Iranians, CIA. Gradually those LCD signs in the malls, the ones that warned women to wear respectful clothing, grew more chilling; the slow-handclap footsteps of the security guards on the marble floors more menacing.

Of course, it was someone else's culture, and other people's culture ought to be respected. So if they wanted to divide some car parks by gender, then maybe they should. And if the women really genuinely enjoyed covering up, they could. Yes, there were books on the school curriculum that said non-believers would burn in hell for all eternity. But Isobel would just have to keep a close watch over the twins' reading lists when they grew out of picture books; and if the international crèche saw fit to teach them religious texts, then she'd personally force-feed them *The House on the Hill*.

When she'd first arrived in the Emirates, she'd worn hot pants when she knew she'd be among friends. But her skirts had got steadily longer, her necklines higher. The line between freedom and incarceration was slim, and barely visible. All it took was a quickie in the sand, or a Buck's Fizz in the wrong town. Like being atop the Burj, behind that inches-thick glass, in a high wind: it felt completely secure, but really, you were just inches from certain death. What if, Isobel wondered, she got the uncontrollable urge to leap?

None of this bothered Shauna. Her obliviousness was soothing. She'd blithely dragged Isobel to the races at Meydan, and the eerie extravagance of the bank's VIP box. She'd forced her to try the ersatz skiing at the Emirates Mall, because everybody had to do it once. (Isobel liked the cold, if not the skiing.) And she'd gone on throwing those raucous barbecues on the sandy strip behind her house.

It was for just such a party that they sped sensibly through Sharjah now, the Pathfinder full of contraband, listening to Shauna's John Mayer CD to calm their nerves. They made it back across the border without encountering any makeshift police road-blocks, but by then Isobel was giddy with anxiety, Shauna with anticipation. Isobel chalked it up as a bonding experience.

Brian was at home when they pulled into the driveway. He stood like a lolling tongue in the slack maw of the garage, a pink face atop a sweat-patched polo shirt, waving. He still had the goatee, which looked no better by day than it did by torchlight. 'All right, girls,' he hollered. 'Bloody perfect timing! I was just getting the meat out to defrost.'

In the garage, behind the Escalade and the Lexus, were a waist-deep chest freezer and a stand-up fridge. On a shelf by the door, Brian had made a heap of frozen meat that was already dripping steadily into the sheets of newsprint he'd folded beneath: slab-steaks, pork ribs, fat seven-inch sausages. Obliged to appear manly, he forbade Isobel and Shauna to do any of the unloading, so they stood there in the driveway and watched as he decanted the booze from the boot of the Pathfinder.

'How was your game, love?' asked Shauna, as her husband struggled chivalrously to carry three stacked boxes of Foster's to the fridge at once.

'Yeah, good,' he replied, straining and sliding the boxes awkwardly onto a shelf, forcing the fridge door closed behind them. He strolled back out into the sun, sweat patches spreading.

'You win?'

'Nah. Me fackn swing was off,' and he overfilled his arms with vodka bottles. They watched him waddle back to the open freezer and plop the bottles in, one by one.

'You sure we can't give you a hand, Brian?' said Isobel.

'I'm good, thanks. Don't you girls want an iced tea or something?'

It took him almost a quarter of an hour, but Brian finally emptied the boot of the Pathfinder all on his own, and Isobel drove home to plant five acres of aubergines, consolidate her battery eggs, and change into her outfit. 'I can't wait to see you in that dress, Iz,' said Shauna as she left. 'You are going to be such a *knockout*!'

Clothes shopping with Shauna meant Bloomingdale's and Saks Fifth Avenue, not M&S, and the previous week she'd helped Isobel pick out a new party dress. Isobel had insisted she didn't need one, and she really didn't, but when she saw the striped stretch-dress at Marc by Marc Jacobs, she'd changed her mind. Honestly, she couldn't afford it, but Shauna persuaded her that it'd make her feel better, and that if she couldn't afford it, then Tor could – and he'd thank her for buying it when she put it on. So she'd hidden the credit card receipt under a copy of *Elle*, in a drawer in her office, along with the one for the Stella McCartney sandals. And the rest.

Tor was showered and dressed with half an hour or more to spare, so Isobel had been in the bedroom alone for some minutes, moisturising and making herself up, before she finally put the dress on and looked at it in the mirror. It really set off her soft tan. She was certainly slim enough for horizontal stripes; she'd barely been jogging recently, but had somehow lost weight all the same. On the other hand, did it make her look too much like a tennis player? Maybe. Maybe not. Maybe. Anxious, she took off the Marc dress and threw on her old floral maxi from Topshop. Then she changed her mind again, and changed back, and tugged off her hair-tie, letting her hair fall loose. Better. Probably.

When she came down the stairs, ready to leave, Tor was at the table with Carmen and the twins, watching them finish their dinner. They looked like a happy family, the four of them. Carmen, tiny and quiet and polite, could cook and clean and take care of small children all at the same time. Isobel wasn't much of a multitasker; Pen plainly hadn't passed on all the necessary skills for motherhood.

As the kids chewed the last of their fish fingers, they clambered calmly from their high chairs and onto their father. They already had his athleticism. He sat motionless and calm as they clung to him, entertaining them without effort. Tor had an easy confidence in the family unit. He believed that DNA was destiny, and that his and Isobel's family would be as trusty as the Aryan platoon his own parents had produced. But what if she'd soured the wholesome Meier gene-pool with Manville inconstancy?

'Hey, boys,' she said. 'You like Mummy's dress?'

The twins stared at her, still munching silently.

'It's new?' asked Tor. She nodded, hoping he wouldn't ask what it cost.

'It's beautiful,' he said, and stood to kiss her, the kids still fixed to his limbs. 'Like a sexy tennis player, no?'

They had to park a hundred metres from Brian and Shauna's, because the driveway and the road beyond were already clogged with cars. From behind the house as they approached, Isobel could hear the hubbub of conversation, and a delighted screeching that she identified as her friend's. She fought to suppress her pre-party

jitters. Try as she might, Isobel still got nervous about big gather-
ings – especially ones of bankers and their wives.

The hallway was full of people, pressed around the grand,
faux-antique table, scattered halfway up the broad staircase. Men
and women, drinking and howling with laughter. Beneath the blur
of voices was a bedrock of nineties R&B, thumping and crooning
from the speakers that dotted the house. There was flesh on show,
far too much of it, too crinkled and brown. The lights were
lowered sufficiently that each ghastly, suntanned face looked like
an Italian painting. The unfortunate thought that they'd inadvertently joined a swingers set pinged into Isobel's brain, but there
was no fruit bowl full of car keys to be seen. Just Kettle Chips
and potpourri. She clung to Tor, still close enough to the front
door that they could turn and leave. Tor hadn't even wanted to
come. She'd talked him into it.

'Torsten!' Brian appeared, forcing his way through the crush
of guests. 'Isobel, bloody great to see you!' He kissed Isobel on
the cheek, his goatee gruesomely ticklish, then he glanced at her
breasts and gave Tor a rough handshake. 'You need a stubbie,
mate? I was just setting up a little foosball tournament with the
fellas. Care to join us? Shauna's out by the pool, Iz.'

He handed Tor a beer and hustled him away, leaving Isobel
alone in the crowded hall. She gripped her clutch bag, steeled
herself, and carved a route through to the kitchen. It was crowded
in there, too, clammy and noisy. She smiled at a couple of people
she was pretty sure she'd seen before and ought to remember, but
nobody was bold enough to strike up a conversation, thank God.
She could smell meat cooking on the barbecue outside, and through
the kitchen's double doors she spotted a handful of children in
swimming gear, scuttling around the pool between the grown-ups.
There was a woman in a caterer's apron at the stainless-steel bar,
serving drinks. 'Vodka tonic,' Isobel shouted over the din.
'Double.' She heard a dull splash from outside. The music was

awful. She downed half her drink and picked up a long strip of pitta from a platter of hors d'oeuvres, which she dipped in hummus, ready to devour. But she felt nauseous when she looked at it again – beige gloop clinging to that dry chunk of bread – so she left it on the side of the plate instead.

She found Shauna outside, as Brian had promised, holding court at the poolside table. She screamed with pleasure when she saw Isobel, leapt up and squeezed her.

'Iz, that dress is just *gorgeous*. Isn't she *gorgeous*, guys? Have you met everybody, Iz?'

She did know some of the people at the table. Diane, displaying way too much of her ridiculous cleavage. Mercedes, shovelling chunks of tiger prawn into her mouth with her fingers. That big Irish accountant she'd met at New Year, and next to him, she presumed, his almost-as-big wife or girlfriend. The Irishman stared Isobel up and down as he nibbled on a sticky pork rib. So the dress was doing the trick, then.

'Have you eaten yet, darln? Cmon, let's fatten you up!'

Shauna coaxed her towards the barbecue. Brian appeared to have abdicated that responsibility, entrusting the grill to another aproned Bedouin ('Bedouin') caterer. The man grinned obsequiously and handed her a chicken burger that she didn't want. She was a bit drunk already. The children in the pool were scrapping over the inflatables. Isobel felt guilty for having left the twins with Carmen, but she'd yet to acclimatise them to social events. They worried her too much to bring them with her. What if she got distracted and lost sight of them, and they smashed some host's imitation Ming vase, or fell in the deep end and drowned?

Shauna seemed to appreciate the excuse to escape Mercedes and Diane, so together she and Isobel made their way back inside to find their husbands. They followed the sound of oohing and aahing down the corridor to the games room, where they came upon a horde of bankers crowding the foosball table, intent on an unfolding game. Framed and spotlit on the walls were what looked like Aussie rules football jerseys, three of them, signed by whichever player they'd belonged to. On the big plasma TV, muted, MTV India. There was Brian, face furious with concentration, restless hands whirring and clacking the red team as the ball bounced from end to end; and opposite him, Adonic forearms gracefully twirling the blues, Tor, whose elegant touch suggested either natural aptitude or years of teenage practice. The scoreboard showed blue ahead by nine goals to four. Isobel was suddenly antsy with the contagious thrill of competition. Must be the booze. Without thinking, she took a big bite out of the chicken burger, and chased it with the last of her double vodka tonic. She heard Shauna breathe in sharply through her teeth, a thud of blue plastic boot on ball, a crack as it hit the back of the wooden net, and the sound of Brian's goalkeeper spinning in vain, drowned out by the cheers of his colleagues. Yesssss: Tor, ten to four.

'Dammit! Fackn thing!' Brian yelled, and kicked the nearest table leg. His stubbie, balanced on one corner of the foosball pitch, toppled and fell to the floor, spilling the remnants of the lager onto the laminate. Brian didn't notice. He gripped the sides of the table for a second or two, his knuckles white, composing himself, and then he offered Tor his hand, accepting the defeat. Tor smiled briefly in triumph as he shook it; a pretty rare sight. The other bankers hooted with laughter at their boss's trouncing. Shauna leaned in to her and said, 'He's going to be in a bad mood all night now, you wait and see.'

Brian was in a bad mood all night. He did his best to disguise it until he went up to bed at 1 a.m., which was, said Shauna, dead early. Some time in the small hours, Isobel left her husband and his busted-drunk colleagues in the kitchen, reciting numbers to one another. Out by the pool, the crowd had thinned. The caterers were gone, the barbecue cooling, just a few still-warm sausages sitting in tinfoil on the rack. At the poolside table, a cluster of bleary guests were smoking apple tobacco through a shisha. Diane sat on a lounger, a towel wrapped around her shoulders, clothes still damp from when she'd gaily gone tits first into the pool earlier. On another lounger, Mercedes was slumped, snoring. A couple of kids still sat at the edge of the pool, tired and despondent, kicking their feet in the water. Isobel went on down to the beach behind.

Shauna was by the shore, staring across at the houses on the far bank of the canal. They were slightly bigger than hers. Two turrets instead of just one. Isobel stood beside her friend in silence for a minute. In the city, the desert's incredible night sky was soiled by light pollution. Was that the Milky Way she was seeing, or just the phosphorescent haze of downtown?

'He's got so much enthusiasm,' said Shauna suddenly, apropos of whatever. 'Sometimes he just lets it run away with him, y'know?'

'Yeah.'

She didn't know. Honestly, she didn't give Brian that much thought.

'Does Torsten talk to you about work?'

'Not really.'

But Tor didn't really talk much about anything. Not his style.

'Brian used to just love it there. At the bank. I don't know. He prefers the golf now.'

'Well, the golf here *is* really good, right?'

Shauna laughed at that, sort of. She put her arm around Isobel.

'Y'know, darln, I think you're the best friend I've made here. No, seriously. You're real, Iz. You're just so fackn *real.*'

That had to be bullshit. They barely knew each other. But she felt horribly sorry for Shauna in that moment. And horribly sorry for herself. Because, truth was, Shauna was probably her best friend, too. On a technicality, maybe, but still. She couldn't just rely on Tor and the twins for human contact, could she? Jonathan was in London. Cindy Welch was in Boca Raton. Home was so awfully far away. And in the end, maybe the only friend worth having is the one standing next to you.

24

3:11 p.m.   **me:** whats up

Conrad: not much. saw jerry @ the wkend

me: dad you mean

Conrad: ok ok

me: and?

Conrad: pissed

me: you?

Conrad: him.

me: how pissed?

3:12 p.m.   **Conrad:** majorly. fell over in pub, cracked head . . .

me: wha??!!

Conrad: vommed. alot. took him to a+e

me: holy shit!!

Conrad: yep. Fine, though. Din't even see doc, just decided he was better + left. still bleeding a bit. Fkin weird.

me: hahahaha.

Conrad: not funny. Embarrassing. was with polly etc

3:13 p.m.   **me:** :(

Conrad: f off

me::o

Conrad: nnnngnggg

3:14 p.m.	**me:** so theyre selling the house then
	Conrad: fkin finally. Viewings next wk
	me: not a bit sad?
	Conrad: pfft. could do with the cash
3:15 p.m.	**me:** me too. be strange tho.
	Conrad: for u? ur never even here1
	me: true but thats why its strange. No home
	Conrad::(
	me: ha.
3:16 p.m.	**Conrad:** howre the kiddies
	me: hang on kettles boiling
3:19 p.m.	**me:** back
	Conrad: twins?
	me: doing iPad mainly.
	Conrad: they have ipads?!
	me: no. theyhave *my* iPad. most of the time anyway
	Conrad: oh ok. *You* have an iPad?
	me: y
	Conrad: Are you writing this on ur iPad?
	me: y
3:20 p.m.	**Conrad:** nice. from torsten?
	me: y
	Conrad: sexface
3:21 p.m.	**me:** U got a girlfriend yet
	Conrad: er. Wokring on it. as per
	me: Polly?
	Conrad: pfft.
3:22 p.m.	**me:** r u growing a moustache btw?
	Conrad: er. might be

256

me: such a hipster

Conrad: whatevs

3:23 p.m. **me:** but wait is dad ok tho, srsly?

Conrad: well some1 wd call us if hes dead. So I guess hes ok

me: charming. I'll call him

Conrad: be my guest

3:24 p.m. **me:** so how much will the house be

Conrad: It's on for like 2 mill

me: WTF

Conrad: I know

3:27 p.m. **Conrad:** cooee

me: sorry daydreaming. maybe I shd come visit 1 more time b4 its sold

Conrad: homesick?

me: bit

3:28 p.m. **Conrad:** Mums back in ldn next wk. w the colonel I guess.

me: hahahaha. Lucky you. when u coming to visit me

Conrad: no $$$

me: right. so hows work?

Conrad: v funny

3:29 p.m. **me:** want to join acres? Make some fake $$? I cd lend you my old tractor x

Conrad: F off.

me: :(

25

When the telephone rang at 2 a.m., her first thought was that it was watering time. Did she forget to fertilise her loganberries? Her second was that her dad had actually died, of an epidural haematoma or something, and that she'd never called him like she told Conrad she would. But it was Shauna, and something was horribly wrong.

'Oh, Iz. Thank God. I'm so sorry to call . . .'

'Shauna? What is it?'

She switched on her bedside lamp. Tor's breathing stayed low and regular beside her.

'Could you come over, darln? Is there any way . . . ?'

'What, *now*?'

'I wouldn't ask, but it's really. It's kind of.'

Isobel heard her friend's voice fracture. She sounded manic.

'Shit. Are you okay? Is Brian okay . . . ?'

'Yeah, yeah. Fine. Fine. It's just. I'd rather not talk about it on the phone. Y'know?'

Isobel was up out of bed now, whispering into her iPhone in the en suite. Woken unexpectedly, her body had taken emergency measures, flooding her arteries with adrenalin.

'Should I bring Tor?'

'NO,' said Shauna quickly. 'No no, don't wake him. It's not like that. It's.'

'Okay, okay. I'm coming. Give me an hour. Half an hour.'

Palms clammy, fingers trembling, she almost dropped the

iPhone in the loo as she tried to end the call. She tiptoed back into the bedroom. It was hard to tell whether she was being quiet or not, what with the blood pumping in her ears, but Tor was still fast asleep. Unless they'd been out late on some rare excursion, he always slept non-stop from 10.30 p.m. until 6.00, and could not be woken between those hours, except in an emergency. (In fact, this had happened only once, when Isobel's waters had broken after midnight and he'd risen instantly, uncannily alert.) If she wanted sex on a weekday, she had to be sure to creep into bed no later than 10.10 p.m. Recently, due to the time pressures of Acres, this had been happening less and less.

She pulled on some sweatpants and a T-shirt, thrust her feet into her flip-flops, grabbed the phone and her iPad and slipped downstairs. The house was dark save for the night lights placed strategically at sockets along each corridor, to guide the kids to their parents or the potty in the middle of the night. In the kitchen, she poured herself a glass of water and gulped it down quickly while she checked the iPad: in Acres it was broad daylight, like always. The loganberries wouldn't have to be watered for more than three hours, but who knew how long she was going to be at Shauna's? She put I22y and her crew to work, and then wrote a jittery note to leave on the kitchen table for Tor: '*Gone to Shauna's. Some kind of emergency. Will call/text when I know more. XX*'.

Out in the garage it was breathtakingly humid, oven hot even at this hour. Isobel winced at the noise of the big metal door grinding open. The outside light came on automatically, bathing the driveway in bright white. She listened for any stirrings from back in the house. Nothing. She jumped into the Pathfinder and winced again as she started the engine. The throb of the a/c cooled her anxiety briefly as she pulled out into Blue Sky Grove.

Shauna practically ran to meet her as she drew up at the house in Jumeirah Park. The lights were all blazing inside, and, as she parked next to the Escalade, she saw that its boot was hanging open, half-full of suitcases.

'Aw, darln,' said Shauna. 'Thank God you brought the SUV! I completely forgot to ask . . .'

Her eyes were wide and bloodshot. She'd been crying, and her attempts to remove her running mascara had not been entirely successful. Her hair was tangled, and she wasn't wearing a bra under her blouse, which wasn't like Shauna at all.

'Would you be able to fit the foosball table in there, d'you reckon?'

From inside the house Isobel heard a thud and a clatter, followed by Brian's almighty '*FACK!*' Shauna flinched and looked back at the porch. Isobel, her own night terrors taking hold again, grabbed her friend by the shoulders. She stank of booze.

'Shauna, what is going on?'

'It's Brian,' she said, in a gin whisper. 'He got the sack.'

'What?' said Isobel. 'I mean. Tor didn't say anything.'

She rewound her memory of the previous evening: they'd eaten supper, penne and pesto, though Tor had ended up eating most of her portion; watched an episode of *24* together; and then she'd spent an hour or two on Acres. Tor had been asleep by the time she got to bed. Had he mentioned anything about Brian? She didn't think so. What had they talked about, anyway? She couldn't remember. She felt shattered, keyed up, both at once.

'I thought,' muttered Shauna. 'I thought. I thought maybe you could take a couple of things for us. Y'know. Ship 'em to Brisbane after. I'll give you the cash to cover it.'

'What? Wait. Shauna. What the fuck.'

Brian came clumping out of the house, towing another big suitcase. Shauna shied from him as he heaved it into the back of the Escalade. He looked beat, as though he'd been crying as well. He slammed the boot closed and held out his hand wearily to his wife.

'Brian, will you tell me what the fuck is going on?'

'Shauna, darln,' he said, ignoring Isobel. 'Cmon or we'll miss the fackn flight.'

'What flight?' said Isobel, as Brian yanked Shauna back to the house. She chased them into the floodlit hallway. A large carpet was folded haphazardly against the wall. The pictures of their kids had vanished from the faux-antique table. 'Brian. WHAT FUCKING FLIGHT?'

Brian rounded on Isobel and raised his fist, face scarlet and glistening, veins popping in his forehead. He could've taken a swing, but instead he extended his index finger, jabbing at the air in front of her as he spoke.

'When you lose your fackn job round here, right,' he said, spittle collecting in his goatee, 'your employer automatically tells your bank, stat. And if your savings don't cover your debts, all your fackn accounts get frozen. The lot. And this fackn country forbids you from fackn leaving it. So unless we catch the six-twenty flight to Brisbane, I am going to fackn jail in the morning. Now, I have been spelling this out to Shauna all fackn night. So if you don't understand, Iz, then ask your own fackn husband to explain it. All right?'

He sighed violently and strode off down the corridor towards the games room. Shauna had started crying again. Wait, wait. Isobel knew about this. She'd almost pitched a piece about it to *Grazia*. There were people getting locked up for bounced cheques and unpaid credit card bills. But Brian? Really? Wasn't he Senior Fund Manager? She took the two steps across the tiled floor to Shauna and hugged her. Her friend was trembling, or was it her?

'Are you sure about this, Shauna? Is this really? I mean.'

'I don't know I don't know I don't know,' Shauna moaned. She was melting down. 'We have a lot of credit, Iz. A lot of debts. That fackn condo. I don't know.'

'But it's Saturday tomorrow. Today even. Can't you wait a day? Something.'

'I don't know.'

'But what happened? Why'd he get fired?'

'I don't know!' Shauna moaned again, and broke the embrace. She retreated to the folded carpet and pulled it out flat, knelt on the floor and began, between sobs, to roll it up again neatly. Isobel didn't know what to say. From the games room came the howl of something heavy being dragged across the floor. So she left Shauna and followed Brian's muttered facks down the corridor. He'd managed to get the foosball table as far as the doorway, but it was much too bulky for him to wrap his arms around and carry alone. He was resting against the jamb, breathing heavily. The plasma TV was still there on the wall behind him, but the autographed Aussie rules shirts had been removed from their frames, which lay splayed and empty on a leather sofa. Brian looked at her, pride hollowed out, pleading. Okay, she thought. Fine. I surrender.

'Let me help you,' she said, and picked up one end of the foosball table. God, it was heavy. The old carved names of Brian, his brothers and his son sat level with Isobel's eyeline as they lugged it down the corridor and through the hallway and out to the Pathfinder, stopping twice to set it down and rest on the way. Brian was silent as they went. Sweating profusely in the heat and dark, she clambered into the back of the SUV and forced down the seats to make space for the game. With a final mutual grunt of effort, they shoved the damn thing into the car sideways. Somewhere in its hardwood interior, she could hear the little plastic footballs clacking around.

'Thanks, Iz,' said Brian, staring at the driveway concrete. 'Sorry. Thanks.'

They went back into the hallway. The carpet was now rolled up carefully at the foot of that stupid staircase, but Shauna was gone. 'Aw, where the fack is she? Shauna? Shauna, love!'

Brian went right; Isobel went left. The kitchen looked as though it'd been burgled. Cupboards and drawers sat open, still full of food and cutlery. A smashed tumbler lay scattered on the stainless-steel counter, slivers glinting in the light from the patio. Shauna was by the pool. Isobel went out there to put an arm around her. She was gazing into the dark, towards the sort-of-beach at the back of the yard. Isobel looked around at the pool furniture. The barbecue. That bloody great pizza oven they never used.

'We have to go, darln,' said Brian, behind them. His wife, it seemed, could barely look at him.

'Shauna,' said Isobel softly. 'Shauna, come on. I've got the foosball table. You guys should really go.'

Shauna hoisted another sob from the depths of her throat.

'Darln,' said Brian impatiently, moving towards them, but Shauna waved him away with a strangled 'No!' and took a step back towards the pool. Isobel thought she might topple in.

'Brian,' said Isobel. 'Maybe. Maybe I should drive her. You go and check in. Check in the bags. I don't know, get the tickets. Whatever. We'll be right behind you. I promise.'

He stared at her, impatience and distrust tussling visibly behind his eyes. His shoulders sagged.

'All right. All right. Shauna . . .' She was biting one of her huge red nails. 'Shauna, love. I'll meet you at the terminal. Call me when you get there. Shauna?'

'I don't know,' said Shauna again.

'It's fine,' said Isobel. 'I'll bring her right to you.'

'Okay,' he said, deciding. 'Thanks, Iz. Sorry.'

He pulled a set of house keys from his pocket and cradled them for a moment. Then he handed them to her, dipped his head and went back inside. Isobel stayed there by the pool with Shauna, and they listened anxiously as the Escalade started up, sped off and died away in the night. Shauna was mute, but Isobel coaxed her back inside. She locked the patio doors behind them. Quietly, methodically, she helped her to work through the house, checking each room for forgotten trinkets – a lipstick, a brooch – turning out the lights one by one. Shauna steadily became more functional, and eventually she was able to walk out to the Pathfinder without being cajoled or reassured, while Isobel double-locked the front door. Who was going to be here next? Bailiffs? Secret police? Why bother locking it at all? But she did, all the same. Shauna slumped in the passenger seat, staring back at the house. There was one light still on, in that ridiculous turret. Fuck it. Isobel started the engine and checked her phone for the time: 3.45. She began to reverse towards the road.

'WAIT!'

Holy shit. Isobel's heart smacked against her ribs.

'What? What is it, Shauna? Jesus.'

'The rug. Would you . . . Could you take the rug, as well?'

Isobel exhaled.

'Fine,' she said. 'I'll take the fucking rug.'

So they jumped out of the car again, unlocked the front door, dragged the carpet to the SUV and draped it unceremoniously over the foosball table. Isobel thought about driving straight back to her place with Shauna, calming her down, discussing the situation with Tor. He'd know the right thing to do. But then, maybe the right thing to do was to have Brian yanked off the plane and taken to jail. She could almost see Tor recommending it as a logical course of action. And when she considered the consequences of that, for Shauna and herself, if not for Brian, she knew straight away that she would take her friend to the airport just as she'd promised.

They hurtled up Sheikh Zayed Road with the slick black coastline on their left, through the valley of downtown skyscrapers, still aglow in the small hours. A vast, illuminated billboard bore down on the multi-lane highway, of a benign Sheikh Mohammed and something in Arabic. '*All Hail the Dear Leader*', it might've said, or '*Big Brother is Watching You*', or '*Have a Nice Day!*' Isobel still wasn't sure if she believed all the scare stories, the conspiracy theories, the rumours of the city's dark heart. But Shauna's terror was real, and it was infectious.

'Thank you, darln,' said Shauna shakily, as they were nearing the airport. 'You saved my life. That rug is my favourite. I'll give you my mother's address. Y'know, in Brisbane.'

'Sure, 's fine. Just email it to me or something. I'll sort it out. The foosball table, too.'

'Yeah. That fackn game. It really. It means a lot to him. I wouldn't have asked otherwise. I'm so sorry, Iz. About all this.'

Isobel felt a flash of anger as she thought of the task ahead of her, smuggling the carpet and the foosball table all the way to Australia. Was it even legal? Would it put her at risk?

'Why call me?' she asked. 'Why not Mercedes, or Diane?'

'I don't know,' said Shauna again. 'I trust you. I wanted to say goodbye. Y'know. To *somebody*.'

The anger turned to shame and pity, and then to sadness. Isobel wanted to say something to mark her friend's departure, but now the airport loomed ahead of them, monstrous and marbled, the Emirates' prize carbuncle. She turned in at the Terminal 3 drop-off and let the Pathfinder idle in the taxi lane. Her phone said 4.30.

'You'd better go,' she said. 'Think you can find Brian?'

'Yeah,' Shauna replied, gripping the door handle, seemingly scared of whatever lay beyond it.

'Could you,' she whimpered. 'I mean. I don't know. Could you not say anything to Tor? Just for a few hours, y'know. I don't know. The bank.'

'Er. Okay,' said Isobel, uncertain. There wasn't really time to ask why. Something occurred to Shauna. She seized her handbag from the footwell and rummaged through it feverishly, her fist emerging full of dirham notes. 'Here,' she said, thrusting them at Isobel. 'For the shipping. It's the last of my cash. Take it.'

'Shauna . . .'

'Take it!'

So she took it, and she stuffed it in her sweatpants pocket, where she thought it might stop embarrassing her. Shauna cupped her face in her hands.

'You are a good, beautiful person, Isobel. I hope I see you again.'

'You will. Of course you will,' she replied, a wobble climbing into her voice. And then Shauna was gone, tottering from the car towards the terminal.

Isobel's mind was elsewhere, and she made a wrong turn on her way out of the airport. When she realised she'd been heading north, away from the city, she turned down a side road, thinking it might take her back towards home. But as the midsummer sun began to fringe the horizon, she found herself lost in Sonapur, skirting along a mile or more of low, concrete apartment blocks. She pulled over and parked at the side of a large patch of rubbled waste ground to reset the satnav. But she couldn't concentrate. What was her address again? Her fingers shook too much to work the touchscreen. She was shivering. Maybe the a/c was on too high. She opened the door and stepped out into the twilight and took a deep breath. The humidity almost choked her. A pair of flies buzzed around her head. Out on the waste ground, skeletal cats were circling. She could smell her own sticky armpits, her unshowered skin. It made her feel sick.

As she caught her breath, doubled over and leaning against the side of the car, she heard a far-off rumble of engines and a creak of brakes. In the distance, lined up outside those endless low-rises, she could see ranks and ranks of dark-skinned men in sky-blue boiler suits: labourers, filing onto buses in the dawn. Surging into the city, remaking it and remaking it and remaking it. Working for pocket change on a Saturday. Not so very far away, people like that were dying to undo the status quo, to topple the wicked and the venal. And maybe, she imagined in her delirium, there was another Isobel, a doppelgänger who'd made different choices and was right now reporting live from Cairo or Tunis or Benghazi. A serious person. She wanted to care, to correct injustice wherever she found it, to shrug off her sickly privilege. But no, here she was, watching the maid bring up her kids in a glorified beach resort.

The distant buses began to move off, guts clogged with workmen. Isobel remembered her address, repeated it to herself under her breath, and climbed back into the car.

26

The house was still quiet when she got back to Blue Sky Grove. She tore up the note she'd left on the kitchen table into pieces so small as to be illegible, and then stuffed them into the bin. The kettle boiled quickly, but the tea was no comfort. It tasted bitter, sterile. She blamed the Gulf water, pouring half of it back into the sink. Distraction, she needed distraction. No. She needed a shower. She used the downstairs bathroom rather than wake Tor, and scrubbed away the sand and perspiration of the night with soap and a pumice. Her eyes were dark circles in the steamed mirror as she gargled mouthwash. She put on her sweatpants again, and padded up to the bedroom to get a fresh T-shirt. Tor woke up as she was foraging in the HEMNES chest of drawers. She looked at the bedside alarm clock: 6 a.m., on the nose. He slid himself up into a sitting position, baring his olive brown torso. His lovely blond hair was the littlest bit ruffled. He smiled softly, as if he knew something she didn't.

'You're up early again.'

'Yeah!' she replied, as brightly as she could, pulling the clean T-shirt over her head. She hadn't decided what to tell her husband yet, if anything. So she leaned down and kissed him instead.

'Shower's all yours,' she said.

The twins were in the sitting room when she went back downstairs, watching the Cartoon Network. She sat with them awhile as they gaped at the television, hoping they'd divert her attention. She could smell coffee percolating, which meant Carmen was up, too. Anton squatted on the carpet, building something out of Duplo.

'What's he making, Jonas? What's Anton making?'

Jonas just shrugged, blue eyes glued to the cartoon. It was Japanese, and bafflingly noisy, and it did nothing for her nerves. Maybe Anton wasn't making anything at all, she thought. Maybe he was just sticking the blocks on top of each other, one by one, as many as he could manage without it toppling under its own weight. That would be more logical, somehow, than a Duplo castle, or a spaceship. More Meier.

'Mummy helped her friend run away in the middle of the night,' she said. 'She drove her to the airport so that she could fly home on a plane.' Nothing. Not a thing.

When Carmen came to call the twins to breakfast, they toddled off to the kitchen without a word, leaving the TV on and the Duplo monolith unfinished. Isobel was still sitting there on the sofa under the flamingo paintings, staring out the window with the Cartoon Network on, when Tor came down in a shirt and trousers.

'Isobel? I'm sorry, I have to go to work,' he said.

She hauled herself back into the moment.

'Work? On a Saturday?'

'Yeah. There's a few things to sort out at the office. I'm sorry.'

His features were a total blank. She'd always thought he'd make an amazing gambler, if that weren't illegal here like everything else.

'Why?'

'*Ach*, I'll explain it all later. But are you okay with the twins?'

'Yeah, yeah. But. All day?'

'I expect so, yeah. I'll tell you about it later.'

Tell me about what, she wondered. About Brian, surely. She wanted to ask him exactly what had happened at the bank. She wanted to tell him all about the night she'd had. But she didn't want to jeopardise Shauna – or herself, for that matter. What if their plane had been delayed? What if there was still time for the secret police to catch up to them? Had she already betrayed Tor, by not confessing immediately? There was a lie now, between Isobel and her husband: the last fully sentient, English-speaking person in the city who'd help her. How had it come to this: protecting a man like Brian from a man like Tor? Her iPhone was still in her sweatpants pocket; Shauna's wad of dirhams rustled ominously as she pulled it out and checked it. Tor just stood there, waiting for her permission to leave. No text from Shauna. But they ought to be in the air by now, somewhere over southern India maybe.

'Okay, cool,' she replied. 'See you later.'

'Okay.'

She heard him go through to the kitchen and say goodbye to his sons. Then came the grinding of the garage door. FUCK. SHIT. The foosball table. The carpet. They were still in the back of the Pathfinder. She sprinted through the house to head him off, but as she got to the front door, Tor was already reversing out of the drive in the Audi. He spotted her in the doorway, gave her a puzzled look. In her horror, she hesitated a second, and waved. He smiled, waved back. Then he drove away.

Distraction. She booted up the laptop, then the Web browser, then Acres. The jingle started to play. She tapped in her Facebook password. The loganberries were flourishing, almost ready to be reaped. She zoomed out and out into a bird's-eye view, and then roamed across her 800 acres from above. Squares of wheat and soya beans, rectangles of aubergines and squash. Her prize-winning marrows. The grey, gloomy barnful of battery chickens to the south-east, the meadows of free-range cattle and sheep to the north. Glossy shire horses, lumbering backwards and forwards. Her farmhands, hard at work in the fields with watering cans and scythes. I22y, sitting proud upon the AcreMaker500, ready to plough new furrows.

More acres. She needed more acres. That meant more coins. The loganberry harvest was going to take some time, and she wanted that hit of dopamine right fucking now. She felt the prickle of cold sweat on the palms of her hands. At the marketplace she bought 10 new acres ($20) and strawberry seeds to plant in them (also $20). Strawberries grew fast and hard. She'd have 250 coins back from the sale of the strawbs by the end of the day. She paid for it all by Mastercard on her Acres account, and then set I22y to work.

Her Mastercard. Fuck. She leaned down and opened the desk drawer with the copy of *Elle* resting on top of it. It was the January issue. Six, seven months old. She lifted it out gingerly to survey what lay beneath. A fat stack of receipts. She picked them up with both hands, quaking, and fanned them on the desk beside the laptop. There were the Stella McCartney sandals, the Marc by Marc Jacobs dress, the Ray-Bans (real ones), the other Marc Jacobs dress, lunch at that rip-off Gary Rhodes place. Too many to tot up in her head, but enough to know it came to a lot. It didn't even include her Internet shopping, let alone Acres; the receipts for all that were hidden away in her Gmail somewhere. Could she cover all of it with her savings? She didn't even *have* savings! Could she go to jail for all this? This country. Why had she never told Tor she was spending so recklessly? He could've stopped her. Told her the risks. He could've slowed her down. He could've. Now it was too late.

Distraction. Distraction. The jingle was still playing. Screw it. She was in so deep now that it hardly mattered. She clicked through to the marketplace. There it was: the AcreHayMaker1000 combine harvester. It came in ten different colourways, and she scrolled down to yellow, with a blue stripe. It would match her AcreMaker500. '*Are you sure you want to buy the AcreHayMaker1000 for 1,000 Acres*

271

coins (100 USD)?' She let her mouse arrow hover for a second, then clicked YES before she could change her mind.

The massive vehicle materialised, as if by magic, at the door of her barn, and she sent I22y to start it up post-haste. As her avatar motored the monster across the farm towards the loganberries, Isobel went back to the market and bought ten more acres and ten more sacks of strawberry seeds. She dispatched the shire horses to plough the new western fields, and a dozen workers to plant and water them. The AcreHayMaker1000 began churning the fruit into its vast belly. (Unrealistic, Isobel thought, in a brief moment of clarity: a combine harvester collecting berries. But she was beyond demanding plausibility.) The coin counter in the top right-hand corner of the laptop screen started to climb. A minute later, a message appeared in her Facebook inbox. It was Cindy Welch in Florida. The purchase must've shown up in her news feed.

Cindy Welch
You got an acrehaymaker1000?! Omg amazing!!

Fuck you, Cindy Welch. I will fucking own you. Isobel scanned her friends' Acres rankings. She was still behind Cindy, who'd already had her own combine harvester since Christmas. And she wasn't far enough clear of Karen Pinsky for comfort, even now that her loganberries were flooding the market. Maybe she should hire more workers to do the watering. Her AcreSprayer crop sprayer, once so coveted, seemed to her now to be sluggish and inefficient. She tabbed back to the marketplace, scrolling up and up through the farming equipment for sale. There: the AcreSprayer1800 crop-dusting biplane, in red. $180? Done.

She needed new fences in the strawberry fields, and having her staff make them manually was laborious, so she bought an AcreBreaker650 mechanised fence-builder for $65. What next?

She almost forgot: with her Acres log-in, she could also surf the marketplace in Safari Town: another, synergised game. Lions were 250 coins, $25: the same as a shire horse. She bought two, and an acre enclosure (20 coins, $2), which she put next to one of her sheep pens, just to see what would happen. She erected a ticket office with a few clicks of the mouse, and hired a new staff member to manage it. Virtual customers began to arrive at the turnstiles in ones and twos, each of them trickling more coins into her coffers as they came to admire the animals. Not enough, though. Not enough. She clearly needed more attractions. A giraffe, $20! An elephant – a novelty one, in Indian ceremonial dress, with tassles – $60! A penguin enclosure, including five penguins, $200!

Cindy Welch
Hey hon bun. What's going on? R u ok?

Isobel paused and looked at her iPhone clock. Was she okay? She'd been at the screen for over four hours. She blinked. Through her office window she could see Carmen keeping watch over the twins, as they bounced in their armbands at the shallow end of the pool. She tabbed back to her Acres rankings. Cindy was left in the dust. She was number one: I22y, valiant virtual farm worker, remaking the world as she wanted it to be – a place with fields and trees and rivers and wildlife. Just as she'd once been Izzy, child star of the *The House on the Hill*, always on hand to help Conrad out of a scrape. The house on the Hill. Home: she was a hero there. Home: her Britpop posters and her gap year collages, her mum and her dad and her brother. Isobel was old enough to remember her parents being happy. To remember what a real family was like. She couldn't believe they were selling it. The bastards. The complete fucking bastards.

* * *

She opened a new browser tab and found a KLM flight to London via Amsterdam, leaving in a few hours. If she was quick, she could still make it. She paid for a one-way ticket with the Mastercard, miraculously undeclined, and then ran upstairs to throw some clothes into a wheelie case. She wrote another note for Tor and this time left it on top of the HEMNES chest, where only he would find it, by which time she'd be airborne: 'Gone to London. Emergency. Will call when I get there. A&J fine with Carmen. Love you, xxx'.

And she did love him. She did. But then, she was pretty sure her mum and dad had still loved each other when they split up. That's what they'd claimed. So is love enough, she wondered, when you hate everything else? Hate the country, hate the Grove, hate the house, hate the Ikea furniture, hate the Sheikh, hate the sand, hate the wind, HATE the heat, hate the Lifestyle (hate the clubs and the malls and the brunches and the booze and the traffic), hate the maid for making her look bad, hate the twins for loving the maid, hate herself for hating all three of them? Hate everything but Tor: good, strong, boring, *beautiful* Tor?

In her office, she dithered over the credit card receipts and, in the end, thrust them all back into the drawer with the magazine. She shut down the laptop and left it on her desk, but she tossed the iPad into her bag. The twins would just have to do without *Angry Birds*. They were eating their lunch in the kitchen when she came to say goodbye. Mini chicken Kievs. She kissed them both on the tops of their heads. They ignored her. She was jittery again, her blood sugar low, but she didn't think she could eat anything. There'd be a meal on the plane, maybe. She told Carmen she was going to see a friend.

There was the painting her mum had given her for Christmas, still wrapped in brown paper and propped against the wall of the garage. The oils had probably melted by now. Tor had taken the Audi, and there wasn't time to call a cab. She dithered anxiously again in the heat, then she put the suitcase in the front seat of the SUV and opened the boot. Shauna's carpet was easy enough to extract; she slid it out of the car and lay it next to Tor's rowing machine. The foosball table was another matter. She let it tip slowly out of the boot onto its side, and then rocked it back to its feet. She wasn't strong enough to combat gravity, and it made a great crashing noise as it landed. But it seemed to have survived intact. She pushed it, groaning and scraping, across the floor and up against the wall, and then wondered what her husband was going to make of it when he got home. Yet another thing to explain. But her mind couldn't hold any one thought for long. She blamed the game; distraction had decimated her attention span. She was already sticky with sweat again.

At the airport, she left the Pathfinder in the long-term car park. Tor could arrange to have it picked up if necessary, she was pretty sure of that. She wondered where Brian had abandoned the Escalade. There was a Corvette in the space next to hers, its banana-yellow bodywork already crusted with sand. Someone had scrawled a message with their finger in the dust of the driver's side window: 'So Long, Farewell, *Auf Wiedersehen*, Dubai!'

5:32 p.m. **me:** what u up 2

     Isobel: watching 24

     me: w tor?

     Isobel: yep

     me: say hi

5:33 p.m. **Isobel:** He says hi back. What's up

     me: not much

     Isobel: Shit never called dad. He ok?

     me: don't kno. Guess so

     Isobel: you haven't called him?

     me: nope

     Isobel: talked to mum?

     me: nope you?

5:34 p.m. **Isobel:** no

     me: hows things

     Isobel: hot

5:35 p.m. **me:** so let me ask u this

     Isobel: hang on, exciting bit

5:38 p.m. **Isobel:** ok back soz

     me: what happend?

     Isobel: Jack Bauer killed someone

     me: obvs

     Isobel: With an *axe*

5:39 p.m.   **Isobel:** anyway carry on

                me: do u ever turn down an FB friend request?

                Isobel: Not if they have Acres.

                me: pfft.

5:40 p.m.   **Isobel:** Why?

                Isobel: r u ignoring s.o. or r they ignoring u?

5:41 p.m.   **Isobel:** is this about a girl?

                me: er. Might be.

                Isobel: haha. She blocked you?

                me: no! prob just taking her time accepting.

                Isobel: :(. . . omg why? What did you *do*?!

                me: NOTHING!

5:42 p.m.   **Isobel:** Maybe she didn't like your new moustache

                me: f off

                Isobel: xoxo

28

On Saturdays, Conrad cleaned his bikes. When he was out of work, it gave his week a structure that employment might otherwise have provided. When he'd spent the past few days at the supermarket, it was a way to wind down and empty his mind. He shunted the coffee table and the reclaimed antique armchair to one side and laid sheets of newspaper on the wood-imitation linoleum in the middle of the sitting room. He opened the front window a touch to let out the scent of commercial cleaning products. He lifted the bicycles from their rack, high on the wall in the corridor, and set them on the newspaper, bellies up, wheels aloft.

He sprayed the chains, rings and sprockets with degreaser, and then wiped them down with a dry rag, which had once been a pair of Calvin Kleins. He cleaned the frames – first the Giant, and then the Peugeot – with a soapy cloth and an old toothbrush for the hard-to-reach crannies. He pumped the tyres to a supple 95-100psi. He lubed the chains and turned the pedals a few times to let it work into the links. If the drive train was saggy, he adjusted the tension, loosening and tightening the rear wheel of the Peugeot with a crescent wrench. He checked the brakes: one caliper on the fixie, two on the racer.

Polly was always the next to wake, and ever since she'd hired her first employee – an art student who looked after her stall at Broadway Market on Saturday mornings – she liked to watch Conrad at work. She'd empty the ashtrays and make them both coffee, and then curl her legs beneath her on the sofa to study his routine. Occasionally she persuaded him to see to her Pashley as well. Most weeks, once he'd returned the bikes to the rack and cleared away the tools and debris, the two of them went out for brunch while Beagle and Dennis and Jamie were still sleeping off the previous evening's MDMA.

Conrad found that fixing up his bikes engaged not only his hands, but also his brain. It sent neurotransmitters whizzing across synapses that went unfired during a day on the shop floor, or in front of a computer screen. It staunched the flow of his neuroses. It was calming to connect with the real world, even if all he was doing was replacing a tyre or repairing the bar tape. He felt more like a participant in his physical surroundings, more aware of breathing and walking and eating, more alive in the moment. Maybe, he thought, this is what it's like to be Buddhist.

Except that Buddhists were probably supposed to forsake all worldly possessions, and despite having divested himself of most of his stuff, Conrad couldn't help but crave another new bicycle. Some nights, he found himself awake into the small hours, surfing eBay and the specialist sites in search of vehicular porn. Classic road bikes with lugged steel frames; punchy fixed-gears; refined single-speeds with intriguing colourways. He had his eye on a custom cyclocross hybrid being auctioned by a guy in Scotland, though he knew full well that he couldn't afford it without extending his credit card limit or refinancing his existing bank loan.

He disdained BMXs, because most BMX riders could barely do a wheelie. And without tricks, the squat little bikes were no more than an impractical pose. (Conrad placed a high value on practicality: he'd bought his first fixie for its minimal maintenance requirements. Only later had he developed his hypothesis regarding its spiritual virtue.) He had no problem with commuter hybrids and Bromptons, nor with their riders; he didn't look down on

279

rucksacks or hi-vis jackets. There was a straightforward honesty about their purpose. Those people weren't trying to be anything other than themselves; they were just trying to get to work. Sometimes they clogged up the junctions, but Conrad was sufficiently silky to slip to the front of the peloton at any set of traffic lights.

Polly deposited Conrad's coffee cup on top of a copy of *LOVE* magazine and sank onto the sofa's cracked, shabby pleather. Tumbleweed bundles of black dust were collecting on the windowsill, reminders of the neighbourhood's industrial backstory. It was hot in the flat, which was east-facing and hoarded the morning sun, so she was dressed only in a grey marl T-shirt and boxers, squinting through her hangover. Conrad could see the tattoo of the Joni Mitchell lyric near the top of her thigh, just below the tanline where her hot pants normally ended. It was for her mum, she'd always claimed, that classic sentimental excuse for bad body art. Conrad thought it was pretty cool, actually.

'Can you believe this?' she said.

Conrad looked up from his lubing. She was pointing at a large spot on her forehead. He'd known Polly long enough to recall an unjustly awful acne spell in their teens. She was still sensitive about her skin.

'Believe what?' he replied.

'This fucking massive *spot*!'

'I can't really see it,' he said, though he could see it just fine.

'Don't lie.'

'Okay. It is pretty massive.'

'I *know* it is!'

'Have you washed your hair recently? Maybe it's your greasy fringe.'

'Fuck off,' she said, grinning, and put a hand through her tousled morning hair.

Conrad knelt on the newsprint and pushed the MKS pedal,

turning the Campag crank, a clean clackety-clack. Polly watched, mesmerised by the blur of the back wheel spinning. He put two fingers to the tyre and let the friction slow it gradually to a stop. He wiped his hand on the dry rag, careful not to get oil or dirt on his Breton-striped top. Then he picked up his coffee and sipped it. It tasted wrong.

'Is this my Kenyan stuff?'

'No, sorry. We're out. It's Tesco ground.'

'Oh.'

'Does that seriously bother you?'

'No, it's just.' He could see that she was trying not to laugh. 'No. It does not bother me.'

He sipped again. It bothered him slightly.

'First-world problems,' she said, and reached out to ruffle his quiff.

Conrad clenched and unclenched the brakes on both bikes; they were solid.

'Music?' said Polly, pulling her iPhone from the elasticated waist of her boxers.

'Okay.'

Conrad was pretty chuffed with the sound system he'd networked through the flat. Using an old Airtunes base station and a set of phono leads, he'd hooked up the home cinema amp to the Wi-Fi, which let them all play their iTunes and Spotify playlists wirelessly from anywhere in the flat, using only their smartphones. Polly put on some Grizzly Bear. It was that kind of morning.

'So what's new on the stall?' said Conrad, fitting his foot-pump hose to the front tyre valve.

'Soviet alarm clocks,' she replied, and blew cool air across her coffee as he started to pump. 'I ordered a stack of them from this Etsy shop in Latvia. Really cool. They're wind-up, but still. Awesome, old-school typography on the numbers. And this girl

I use in Bristol found like a hundred of these funky old church kneeler cushions in this charity sale – you know, with those kitsch embroidered pictures on them? I put them on the website and this design blogger tweeted about it, so people are going wild for them. I'm nearly sold out already. So I'm gonna see about sourcing some more from somewhere. But I don't know where you would get those. I mean, do churches have closing-down sales?'

'Dunno,' said Conrad, who by now had finished pumping the back wheel. 'I guess so.'

'Hm,' she said, and drank some more coffee.

Conrad never ceased to marvel at Polly's acumen. As a teenager, she'd been a game, intermittently pimply ditz from the girls' school, who could be relied upon to provide friends for Conrad and Co. to lust after with sporadic success. Like the boys, she'd decant the contents of her parents' drinks cabinet into jam jars to smuggle to the Heath on Saturday afternoons. But when she came back from university, stylish and sorted and hanging from that braying public schoolboy like a striped blazer, Conrad was confounded. All those bold schemes of his. Who'd have thought Polly would end up being the business brain?

Her success made her continuing fondness for Jamie Doohan all the more galling. His confidence, his pseudo-military poise: endorsed by Polly's affections. Conrad couldn't bear the way Jamie let her do the cooking and the laundry, the way she baked him fancy cupcakes and knitted him Skandi pattern scarves for almost no credit. (She did most of these things for Conrad as well, but he always said thank you.) Craft was cool right now, so she believed she was being progressive and empowered, when really she was acting like a fifties housewife. Conrad, of course, kept these opinions between himself and Beagle.

The chain on the fixie was a bit loose, so Conrad fetched the wrench from his toolbox. He fitted it to the bolt on the back wheel and worried at it until it gave a little.

'Er. So. Does Jamie still hang out with that girl Flo?'

'Oh, my God. Seriously?'

'What?'

'Flo Dalrymple? Have you *still* not given up on that one, Conrad?'

'Actually, she came into the shop. Like a fortnight ago.'

'A *fortnight*?! I'm AMAZED you haven't mentioned this until now.'

'Very funny. I told Beagle. Maybe I just knew how you'd react.'

He started to loosen the left-side bolt. 'But seriously,' he went on. 'She was with this bloke. I dunno. I just wondered if she had a boyfriend.'

'Wow. You are such a loser.'

'Okay, okay. I was just *asking*!'

'Seriously, though. I mean, I know you fancy her or whatever, but didn't you think she was kind of a douche? I think she's kind of a douche.'

Well, Conrad thought Jamie was kind of a douche, but he didn't go telling her that, did he?

'What's so douchey about her anyway?'

'Well, doesn't she strike you as sort of up herself?'

'Pfft. You mean confident?'

'*Nooo*. There is a difference. She's a know-it-all. And she's like super self-righteous.'

'Why does Jamie like her, then?'

She laughed. 'Same reason you do, I expect.'

Speak of the devil: at that precise moment, Jamie sauntered in, wearing only a pair of carrot jeans, stretching and yawning. He had exemplary abs, obvs. He effortlessly inspired feelings of inadequacy. But where Polly presumably saw a hot bod, Conrad saw a guy who spent way too much time at the gym.

'Morning, babes,' he said to Polly. 'Hello, Conrad mate.'

Conrad's loathing of the term 'babes' knew no bounds.

'Conrad was just asking about your friend Flo,' said Polly.

'Oh, yeah?'

'No,' said Conrad. 'It was just. Forget it.'

But Polly would not forget it. 'Do you know if she has a boyfriend?' she said.

'No,' said Jamie quickly. 'I mean. I don't think so, no.'

He ran a hand through his hair, as if he was starring in an aftershave ad or something. 'Oh, *yeah*, Conrad mate. I remember. She asked to meet you at the show opening that time, right?'

'Right. Wait. *She* asked to meet *me*?'

'I think so, mate, yeah.'

'Don't encourage him,' said Polly.

Jamie sat down on the sofa beside her and gave her a squeeze. He was way too naked for comfort. Conrad tried to keep his back wheel true as he tautened the chain. So: no boyfriend.

'I think she's just a fan of my mum's books,' he said.

'She's having a party tonight, actually,' said Jamie. 'Squat party. You should both come.'

'Really?' said Conrad, failing to project the necessary nonchalance. Polly rolled her eyes at the idea. But Conrad was all ears. Party+Flo: it sounded like an excellent equation. Jamie had his phone out now and was poking at it, apparently searching for the details.

'You know,' he muttered, concentrating. 'I think her dad is a Lord.'

'What?' said Conrad. 'No way.'

'Not like a proper Lord, though,' said Polly. 'Like a Lib Dem peer or something.'

'Right,' said Jamie, looking up from his keypad briefly. 'Do the Lib Dems have Lords?'

'Er, yes,' said Polly.

'Weird,' said Jamie. 'Yeah. Here it is, mate. Facebook invite: *"Houseparty on the Hill"*. She's living in this squat in Highbury somewhere.'

So Flo clearly *did* use Facebook, after all. But wait, something was . . . Conrad felt a bit light-headed all of a sudden. His bowels shifted. Maybe Polly made the coffee too strong. Hang on. Er. Highbury. Huh? Polly threw Jamie a peculiar look.

'What did you say it was called?' she said.

'What, the party?' Jamie checked his phone again. '"Houseparty on the Hill". Why?'

Conrad's spanner clanged off the bike frame, on its way to the floor.

29

Conrad cycled fast and hard on his fresh-lubed fixie. As a rule he'd ride somewhat defensively: mindful of the cars on his shoulder, swinging wide at blind corners to prevent them overtaking. But today he took a racing line. The house on the Hill was only twelve or so minutes from his flat at a clip – up Kingsland Road, hang a left at Haggerston, cross the canal and Essex Road, shoot up through Canonbury and on into High & I – but it seemed a lot further than that in Conrad's personal psychogeography. Years. Light years. All this time spent trying to distance himself from his youthful caricature, and in fact he'd moved no more than three miles.

He rode with his hands on the drops, narrowing his elbows and flattening his torso to the wind, long-sleeved Breton T-shirt tucked into his plum chino shorts to reduce drag. He'd sometimes thought of shaving his legs like a real pro, but they were already hairless enough. Turning into a skid stop outside the house, he rolled over the kerb into the drive, hopped off the bike and left it leaning against the gatepost. He broke instantaneously into a post-workout sweat, fearful pores gushing. The wheelie bins were lined up on the pavement, and Conrad could see fat black sacks hulking beneath their lids. Who was leaving out rubbish?

'Nonononono,' he muttered under his breath. 'Shitshitshit.'

Music. There was music coming from somewhere. Ska. Conrad couldn't stand ska. He looked up at the house. His mum and dad's bedroom window was open. Not much: just enough to let the air in, and the ska out. NONONONOSHITSHITSHIT. He stole

286

coyly across the gravel, eyes sweeping the house. The sitting-room curtains were closed, but there was a piece of paper taped to the inside of the window, which settled the question at last. He adjusted his non-prescription specs instinctively, though they served no purpose whatsoever. He could read the declaration just fine with or without them: '**Section Six**,' it said, in bold type, underlined. '**Criminal Law Act. 1977**.'

'Fuck,' he said. 'Fuck.'

His innards gurgled with anxiety – and something else, something he didn't recognise, something that seemed a lot as though it might be rage. Polly had tried to reassure him as he rushed from the flat, but she'd been right about Flo after all. THIS was why she'd never accepted his *friend request*. And he thought she'd been *into* him! He thought they'd had a CONNECTION! As he'd spilled his guts there on the pavement in the April drizzle, she'd, what, been scoping the house for occupation? How could anyone *do* that? He clenched and unclenched his fists. Was this *his* fault? His parents were going to kill him. Shit. Conrad's chest was knotted tight. He became conscious of badly needing the loo. Was it Polly's coffee? Or was he having a panic attack? Deep breaths, Conrad. Deep breaths.

He could still hear the music over the blood beating in his ears. So, he thought, there were people in there RIGHT fucking NOW. He steeled himself and mounted the front steps, heart pumping hysterically, like a time-trial racer with a flat tyre. No keys. Why-oh-WHY didn't he carry *house keys*? He pressed the buzzer, but it didn't seem to be working; normally you could hear the ring from within. Jumpy, he banged the knocker twice instead, and then he put his ear to the door. There was movement inside, approaching. He could hear footsteps on the floorboards in the hallway, hushed voices. An argument, maybe. A girl and a boy. He couldn't make out the words. The bolt clicked in the lock, and Conrad took a step back, bracing himself for whatever emerged.

He should've prepared a tirade. Too late now. Too late.

Flo was beautiful: he'd remembered that much correctly, and, as she opened the door, he was distracted just long enough for her to step out and throw her arms around his neck. He flinched. But it was a hug. Definitely a hug. He could feel her perfect breasts pressing against him beneath her grey sleeveless sweater. Her perilous cheekbone grazed past his ear. He wanted to give her a piece of his mind – but which piece, exactly?

'I knew you'd come,' she said.

'Oh,' he said. 'Er.'

There was a man shaded by the doorway behind her: Austin. Stubbled, skinny, in a vest and weathered cargo pants. A roll-up dangled from his lip, and he looked Conrad up and down as Flo pulled away. Conrad felt as though Austin might attack him, if not for his human shield. But instead he traipsed past them down the steps and into the driveway. Conrad looked at Flo. She was smiling. This was weird, right? This was definitely weird.

'You're blonde,' he said, because he couldn't think of anything else to say.

'And you have a moustache. Sort of.'

He put his fingers to his top lip, to check that the modest growth was still there. He didn't think Flo would've heard of Eugène Christophe, the mustachioed Old Gaul, and his Tour de France heroics.

'But wait,' he said, coming to his senses. 'What. I mean. What is going ON?'

She slid her hands into her back pockets, almost sheepish.

'Weeell . . .' she began.

'You squatted my house! My *parents'* house.'

He was whispering through gritted teeth, as if Jerry and his mum might overhear.

'It was empty, Conrad. An empty house! Someone *ought* to live in it. You said that!'

'Did I?'

'*Yes!*'

'Well, I didn't mean *this*, did I? You can't honestly think I meant THIS?'

'No, not quite. But.'

Conrad glanced past her and saw movement in the corridor: shadows flung up from the kitchen-diner at the back of the house, indistinct shapes beyond the sitting-room door. Oh, man. He was in so much trouble.

'How many people are *in* there?!'

'Just come inside.'

'Pfft.'

'Conrad. Conrad. Cmon. You said they'd never sell it.'

'Yes. I know I said that. But now they *are* selling it!'

'Yeah, well. We know that now. Your dad's getting the lawyers on us. We'll be chucked out soon. But that's the point of the party. You *know* about the party, right?'

'Wait. You met my *dad*?'

'Yeah, he came to the house last weekend.'

Of course he did. Of course. Shit Shit Shit. Conrad was anxious. He was agitated. He was hurt, although that was somehow melting under the warmth of Flo's welcome. And he ought to have been angry. He really ought to have been. But he just couldn't muster it. The rage, if that was what it was, had been transitory, deflated at once by Flo's embrace. More than that, though: he couldn't help but wonder whether, given that she'd stolen his house, she might feel she owed him a shag. A handjob, at the very least? Something. Maybe she really had been into him, all along. He was terribly confused.

'You cannot have a party,' he said. 'You absolutely *cannot* have a fucking party.'

'Just. Come inside, Conrad. Please. Come inside.'

He was about to relent when he remembered his bike. He turned and saw Austin standing in the driveway, holding it by the handle-bars, studying it.

'Excuse me,' said Conrad, moving warily down the steps and across the gravel towards him. Normally he enjoyed the attentions of his fellow bicycle enthusiasts, but this one did not seem especially trustworthy.

'That's a nice bike,' Austin growled, gesturing at the frame with his depleted cigarette. 'Peugeot, yeah? Did you do all the restoration yourself? The welding and that?'

Conrad paused. He did seem genuinely interested.

'Er. Yeah,' he replied finally. 'I mean. No. Not the welding. It was this guy in Brick Lane.'

'Oh, yeah. Bananaman, was it?'

'Er. Yeah, how did you . . . ?'

'I know the bloke. Nice job. I like the colour scheme. Racing Green?'

'Oh. Yeah. Yeah, that was my choice. And I built it up myself, actually – the cranks and the bars and the rims and all that stuff. Did the same for my racer. It's vintage.'

'Yeah?' He nodded appreciatively, then he winked at Conrad. 'You might want to take it inside. Don't want the local lowlifes taking a fancy to it, do you?'

Conrad had never been allowed to keep his bikes inside when he lived with his mum; he always had to put them in the garden passage, where they were apt to rust.

'Er, no,' he said, agreeing. 'Okay.'

Austin stubbed his cigarette out on the gatepost and picked up the bike. Conrad followed him up the steps to the front door.

'Conrad, remember Austin?' said Flo as they passed her. 'Austin, this is Conrad.'

'I know who he is,' said Austin, propping the bike against the radiator in the hallway.

Conrad stepped inside. Austin disappeared up the stairs.

'Are you sure he's not your boyfriend?' Conrad mouthed, pointing after him.

Flo laughed. 'No,' she said, and his heart beat fast again. Boom-boom.

He looked around. The place seemed clean enough. The floorboards, the walls: unmolested. There were melted candles on the radiator unit, though. He got a pretty strong whiff of skunk, and he frowned at Flo.

'Is that . . . ?'

'Yeah, sorry,' she said. 'We try to keep it to the garden and the kitchen, but people don't always abide by that particular rule.'

'You have rules?'

'Of course, we have plenty of rules.'

'I guess I thought you'd be anarchists or something.'

'Well, we don't really define ourselves like that. But even anarchists have principles, you know. Every decision here is voted on by the housemates – including who the housemates are. I should've probably held a vote on whether to invite you in, but I didn't have time.'

'Oh. Sorry.'

'Cmon. Come see.'

The sitting room was dark, because the maroon curtains were pulled closed. But sunlight spilled in from the open French window at the back, enough that he could see a dude with ill-advised ginger dreadlocks twiddling the knobs on a set of mixing decks in the bay window where his mum's chaise longue used to be. There were two vast speakers to either side of him, presently burbling the dreaded ska. The sight of the amps made Conrad anxious again. They could not have a party. Absolutely not. No way.

'That's Henrik,' said Flo. 'He's the DJ. And our resident legal expert. Training to be a barrister, aren't you, Henrik?'

The dreadlocked trainee barrister waved hello. Conrad waved back, because what else could he do?

'This is Conrad,' said Flo to Henrik. 'He's come for the party.'

Somebody had stapled a parachute to the ceiling; the white silk billowed gently in the breeze. Probably a fire hazard, was Conrad's first thought. On the mantel above the cast-iron fireplace was an ashtray, with a half-smoked joint slumbering. Flo noticed it, too, and she stubbed it out. There was no sign of the telly. Had it been stolen? Best not to ask. The hardwood floor had been cleared: for dancing, he supposed. He could see a couple of scrapes in the veneer where they'd moved the coffee table, deep enough to give his mum palpitations. He looked again at the walls.

'Hang on, were they . . . ?'

'No. They were white before, but we thought that was sort of boring, so we repainted them. Austin's idea: he's responsible for interior design. He's done some UV stencils in the kitchen, too. You'll love those.'

I probably won't, he thought. All the remaining furniture had been shifted to the back half of the room with the dining set. On the Habitat sofa sat two girls, talking quickly in low voices. Conrad almost tutted at a stain on the fabric, but then remembered that he'd once tipped over a cup of Ribena in that exact spot.

'We have educational workshops and discussion groups in here,' Flo explained. 'Urban disruption; virtual utopias; deschooling society. And we teach woodwork and gardening out the back as well. This is Freya and Cass. They were kettled in Whitehall last winter.'

The girls stopped talking momentarily to nod hello at him, both bearing sombre, world-weary expressions. Cass had a pierced lip. They looked about seventeen.

'How did you get in here in the first place?'

'The front window was unlocked,' Flo replied. 'Totally legal. Ask Henrik.'

Did Conrad believe that? About the window? He wasn't sure he did. Did it matter?

The kitchen made him queasy. They'd set up three giant industrial wooden spools as tables, using his mum's garden furniture and some empty plastic water barrels as seats. Something was cooking in a toasted sandwich maker; a string of melted cheese oozed onto the worktop. Boxes of herbal teas sat open beside the kettle. The sink was full of washing-up. The bin was spewing surplus waste. Two more twenty-somethings were smoking at one of the tables. One had dyed hair; the other no hair at all. He didn't seem like a skinhead, though. No Ben Sherman gingham, no braces, no Doc Martens. Converse trainers, in fact. Just an ordinary guy with a grade zero buzz cut and an 'Obey' T-shirt. Conrad was baffled. Weren't squats meant to be full of crusties and tie-dyes?

'That's Waingro and Spooky: Waingro's a film studies dropout; Spooky lost his job at a carpet warehouse in . . . Where was it, Spooks? Sunderland?'

'Gateshead,' said Spooky, grinning.

'We recycle all we can. And we get a lot of food from supermarket skips,' said Flo, to Conrad's quiet revulsion. 'But we're trying to grow some of our own as well. Cmon.'

A couple of people lay sunbathing on the lawn, or what was left of it. They were murmuring to one another in a foreign language. The whole back end of the garden had been dug up, along with the flower beds. Conrad's mum would completely lose her shit if she saw this. They'd planted veg, Flo explained: tomatoes, carrots, courgettes, lettuce, potatoes. She'd wanted to get some chickens, she said – to lay eggs, to make the residents' diet more sustainable.

'We planned to make this whole place into a social centre. With a café and a garden. Classes and talks. For disenfranchised young people. But that's not going to happen now, obviously.'

Conrad looked around him. The soil was arranged in neat ridges, most of them sprouting something green. The tomato plants, tied to bamboo sticks by the garden wall, were ready to bear fruit. He had to admit he was impressed. Flo seemed to have executed her business plan impeccably. He turned to tell her so, and saw Austin standing by the back door with a bicycle. It was a beautiful machine: turquoise frame, black forks, gleaming steel lugwork. The seat stay and chain stay were both curved like a flattened 'S'.

'Holy shit,' said Conrad. 'Is that a Hetchins?'

'Good knowledge, my friend,' Austin replied. 'Thought you'd be interested.'

Conrad approached the bike and knelt before it. The design detail of the lugs was fine and delicate, and there was a florid turquoise 'H', rimmed in silver, on the front of the head tube.

'That is a 1985 Hetchins *Scorpion Bonum*,' said Austin.

'What's so special about it?' asked Flo.

'It's a collector's item,' Conrad replied, thrilled. 'Hetchins. They make these curly frames.'

'Restored it myself,' said Austin.

'Really?'

'Austin used to be a welder,' said Flo.

'Apprentice welder,' said Austin. 'I custom-painted it. Added the reproduction decals.'

Wow, thought Conrad: Austin was not only a genuine working-class person. He was a real artist, too. The bike was maybe the most beautiful thing Conrad had ever seen. It was all too much. This whole thing was too much. He thought he might blub, so he took some more deep breaths as he stroked the soft, tan leather saddle.

The master bedroom was now a dormitory, with sleeping bags and open rucksacks smeared across the floor. On his parents' kingsize bed, two unconscious girls were sleeping in their underwear. Conrad tried not to look; he didn't dare ask who they were.

In Jerry's study the squatters had started a library. There was an Italian kid in there on the Barcelona chair, reading a book of Slavoj Žižek essays. A few of the housemates were European students, said Flo, showing him her complete collection of *The House on the Hill*, which had pride of place on a top shelf: all twelve titles. She assured him that the house-cleaning rota was rigorously enforced, though he could see a line of scum around the tub in the brand-new first-floor bathroom, and a quiver of grotty toothbrushes in a mug on the marble basin surround.

In his mum's studio – now, apparently, the digital hub – were two studious-looking nerdalikes on laptops, whom she introduced as Ben and Benjy, anthropology postgrads with responsibility for the squat's Web presence. They'd been hijacking Wi-Fi from the neighbours to maintain a Twitter feed and a Facebook page. Among other things, they proudly explained, they'd used the social networks to help organise protests at tax-avoiding retail outlets.

Conrad had expected the squatters to be more confrontational, more conspicuously irate. But Ben and Benjy were gentle and geeky. He found himself in awe of their commitment, amazed that they cared enough to organise a protest about something, anything. He didn't think he had sufficient confidence in any of his opinions to inflict them on anyone else.

Isobel's bedroom, Flo explained, was reserved for travellers.

'"Travellers" as in *pikeys*?' Conrad asked, aghast.

'No! Just people who turn up unexpectedly. Who need a place to stay.'

'Oh. Okay.'

'Guess there'll be a few of those tonight.'

'Er. How many people have you invited?'

She grimaced. 'I'm not sure. A few.'

Up in the loft conversion, the playroom floor was half-covered with old mattresses, apparently salvaged from skips and jumble sales. A girl was playing a guitar, a guy in a linen smock slapping a pair of bongos. Jules and Karim, said Flo: they went busking most days, adding their profits to the household pot. She pulled open the plate-glass balcony door and stepped out into the blue afternoon. Conrad followed her. As she leaned on the wooden rail between two window boxes, her sleeveless sweater rode up to reveal a pair of dimples, framing the small of her back; they spoke of musculature, of health and flexibility.

'So, what do you think?' she said.

What did he *think*? He thought she was trouble, just as Beagle had said. But his views on trouble and its attractions were unaltered, despite everything. Flo had somehow packed away the facts of her past and modelled herself a new and elusive persona: black hair, red, pink, blonde. What nerve. He was defeated, utterly.

'Er,' he said. 'Not exactly "Workers of the World", is it?'

Flo made a serious face.

'You know, Conrad,' she said. 'You live in a democracy so you think you're free. But the government, your parents, everyone told us to take on debt: that's how we'd get through being students, or just being young people. Overdrafts and student loans and credit cards. So you get into debt, and then you think: I might as well go into more debt. Because some day at the end of all this my fine education is going to get me a job that pays it all off. But then that doesn't happen. That might never happen, not for any of these people. And now the debt owns us. The banks own us. The government owns us, and we're not free at all.'

Conrad was watching her lips, not really listening. A question occurred to him.

'Does Jamie know about all this?'

'Jamie Doohan?' She seemed puzzled. 'No. I mean, he knows I'm squatting, I suppose. I invited him to the party. But Jamie and me don't really . . . We're not best buds or anything. He was at school with my big brother.'

'Why do you need to be a squatter? I saw you pay for all that

296

shopping at the supermarket. You had a *gold card*. And Jamie said your dad's a Lord or something?'

'Ha. Well, me and my dad don't exactly get on right now. I mean. I don't *need* a place. But these are my friends. This is what I do.'

'You're the leader.'

'There is no leader.'

'They're going to sell it, you know. My parents.'

'I know.'

'So what'll you do?'

'Find somewhere else. There are a *lot* of empty houses, Conrad. It's just, this one's special.'

'Pfft. Not that special.'

She turned back to the view, out over the Emirates Stadium to the city beyond. Okay, thought Conrad: it was *quite* special.

'So, your dad,' she said. 'Tell me about him.'

'Jerry? Oh, I dunno. I don't see much of him. He has another family now. Although, well . . . Anyway, I don't see much of the others, either.'

'Not even your sister?'

'She lives abroad. So does my mum.'

'Do you even get *on* with your dad?'

'We got on fine when I was a kid, I guess.'

'And now?'

'Isobel's the perfect one. You know. You've read the books.'

'Why do you call him "Jerry"?'

'Because that's his name.'

Flo pulled her phone out of her jeans pocket and started to type something.

'Is that a BlackBerry?'

'Yeah.'

'I thought you said you lost your phone.'

She shrugged.

'Who are you messaging?'

She ignored him, concentrating hard on whatever she was writing.

'Cmon,' she said when she'd finished. 'Let's go to my room.'

There was a makeshift padlock arrangement on the door to Conrad's old bedroom. Jem, the guitar player, had started to warble an unfamiliar folk tune, and it wafted pleasantly down the corridor from the playroom.

'Not really in the spirit of things, is it?' he said, watching as Flo produced the key to the padlock.

'My laptop is in here,' she said. 'And the big TV from the assembly room.'

'The sitting room, you mean.'

'I figured it might be valuable. Didn't want people getting ideas. So I brought it upstairs.'

'So you get the best room? I thought there were no leaders.'

'Well, I found the house. So I got the pick of the rooms. That's a rule.'

'Whose rule?'

She turned the key and the padlock came loose. Was this flirting? wondered Conrad.

'You know,' he said. 'This is my room.'

'Was. Now it's nobody's. I'm just passing through.'

'Right. Passing through. Of course.'

She slipped inside, but Conrad waited on the threshold for a moment, recalling another time when he'd entered this selfsame room without nearly so much trepidation: coming home early from school to recover from an embarrassing diarrhoea spell, only to find his father's bare arse-cheeks bobbing up and down like two bald swimmers breaststroking; the au pair, Barunka, gazing up at Jerry silently, raptly – so engrossed that it had taken her a second or so to spot the boy standing in the doorway. That was pretty much his worst memory.

Barunka, by then, had belonged exclusively to Conrad – Isobel was too old to require the services of an au pair any longer. Young though he was, Conrad had been old enough for love, and he had fallen hard for his Czech governess: his first, worst, doomed crush. He'd never told anybody about the incident, at Jerry's express request. And so, while most children of divorce went about blaming themselves for their parents' problems, Conrad beat himself up instead for delaying the inevitable: for lying obediently to his mum, rather than yanking off that Elastoplast when he had the chance.

In the end his parents' marriage had cracked and split slowly, painfully. They'd staggered on, arguing and not, for a year or more afterwards, their relationship devolving into epic silences and petty disagreements. His mum had gone on propagating the myth of *The House on the Hill*, squeezing out two or three more fictions in spite of the sad truth. By the bitter end, Jerry pretty much lived in the spare room, and Barunka was long gone. Conrad really ought to have asked Pen – at some later date – whether she'd known about Jerry and the last of the Czech au pairs. Perhaps he could've purged the awful recollection by passing it on. But he'd never got around to it. Had the long-drawn-out divorce scarred Conrad mentally, emotionally? Maybe. Probably. But he couldn't say how. He was who he was: Conrad; 'Conrad'. One way or another, his mum and dad were to blame.

'So,' said Flo, hands on hips beneath the skylight. 'Are you staying for the party?'

EXCHANGE

30

Flo's first guests were her fellow housemates. They came bearing beer crates, back from whatever they did with themselves during the day. Some had low-paid jobs, she said, in bars or on building sites. Some were artists and thinkers. Some had simply been side-lined by society (her words). Like the others, they seemed to be mostly well-adjusted, middle- to lower-middle-class students and assorted youth. They were people almost like Conrad. Like hipsters, but with a cause. He still hadn't grasped precisely what the cause was just yet, in spite of Flo's repeated, semi-abstract explanations. But he knew that it had something to do with the government, and the banks, and her dad. And possibly Conrad's dad as well.

The dining table became the bar, set up in front of the French windows, with the cans stored in cool-buckets out back. Flo wrote a price list in black marker pen on a piece of cardboard: *Beer £2*. The armchairs and sofas were pushed back around the walls to create a chill-out area. The sitting room, empty but for Henrik's decks and speakers and a lighting rig sourced from who knows where, was indeed set aside for dancing. Conrad had texted Polly to tell her he was all right, and she and Jamie arrived with the first wave, as the skies darkened and the street lamp opposite flickered pinkly on.

'Mate,' said Jamie, who was wearing his keffiyeh and aviators. He gripped Conrad by the shoulder: a classic Alpha move. 'So this is *your* house! That is . . . awesome?'

'Er. Yeah,' Conrad replied. 'Awesome.'

Jamie spotted Flo in the kitchen and went to inflict himself on her instead. Polly yanked Conrad into the little downstairs loo and locked the door. He'd asked Waingro very nicely to disinfect all the toilet bowls in the house before the guests arrived, and Waingro appeared to have complied. The bleach fumes crackled in Conrad's nostrils.

'It's okay, it's *okay*, Pols. They'll leave after this. My dad's having them thrown out.'

'You can't be serious.'

'It's my house, too. I *choose* to have this party.'

'That's ridiculous.'

'Why?'

'It just is.'

'It's not. But anyway.'

'Are you sure, Conrad?'

'Yes.'

'Are you *sure* sure?'

'Well, no. But . . .'

'Are you doing this because you think Flo . . .'

'No. No, absolutely not.'

'Because she is *totally* taking the piss.'

'Well. Be fair.'

'Oh, come on.'

'Seriously, though.'

'What?'

'It's fine.'

'Really.'

'Er. Yes.'

'You're sure.'

'Pretty much.'

'Pretty much?'

'Pretty much.'

'Pretty much.'

'I don't know!'

'You don't know.'

'How can I *know*? But look. How much can you trash an empty house, anyway?'

'I guess we'll find out.'

'Nonono. These people aren't like that.'

'Ha.'

'Seriously, though.'

'Right.'

'I've had house parties before, Pols. You can clean up afterwards, you know.'

'But this is a squat party.'

'Sort of.'

'It's a squat. It's a party.'

'It's a house. My house. It's a house party. And anyway, Flo's right. It *has* just been empty. Why should my parents . . . ?'

'This is amazing. She's totally brainwashed you.'

'She wants to make it into a *social* centre! With WORKSHOPS!'

'Oh, my God. I can't listen to this any more.'

Polly unlocked the door of the loo.

'*Seriously*, Polly. You need to meet some of these people. They seem very nice.'

She walked out and left him there, and he contemplated following her. But then he locked the door again and sat down on the lid of the loo. He needed a few moments alone to collect himself. Deep breaths, Conrad. Deep breaths. If his parents found out that he was involved with the group who'd squatted their house, he'd surely be in deep shit – party or no party. So eventually he'd decided: why not just let them have the party? It felt a lot simpler than trying to stop them. Flo was inflexible, and he didn't want to upset her; he still had his heart set on a snog some time in the small hours, if she was keen. Thanks to his continuing anxiety, he was in dire need of a dump. But he always felt too self-conscious to void his bowels at any large gathering; the fear of exiting the bathroom to find a pretty girl next in line was just too great. So he flushed the empty bowl, splashed water on his face and stepped out into the corridor.

Beagle and Dennis had arrived and were in the kitchen. Beagle was wearing his *Pokémon* onesie and sucking a lollipop. He opened his paw to show Conrad a sheaf of grey plastic strips.

'We brought glow-sticks,' he said. 'To show our solidarity. Here, take some.'

Polly came back, with Jamie and an armful of beers, partially mollified. Beagle snapped a couple of the sticks so they blushed neon pink and cyan, and he threw shapes at her face until she broke into a smile. It was weird, thought Conrad, when Polly didn't smile. The music was cool: Henrik had promised Nu-Disco and Funk, segueing into some credible Funky House, which all sounded perfectly innocuous. So as more guests appeared, and then more, and then more again, they cracked open their Kronenbourgs and toasted the house on the Hill. Conrad chilled out, easing into the evening as if it were an ice bath.

Flo grinned at him as they collided gently at the bar, collecting more beers.

'Enjoying yourself, then?'

'No,' he grinned back.

He and Flo were co-hosts, Conrad decided, reclaiming the rooms where his parents once held their poncey dinner parties; their relationship, he felt certain, was now threaded with inevitability. He kept to the kitchen, mingling, admiring Austin's luminescent stencil paintings by the light of the UV bulb the gifted Brummie had installed. He introduced Beagle and Dennis to Spooky, the skinhead-but-not-that-sort-of-skinhead from Gateshead. He locked eyes with Flo as she chatted to Jamie somewhere over by the kitchen sink, and they shared a look that seemed to mock Polly's boyfriend for his preposterousness. Three or four drinks down, he experienced a rush of euphoria. And he hadn't even taken any drugs yet.

And then, he couldn't say how much later, his beer can empty again, Conrad looked around for Flo and couldn't see her. He'd been telling Karim the bongo player about the summer he went InterRailing in Morocco, and he'd failed to notice the growing crush of bodies in the kitchen-diner-slash-café. The music was getting seriously loud. The chat was a deafening drone. 'Excuse me,' he said, to whomever was in his way, and elbowed out through the back door and into the garden. It was hardly less crowded than indoors, but through the thickets of people he could see a row of guys using the back wall as a urinal. The tomato plants had been trampled. Crushed cans and cigarette butts dotted the lawn. He spotted Ben and Benjy, the computer nerds, cringing beneath his mum's gazebo.

'Exactly how many people were invited to this party?' he asked them, raising his voice to be heard over the throb of deep house.

'Ummm, we don't really know,' replied Ben or Benjy. 'It was an open invite. So . . .'

'Could be five hundred,' said the other one, as if that was somehow helpful.

Who were they all? Facebook funnelled out through six degrees of separation in seconds. How could you tell who the gatecrashers were, when you had no guest list? Polly was right, again. Conrad's dread deepened. He fought his way down the side of the house to the French windows, where a pair of squatter girls were trying to maintain control of the bar. The beer was almost out, but most people had BYO booze: quarters of vodka, bottles of wine. What were the girls' names again? One of them had a lip piercing. She looked at him bleakly.

'This is what it's like being kettled!' she shouted into his ear.

Conrad was cool with MDMA, laughing gas, a bit of coke and weed and ket. But as he battled on past the bar into the dining-room-slash-chill-out-area, his arms machetes parting the bodily undergrowth, he began to get the sense that stronger things were being taken, or that the cool things were being done in unhealthy doses. Smokers were ashing on the sofas. He scented the un-ambiguous tang of puke. Like milk left out overnight, the party was on the turn. The crowd contained an unsavoury element: sneering kids, capable of at least low-level criminality. Where had they come from? He heard a bottle smashing somewhere, pursued by an excitable screech. There was something in the air, a thin mist of insanity.

On he went, into the sitting-room-slash-dance-hall, where the floor was sticky and spiked with broken glass. Dancers flailed, flinging sweat beads as they scythed the air. The coloured lights pulsed across the wall and the parachute ceiling, and he could see splashed red wine stains along the skirting boards. Oh, and puke. Yep, definitely puke. Henrik had started playing what sounded suspiciously like Dark Electro House, which was well beyond his remit. Conrad was about to go and request something softer to wind the night down – like Leonard Cohen, maybe – when he spotted a teenager in a beanie spray-tagging the hallway wall.

'What the fuck are you doing?!' he said, trying to yank the spraycan from the kid's grasp, instead propelling a stripe of black paint up the wall, disrupting both the tag and his mum's precious sponge effect. He instantly regretted his haste. The kid squared up to him; he was some inches shy of Conrad, but he looked considerably tougher. As did the two behind him in hoodies, arms crossed, sticking their jaws out.

'Oi, fuck off, bruv,' said the graffiti artist, jabbing Conrad in the chest with an index finger. ''S not your fucking house, innit?'

Conrad was unable to correct him, because he'd briefly mislaid the power of speech. He didn't think he'd ever been quite so scared in his whole life. Not even when his wallet was snatched in Morocco. So he was really jolly grateful when Austin materialised next to him.

'There a problem here?' said Austin.

'Oh, my days,' said the kid. 'Tell your boy to back off, yeah?'

'Okay,' Austin replied. 'Long as your boys back off, too.'

The kid sucked his teeth and turned towards the front door. They were leaving. Austin patted Conrad on the back, and he welled up with relief. He needed a hug.

'Getting a bit out of hand, this,' said Austin.

'Who are all these *people?*'

'I don't know, my friend. I do not know.'

Conrad remembered the bikes. They'd stashed them in the playroom at the top of the house to keep them safe during the party. But now nowhere was safe. He left Austin in the hallway and started to climb: up two steep flights of stairs, over and around the craggy sprawl of partygoers. The kid with the spraycan had already been up here; there was a flamboyant tag on the door of Jerry's old study. The first-floor bathroom was now reserved almost exclusively for drug use, so the queue for the newly fitted loo on the second floor was a snake. At its tail end, Conrad came across Polly, Beagle and Dennis. Polly looked glum. She grabbed his arm and yelled at him over the music. The bass line rippled through the carpeted floor beneath them: WUB, WUB, WUB, WUB-WUB-WHOMP.

'Where are you going?' she said.

'The bikes. Checking on my bike.'

'Have you seen Jamie anywhere?'

He had not, and so the three of them climbed the final set of stairs with Conrad, to try their luck with the shower room in the loft conversion. The crowd thinned as they reached the top of the house, and the loo was unoccupied. Conrad left his friends to piss and proceeded to the playroom at the end of the corridor.

The Peugeot and the Hetchins were both still propped against the wall behind the door, uninjured. He looked them over, breathing a deep sigh of relief. There were some people smoking a fat joint on the grotty, second-hand mattresses. I could really do with a toke right now, he thought.

He looked out at the balcony beyond the plate glass, where a band of drunken lads was laughing wildly. One of them had his arms wide, hands gripping the two ends of one of Conrad's mum's wooden window boxes. It had little sunflowers in it, which the squatters had planted. The guy was straining, egged on by his mates, ripping the box from its moorings. It came away, finally, with a crack, and he held it above his head like a triumphant weightlifter, lapping up his spectators' applause. Conrad did not crave another confrontation. So he watched, powerless and dizzy with vertigo, as the guy launched the box over the end of the balcony, sunflowers and all, into what must have been next-door's garden.

Maybe if he could just get Henrik to turn the music down. Maybe then the crazies would leave. Maybe. He turned back to the corridor, bracing himself for his descent. The others were waiting for him at the far end of the loft conversion, near the stairs. The padlock on Flo-slash-Conrad's door was missing.

'Dude,' Beagle called down the hallway. 'Isn't this your room?'

He shrugged, so Beagle opened the door and went in, Polly and Dennis behind him.

Conrad reached the doorway just as Polly was storming out.

'Wanker,' she said as she made for the stairs, and Conrad, hurt, presumed she meant him.

He stepped into the bedroom, where, by the dim light of Flo's MacBook, Beagle's fistful of glow-sticks, and a cluster of candles on an upturned packing case, he saw Beagle, the hood of his *Pokémon* onesie pulled back; Dennis, hand over his mouth in shock; Flo, sitting on the bed, mussing her cropped blonde hair; and beside her, Jamie Doohan. The floor rattled with every thump of the bass from below. WUB WUB WUB WUB-WUB-WHOMP. Conrad was confused for a moment: had they been doing coke? But as Jamie stood to follow Polly, his belt flopped loose, and Conrad's eye was drawn unavoidably to the bulge in the crotch of his carrot jeans. Ah, he thought. Maybe *this* is what anger feels like.

'Dude,' he said grimly. 'Not cool.'

'Hey, *fuck* you, Conrad mate,' said Jamie, and started towards him across the room. Conrad, still a coward by instinct, backed up into the door, which closed behind him. All of a sudden, Jamie was falling forwards, and Conrad saw Beagle's foot outstretched, tripping the fucker face first onto the carpet. He made a dull thud as he hit the floor. Dennis shrieked with laughter and high-fived his boyfriend. Jamie moaned and curled up at Conrad's feet. Flo just sat there quietly: trouble. Conrad could see now that he wasn't going to get that shag, after all.

Funny, he reflected, how you could bet so long on someone you barely knew. Funny how much you could invest in a fantasy, even when reality was staring you down. As he was considering his position, the music stopped mid-beat. WUB, WUB, WUB-WUHhhhh. The silence was like fresh air sucked into a vacuum. There were shouts and catcalls from the lower floors. They all looked at one another, blankly, as if any of them knew what was going on down there.

'Shit,' murmured Flo.

'WTF?' said Beagle.

In the square of moon that the skylight threw across the floor, Jamie was quaking in a ball. Conrad heard a whimper. Was he crying?

'Jamie? Are you okay?'

Dennis snickered. Beagle shushed him.

'Jamie?' said Conrad again.

'Fuck*sake*, Conrad mate,' said Jamie, hauling himself up into a sitting position. He dragged his sleeve across his face, and Conrad was sure he could see snot and tears there, gleaming.

'You don't understand what it's like,' Jamie went on, his voice wavering. 'You and Polly. It's like you talk in this secret language. Like, whenever I come into a room or whatever. It's like you're both laughing at me or something. It makes me really, really insecure, *okay*?!'

Conrad could tell that Beagle and Dennis were both trying hard not to laugh. He looked at Flo, who just raised her eyebrows, unimpressed. He could hear somebody stomping up the stairs, and he hoped it was Polly, come to take control of the situation again. But no: it was just someone using the loo next door.

'Jamie,' said Conrad. 'You've got it all wrong. Seriously. Mate. I really. I really respect you, Jamie.' (He did sort of respect him, he supposed. He didn't like him. But he respected him. Or at least he had, until about two minutes ago.)

'Really?' said Jamie, so hopeful it was almost heartbreaking.

There was an enormous crash from the loo next door, as if someone had tumbled over and totalled themselves in the shower cubicle. They all chuckled, the tension momentarily relieved. Conrad leaned down and gripped Jamie's shoulder to reassure him: classic Alpha. Then there was another bang. The wall behind the bed shook. Flo turned around. A third: BANG.

'What the hell is that?' she said.

Another, and another. BANG. BANG. A crack appeared in the wall. Conrad tried to flick on the bedroom light, but the bulb had gone, or the fuse had blown, or somebody had cut the electricity. BLAM. POW. To Conrad's horror, the crack split and crumbled, and a chunk of wall dropped out of it. Then water started to spray through the seam and into the room. Flo screamed, and so did Dennis. Beagle's eyes opened wide. THUNK. CRUNCH.

312

Someone is actually destroying the house, Conrad told himself. Someone is taking my home apart. The graffiti kids. Or the window-box yobs. Or worse. Shit shit shit. It's my fault. It's my fault. I let it happen. I did this. It's my fault. Head spinning, he opened the door to step out into the corridor. It was dark, but he could see that the water was creeping in from outside, too. WHAM. KABOOM. It flowed like a mountain stream along the corridor of the loft conversion; he could hear it cascading down the stairs to the second floor. BANG. BANG. BANG. Flo was up and off the bed now, and she pushed right past Conrad, out of the door and into the flood.

31

As the plane banked towards Heathrow, the scattered lights of the Thames Estuary rolled across the window and back, rousing Isobel from an anxious slumber. A stewardess leaned over the snoring Dutchman in the aisle seat and ordered her to buckle up. The cabin stank of stale a/c. They were in a holding pattern, spiralling down in the darkness towards the green fields of her imagination. Shire horses, tractors, loganberries. Tor would be panicking by now. No, that was wrong: she couldn't imagine him panicking. But he'd try to call. She would leave her iPhone switched off after landing, she decided, at least until she'd pulled herself together, made it back to the house on the Hill, worked out what the hell she was up to, exactly.

She'd poked at her in-flight meals, unable to swallow more than a few mouthfuls. She couldn't read a word of the airline magazine. On the DXB–AMS leg, she'd watched parts of a Rachel McAdams movie, which she could now no longer recall, except that the guy in it was cute. The flight had calmed her, as she'd watched the desert give way to the Med, and then to the Alps in late afternoon. But the layover at Amsterdam had been excruciating, dead time. She'd been wearing the same sweatpants for twenty-four hours, the same T-shirt almost as long; they clung to her, still clammy with the remembered heat of the Emirates. There was sand in her trainers when she'd removed them to put on her complimentary socks.

The captain announced their final descent. Isobel raised her seat-back as instructed, switched off the reading lamp and turned her eyes to the night. A shudder of turbulence, and then the plane swam out from under the cloud cover. She thrilled to the sight of London unfolding beneath her, awash with brilliant light pollution. They sank lower, and lower again, her stomach lurching with each gentle altitude adjustment. Soon they were gliding west along a reef of landmarks. There! The Dome! There! Canary Wharf! They followed the dark, winding path of the river down over the City, St Paul's, the West End. Wembley, off to the right, past the wing-tip's blinking red beacon.

Isobel craned her neck and searched and searched and was certain she could see the tiny gap in the dots that signified Highbury Fields and, nearby, the floodlit Emirates Stadium, which meant the house on the Hill had to be right . . . there! She was sure of it. Her heart leapt at the thought. She didn't know what she planned to do when she arrived. Persuade her parents not to sell? Or just curl up beneath the covers in her old bedroom and hope that whoever bought it wouldn't notice.

A soft landing. It hit her as she hurried down the covered gangway into the terminal: the cool of the night, even in midsummer. Oh, to be home! She was briefly thwarted by the queue at passport control, but once free of officialdom, she cantered with her wheelie case through baggage reclaim and out into the arrivals hall. She found an ATM and nervously withdrew £250, thinking she ought to grab what she could before the banks cut her off completely. The Heathrow Express was at the platform as she reached it; while the jet-lagged faded into sleep around her, Isobel's nervous energy remained undimmed by the motion of the train, speeding them into the city. Closer, it seemed to whisper: closer, closer.

At Paddington, she rushed for the taxi rank, wheelie case rattling over the adorably uneven pavement. There was slow-moving traffic on the Marylebone Road, even at this late hour, and she willed it to disperse. She tried to focus on where she was going, not on where she'd been: Tor, Anton, Jonas. The twins would hardly notice she was missing. As the taxi passed close to her dad's flat in King's Cross, Isobel remembered she'd no keys, and worried all the way down Upper Street: how would she get in? She'd have to call him, or Conrad. She yearned to see them both, yet she didn't feel quite up to it, to explaining herself. And anyway, if she turned on her phone, she might have to screen calls and voicemails from her husband. Maybe she could climb in through an open window instead. Something. *Something*.

'Sounds like a party,' said the cabbie, as they drew up. 'Bloody hell. Looks like one, too.'

Isobel had been too busy fretting, too busy anticipating the house of her dreams, to appreciate the dawning reality, so it took her a few moments to fully compute that the home she was looking at – the one with the coloured lights blazing behind the condensation on the bay windows; the people spilling like smoke-dazed firemen from the dark of the front door; and the music quaking the whole fucking taxi with its bass line – was her own.

'Oh, my God,' she said, but she could barely hear her own voice. The cabbie was saying something. Cash. He wanted cash. Should she stay, or flee? What the fuck was going on? What *was* that *music*? She fumbled for her purse and finally peeled £40 from it for the driver, then she clattered out onto the pavement with her wheelie case. The noise! It swallowed her like fog. The taxi swung quickly away from the kerb and was gone.

'Oh, my God.'

Her head was light, her legs buckling. She felt sick again, but there was nothing in her stomach to bring up. By the glow of the street lamp, she could see a fat, illegible graffiti tag on the brickwork by the gatepost, next to a crudely sprayed outline of a cock and balls. The people on the front steps. They were what, teenagers? A couple of them were staring at her, curious, hostile maybe. One of them was laughing about something. She could smell marijuana. Shadows jittered behind every blurred pane. Shouting. She heard shouting. In the shadows beneath the bay window, she noticed a man slumped against the wall. Slumped? No, leaning. No – pissing. Pissing against the wall. A wine bottle landed on the gravel driveway and shattered. Isobel recoiled. Oh, my God. Where had it come from? Mum and Dad's bedroom?! She wheeled around to the street, the dark surrounding houses, as if for someone to scream at. But there was . . . Dad's car? Is that *Dad's* car? She ran across the road to the red Lotus. He wasn't inside. But wait: a tiny, cowering shape. Is that . . . ? It had to be.

'Oh, my God. Alice?'

A strange calm took hold of her then, and she knew that she was in shock. Knew that in fact she'd been in shock for probably a whole day, maybe even longer, maybe years, and that her body's psychic defences were only now kicking in, just as the moment demanded it. She plucked the quivering little girl from the passenger seat, and hugged her, and kissed her cheeks where the tears threatened to fall, and asked her what the fuck was going on. But Alice couldn't say for sure, except that her dad – *our* dad – was inside. Isobel slung her wheelie case into the car and, leading Alice by the hand, walked coolly back over the road, the music throbbing in the air, the eyes of those teenagers following them across the granite paving of the next-door driveway, past the tiny electric car and up the neighbours' front steps. In Dubai, she'd feared the power of the police to prevent parties, to call a halt to fun. Now she prayed the Met could do the same, and with comparable efficiency.

She had to ring the doorbell twice and bang the knocker viciously before anyone came to the door. It opened halfway to the dim-lit hall behind, and a woman peered around it, her mousy hair tied back, her face free of make-up, her expression, frankly, terrified. She looked wide-eyed at Isobel, and then at Alice, and she seemed to understand.

'Oh, no,' she said. 'You must be . . .'

'Isobel. Can I use your phone?'

'I'm sorry?'

At that moment, the music from next door went abruptly quiet. It was replaced, almost at once, by the roar of conversation. It sounded like hundreds of people.

'I need to use your phone, right now.'

32

Jerry tried to avoid South London wherever possible. Just look at the Tube map: all those underground lines tailing off below the Thames like paint dribbles. Nobody wanted to go to South London, not really. But after he took Glassop's advice, and called 'John', the bloke on the back of the property developer's business card, he was told by a gruff voice to come to a builder's yard by the railway line in Camberwell, at lunchtime on Saturday. Jerry feared for the Lotus chassis as he turned in through the gate and parked on the potholed waste ground. The yard was fringed with coils of corrugated tubing and empty wooden pallets. There was an ancient, unwheeled Sierra Cosworth sitting on stacks of bricks at the far end, but Jerry put his car next to the white van by the Portakabin office. He hated white vans, and all they stood for.

He'd dressed down in jeans and a T-shirt, aware that he'd be interacting with the common man. Nerves jangling, he climbed the three noisy metal steps to the office door, knocked once and, receiving no response, timorously pushed it open. The little room was gloomy and spartan. A shelf ran down one of the chipboard walls with nothing but an *A–Z* on it, lying flat; on the opposite wall was a single hook, from which there hung a leather jacket. The window at the back had a view of the bricks between the railway arches, and seated at the desk in front of it was a large man with dark hair in a denim shirt, eating a packet of Quavers and reading the *Daily Mirror*. Jerry thought he could hear *Test Match Special* coming from somewhere.

'John?' he said tentatively.

'Ah,' said the man, looking up only now, as if he'd not noticed the door opening, which he plainly must have. 'Mr Manville?'

Jerry nodded. The man slapped the Quaver dust from his palms and held out a big, calloused hand for Jerry to shake.

'Sit down,' he said. 'Can I get you a coffee or something?'

'No, thank you,' Jerry replied. John had a South London accent. Slumbering on the threadbare carpet squares beside the desk was a South London dog. One of those horrible mutts with muscled, mottled-brown bodies and clanking hyena jaws. Never trust a man with a dog, that would be Jerry's advice. He pulled the chair away from the beast so that he could sit down and cross his legs without the movement engaging its protective instincts.

'So,' said John, smiling. 'You've a bit of a problem.'

'That's right.'

'Well.' John picked up his dwindling mug of coffee from the desk and slurped it. 'I expect we can sort that out for you.'

'That would be . . . extremely helpful,' Jerry replied. The dog was wide awake now, and staring at him steadily. 'Could you tell me a little bit more about your methods, perhaps?'

John chuckled. He laid the packet of Quavers flat on the desk in front of him, then he brought his fist down on it with a thud. And another, and another. Jerry could hear the crackle of the crisps being ground to pulp. John picked up the packet again, tipped the smithereens into his mouth, and chewed them, grinning. Jerry's heart was beating rather fast.

'So,' said John, finishing his mouthful. 'You said you wanted this done sharpish.'

'That's right. Er. Tonight, if possible.'

John sucked his teeth. 'I think we might be able to manage that. Sammy!'

'Hold on!' said a muffled voice from behind the door in the corner of the office. Jerry heard a toilet flushing. John waited, and so did Jerry. (And so did the dog.) The door opened, and through it emerged another man, younger than John, and even larger. In his fist was a pocket radio with the cricket on, and with him came the wafted smell of ripe shit.

'Sammy,' said John. 'Reckon you can round up some fellas for a job this evening?'

Sammy looked at John, and then at Jerry, his eyes blank. Jerry shrank into his chair.

'Yeah,' said Sammy, in an Eastern European accent. 'Should not be problem.'

'Er,' said Jerry. 'Can I possibly. Er. Get a quote for that?'

John considered the question for a second. 'Three thousand,' he said.

'Fuck me,' said Jerry.

'Fuck you, indeed,' John replied. 'I ought to charge more for the short notice. My lads have to get paid, you know.'

'Of course,' said Jerry, flustered. 'Of course. Er. How many "lads", exactly?'

'Ten, normally. Strength in numbers. Shock and awe.'

Jerry breathed out. He thought about the girl. Ulrike. She'd love this, wouldn't she? Martyrdom. Getting dragged from the house, kicking and screaming. But then he thought of Sammy's steroidal Polish fist, and her pretty porcelain face, and it gave him pause. And it wasn't just her, was it? There were others. Students, some of them. Kids. Did he really want to send these thugs in to crush them? Was he *that* man? He was a Labour voter, when he bothered to vote. And this, he supposed, would count as tyrannical right-wingery. Fascism. He stood up, and all three pairs of eyes followed him as he backed around the chair, putting it between them and him, and putting him closer to the exit.

'Hmph,' he said. 'You know. I'd. Er. I think I'd like to . . . consider it, for a while. Perhaps. Um. Perhaps it's not quite as urgent as all that. I'm not sure. Er. Um.'

John looked at him levelly. 'Go ahead,' he said. 'Think about it all you want, Mr Manville. You have my number.'

'I do,' said Jerry, 'I do. Thank you.'

He backed through the door, and then turned and clanged down the metal steps to the Lotus. John had his number, too, he supposed, but not his address. That was some comfort. What the hell was Glassop thinking? It took him two attempts to start the engine and, as he swung away from the Portakabin, Sammy was standing in the doorway, filling it, watching.

Jerry drove around a while, then he parked back at the flat and went for a walk. He walked to his club, where he drank a Guinness and a whiskey to steady his nerves, ate a BLT and stared at a long story about phone-hacking in *The Times*, taking in none of it. He walked to Liberty and bought some expensive stationery, thinking a new Smythson notebook might calm him down. He was going to have to tell Pen. There was no getting around that now. It was past eight when he got back to the flat, and his BlackBerry was out of juice. He plugged it in and booted up the iMac to watch something on YouTube. There was a video of Emily Maitlis uncrossing her legs on *Newsnight* that he thought might relax him. Before he could find it, however, a ping announced the arrival of a new email. He knew who it would be from before he opened it, and he could feel his bile rising already. He ought not to give her the satisfaction of reading them. But he did anyway. It was brief, like the others.

From: 'Ulrike' <71117@dotmail.com>
Sent: 16 July 2011 15:02
Subject: You/Us
You are wealthier and freer and more powerful than any other generation in history, and you've screwed your own kids. It's practically child abuse.

Jerry's BlackBerry rang as he read the email, twice, his anger engorged. The ringtone: 'Rockafeller Skank'. He ignored it until he was done, and the blinking red light on the phone informed him of a voicemail. It was Genevieve, and she was irate: Why the *hell* hadn't he picked Alice up yet? Wasn't she supposed to be spending the *night*? He *knew full well* that she and Xander had reservations at Heston Blumenthal's! He was about to throw the phone across the room when a text arrived from Pen:

> Catching the night ferry. Will be at the house in the morning. See you then? P

Fuck me. Women. A triple whammy. Accusations, demands, disapproval. Jerry's outrage was all-consuming. He gripped the BlackBerry as tightly as he could, imagining himself a superhero, able to crush complex electrical devices with his bare hands. But it was too robust. He made to throw it across the room, and then the cost and the hassle of replacing it flashed across his consciousness, so he slammed it back down on the desk instead. He stood and stormed into the kitchen and opened the fridge. He needed to Feel Better. But he appeared to be out of *Ppalleena!*s. What day was it? Saturday. There ought to be one left. Where was it? Where the bloody hell was it?! How was he supposed to Feel Better?! He spotted something orange, lurking at the back of the shelf behind a Waitrose ready meal. Not a *Ppalleena!*, but a half-eaten Toffee Crisp. How the hell did that get there? he wondered. He fished it out and ate it.

On Marylebone Road he put his foot down, weaving the Lotus perilously between the sluggish lanes of traffic. When he reached Notting Hill, there was a scrawled note stuffed into the letter box: '*Let yourself in. G.*' Jerry still had a fucking key for the house, which he fucking *owned*, by the fucking way, and he grappled with his fucking fob in the fucking dark until he fucking found it. Alice was alone on the seashell-white sofa in the snow-white sitting room, reading a picture book.

'Where's your mother?' he asked.

'She went to Heston Bum-Mentals with Xander.'

'Get your things. We're going.'

While Alice collected her rucksack, Jerry went out into the back garden. At the bottom of the lawn there was a shed, its wood walls crisped to black charcoal: Japanese weatherproofing treatment – Genevieve's idea. The door was unlocked, and he pulled the cord that switched on the ceiling's bare light bulb. He soon saw what he was looking for, propped in the corner: a sixteen-pound sledgehammer. Long, scarred hardwood shaft; rusting, double-faced iron head. One of the workmen had left it behind after they knocked through half the walls in the house to satisfy his second ex-wife's minimalist vision. Jerry had never used it – too scared of its destructive power – but he'd kept it all the same. A pair of gardening gloves rested on the lip of a terracotta plant-pot. He picked them up and stuffed them into his pocket. On the cluttered workbench in the corner, he found a pair of safety goggles and a painting mask with an elastic head-strap. He grabbed both of those as well.

He thrust the gear into the tiny boot of the Lotus along with his daughter's rucksack, and lowered himself awkwardly into the driver's seat again. Ridiculous car, he thought. I should just bloody buy a new one. Alice had a book on her lap. There was a picture on the front of a frightened little boy, frantically chasing a herd of bouncing green orbs down a slope. He recognised it at once, the book and the boy. *The House on the Hill 4: The Wheelbarrow and the Watermelons*. He started the engine.

He kept thinking about what Glassop had said. About how he'd ballsed everything up. He knew it, of course. He'd always known it. He didn't know that it was quite so glaringly obvious to everyone else. Jerry never wanted to do it. Not to Pen. Not when they were kids, anyway. He loved her. He did. He'd never so much as petted the supermodels on those ad shoots in the desert, or in the South of France, or in the former Soviet Union. Oh, I don't know, he thought: maybe I would have, if only Brandt and Glassop hadn't got in there before me.

Because there was always, wasn't there, that unfortunate urge to shag somebody new, somebody unfamiliar, somebody still at the brink of fantasy. Somebody still dazzled by the imagined Jerry, and not yet disappointed by the substandard reality. And so, okay, he'd bonked Barunka, the chunky Czech au pair. And Glassop's secretary. And a couple of other tedious blondes, once it became clear that he was in his prime and ought not to waste the opportunity. Flings, crushes, cured instantaneously by consummation. But that period of sexual allure had been brief and unsatisfying: a fairground firing range, with Genevieve its booby prize.

When he looked back on it now, the emotion he recalled most viscerally was not the happiness of marriage, nor even the sadness of divorce, but the shame that came between them. If he let one guilty memory in, the rest always came tumbling after: Conrad, catching him as he climaxed inside the nanny. Pen, bottom lip trembling, banishing him to the spare room. Isobel, hanging up when he called to applaud her GCSE results. Barunka, blubbing love haikus in broken English as he drove her to the airport. Those were the things that kept him awake at night. The shame. The guilt.

He really thought that he and Pen could have got past it, if they'd made the effort. For the children. For themselves. But divorce was the path of least resistance. They were lazy. He was lazy. He ballsed it all up. The guilt was too much. It was *too much*. He had to get it out somehow. Had to get it all out. He had to Feel Better.

* * *

325

The music was louder than it had been last weekend. A lot louder. And it wasn't Peter Tosh. It was some sort of dum-thwack, dum-thwack bollocks that only people on drugs could possibly enjoy. Jerry parked the Lotus in the same place, opposite the house, and levered himself up and out to see what those bastards were doing to his home. He didn't really know what constituted a rave, but he guessed this was one. The house was aflame with light and sound.

'Dad,' said Alice timidly, rolling down the passenger-side window. 'Daddy? What are you doing?'

'It's okay, Alice,' Jerry replied over the noise. 'Dad just has to go inside for a few minutes. You stay here.'

This time, she didn't argue. He walked around to the back of the car. He was still in his jeans and T-shirt, but his loafers had cost £400. Couldn't be helped. There was a waterproof camping lantern in the boot that he kept there for when the car broke down at night. He strapped on the painting mask, slowly, cautiously, as if he were about to go over the top at Verdun. Then the goggles; they were scuffed, and most of the world became a blur when he snapped them on over his specs, but they'd do. He pulled on the gardening gloves, picked up the sledgehammer and the lantern, closed the boot, and strode towards the house.

Through the goggles' haze he could see some kids kneeling on the pavement near the gatepost, studying the brickwork. They jumped up and ran off down the street as they spotted him approaching. There were more on the front steps smoking as he walked up and in through the open door. They looked at him oddly, and one of them started to laugh. He knew this would happen. He bloody knew it. The bastards wanted to destroy the place. Well, he thought, not if he beat them to it. If he couldn't live in it, then nobody could. He made this place what it was. His legacy: the only thing he ever built with his own two hands. He knew every wire, every pipe, every floor and wall – every weakness.

The hallway was dark and jammed with people. There were

candles on top of the radiator box where they'd once left keys and post, the wax melting onto Pen's paintwork. The hardwood floor was sticky with trampled gunk. The sound system seemed to have been set up in the sitting room, and the music was so loud as to be a mere buzz, indistinguishable from itself. Jerry ignored it and barged through the clumps of kids to the back stairs, making his way down into the kitchen-diner. Some of the partygoers complained as he pushed past, but nobody tried to stop him. In fact, the few faces he could make out looked surprised and scared to see the man in the mask with a hammer at his side, bearing down on them. He suppressed the urge to split their heads open.

The kitchen was almost unrecognisable. Pen's diner-style Formica table had been dragged to one end and smothered under smokers' ash and empty booze receptacles. There were vast wooden industrial spools being used as tables, each of them awash with more melting candles. The strip-lights over the worktop had been replaced with UV, to illuminate the stencilled graffiti on the walls. The air was clogged with dope smoke. So this, Jerry surmised, was the 'drugs' room. He hoped he wouldn't step on any hypodermic needles. The people crowding the tables studied him warily as he made his way between them. Outside, in the garden, he could see yet more of the bastards milling around. There was a small airing cupboard on the far side of the kitchen-diner. Some bald little twat in a logo T-shirt was leaning against it, drinking lager and shouting to his mate over the music. Jerry put his lantern on the floor.

'Excuse me,' he said.

The kid frowned at him, and then at the hammer. Jerry removed the painting mask.

'EXCUSE ME,' he said again, and the kid moved away. He and his friend sidled towards the nearest table, staring. Jerry put the painting mask back on and opened the cupboard. They'd once kept an ironing board in here, and spare towels. There was nothing in the darkened recess now but the fuse-box. It was mounted high on the wall, just out of arm's reach. There was a long row of black circuit-breakers: kitchen; hallway; sitting room; master bedroom. Jerry knew each of them by heart. At the right-hand end, the main switch pulsed red like a bull's eye.

He checked behind him, and saw that people had started to back off. The dum-thwack music from upstairs was reaching some kind of crescendo, rumbling the very foundations. He hefted the sledge-hammer onto his shoulder, spread his feet for optimal balance, and then swung it at the wall. Missed. Fuck. A chunk of masonry tumbled to the floor. The people around him started to shout at him to stop. He swung again – KAPOW! – and the lights went out.

The music ground to a halt as well, and there was a momentary lull in the hubbub as the partygoers all came to terms with the silence. Then the chatter restarted, this time with purpose. Cries, complaints, queries. The people nearest Jerry were swearing at him, but nobody dared come close in the ebbing candlelight. He reached up and wrenched a handful of cables out of the shattered box, like weeds from a flower bed, just to be sure. The point was to make the place unlivable, even for barbarians. The electrics were gone, but that wasn't enough on its own to render the house inoperative, so Jerry dropped the sledgehammer to his side once more, picked up the lantern and made for the stairs.

Even in the dark, he knew his way around the building using simple sense memory. He clambered over the slumped kids on the stairs to the ground floor, and then to the first floor, where shadows were jostling in his study and the master bedroom. As he ascended, smartphone screens clicked on all around him, their owners' faces glowing in the dark, recoiling as they saw the madman in the mask and goggles. He stamped on, to the second floor: Isobel's bedroom; Pen's studio. His hands were getting sweaty, so he took off the gardening gloves and stuffed them in his pocket.

As he made his way to the very top of the house, Jerry flicked on the lantern. The detail began to bleed back into his vision, the lamp's beam swinging side to side as he climbed the last set of stairs to the loft conversion. He trudged past Conrad's closed bedroom door. It was almost quiet up here. In the playroom at the end of the corridor, he could see some people lounging on what looked like old mattresses, illuminated by the moon through the balcony window. One of them came to the door, and then closed it in a fright when she saw him. No matter. The shower-cum-loo was empty. He put the lantern on top of the bathroom cabinet, where it would light the whole room. Somebody appeared to have pissed on the floor. When they'd originally installed it, the plumbers had boasted of the power shower's excellent water pressure. Jerry decided he'd take that out first. He slid back the Plexiglas door of the cubicle and lined up as long a swing as he could in the cramped space. His first hit was pathetic, and the hammer smashed nothing but a handful of aquamarine mosaic tiles. The second was better. The fourth hit pipe. The sixth drew water. The eighth or ninth burst the plumbing wide open.

Jerry turned his attention to the sink. He was finding a rhythm now. Blood pounded in his ears. The exercise was probably doing him good. As he swung, he sensed his dull, week-long headache dispersing. He threw jagged silhouettes across what was left of the walls. He could hear people hurrying, scared, down the corridor from the playroom to the stairs. He was flushing them out, flushing them out like the little turds they were. Water began to gush from the washbasin's open wounds. His clothes were sodden. It was coming in over the tops of his ruined £400 loafers. He decided he might as well trash the toilet, since he was enjoying himself, so he went at that as well.

'What the fuck . . . ?'

Jerry stopped what he was doing and turned to the voice in the doorway. He wrenched off the goggles and the painting mask.

Ulrike stood there, blonde, gawping, loose mosaic tiles floating out into the hall between her black-jeaned ankles.

'Oh, right,' she said, understanding. 'Yeah. Of course.'

As she backed away from the door, Jerry saw that she was beaten. He'd reduced his own home to wreckage, but he'd won it back. Weary but triumphant, he let the hammer drop, and it splashed loudly as it hit the deepening puddle. Water still sprayed from the smashed appliances, but the pressure was starting to abate. Jerry was drenched, his clothes clinging to every unsightly inch of his frame. With a final crooked grimace, Ulrike ducked out of the lantern-light and was gone. Jerry tried to find something to wipe the droplets from his glasses, but everything was wet. He reached for the lantern and followed her out into the corridor. She'd vanished. Instead, he saw a boy in shorts at the end of the hall, looking at the stairs as if about to follow the girl and the water down them. The Breton-striped top seemed familiar. And the quiff. And the bum-fluff moustache. The boy turned and squinted fearfully into the lantern through Elvis Costello specs. His eyes went wide.

'Jerry, is that . . . ?' he said.

Jerry stared back at his son, uncomprehending. What did this mean? Conrad looked as though he was about to faint.

'Dad?' he said weakly. 'I don't get it.'

The hubbub downstairs increased, a rumour rattling up from the floors below. Someone was yelling something about pigs. Then Jerry heard the whoop of a siren.

33

Six months since his accident, and Bruno was still limping, but his niggling injury had not kept him from erecting the new wood-shed. In just a few days, he'd sawed and stained and sealed an elegant pine frame, and now three long, rectangular sheets of corrugated plastic leaned against the back of the house, ready to become its roof. He'd stripped out the rotten beams from the old structure and heaped them onto a bonfire up the slope on the back lawn, close by Bennett's grave. And he was still at work after lunch on Saturday, when David left for the market in Agen, to buy more jam labels for the batch he planned to hand out at church the following morning. Pen sat at the refectory table, the scent of the bonfire creeping in through the kitchen door, and waited as the noise of her husband's Volkswagen was replaced by the buzz of far-off farm machinery.

She drained the rest of her elderflower cordial into the sink, and then wheeled her mid-sized suitcase out past the pots of petunias and cascading nasturtiums to the gravel driveway, where she lifted it into the boot of the BMW estate. Like David, the big car now spent more and more time at Le Boqueteau, but he'd gently insisted she drive it back to London, to help collect the last of her things from the Highbury house before the sale. It was parked next to Bruno's old jeep, and she could see the Frenchman up near the treeline, holding his weight on his good ankle, prod-ding the bonfire with a pitchfork. The smoke wheeled and twisted into the blue sky. He was working on a Saturday because he wanted to finish the job. He was skilled and conscientious, and he took pride in his work. She still admired all that.

She should say goodbye, she thought. She strolled to the foot of the back lawn, and Remy came hurtling excitedly down the slope to meet her. The little pointer trotted with her towards his master, nudging at her heels. Pen's relationship with Bruno had almost returned to its proper, pre-coital state. When they were alone on the property without David, which was often, they were quietly polite to one another. And they had achieved an easy naturalism around her husband whenever he was in residence, so that he never seemed to have suspected a thing. Bruno's limp, and his occasional, unprompted deliveries of foraged *cèpes*, were the sole physical reminders of their romance. She never quite knew whether he was taunting her, or trying to win her back.

Sometimes, when she spotted Bruno and David out in the garden, gravely conferring on household matters, she felt a twinge of concern that he'd suddenly reveal everything: the whole sorry, scandalous affair. But to his very great credit, he had never once threatened to spill the beans. She supposed he still needed the work. And she could never fire him, in case he chose to expose her. Mutual Assured Destruction.

She stopped halfway up the lawn, forty feet from her former lover. He was watching the flames, with his back to her, the pitchfork thrust into the earth beside him.

'I'm off now, Bruno,' she said.

He didn't seem to have heard her over the breeze and the bonfire's crackle.

'Bruno!' she said loudly. He turned to face her.

'I'm leaving now,' she said.

He nodded. 'To England.'

'Yes. To London.'

Remy wagged his tail, halfway between them, agitated by the unnatural distance.

'The woodshed looks beautiful,' she said. 'Thank you.'

Bruno nodded again, and stared at her. She tried to engage some of that old sensual longing, but it was gone now. Gone for ever, perhaps. She smiled, waved once, and then turned and walked back down the slope to the car.

Bordeaux, Poitiers, Tours, Le Mans. Pen drew ever closer to the Channel, and to London, and to the house on the Hill. Somewhere along the Loire Valley, she stopped at a picnic spot beside the autoroute and unwrapped the aluminium foil from one of the damson jam sandwiches that David had made for her. It was sickly sweet, and she didn't think she could manage the second one, so she threw it in the bin and ate a small triangle of Saint-Paulin to try to make the taste go away. She washed it all down with mineral water. The further north she drove, the clearer the Radio 4 long-wave signal became. *Woman's Hour* was half-static; *PM* was listen-able, in spite of the high-pitched background hum; *Loose Ends* was crystal clear. She was time-travelling, back into her old life. It had taken her six months to get the house on the Hill to market, what with the bathroom refits and certain other semi-crucial details. She'd been in a diminishing state of denial, she supposed, about finally giving it up. But the time had come at last.

Waiting in the queue for the boat at Caen, she considered the significance of the coming few days. It was important to take her leave of the old house, she thought, properly and reverently. To bathe awhile in the light from the bay window; to soak up the view from the loft conversion. She hoped she might persuade Conrad to come and be cooked one last supper on the eight-ring stove in the kitchen-diner. Perhaps even Jerry. Isobel's commu-nications had been dreadfully intermittent of late, but wouldn't it be wonderful, Pen thought, if we could all say farewell to the place as a family? She sent Jerry a text, to let him know she was on her way.

After boarding, she found her little cabin and freshened up. She checked her phone again: a voicemail from David, checking that she'd made it to the port in time, but nothing from Jerry. She went to have dinner at the more salubrious of the ship's self-service restaurants, and consumed what passed for a Caesar salad with a half-bottle of cheap Sauvignon. A calm crossing ahead, announced the captain over the tannoy, and Pen watched the people around her exchange their smiles of relief. Back in the cabin, she checked her phone again. Still no answer.

As she lay on her narrow bunk, waiting for sleep, Pen thought once more of her first husband, that ambitious boy who'd installed the electrics and the central heating himself, who'd plumbed the kitchen and slated the roof. Who'd built the shelves, carpeted the floors, plastered and painted the walls. Such a big house, too. It was almost selfish of them to have had only two children, when there was so much space. But then, they'd had to accommodate Jerry's study, and Pen's studio, and a spare room – and the au pair had to sleep *somewhere*.

When the divorce arrived, she'd been made to feel that she had somehow swindled Jerry. She'd acquired him at the bottom of the market, when she was a worldly art-school grad, and he a shy Northern lad from the middle ranks of the creative department at Wilson Watson Jarvis Dunn. But he'd appreciated in value over the years, and prospective buyers had begun to circle. Some wives blithely consent to such behaviour. To their husbands' pathetic, ego-sating affairs. Some even manage to be happy. But not her. Not Pen.

She cast her mind back to that succession of sad, late-night conferences at the table in the kitchen-diner after the children had gone to bed, she and Jerry drinking boxes of middling claret as they hashed out the terms of their separation. They'd decided then that Jerry would leave and Pen would stay with the children, but that they would maintain the house as a mutual concern, given how much they'd both invested in it: financially, physically, emotionally. And in the weeks before he found himself a flat, when they were still only semi-detached, Pen had lain alone just like this, night after night, willing him to creep down the single flight of stairs from his spare-room exile, to push open the door of the master bedroom and slide back between the covers, with an apology and a simple promise. But of course he never came.

The gentle movement of the ferry rocked her into unconsciousness.

Portsmouth. Pen woke at 5.30 a.m. Greenwich time, as the boat was docking. She packed her wash-things into her overnight bag and made her way down to the car deck. Still no text from Jerry. But the weather was fine, the air was clear, and the roads into London were empty.

34

Alice was exhausted. Her mum and Xander never let her stay up all night. Sometimes she stayed awake after bedtime reading a book under her duvet, but she couldn't keep her eyes open for long, even if the book was a really good one. Today was different, though. She would not fall asleep, could not fall asleep – because, if she did, then she would miss the excitement of being in the real-life house on the Hill, with real-life Conrad and real-life Izzy. The *real* Izzy! Alice had to keep stopping herself from giggling, she was so delighted.

She liked the first book a lot, the one where Conrad drew all over the walls. But she thought they got better after that. The one where the melons fell out of the wheelbarrow was so funny. And the one with the bees! She loved the one with the bees. But she thought her favourite *House on the Hill* book was probably *Rover and the Roller Skates*, because it had a dog in it. Alice loved dogs. Her mum wouldn't let her have a dog. She said that Xander was allergic to the hair. Which was weird, because Alice's mum had lots of hair, and Xander wasn't allergic to *her*. Maybe her dad would let her have a dog and keep it at his flat. Her friend Matilda had a dog.

The lady from the house next door had given her a hot chocolate. She smiled a lot and stuck her tongue out through her teeth and asked Alice if she wanted to have a sleep, but Alice said she didn't. Alice thought she was ugly, but the hot chocolate was nice. The lady's husband was there as well, but he didn't talk to Alice because he was a grumpy guts. After all the horrible people left and the noise stopped, Izzy and her dad had come and collected her and taken her back to the house on the Hill. There were some policemen there, asking questions, and one of them showed her his handcuffs and his walkie-talkie and told her to be a good girl.

Conrad and her dad had a Big Shout after the policemen left, because Conrad had been naughty, as usual. Alice wanted to giggle when she thought about it. But Izzy – clever, sensible Izzy – had calmed them both down in the end and given them big hugs, even though her dad's clothes were all wet. Good old Izzy. She always sorted everything out. She'd put Alice to bed in what she said was her old room, and Alice lay awake for what seemed like for ever, listening hard to the three of them tidying up, and wondering why Izzy's bedroom smelled like boys.

Maybe she had slept for a little while, actually. By mistake. Because suddenly it was light outside, and Alice got up and pulled her shorts on and went out into the corridor. It smelled bad out there as well, the way her mum smelled when she came home late from a big party and sat on the end of Alice's bed while Alice pretended to be asleep. The carpet made a squelching sound when she walked on it, so she went back into Izzy's room to put on her Crocs.

She could hear voices from downstairs, so she followed them down until the carpets didn't squelch so much, and then down again until the carpets turned to wood. She found the three of them – Izzy, Conrad and her dad – sitting in the kitchen at those funny big round tables, surrounded by bulging black rubbish sacks. (At least, her dad had told her it was the kitchen, but it didn't seem like any kitchen Alice had ever known. It was very dirty, and the water wasn't working, and nobody had mopped the floor.)

They stopped talking when Alice came in, and she rubbed her eyes and said hello. She thought she might have interrupted a Serious Conversation, but Izzy said to come and sit on her lap, so she did. Izzy was quite skinny and bony, so it was a bit uncomfortable for Alice to balance on her knees, but she didn't complain because she was so excited to be there. Izzy put an arm around her, and Alice supposed that they would soon be very good friends. It was quiet. When Alice's dad shifted on his stool, his clothes made a funny whooshing sound because they were still a bit soggy.

'Were you not in love any more?' said Izzy, after a while. 'You and Mum. When you decided to get divorced?'

'Fucksake, Isobel,' said Conrad, and Alice tried not to giggle at the bad word.

'No. Seriously. I think I need to know.'

Alice's dad was looking at the floor and breathing through his nose. Alice knew exactly why he and her own mum had got divorced: because Daddy was a bad word, and Mummy was a bad word (and Xander was a *complete* even-worse-word), and they couldn't bear each other, even though they both still loved Alice very much. So maybe it was the same with Izzy's mum.

'Hmph,' said her dad in the end. 'I don't know, Isobel. It was the nineties. Everybody was doing it.'

It was quiet again, and then Izzy started to sniffle. Alice looked up at her. She was crying.

'Oh, balls,' said Alice's dad. 'Sorry . . .'

Izzy sobbed and laughed at the same time, and Alice felt a little flick of spit land on her face.

'No, no,' said Izzy. She shivered. 'I'm fine! I just. I miss my kids! I miss Tor.'

'Oh, dear,' said her dad.

'No! It's good. It's good, Dad! I guess. I don't know. I was worried that I wouldn't miss them, but I do. I do.'

Conrad reached over and put his hand on Izzy's shoulder, and Izzy suddenly squeezed Alice very hard. Alice thought it was pretty weird that she was crying, even though she was happy. Izzy lifted Alice off her lap and stood up and said that she needed to make a phone call. Then she went out into the garden, closing the back door behind her. Alice sat down on the stool and watched through the glass as Izzy dialled. Cool, she thought. An iPhone. Alice really wanted an iPhone, but she wasn't allowed to get one until she was ten, which was still seventeen months and two weeks away. It was jolly unfair that her parents – all three of them – paid for her to have loads of boring lessons in Spanish and acting and music, but wouldn't pay for something actually useful like an iPhone. Her friend Matilda had an iPhone.

'Should I . . . ?' said her dad.

'No, leave her,' Conrad replied.

They were quiet again. Alice thought she could hear birds singing outside, and the muffled sound of Izzy talking into her phone, and the slam of a car door somewhere.

'The plumber will be here in a bit,' said her dad. 'Did you have a nice sleep, Alice?'

'Yes, thank you,' Alice lied.

Isobel came back inside. Her eyes were all red but she was smiling.

'Everything okay?' said Conrad. 'Was that Tor?'

'Yeah, yeah,' she replied. 'Everything's fine. You okay?'

'Yeah,' said her naughty little brother. 'I guess.'

Izzy ruffled Alice's hair, which was what Xander always did. Alice found it very annoying. But because it was Izzy, she decided not to say anything. She hadn't brushed her hair yet this morning anyway, because all of her things, including her hairbrush, were still in her dad's car.

There was a noise from upstairs. The front door swinging open, and a footstep in the hallway, and a gasp, and a scream. Alice jumped: what a shock! Her dad stood up suddenly, his wet jeans whooshing again as they rubbed together. He ran out of the kitchen and thundered up the stairs. Conrad and Izzy looked at each other.

'Shit,' said Conrad.

'Mum,' said Izzy.

They hurried after their dad, and Alice followed as fast as she could. She wanted to giggle all over again with the excitement. Could it *be*? Could it *really* be Auntie Pen, who made up *all* of *The House on the Hill*? There was a funny doodle on the wall in the hallway. Alice's Crocs stuck to the gummy wooden floor. Izzy and Conrad were standing at the door of the sitting room, looking in. Through the gap between them, Alice could see her dad, hugging an old lady. Alice just about recognised her from the black-and-white photo that was on the back cover of all her books, but she looked very different now. She was sad and moaning, her legs like wobbly jelly, her face twisted into a frown. Alice's dad was holding her up in the light from the big window at the front of the house, smothering and supporting her at the same time.

'I'll pay,' he was saying, over and over. 'I'll pay, I'll pay.'

COMPLETION

In the months and years to come, the French investment banker who'd bought the house on the Hill would woo his dates with a trip to the loft conversion. From the basement kitchen-diner – which he'd extended into the garden with a glass-box conservatory and granite paving – they would climb the stairs, the date carrying her heels in one hand and her champagne flute in the other. The upward journey would take them straight past the door of the master bedroom, to which the French investment banker might allude suggestively, if he thought the date was already sufficiently pliant. With any luck, she'd ask if she might freshen up, and he would direct her to his splendid marble wet-room.

He'd bought the place without even having seen it, he would say as they ascended to the second floor. He just knew it would be perfect for him. West London, he'd explain, was full of investment bankers, and he'd wanted to live somewhere that wasn't so gentrified. The old man who sold him the house, he'd tell his dates, laughing, made him promise to be kind to it. But once he had the keys, he'd hired artisan builders to tear out all the non-load-bearing walls; he wanted his home to be light, white, airy and *minimaliste*. The loft, for example, was a single, vaulted space, containing his hi-tech home gym and sports room.

Finally, the French investment banker would slide open the large, plate-glass door and let his date step out onto the long balcony ahead of him, where she would gasp and then chuckle at the spectacular city view. How on earth, they tended to ask, did you find this house anyway?

The French investment banker had found the house by offering the asking price, in cash, before it officially hit the market. Jerry was extremely grateful, given that he'd already forfeited around £100,000 of his share to have it repainted, replastered, re-plumbed, re-carpeted and rewired. He paid for the locks to be changed, and for a security firm to monitor the house and prevent the squatters' return. The builder and the plumber and the electrician all breathed in through their teeth at the destruction he had wrought. And so he paid, and then he paid again.

That morning in July, as the Manvilles assessed the wreckage, Isobel had eased her distraught mother down onto the desecrated Habitat sofa. Jerry insisted he'd no idea whatsoever who the squatters were, nor how they'd known the house was empty, nor how they'd been able to break in. But it was his fault. It had to be his fault, all of it. He must have left a window open, a door. He'd been remiss. He'd neglected his responsibilities. He found that he had a hitherto unplumbed capacity for contrition. Conrad looked on in grateful awe, as his father hoovered up the blame that ought to have been his.

Later, somewhat recovered, Pen led the forlorn procession of family members from room to room, weeping and gnashing her teeth once more at the graffiti and the vomit stains and the water damage. And yet, deep within herself, she felt an ancient weight lifting. Finally, *finally*, she was able to let go of her lingering affection for Jerry. The old fool had located the last straw. Now, at long last, she could move forward unburdened to the future.

Isobel spent two nights at Jerry's flat before flying back to Dubai. He gave her what advice he could about marriage, which was not much, and she hugged him to let him feel wise. But she'd reached that point in life when she knew that all relationship advice

344

was fatuous, from her father or from the pages of a glossy magazine. No one could really give you sound, copper-bottomed guidance: your parents didn't know shit; your friends didn't know shit;
and any therapist would be biased by their training and their fee.
You were on your own. So you followed your instincts, and Isobel
followed hers back to Tor.

Tor was calm and somewhat baffled, and he bailed her out of
her debt hole at once. She promised to pay him back as soon as
her share of the house sale came through, but he wouldn't hear
of it. He'd been given Brian's job, Senior Fund Manager, and was
finally earning real banker money. Brian, she gathered, had left
things in a parlous state, and Isobel's husband had cleaned them
up as he always did, coolly, efficiently, without complaint.

After six months, the bank offered Tor his reward: Zurich. The
house was another semi-furnished rental, close to the lake in
Kilchberg, and it was sterile in its way. But Isobel knew in her
bones by now that home was not a house. And at least Switzerland
was European, cold, a democracy – a four-hour drive to Munich,
and a short flight to London or the Dordogne. Pen had converted
her barn into a gîte, and Anton and Jonas adored her Labrador
puppy. And as Isobel toured with the twins to the lakes, or to the
mountains, her arable fields lay fallow, her animals roamed free,
and I22y lazed in the endless Acres sunshine.

Conrad came to the same understanding as his sister: that there
was something honest and true about family that had nothing to
do with the house or the Manville name. He thought he might let
Polly call their kid by her own surname when it was born. Because
the name didn't much matter to him, as long as they shared that
basic, biological connection: the genetic strands and DNA double
helixes that strung them all together like brightly coloured spoke
beads.

When Polly opened her first pop-up shop, she gave Conrad
and Austin half the space to trial Tinville, their bespoke bicycle

repair and restoration business. Conrad had used some of his share of the house sale to lease a workshop in Hackney Wick, where Austin was content to sleep. Squatting would soon be criminalised, and Conrad did not wish to see his new friend and partner arrested unnecessarily. In lieu of rent, he taught Conrad welding, brazing and silver brazing, and between them they were soon creating machines that were as much their own as they were the original manufacturers'. In time, Austin slowly began to build his own bikes from scratch. They conceived killer colourways and cool detailing, like the hand-carved flourishes on the seat clusters. They perfected the Tinville emblem, and melded it seamlessly into their designs.

Conrad thought he was probably undercharging his customers for labour, but he decided that was okay, because he was still learning – and besides, he wanted people to come back, and to tell their friends. His clients became a community, and he trained himself to match each bike not merely to its owner's inside leg, but to their character. Some remained little more than acquaintances to whom he'd nod if ever he pulled up beside them at a traffic light; others bought him drinks at the Cow-Shed. A few even became friends, who'd join him and Austin now and then for Sunday rides beyond the city. Fixing up bikes started to come so naturally to Conrad that he could lose himself in it. His intellectual and physical faculties became unmoored from active thought; he worked without thinking, his mind and body flowing as if lost in the happy repetition of a video game.

Beagle moved out and shacked up with a synth player; the Kingsland Road flat seemed bigger all of a sudden, with just the two of them in it, sharing a bedroom. The pho noodle place became an estate agents' office, so the smell disappeared and the plumbing miraculously improved. They redecorated with Ali the landlord's consent, and decided to stay rather than weigh themselves down with a mortgage. Besides, Conrad had spent a lot of his remaining capital on the refurb for his first permanent Tinville shop. And sometime after Jerry's second heart attack, Conrad relented and allowed Polly to invite his father for dinner.

The first attack, Jerry admitted, as he declined Polly's offer of an aperitif, had come as a shock to no one but himself. The second was a shock to everyone but himself. But he was finally following his doctor's advice, he'd shed two stone, and he felt a lot better, thank you. His solicitor had put his post-mortem affairs in order, for a price. And he was content to know that at least five people, his wives and children, would be at his funeral. (That was the thing about children: even if they despised you, they really had to turn up. And so did their mothers.) Nine, if their other halves all came to support their partners. Eleven, if Isobel brought the grandchildren. Twelve if Tony Glassop outlived him and agreed to deliver the eulogy. Twelve: no more or less than he deserved.

Jerry picked his way through Conrad's fruit salad, the only dessert in the son's repertoire that conformed to the father's strict dietary requirements. He could smell the coffee percolating on the stove, but his delicate condition demanded he settle for camomile tea. He glanced again at Polly's five-month bump, his next grandchild. He hoped that he'd survive long enough to meet it. He put down his fork.

'You know,' he said. 'I remember being very happy when your mother and I lived in our crappy little flat in Kentish Town. Before your sister was born. Very happy indeed.'

'Are you calling our flat crappy?' said Polly, and laughed.

The French investment banker's date would shiver a little, and he would remove his suit jacket and wrap her into it to fend off the cold. If a date seemed intrigued, he might point out the BT Tower, or the tip of the Shard (which she could see if they leaned out far enough, with the French investment banker holding her firmly by her waist for safety), or the Emirates Stadium, home to his beloved Arsenal. Then the date would wiggle her empty champagne flute at him, and he'd follow her as she stepped back inside and slipped downstairs to pour some more Moët, moving inexorably towards the master bedroom and the French investment banker's 1,000 thread-count bed linen. For what the French investment banker knew beyond doubt was that the house, and the loft, and the view, bestowed upon him an imagined value that his face and body and charm alone could never achieve. It projected a lifestyle that any sensible woman would lust after. It *almost* always got him laid. Although, of course – and just to be sure – he would also have paid a very great deal for dinner.

THANKS

To my agent, Jane Finigan, without whose encouragement, enthusiasm and soft deadlines, this book would still be a half-finished .doc in the depths of a hard drive. To editor, publisher and accidental property expert Jason Arthur, for his invaluable guidance beyond the first draft. To everyone else at Lutyens & Rubinstein and at William Heinemann for their effort and time. To those who read and reviewed the work in progress, particularly fellow scribblers Neil Burkey, Jon Digby, Grant Gillespie and Philip Kidson. To Bea, for the loan of her desk – and for everything else.

In writing about Dubai, I drew inspiration from several nonfiction sources, including two excellent accounts of the history and culture of the emirate: *Hello Dubai* by Joe Bennett (Simon & Schuster, 2010), and *Dubai: The Story of the World's Fastest City* by Jim Krane (Atlantic, 2009).